Beatrice Cenci

By

Francesco Domenico Guerrazzi

Published by Forgotten Books 2012
Originally Published 1906

PIBN 1000421804

THE LITERATURE OF ITALY

consists of sixteen volumes, of which this one forms a part. For full particulars of the edition see the Official Certificate bound in the volume entitled

"A HISTORY OF ITALIAN LITERATURE."

Edited by Rossiter Johnson and Dora Knowlton Ranous

With a General Introduction by William Michael Rossetti and Special Introductions by James, Cardinal Gibbons, Charles Eliot Norton, S. G. W. Benjamin, William S. Walsh, Maurice Francis Egan, and others

New translations, and former renderings compared and revised

Translators: James C. Brogan, Lord Charlemont, Geoffrey Chaucer, Hartley Coleridge, Florence Kendrick Cooper, Lady Dacre, Theodore Dwight, Edward Fairfax, Ugo Foscolo, G. A. Greene, Sir Thomas Hoby, William Dean Howells, Luigi Monti, Evangeline M. O'Connor, Thomas Okey, Dora Knowlton Ranous, Thomas Roscoe, William Stewart Rose, Dante Gabriel Rossetti, William Michael Rossetti, John Addington Symonds, William S. Walsh, William Wordsworth, Sir Thomas Wyatt

THEY ALL MARCHED ON TOGETHER. BEATRICE BEGAN TO CHANT WITH A SONOROUS VOICE THE LITANY OF THE BLESSED VIRGIN

From a Painting by P. Delaroche

BEATRICE CENCI

BY

FRANCESCO GUERRAZZI

TRANSLATED BY LUIGI MONTI

THE NATIONAL ALUMNI

CONTENTS

CONTENTS

ILLUSTRATIONS

INTRODUCTION

FRANCESCO DOMENICO GUERRAZZI, the Italian patriot and writer of romances, was born in Leghorn, Italy, August 12, 1804. At fifteen years of age he had abandoned his home and become a student in the University of Pisa. From these earliest days of young manhood he had conceived a hatred of the monarchical form of government; and an acquaintance formed with Lord Byron, while he was still a student at the University of Pisa, had a marked effect in turning his mind toward literary work, both political and imaginative. In 1827 he wrote *La Battaglia di Benevento,* a romance filled with fulminations against tyrants and all forms of tyranny. In the following year he published a violent attack upon the Grand-Ducal Government, in consequence of which he was compelled to remain six months within the confines of Montepulciano. During his sojourn there, Giuseppe Mazzini, the distinguished Italian patriot and revolutionist, visited him, and influenced him to take a fresh step in the path of politics. When the term of Guerrazzi's confinement was over, he was hailed as a new leader by the more daring and dissatisfied among the Italian people. In 1831 the Grand Duke of Tuscany appointed him to a place in his cabinet, but he soon drew upon himself the displeasure of the Duke because of his ultra-liberal views and desires, and he was not only dismissed from the cabinet, but imprisoned, and later was exiled to Corsica. During this second period of exile, Guerrazzi wrote *L'Assedio di Firenze* ("The Siege of Florence"), in 1836, a powerful political work, which revealed his real literary genius and impelled fiery Young Italy to rebel against the yoke of strangers. This was followed, in 1844, by a striking historical romance, *Isabella Orsini*, and by other novels, less widely known. In the field of romance, he had sufficient force and originality to deviate from the style of Manzoni, which had so long been the model for Italian novelists, and his brilliant diction was extolled by all the critics of his time. He had a vein of humor, which is shown in some of his short stories—as *The Little Snake* and *The Hole in the Wall*—written in early life. The latter is supposed to be a little chapter from his own experience. Because of a severe reprimand, the boy leaves home and establishes himself in a garret. To decorate the place, he buys a cheap print from a hawker in the street—a Madonna which he fancies resembles his mother. He would not hang it on the wall of the room, as that would make it seem too common, and instead determined to hang it in a closet, which he resolved "should contain nothing else, my principal reason being that I possessed nothing else to put there. With a stone for a hammer I drove in a nail. But the point of the nail pierced through a joint, and the plaster gave way as if it had been cheese, leaving a large hole." Peeping through into the next apartment, he sees an attractive young woman, who of course becomes the heroine of the story.

The emotional and enthusiastic side of his nature is

shown in his estimate of Byron, of whom he writes: "Reports had spread that a most remarkable man had come to Pisa. He was spoken of in a thousand different ways. He was of noble descent, wealthy, powerful, having a ferocious nature, and yet highly chivalrous. They said he had a more than human intellect, and yet was a very genius of evil, wandering to and fro in the world and going up and down in it, like Job's Satan, challenging anyone to slander him. This man was Lord Byron. I saw him, and he resembled the Apollo of the Vatican. Then I said: 'I will never believe that the Creator has put an evil soul into a body so beautiful.'"

On leaving Corsica, Guerrazzi settled in Florence, and for a time he was occupied with the practice of law. When the revolution of 1848 broke out, he was one of its moving spirits, and was again imprisoned for a short time. As soon as he was released, he joined the party of Mazzini, Gioberti, and other revolutionists, founded a republican newspaper in Florence, was elected deputy to the national assembly of Tuscany, and on the fall of the Capponi cabinet was appointed Minister of the Interior (1848). After the flight of the Grand Duke, in the same year, when the Italian duchies were republicanized, Guerrazzi became dictator of the temporary government, which one month later was overthrown. He was arrested illegally, and was unjustly sent to the state prison at Volterra, where he remained until 1853, writing while in prison a defense of his political conduct, entitled *Apologia della vita politica di Francesco Domenico Guerrazzi* (Florence, 1851). Notwithstanding the good sense and complete self-justification of this "Apology," he was condemned to perpetual exile, and went to Corsica, where he wrote his world-famous historical romance, *Beatrice Cenci* (1854). This was followed by *L'Asino,* a biting politico-social satire, and other lesser works. After Italy became a united kingdom (1861), Guerrazzi had his rights as a subject restored to him, and was elected several times a member of Parliament. He died in Rome, September 23, 1873. His Letters were edited by Giosue Carducci (1882).

D. K. R.

CHAPTER I

FRANCESCO CENCI

AN artist that might have attempted to paint the group that awaited Francesco Cenci in the hall of his palace would have depicted it, I know not whether more charmingly, but certainly in the manner of the *Madonna della Seggiola* of Raphael. A young woman sat near a large window, clasping a baby to her breast; behind her a youth of noble bearing looked down upon this spectacle of love. He clasped his hands, and, raising them toward Heaven, thanked God that so much happiness was his. His aspect and attitude expressed in that moment the three affections that make man divine: his hands were lifted toward God, his look was given to his child, and his smile to his wife. The woman did not see the smile, for the duty and dignity of a mother absorbed her. The child looked like an angel strayed from heaven.

On the opposite side of the hall, stretched upon a bench, lay a man that might have furnished to Michelangelo the model for one of his famous *chiaroscuri*. His face was half hidden under a conical hat with a large rim. His beard was long, uncombed, and gray; his skin like that which Jeremiah describes in the children of Zion, of an ashy color, like an oven floor. He was wrapped in a large cloak; his legs were crossed and his feet covered with sandals, after the fashion of the Roman peasant. Perhaps he was armed, but he kept his weapon hidden; for the Roman laws, after Pope Sixtus V, were very severe in such matters.

He that might have gazed, first upon the lovely family group, and then upon the man, would have recalled the words of Scripture—"He divided darkness from light."

Two young cavaliers walked restlessly through the hall, conversing sometimes loudly, sometimes quietly. One had a spotted skin, like that of a leper; his black eyes, glittering through inflamed lids, were fierce, and showed indications of mental wandering; his hair was straight, his teeth were black; while his flat nose and flaccid cheeks gave him the look of a hunting-dog. His dress, although elegant, was disordered; his voice came from his parched lips impetuous and harsh; his speech was coarse; his shoulders, arms, and head were continually in motion. Crime was there, like a wild beast, ready to burst forth at any instant.

The other, on the contrary, was pale and refined, with a large head and luxuriant light hair. His look and speech were slow and sad; he appeared distracted, and often sighed. He frequently stopped in his walk, started, and showed his emotion by the trembling of his upper lip and the quivering of his moustache. His clothes, ribbons, and the lace of his collar and sleeves were elegant, but whoever saw him would exclaim at once, "He is unhappy."

Clad in a black tunic, without a cloak, looking like a magpie flitting uneasily through the house, a priest moved here and there, taking the greatest pains to attract the attention of the bystanders. He talked of the summer, of the winter, of heat and cold, of seed-time and harvest; but no one listened to him. Then he asked whether he might have the honor of speaking to his Excellency, the most noble Count, that day; inquired at what time he usually rose; when he breakfasted; whether he were accustomed to spend a long time upon his toilet; and whether he gave audience every day. It was breath wasted; no one answered him, for the young pair were absorbed in their own happiness; the peasant seemed a bronze statue; the gentleman with the red face had stared at him in such a manner as to make him shudder; the youth with the pale face looked upon him as if he were a man fallen from the clouds. The poor priest knew not what to do; in despair, he now and then opened his breviary and read, but with the aspect of one that swallows bitter medicine.

The curate (for this priest was properly a curate) after discovering that the words of Scripture, "Knock and it shall be opened unto you," are not always verified, addressed himself for the third or fourth time to a certain *valet de chambre* who seemed somewhat disposed to listen to him, when the dark and repellent cavalier called haughtily:

"Cammillo!"

It is the nature of servants, when they have no worse motive for bowing, to obey the commands of him who orders them the most proudly; and Cammillo, belonging to the vast family of servants, was certainly not an exception. Whirling suddenly, as if he had springs in his heels, he turned his back upon the poor priest, and bending low toward the cavalier, with the most obsequious voice replied:

"Your Excellency?"

"Did the most noble Count sleep badly last night?"

"I do not know—I believe not. Several letters were brought to him early this morning, some from Spain, others from Naples—it may be, though I do not know, he is perusing them now."

At this moment an infernal barking deafened the ears of the bystanders; suddenly the doors of the Count's room were opened, and an enormous mastiff came out, frightened and at the same time furious. The peasant lying near the door started to his feet instantly and, disentangling his arms from his cloak, drew a large poniard, ready to defend himself. The young mother pressed the child to her bosom, sheltering him with her arms. The father placed himself before his wife and child, in order to protect them with his own body. The cavaliers drew aside with decent haste, like those who wish neither to meet a danger nor to show fear. The curate ran for his life.

The dog, following his instinct, rushed after the fugitive, seized him by the folds of his tunic, and tore it; he would have done worse had not two valets, running after him, held him firmly by the collar. The breviary had fallen to the ground. The poor priest screamed grievously, and, like Shylock, crying, "My daughter, my ducats!" he exclaimed, "My cloak, my breviary!" The irritated dog barked louder than ever. An old man appeared at the threshold.

This was Francesco Cenci.

Francesco Cenci, of Latin race, from the ancient Cincia family, counted among his ancestors Pope John X. As in age, so in crime, this family was old: for, if history speaks the truth, Marozia, sister of Theodora, wishing to take away from the Pope the dominion of Rome, treacherously occupied the Adrian fortress, and, having invaded the Lateran with a large number of ruffians, put to the sword Peter, brother of John, and shut John himself in prison, where, either by poison or other means, he died.

Francesco Cenci had inherited an immense fortune; his income was estimated at more than a hundred thousand crowns, which in those times was an enormous sum, and even in our own day would be no ordinary one. His father held the office of treasurer of the Church under Pius V, and while the latter was trying to clear the world of heresies, the elder Cenci was busy in clearing the public treasury of its crowns, both being well skilled in their different employments. As to Count

Francesco, his fellowmen hardly knew what to think of him, for the reputation of no man differed more than his. Some said that he was pious, liberal, mild and courteous; others called him avaricious, cruel, and wicked. The truth is that proofs could be given in confirmation of both opinions. He had sustained several law processes, but had always come out absolved *ex capite innocentiæ;* many, however, were not satisfied with such judgments, and complained that the Roman Court never had been known to condemn a man with a yearly income of one hundred thousand crowns. But, however mysterious his life might have appeared to the public, his family knew it but too well; although through decency, and still more through fear, they dared not speak a word. They understood how much he liked to imagine terrible deeds, and the more frightful and contrary to the opinions of others, so much the more pleasing to him. As soon as conceived, they were executed at any cost, even if in accomplishing them a treasure must be expended, or arson or homicide committed. His will was the flash, his deeds the stroke. He was accustomed (to such a point of audacity had he come) to keep an exact account of his expenditures in crime; and in a certain book were found recorded the following items: "For the affairs and accidents of Toscanella, 3,500 sequins, and it was not dear. For the undertaking of the banditti of Terni, 2,000 sequins, and they were thrown away." He always traveled on horseback, and alone; when he thought the horse was tired, he would dismount and buy another; if a man refused to sell him one, he took it, giving in exchange a blow with his poniard. No fear of banditti ever preventing him from traversing alone the dangerous forests of St. Germano or Faiola, and often, without stopping by the way, he might be seen going from Rome to Naples on horseback. Whenever he made his appearance in a place, a rape, a fire, an assassination, or some other catastrophe was sure to follow. He was strong, and skilled in all manner of manly exercises, so that he often provoked his enemies with insults and mockery; but he had few acknowledged enemies, for he was much feared, and before compromising themselves with him, men would think twice. He always kept at his own expense a company of *bravi*. These were men whose business it was to protect their master, and to aid him in his evil designs. The courtyard of his palace offered an infamous asylum to all manner of banditti. Among the fierce Roman barons he was the most brutal.

In person he was very stout, and although somewhat advanced in years, still in a robust state of health, except that he limped, for his right leg had been hurt. He was rich in ideas, eloquent in speech, and might have acquired the fame of a splendid orator, had the times and his tongue permitted; for on the slightest agitation the latter seemed to be entangled in his teeth, and his tones became harsh and halting. He certainly could not be called ugly, yet his expression was so sinister that it never could inspire love; sometimes it inspired reverence, but more often fear. Except for the color of his hair and beard, now changed from black to white, for a wrinkle more, a greater paleness, and a complexion more yellow and bilious, his face was the same as it had appeared in youth. His eyes, ordinarily sad, were a dull gray, surrounded by circles of an ashy color, and lined with veins of violet and red. His face would have been equally adapted for that of a saint or a bandit; its expression was as deep and inexplicable as that of a sphinx.

The Count had retired early to his apartments the evening before, without saluting his wife or his children. To Marzio, who had offered his usual services, he had replied:

"Go; Nero is enough for me."

Nero was an enormous dog, and fierce. Cenci had

named him thus less in memory of that bloody tyrant than to signify "strong" or "powerful" in the old Samnite's language.

Hardly had he gone to his bed, ere he began to turn on each side and groan with impatience; by degrees his impatience became fury, and he began to rave. Nero replied by growling. A little later the Count, starting from the heated bed, exclaimed:

"Perhaps the sheets are poisoned! I have read somewhere of this having formerly been done. Olimpia! Ah! you have escaped from me, but I will reach you; no one can escape from my hands—not one. What a silence there is around me! What peace in my house! Do all rest? Then do I not frighten them? Marzio!"

The valet answered the call immediately.

"Marzio," said the Count, "what are the family doing?"

"They sleep."

"All?"

"All—at least I judge so, as all seems quiet in the house."

"And dares any one to slumber in my house when I cannot sleep? Go, see if they really sleep; listen in the rooms, particularly in Virgilio's; bolt them softly on the outside, and return."

Marzio disappeared.

"That fellow," continued the Count, "I detest above all others; under that surface of icy mildness the waters of rebellion run no less swift. Reptile without a tongue, but not without poison, how I long to see you dead!"

Marzio, returning, said:

"They all sleep, even Don Virgilio: but, from their feverish breathing, it is but a troubled sleep."

"Have you bolted the doors on the outside?"

Marzio nodded an affirmative.

"Very well! Take this arquebuse, fire it near the door of the room of Virgilio, and then cry with your loudest voice—Fire! Fire! Thus will I teach them to sleep while I watch."

"Your Excellency"——

"What is the matter?"

"I will not say have pity for the boy, who seems very ill—"

"Go on!"

"But it will raise the neighborhood."

The Count, without being in the least disturbed, put his hand quietly under his pillow, drew out a pistol, and suddenly leveled it at the valet, who turned pale with fear.

"Marzio, the next time you attempt to contradict me instead of obeying, I will kill you as I would a dog—go!"

Marzio went in haste to execute the command.

It is impossible to describe with what terror the women and the child awoke. They jumped from their beds and rushed to the doors; and, not being able to open them, they screamed, praying some one to tell them what had happened, and to open the doors. But no answer came; and at last, exhausted, they threw themselves again on their beds.

Having filled his house with terror, he returned to his chamber, where nature, conquered by weariness, forced him to a short and broken sleep. When he arose, he appeared gloomy.

"I have slept badly, Marzio—I dreamed I was sitting at table with my dead ancestors. This signifies approaching death. But before I go to dine there many others, Marzio, many others shall precede me to prepare the table."

"Your Excellency, letters have arrived by express couriers from the Neapolitan State."

The Count reached out his hand to receive them. Marzio continued:

"And also from Spain by the usual courier; I have placed them all upon the desk in your study."

"It is well. We will go."

Supported by Marzio, and accompanied by Nero, he went to his study.

A magnificent August sun just tinged with its dawning rays the azure heavens.

The Count approached the balcony, and gazing upon the majestic luminary murmured words to himself. Marzio, charmed with the beauty of the heavens and the light, could not help exclaiming:

"Divine Sun!"

At these words the eyes of the Count, usually so dull, flashed forth like lightning from a cloud, and he turned them toward the heavens. If it is true that the Apostate Julian threw to heaven the blood that issued from his mortal wound, he must have hurled it with the same look and intention.

"Marzio, if the sun were a light, which, by blowing, could be extinguished, would you put it out?"

"I? your Excellency, it seems to me I should leave it burning."

"I would extinguish it."

Caligula wished the Roman people had but one neck, that he might kill them with one blow. Count Cenci wished to crush the sun.

He sat at his desk; opened and read one, two, three letters, quietly at first, then hastily; finally, after finishing them all, he broke forth with a horrible oath:

"All are happy! Heaven! you do it almost to spite me!"

And closing his hand, he brought it down with all his strength; it chanced to strike Nero, who with raised mouth and quick eyes followed every movement of his master. The dog gave a furious start, then rushed against the door, burst it open and fled growling. The

Count, calling him, followed, not without first observing with a bitter smile:

"You see, Marzio, if he had been my son he would have bitten me."

CHAPTER II

THE PARRICIDE

MARZIO invited the cavalier with the red face to pass into the Count's study. The Count awaited him standing; and as soon as he saw him he saluted him with a refined and elegant manner, saying:

"Welcome, Prince; of what service can we be to your lordship?"

"Count, I must speak with you; but here is one too many."

"Marzio, retire."

Marzio, bowing, went out. The Prince followed him in order to assure himself that he had carefully shut the door; he then drew the curtain and approached the Count, who, wondering not a little at these precautions, invited him to sit down, and, without saying a word, waited to hear him.

"Count, like Catiline, I will begin my oration *ex abrupto*. Therefore I tell you at once that, considering you deservedly a man of courage and counsel, strong in mind and in arm, I turn to you for both, and hope you will courteously aid me with both."

"Speak, Prince."

"My shameless mother," he began, in a low voice, "stains with despicable acts my house, and even your own, by the tie of relationship which exists between our two families. Age, instead of extinguishing her passions, causes them to burn more fiercely. The large revenue which she possesses, by the disposition of my stupid father, she squanders on her lovers. Throughout Rome pasquinades may be seen continually. I see mockery painted upon the faces of the people; wherever I go terms of reproach wound me—my blood boils in my veins; to such a degree has the evil reached that there is no remedy, save one. Now, tell me, Count, what you counsel me to do?"

"The illustrous Lady Costanza di Santa Croce! Can you think so? Come, if you do this for a joke, I advise you to take a more suitable subject for it; if, however, you speak the truth, then, my son, I warn you not to let yourself be deceived by temptations of the devil, who, as the father of lies, disturbs the mind with false fancies."

"Count, let us leave the devil in his own house. I can show you manifest proofs, and by far too shameful ones."

"Let us know them."

"Listen. She leaves me, if I may say so, drowned in penury, while with the income of the family she brings up servants and valets, and a crowd of their children, who have made nests in the palace more numerous than swallows'; she banishes me from her presence; does not even wish to hear my name—I, Count, you understand, who never would have given a single thought to her affairs if she had borne herself as a worthy mother should toward a dutiful son—and, to tell you all in a word, last evening she drove me from the house—my own palace—the dwelling of my illustrious ancestors."

"Go on; is there anything else?"

"And is not that enough?"

"It is too much even; and truly, to confess it to you in secret, I have noticed for a long time that the Princess Costanza, God pardon her, cherishes for you a natural aversion. About eight days ago she spoke a long time to me about you."

"Indeed; and what did this miserable woman say of me?"

"To add fuel to the fire is not a Christian act; therefore I am silent."

"In this case, Count, the fire kindled by your words is so great that you can add but little; and this you may easily understand by your own judgment."

"Too well; and besides, silence is grievous to me, since my words will serve as a guide for you and prevent your getting into trouble. The Lady Costanza expressly declared, in the presence of several distinguished prelates and Roman barons, that you are a disgrace to the family; that you are a thief—a murderer—and, above all, a liar."

"She said that?" The voice of Santa Croce trembled, and his face had become like a burning coal through rage.

"And she said also that you were a most miserable spendthrift of all your property; that you had borrowed money at great usury from the Jews, securing it upon the palace of your illustrious ancestors, from which she was obliged to free it with her own money, in order to avoid the shame of dwelling elsewhere; that she had many times paid your debts, and that every day you contracted newer and heavier ones, and more disgraceful than ever; that you are a desperate gambler; and in every vice you have plunged deeply, a scorner of God and of all human respect."

"She said so?"

"And that the immorality of your life had reached such a point that reverence to your mother or respect for your home had not prevented you from bringing infamous women to the palace of your ancestors; together with many other depravities, which only to remember make my cheeks burn."

"My mother?"

"And she added that she believed you incapable of reform; and although it grieves her maternal heart, she has decided to have recourse to His Holiness, that he may imprison you in the castle—to make a visit to the Emperor Adrian. On the word of a gentleman, this is being in prison with the best of company."

"She said thus?" again the Prince interrupted, with a choking voice, while the Count replied with the same malignant and irritating voice:

"Or at Civita Castellana—for life."

"For life! Did she really say for life?"

"And soon; this being due to the honored memory of her illustrious husband, to the reputation of the ancient family, to her noble relatives, her own conscience, and to God."

"Excellent mother! Have I not a good mother?" exclaimed the Prince in a voice which he endeavored to render mocking, although he could ill hide his unusual terror. "And the prelates, what did they answer?"

"Eh! you know the precepts of the Gospel? The tree that does not bear good fruit is cut down—and they repeated it with as amiable a tone as if inviting you to drink a cup of chocolate."

"The affair is more pressing than I thought. Now, Count, give me some counsel—I am poor in expedients—I am in despair."

The Count, shaking his head, replied gravely:

"Here, where flows the fountain of all grace, you may dip with full buckets. Go to my Lord Taverna, Governor of Rome, or if you have much money and little wisdom, to the eminent lawyer, Signor Prospero Farinaccio, who will devour you with costs."

"Alas! I have no money."

"Without money you might as well address yourself to the colossus of Monte Cavallo."

"And then the affair would become public, and I need remedies which make no noise, and, above all, hasty ones."

"And then bow yourself to the most blessed feet, for remember that in the body of the Holy Father every limb is blessed, and hence the feet *et reliqua* of the Pontiff: they call him *insignis pietatis vir,* as Virgil sings of Æneas."

"Lord have mercy on us! Pope Aldobrandino was born at the same time with the she-wolf of Dante, who after eating is more hungry than before. He is old, avaricious, and obstinate, worse than any mule of the Marches; so greedy of money to enrich his relatives as even to try to skin the Colosseum. Before going to him, I would throw myself headlong into the Tiber."

"Yes," ceasing his slight, ironic smile, the Count continued to say, disturbed; "yes, now I think of it, you would throw away your time and trouble. After the sad fault of having given favor to my rebellious daughter against me, he will have become more obstinate in listening to complaints of children against their parents. A father and a king are never in the wrong; children and subjects never in the right. Whence do they derive the right of complaining, whence the audacity of rebelling? They live because their father begat them; they live because their king allows them. Look at Iphigenia and Isaac—these are examples of right subjection in children; as Agamemnon, Abraham, and Japhet, of the entirety of paternal power. Rome kept herself powerful while the father had the right of life and death over his family. These laws of the twelve tables were indeed a blessed invention! By them what did the family represent? The community of the wife, children, and slaves placed under absolute dominion of the father. That was the golden age for Rome, whoever may deny it, when they could sell their bleeding children."

"Then?" asked Santa Croce, astonished at this unexpected rebuff, letting his arms fall in despair. Count Cenci, repenting of not being able to repress the outbreak of his mind, hastened to reply:

"Oh! for you it is a different thing."

Santa Croce, comforted by these words, and more by the paternal look which the Count turned upon him, drew his chair nearer, and, leaning his head forward, whispered in the Count's ear:

"I have heard it said"—and then stopped; but the Count, in a jesting manner, as if imitating the phrases of confessors, encouraged him by saying:

"Go on, my son, go on!"

"I had ever believed, Count, that you, as a discreet and very prudent man, had always succeeded—when any one troubled you, in taking them out of your path with wonderful ease. Well skilled in natural sciences, you cannot be ignorant of the virtue of certain herbs, which send one to the region of the dead without changing horses; and what is more important, without leaving the mark of wheels upon the road."

"The virtues of herbs are wonderful; but of what avail they can be to you I cannot clearly comprehend."

"As to this, you must know that the illustrious Princess Costanza is accustomed to take a little milk every evening to make her sleep."

"Well."

"You can understand, the difficulty only lies whether it shall be a short sleep or a long sleep—a trochee or a spondee—a mere nothing, in fact, simple prosody;" and the villain endeavored to smile.

"*Misericordia Domini super nos*! A parricide for a mere beginning; it would be a good move! Unhappy man! and can you think of it? Honor thy father and thy mother! And there is no disputing that, since it was said by Him who could say it upon Sinai."

The Prince, pretending firmness, replied:

"As for thinking of it, rest assured, for I have thought of it a thousand times; as to its being a mere beginning, I wish you to know that this is by no means the first race I have run."

"I believe it without your swearing to it; but come nearer and let us reason seriously. The art of making poisons is no more in vogue as formerly; we have lost the knowledge of the greater part of those powerful poisons known to our virtuous fathers. The Princes Medici of Florence have labored in a praiseworthy manner about this most important branch of human science; but, if we consider the expense, with but little profit. There is the water *tophana;* good for nothing if one wishes the work done properly—the hair falls off, the nails are loosened, the teeth decay, the skin crumbles to pieces, and the whole body is filled with livid ulcers; so that, you see, it leaves behind too manifest and lasting traces. Alexander Sixth, of good memory, used it, but he did not care whether traces were left behind or not. For my part, I agree with Alexander the Great—with steel one cuts neatly every Gordian knot, and at once."

"What! the steel? And does not that leave any trace behind?"

"There was once a king called Edward Second who had a son of his own, as loving as you, by whom his bowels were pierced and burned, without leaving a single trace behind. In fact, a curious invention! But who advises you to keep secret the death of Lady Costanza? You ought rather to proclaim it, and call yourself openly the author."

"Count, you jest!"

"I do not jest; I speak rather with the best wisdom in the world. Have you never read histories, at least the Roman? Certainly you have. Very well; of what use is it to read books unless you derive instruction to appear well in the world? Remember the threat of Tarquin to Lucretia; he, unless the wife of Collatine would submit to him, declared he would kill her, and then place by her side a dead slave, asserting that he had surprised her with him, and killed her as a just punishment for the offence done to his relative, and in revenge for the sacred majesty of the laws; with a great many other words that honest men are accustomed to use. Thus you, neither more nor less, ought to try to surprise the princess with some one of her lovers, and kill them both. The gravity of the offence excuses the deed."

"But," replied the Prince, visibly embarrassed, "I do not know, really, whether she takes her lovers into her room."

"And where do you suppose she takes them?"

"And then to surprise them at the right moment—it would be impossible."

"Why so? Foxes are always taken in the trap."

"No; I will not, although able, put myself to the risk of doing the thing openly."

"Say, rather," interrupted the Count with a malignant smile, "say, rather, that you have conjured in your imagination lovers for a woman of sixty for the purpose of finding in others the faults which may excuse your own; say, also, that the reason that urges you is the desire that the annuity of your mother should cease; nor do I blame you for this, since I know how fathers eternally crucify their sons, if not with nails, at least with debts. The blame which I do attach to you is, that you have wished to make a fool of a poor old man, and play the sharper with me."

"Lord Count, in truth I swear to you"——

"Silence with your oaths; I believe or not; and oaths, in my idea, are like supports to buildings, sure signs of weakness; hence, without oaths, I do not believe you; still less with them."

"Come! do not abandon me!" And the Prince said this so humbly that Cenci, having tormented him to his satisfaction, and wishing to cut short the conversation, deridingly replied:

> *"'O dignitosa conscienza e netta,*
> *Come ti e picciol fallo amoro morso!'*

I remember to have read some time ago, in a certain case somewhat similar to yours, that the following method was put into execution. In the night, a ladder was placed at the window of the bedroom of the person or persons that were to be murdered; some gold and silver ornaments, and other articles of value, were then stolen and carefully destroyed, in order to give color to the thing, and to have it understood that the homicide was committed for the sake of the theft; finally, the window was left open, that it might be supposed the robbers fled thence. In such manner all suspicions were removed from the person to whom this death proved most useful; and the heir gained the reputation of being a good Christian by ordering a magnificent funeral and many masses. He did not even stop there, but wished also to acquire the name of being a rigid avenger of blood; he instigated justice to make the most diligent search, and lamented the sluggishness of the court; he even promised a reward of twenty thousand ducats to the secret or open denunciator of the guilty person. Thus our excellent fathers had the good fortune in their time of enjoying in holy peace the riches of the dead."

"Ah!" exclaimed Santa Croce, striking his forehead with his hand, "you have truly a great mind, Count! I profess everlasting gratitude to you. That plan will exactly suit my case. But this is not all; you would put a climax to your benevolence and my gratitude if you would kindly call from Rocca Petrella one of those brave fellows to whom you give the charge of such affairs."

"What affairs? of what persons are you talking? The knot is yours; and it is your business to find the thread to loosen it; but take care lest the thread should cut your fingers. We have not seen each other, and we shall never see each other again. Henceforth I wash my hands of it, like Pilate. Farewell, Don Paolo. That which I can do for you, and what I will do, will be to beseech Heaven in my prayers to assist you."

The Count rose to dismiss the Prince; and while with courteous manner he accompanied him to the door, he was thinking: "And there are people who maintain that I do not benefit my neighbors! Calumniators! Slanderers! It is impossible to do more than I. Let us see, now, how many are about to gain by me. The undertaker, *imprimis;* then the priests, whom I love so; then come the poets for the elegy; the preacher for the funeral oration; then Master Alessandro, the executioner; and, finally, the devil, if there is one." Meanwhile, having come to the door, the Count opened it, and taking leave of the Prince with his usual suavity of manner, he added, in a fatherly voice:

"Good-by, Don Paolo, and may God keep you in His holy peace."

CHAPTER III

THE ABDUCTION

THE Count looked into the antechamber, and beckoning to the other gentleman, said:

"My Lord Duke, at your pleasure."

The pale young man entered the chamber like one bewildered; the courteous invitation to be seated he either did not hear or did not wish to accept. But as if he had been seized by a vertigo, he leaned with one hand upon the desk, and gave vent to a profound sigh, which seemed to come from the bottom of his heart.

"What sighs, what pains are these?" asked the Count with flattering voice. "How is it possible at your age to find time to make yourself unhappy?"

And the Duke, with a voice that sounded like the soft murmuring of water, replied:

"I am in love."

The Count, to cheer him, added playfully:

"It is your season, my son, and you do perfectly right to love with all your soul, and with all your body. If you, young and handsome, could not love, who should? I, perhaps? You see that years have sprinkled snow upon my hair, and have bound my heart with ice. To you both heaven and earth speak of love; from all nature a voice comes to you which counsels to love:

'Le acque parlan d'amore, e l'ora, e i rami,
E gli augelletti, e i pesci, e i fiori, e l'erba
Tutti insieme pregando ch'io sempre ami.'

So sang the sweet lips of Francesco Petrarch. Come, cheer up, young man; is this a thing to be ashamed of? Preach it from the pulpit, proclaim it from the roofs; for love is good news. Petrarch, who was a grave man, and a canon of the church, was not ashamed to confess how love had enslaved him twenty-one years for Laura while she was alive, and ten years more after she had taken her flight to heaven. Mercy upon us! That was love to shame the oaks. Nor was he satisfied with having sung his love in a thousand rhymes, for in his declining years he wished he had made them

'In numbers more often, in style more rare.'

To Saint Theresa much was pardoned because she loved much; and some say even too much; this same saint called the devil unhappy, and do you know the reason why? Because he cannot love. Therefore, love *totis viribus;* for doing otherwise you offend Nature, who is, as you know, the first-born of God."

The young man, covering his face with both hands, and giving vent to a deep sigh, exclaimed:

"Ah! mine is a desperate love."

"Don't say that, for even the gates of hell are not without hope. Let us reason together. You have, perhaps, fallen in love with somebody's wife. Be warned! then we should indeed meet with an impediment; two, rather: in the first place the husband, then the commandment."

"No, my dear Count, mine is an honest love."

"Then marry her *in facie Ecclesiæ*, with all due ceremonies, according to the *sacrosanctum Concilium Tridentinum*, and do not come"——

"God knows I would gladly do it; but, alas! so much happiness is forbidden me."

"Then don't marry her."

"The woman I love is of lower birth than I would wish; but if her beautiful form, or rather the greatness of her soul, be considered, she is worthy of an empire."

"Royal soul, worthy of empire, the same Petrarch has said; and if so, you would better marry her."

"Cold ashes and shadows! This love will dwell eternally in me."

"How long will this eternity last? In women, according to the most accurate calculation, the eternity of love lasts an entire week; in some, but rarely, it is prolonged until perhaps the second Monday, and that is all."

The young man, although so engrossed with this love of his, could not help noticing the sneering manner in which Don Francesco spoke to him, and blushing with shame and anger, he replied:

"Sir, you do me wrong; I hoped to find advice. I deceived myself; excuse me!" He made a motion as if to depart. But the Count, detaining him, said gently:

"Please remain, Duke; I spoke thus merely to try you; I see now how truly vehement and fatal a passion burns within you. Unburden your heart to mine; I shall know how to pity you, and, being able, perhaps to help you. I have buried my loves; sixty years and more have associated them with the grave, and sung their *miserere;* for me love is a memory, for you a hope; for me ashes, for you a rose that blooms; but still I nourish within sparks of the ancient flame, and, reasoning with myself, I repeat the lines of Petrarch:

'Ove sia chi per prova intenda amore
Spero trovar pietà, non che perdono'

Non ignara mali miseris succurrere disco, as Dido said to Æneas, who came from Troy to build Rome for the greater glory of the Popes in general, and for Clement Eighth in particular."

Count Cenci, in spite of his protest, sneered; but it was impossible to judge whether he spoke in earnest or in jest, since he appeared so grave; he only half closed his eyes, and his eyelids trembled continually.

"The girl I love lives in the house of the Falconieri. What her lineage may be I know not, but although she is treated as a relative, she belongs to a servile condition. Alas! since I first saw her at the Church of Gesù, adorned with her beauty and modesty, I have lost my sleep; every other woman appears low and common to me."

"Speak in a low tone, if you please, Duke: woe to you if our proud Roman ladies should hear you. They would make of you a second edition of Orpheus torn to pieces by the Bacchantes, with notes and appendix."

"Supposing her an easy conquest," continued the young man passionately, "(and God knows how much remorse it has caused me), I left untried no means to succeed in my desires. Alas! miserable that I am! I fear lest these proposals might have offended her, and perhaps she now hates me!" Here he paused, afraid of sighing; then, with lower tone, he continued. "How repulsive my dishonest propositions must have sounded in the ears of that virtuous girl!"

And the Count, staring at him in astonishment, thought: "I never saw a more simple fellow."

"The Falconieri," the Duke continued, "have made me understand that I should cease passing under their palace windows, since the girl is such that I ought not to marry her, nor will she consent to be my mistress."

"And you, then?"

"I chose to ask her in marriage."

"There is no remedy: I should have done the same."

"My relatives, as soon as they heard of my intention, rose in a fury against me, as if I were about to commit a sacrilege; they asked me to consider the offence to their blood, and the dishonor done to the nobility of their house. The disdain of my kindred, the rage of my companions, and a thousand such deviltries have so worried my brains that I am almost in despair."

"Eh! it is a serious affair; and I should have said the same."

"I wish it could be shown in what way the nobility differ from the common people. Perhaps the rain does not wet, nor the sun warm us; perhaps troubles do not assail us; our cradle is not girded with cries, our deathbed besieged by tears. Can we say to Death, as to an importunate creditor, 'Return to-morrow?' Can we sleep our last sleep better under a marble sepulcher than the people do under the sod? I wish it could be seen whether worms, before coming to gnaw the body of a pope or an emperor, take their hats off, saying, 'By your leave, your holiness;' 'By your leave, your majesty?'

Does my dukedom sow or reap happiness; does not love level all difference among lovers?"

"It is so; 'Love levels all distinctions,' says the poet. Something like it Torquato Tasso sang with his accustomed elegance in his sylvan fable—do you recollect it, Duke?"

"*Dio mio!* What do you wish me to recollect? I have no memory, no mind, no anything more. For pity's sake, my dear Count, you who have so much wisdom and experience of the world, be kind enough to give me a remedy for this evil."

"My dear," said the Count, placing his hand familiarly upon the shoulder of the Duke, "listen to me; you are right."

"Yes?"

"And neither are your relatives wrong. You are right, since the smoke of nobility is not worth the smoke of a pipe. Your relatives are not wrong, for they see, as well as I, the artifice of a woman in this affair, who, by her natural disposition, or by the suggestions of others, plays a game with you. Do not be angry, Duke; you came to consult the oracle, and its responses must be heard, although unpleasant. That which seems to you a sincere resistance appears to me a studied repulse, with the idea that obstacles irritate the passions. The more a thing is forbidden, the more it creates desire, and thus the woman calculates upon the ardor of your passion to bring you where she wishes. In short, it appears the net is stretched to draw profit from the flame that burns within you. To love is human; to allow ourselves to be conquered by blind passion is to be like brutes. When I was young, and gave my mind to such things, people were not so particular. A gentleman like you, when he took a fancy to some plebeian beauty, could persuade her to his pleasure with money. If she denied him, and this I can assure you happened very seldom, at least in my time, he would have her by force. If the friends barked, he would throw a handful of money in their throats and silence them; for the plebeians bark, like Cerberus, in order to have food. When the woman became troublesome—and this happened often—with a little dowry one could get her married; nor were chances wanting; for I do not see how these people degrade themselves in yielding to the wishes of a gentleman; neither do women's lips, after being kissed, lose their beauty."

The Duke made a gesture of horror. The Count, unmoved, kept on:

"No, my son; do not despise the advice of the old. I have seen more of the world than you, and I know how these affairs usually end. Mark me, if you please: I will propose to you a fine way, and one sure of success. First, you must get possession of the girl; and here stands the whole, or indeed, the greater part, you must acknowledge. Then, if she turns out to be a Clelia, a Virginia, or a Penthesilea, why, marry her in holy peace, and there is an end. But if you can avoid this rock of matrimony, do so by all means; since matrimony is in truth the grave of love, which holy water extinguishes. The *Yes* you must pronounce is the feeble cry of Hymen, and at the same time the last sigh of love in agony. Matrimony is born of love, like vinegar from wine; besides, you will escape the indignation of your relatives, and the gossip of the world, which is of no little gain. You may call these the stings of gnats, and I grant it you; but when gnats attack you by thousands they are likely to make you scream by their small but sharp sting, which unpleasantness a discreet man ought always to avoid, if he can."

"No, Count, no; rather would I thrust a dagger in my heart."

"Softly to desperate steps; we always have time to

throw ourselves away. Before taking misfortune for a medicine, consider the business well; you may see that my proposal presents two plans, and at the same time two ways of solving the difficulties. You, with your sound judgment, may govern yourself according to circumstances."

"But if the girl should hate me?"

"You recollect the spear of Achilles. It healed the wound it made; so love heals the wound of love; and beauty is easy in forgiving sins committed for its sake. She will pardon you—do not be afraid—she will pardon you, or is the world now to begin going backward? Don't try to fall into the net like a bird. Women, more than you imagine, often show themselves warlike so as to prove the valor of a lover. In Sparta, if a lover wished to have a wife he had to steal her; nor do I remember any historian who says that the wife was displeased by it. Did not Ersilia perhaps love Romulus? Should we Romans, who are descended from the stolen Sabines, be afraid of an abduction?"

The young man, confused and perplexed by such reasoning, felt as if dragged over a slippery ground. In the frenzy of his passion, he replied:

"And what have I to do? I am not a man for such business. Where shall I begin? Where can I find men willing to put themselves to such risk for me?"

The Count thought awhile, for without help the honest young man would have remained where he was; and besides, an idea had come into his head that had not occurred to him before. He hastened to add:

"What are friends good for in this world? In this affair I can assist you somewhat, if my sight does not deceive me." He opened the door of the hall, and called:

"Olimpio!"

The peasant, like a hound that raises its head at the

call of his master, started to his feet, answering with insolent familiarity:

"Ah, your Excellency has noticed at last that I am still in the world;" and grumblingly added in a lower tone, "he wishes to send some one to heaven, without a doubt."

"Come here!"

Olimpio obeyed. When he entered the room, with that humility which even the most impudent plebeians feel at the sight of lordly halls and furniture, he removed his hat, and upon his shoulders fell a mass of black hair, which, mingling with his beard, gave him the appearance of a river-god crowned with reeds, as sculptors are wont to design them. He had a face as hard as if cut from solid stone; bloodshot eyes hidden under shaggy eyebrows, like those of wolves in their den; a voice deep and harsh.

"We are still alive, eh?" the Count asked him, smiling.

"Eh! certainly, by a miracle of Saint Nicholas. After the last murder which I committed for your Excellency"——

"What are you talking about, Olimpio? Of what murder are you dreaming?"

"I dream, why? On your account, order, and commission," and striking the desk with his large hand, he added, "here you counted out to me the three hundred golden ducats, which was not too much; but so it was. I was contented with it, and there is no use of talking more about it. If I took little, the worse for me. Here"——

And as the Count, with hands and eyes, warned him to stop from saying any more of this affair, he continued undisturbed.

"Oh! that is another thing; you should have advised me in time; I thought we were all friends. I beg your pardon. To return to our subject. The police were round me tighter than my belt; the rope has grazed my neck oftener than the glass has wet my lips; every tree seems to my eyes a gibbet. Now, in this dress I hardly recognize myself; therefore I have dared to return, because you know idleness is the parent of all vices; and I, having nothing to do, am so reduced as to be obliged to work. If in the mean while one of your enemies has a throat more than you wish him to have, here we are at the orders of your Excellency;" and with his right hand he made a horizontal sign at his neck.

"You come like a medlar in October; and I will try to find some little job for you to do, since there is no work of any importance on hand; but I repeat it is a mere nothing—a slight touch of your trade—to keep you in practice."

"Let us hear, then;" and the bandit, with the terrible familiarity that crime gives to accomplices, seated himself. He crossed his legs, leaned his left elbow upon his raised knee, rested his face upon his open hand, and with closed eyes and underlip projecting, he assumed an attitude of profound attention.

"This young cavalier, who is the most illustrious Lord Duke of Altemps"—the Count began.

"Ah, ah!" and without unclosing his eyes, the bandit made a slight sign with his head.

"Is desperately in love with a certain girl"——

"Of your class or ours?"

"How do I know? A chambermaid."

"Neither of yours nor ours," observed Olimpio, shrugging his shoulders in contempt.

"Being sought in love, she has a notion of standing upon her dignity. The Falconieri, who, had they a patrimony equal to their pride, would ruin us, protect her. She lives in their house, and this makes her more haughty; very likely, too, there is some prelate in the affair, which I have neither desire nor time to ascertain;

however it may be, this is an impediment for the Lord Duke"——

"Who calls me?" asked the Duke, starting suddenly.

"Poor youth, see how his passion bewilders him! I wager you have not heard a word of what I and Olimpio have been discussing."

The Duke looked down and blushed.

"In conclusion, Olimpio, it is necessary that you steal her away by force, and carry her where you shall be ordered."

"Is that all, your Excellency?"

"That is all for the present. You will try to enter the palace; if not able, force a door or a grate on the ground floor; if this does not succeed, try a rope-ladder"——

"Poh! that is enough. I know all about these things, with some additions which you don't know. Let me see —one—two—three—I want four companions."

"Those you will find yourself."

"Pistols and horses must be provided. How much do you intend to expend on this enterprise?"

"Well, will not five hundred ducats do?"

"No, sir; they are not enough. After I give a share to my companions, and deduct the expense for horses and weapons, nothing will be left for me."

"Come, we shall not quarrel about that. Say eight hundred ducats, besides the protection and favor which you may expect from me."

"Poh, poh! I shall have to order a cart to carry them home! The feast ended, the flowers are taken away. Sir Count, let us end this nonsense; when I come back to you like a cricket, then you may feed me on dew. Where am I to carry the girl?"

"To the palace of the Duke, or to some one of his numerous country-seats, or wherever he indicates."

"A mistake, your Excellency; if the police get an inkling of the affair, the first places they will visit will be the residences of my Lord Duke. You must then hire or borrow from some person secretly a villa far from the city; and it would be better to hire it by means of some person unconnected with your home."

The Count looked in the face of Olimpio, and smiled in mockery at not having been understood; then he seated himself at his desk and began to write. The ruffian asked some short and rough questions of the young Duke, who answered in a careless manner. He felt like a leaf blown about by the wind; he had fallen under the spell of that kind of fascination which some snakes use toward animals; he wished to protest, he tried to fly, but could not. The Count, although busy with his writing, felt the victory of vice over ingenuous youth; stopping suddenly, he asked carelessly:

"When is the undertaking to be?"

"According to my calculations, it can't be ready until to-morrow night," replied Olimpio.

"To-morrow night, eh? But do you not know that the hour-glass with which passion measures the time of expectation is a torch which throws its burning sparks upon the heart of a poor lover? You are getting old, Olimpio, and are not as you used to be. Once one could stamp upon your face the words *cito ac fidelis*, which motto belongs to the decision of the sacred Roman Tribunal, but which does not prevent litigation from lasting as long as the siege of Troy, and from being treacherous enough to shame Sinon. After a trot we must be contented with a pace; to-morrow, then." A little later, bending his face toward the Duke, he said: "Although by nature I revolt from any kind of indiscreet curiosity, still I cannot resist the desire of knowing the name of your inamorata. Would you be kind enough to inform me, Duke?"

"Lucrezia."

"Oh, Lucrezia! It seems fated that these Lucrezias should always turn our Roman brains. This time, however, she will not cause the expulsion of the King of Rome. We have popes now, who have a better foothold (may God preserve them!) and possess different virtues than those of Tarquin; and Roderigo Lenzuoli is enough for them. Italy can do rather better without the sun than without the Pope; without his blessing, *urbi et orbi*, grain could not grow;" and returning to his writing he murmured, as in excess of merriment, "Lucrezia!

'Crezia, Creziuccia, Crezina,
Ardo per voi sera e mattina.'"

Having finished his writing he arose, saying:

"Olimpio, I believe you have to say your prayers, so you may go now. Be careful that no one sees you leaving my house; for, although you may be sweeter than bread, and as honest as a coat of mail, you can well understand that one may have better friendships than yours. Marzio!" and Marzio entered.

"Marzio, accompany this evangelist by the back stairway to the door of the garden that opens on the lane. Good-by; remember me in your prayers!"

"How are you, my good fellow?" asked Olimpio, slapping the shoulder of Marzio, as he was descending the stairs.

"As it pleases God," replied Marzio, a little harshly.

"What! don't you recollect me, Marzio?" said the other.

"I?—no."

"Look at me better, and then you will see that what I think you think."

"And what do you think?"

"I think that we should be a magnificent pair of earrings to hang upon Dame Gibbet."

"Is that you, Olimpio?"

"The spirit of the gibbet acts like vinegar upon the nose: it clears the intellect and recalls the memory."

"Count," said the young Duke hesitatingly, "I fear I show myself ungrateful to your counsel and aid—but still I feel I cannot thank you—God—(but I do wrong in invoking His holy name in this wicked affair; it were better if He knew nothing about it). May fortune grant that this does not end in evil."

"And fortune is on your side, since, being a woman, she loves the young and bold. If Cæsar had not passed the Rubicon, would he have become Dictator of Rome?"

"True, but the Ides of March would not have seen him slain at the foot of Pompey's statue."

"Every man carries from his birth his star's ascendant. Forward, then! You cannot fail, for a host of Italian, Greek, and Latin authors support you. And why do you fear to trust to Fortune? She rules the world. Look at Sulla! he, more than anyone, knew how to settle differences with the ax, and he dedicated to her the beautiful temple of Præneste."

The Count, as soon as the Duke had left him, took up the paper upon which he had been writing, and read, stopping occasionally to laugh heartily:

"'Most Reverend and Illustrious Monsignore:—

"'The greatest iniquity that ever has stained this most august and happy seat of true religion is about to be attempted. The Duke Serafino d'Altemps, to give sway to some of his passionate desires, conspires to-morrow night to abduct, with an armed force from the palace of the Falconieri, an honest girl named Lucrezia, a servant in the house of that family. The Duke will be accompanied by three or four of the most desperate banditti, commanded by the famous Olimpio, sought for two years by justice for robberies and assassinations, with the offer of a reward of three hundred golden ducats. Be on your guard, for they are people used to all sorts of daring attempts, and danger only augments their boldness. A lover of good government, zealous for order and the exaltation of the Holy Mother Church, warns you of this.

"'Rome, August 6, 1598.'"

"Good! The handwriting never will be known for mine; in one hour this note will be in the pious hands of Monsignore Taverna." He folded it, sealed it, made the sign of the cross over it, and directed it to Monsignore Taverna, Governor of Rome.

"Honor to whom honor is due; he is a duke and must be treated as one. Of that pearl of a Prince, we will think by and by. And so we get rid of Olimpio, if he does not manage to escape this time."

CHAPTER IV

THE TEMPTATION

THE young married pair entered. The man kissed the Count's hand—the woman would have done the same, but the child that she held prevented her by crying. Was it chance or a presentiment? Man knows not the secrets of nature. The Count gazed steadily at the woman, and seeing she was wonderfully beautiful his eyes dilated while they sparkled like the lightning.

"Who are you, good people, and what can I do for you?"

"Your Excellency," said the young man, "do you not recognize me? I am the son of that poor carpenter—do you not remember?—who was ruined nearly four years ago, and had it not been for your charity, would have thrown himself into the Tiber."

"Ah! now I remember. You have grown to be a man, my boy; and how is the good old man, your father?"

"The Lord has called him to himself. Believe me, your Excellency, his last sigh was for God, his last but one for your family and yourself. He was never weary of calling down blessings upon you, and wishing you from heaven all the prosperity man can desire."

"May God keep him in his holy peace! Are these your wife and child?"

"Yes, your Excellency. As soon as my wife recovered, I thought it my duty to bring her to do reverence to you, and to offer thanks with all our hearts, for to you, after God, we owe all our happiness."

"Are you happy?"

"Very happy, your Excellency, except that the memory of my lost father sometimes comes to disturb me; but his years were many, and he died like a child falling asleep. He had no sins upon his soul; and I was a witness how quietly he passed the last night. Poor father!" and so saying he wiped away his tears.

"And you, good woman, are you happy?"

"Yes, my lord, by the grace of the Blessed Virgin, more than thought can imagine, or words express. Michele loves me, and I love him, and we both love very much this beautiful angel of ours. Michele earns enough for our support, and a little more. So your Excellency sees it would be complaining of God's providence not to be satisfied." And the woman in saying this looked almost divine.

"You are then happy?" the Count asked, for the third time, with a deep voice.

"Through your goodness we can say so, your Excellency. When I first entered Michele's house I learned to venerate your name. The first words I shall teach this child will be to bless the name of the charitable Lord Francesco Cenci."

"You fill my heart with joy," the Count said, concealing the rage that choked him; and, to dissemble better, he kissed and patted the little child. "Good people! worthy souls! Still, the little good I did you does not deserve so many thanks; besides, it belongs to us favored with large wealth to help Christ's poor. Of what use is money if not to repair some misfortune? Can it be better spent? Do we not surely invest it in heaven, where it will be repaid to us a hundredfold? I ought then to thank you, my beloved, for having given me an opportunity for doing good." He then, taking a purse from the drawer in his desk, drew out a handful of gold and offered it to the woman, who blushingly tried to refuse it; but the Count, pressing it upon her, said:

"Take it, my daughter, take it. You should have told me before of the birth of this child; I should have wished to be his godfather. But take this, and buy him something handsome, for although very beautiful, still, as the poet says,

'A beautiful robe enhances beauty.'

I would that people in seeing him should exclaim: She is fortunate who has so fine a child, and your mother's heart will exult."

The young mother at first smiled, then, being moved by these gentle words that touched her heart, she wept.

"Continue to love each other," continued the Count, with the solemn voice of a father; "and may jealousy never disturb the serenity of your days, nor may you ever love the house of another better than your own—live peacefully and in the holy fear of God. Sometime in your prayers remember me, a poor old man, for I am not—oh! believe me, I am not as I may seem to you, happy" (and the Count, from being pale, as he usually was, became livid); "and if in any need you should come to me you will surely find me a father."

The young people leaned forward as if to kiss his hand, but he would not consent to it, and with benign voice and gesture he dismissed them. In crossing the hall, they said to each other:

"Oh, the pious lord! The charitable gentleman!"

The valets, hearing these words, looked at each other, shrugging their shoulders, and the boldest among them murmured:

"Has the devil made himself a Capuchin friar?"

"Happy! happy!" burst forth Francesco Cenci, giving free vent to his suppressed anger, "and they come to tell it to my face! They did this to torment me with the sight of their happiness! This is the greatest insult I have endured for a long time! Marzio! run quickly and rejoin Olimpio—bring him back—haste, I say! If you return with him before twelve, I will give you ten ducats. I shall see whether any man, without shedding tears of blood, shall dare to declare in the face of Francesco Cenci that he is happy!"

At this moment, and certainly it was unfortunate for him, the worthy priest entered softly. *Omnes sitientes venite ad aquas*, he joyfully thought, and he held together the folds of his torn robe; but the deep growling of Nero startled him from his joy. The priest (forgetful though he was of even the most grievous offences) remembered that of his enemy, the dog, and he appeared like Lot's wife, when she turned to look back on burning Sodom.

"Silence, Nero! Reverend sir, approach without fear."

The priest, regaining courage, moved a few steps sidewise; and being requested to seat himself, sat upon the extreme corner of the chair, huddled together like an owl on the corner of a roof.

"Speak, sir, I am at your pleasure."

"I am not at all at mine," thought the priest, but did not say it: instead, he spoke:

"The fame"-——

Nero, hearing the priest's voice, began to growl again, and the priest started, frightened; the dog being again quieted, the priest attempted to speak, always watching the brute with a side look and cursing him within himself.

"The fame of your magnanimous deeds, which resounds throughout the world"——

"And through Rome?"

"That is understood, of course, my lord, since Rome is part of the world."

"And for that reason I said so."

"And compares you to Cæsar"——

"Which of the two, reverend sir, Julius or Octavius?"

"Rumor does not signify exactly which, but I mean the one who made so many presents to the Romans, both during his life and after his death."

"And do you know the reason why he could give so much?"

"Eh! I suppose because he had plenty."

"Of course he had plenty of money, since he robbed the whole world; and his debt has fallen upon us, his descendants, and we must pay it with large interest. I tell you"——

"What! does it belong to you to pay the debts of Julius Cæsar?"

"And have you come here to compare me, to my face, to that illustrious robber of provinces and kingdoms?"

The unfortunate priest cursed the hour that had put the idea into his head of repeating a speech composed for the occasion a long time before; it would have been better for him had he spoken in his usual manner. "Ah!" he thought, "if things could be done twice!" Then, mortified, he murmured:

"Pardon me, my lord—I did not intend—I thought to

imitate the speech of my Lord Giovanni della Casa to Charles the Fifth—that"——

"Listen to me," said Cenci, leaving at once his mocking tone, and assuming a severe expression; "I am old, and you are older than I; hence, neither of us has any time to spare; speak distinctly and quickly. All long things tire me—even the thought of Eternity."

The priest, caught thus unaware, knew not where to begin; the sudden change from sweet to sour had astonished him; besides, the last sentence of the Count sounded heretical. At last he said:

"Your Excellency—you see in me a priest—and what is more, a country curate—my church resembles a sieve. The rain pours from the roof and mixes with the wine in the cups. My parsonage is like a baked pomegranate—often when it rains I am obliged to lie in bed with a canopy over me; and that is not all. Can you imagine with what I am obliged to wipe my face? Can you guess?"

"Certainly not."

"With Rodomonte."

"And what is Rodomonte?"

"The cat at my parsonage; and he, at least, gets something to eat on the roof; but for Marco and me who cannot procure food on the roofs, we are often obliged to go without dinner and supper, and I sigh and Marco brays. I have only one robe—or rather—as Chremes says in the *Heautontimoroumenos*, ignorant whether his son were living—I cannot say whether I have or not; it is certainly so shiny that I can see myself in it; but at least with a little mending it might have lasted me until December—and now, see how your Excellency's dog has ruined it!" And in showing the rent, his voice sounded like the intonation of *Stabat Mater Dolorosa*.

"Have you not taken a vow of poverty? Why do you complain of a state which so nearly reaches perfection?

This perfection does not please you, then? You would prefer rather to be imperfect, with some thousand ducats' income, than perfect, and more than perfect, with poverty? Complain to the Author of your precepts, which you priests appear not to understand. Jesus Christ has preached to you that your goods are not of this earth; look at heaven, and select there your field; no space is wanting, thank God! But you shut your eyes and say in your hearts, 'The doubloon is the Father, the half-doubloon the son, the third the Holy Ghost;' and, finally, you believe the one is derived from the other.

'Godete, Preti, poichè il vostro Cristo....
Dai Turchi e dai concilii vi difende.'

Shame, reverend sir, shame upon this continual thought of worldly things! When the Church used chalices of wood, the priests were of gold! Saint Clement of Alexandria said it. Now that the Church has golden chalices, the priests are of wood. And do you know, reverend sir, of what kind of wood? Of that wood which the holy Gospel declares should be cut down and thrown into the fire, because unfruitful."

The poor curate bore this shower of reproaches as veteran soldiers meet their enemies' fire; then he exclaimed, with a sigh:

"Ah! Saint Clement of Alexandria was a very learned saint; but I don't believe he was obliged to lie in bed with a canopy over him when it rained."

"It may be so. Are you in want of the necessaries of life? Then have recourse to the rich prelates. Have not they, perhaps, had too much? But what do you want of us—our last drops of blood? Go! Knock at the palaces of bishops, at the doors of abbots. Knock, I say, and it will be opened unto you; ask and it will be given; *pulsate, et aperietur vobis* has been said by Him who never fails."

"But—it seems these dignitaries are usually busy out of doors. I have tried to knock at their doors, but seeing I might break my knuckles before any one of them would open to me, I gave up the idea."

"You minor clergy are like a flock of sheep, so the fat prelates call you, and they behave like true shepherds to you. Everyone can see that they follow all the shepherds' customs. Do they not milk you? Don't they shear you? Don't they skin, roast, and eat you? Now, be bold, and rebel against this wicked hierarchy; publish to the world the fact that upon one single person are heaped benefices, prebends and abbeys, either by simony, fraud, or some more vile action; which, on the one side, make lazy, proud, vicious, and rascally priests, and on the other, poor, vile, despised, and roguish ones; show that the Councils have not reformed anything; proclaim that this wicked college of hypocritical Pharisees attends to nothing but how to make bread with the devil's flour. Oblige epicures to share with you their table, which they like so well to spread to excess, and which, through the ignorance and folly of others, will continue to be furnished to excess."

The curate, astonished at such a whirlwind of heresies, looked around with fear, and then observed in a low tone:

"For the love of God, your Excellency, be kind enough to remember that here in Rome there is something—that is—a certain holy office of Inquisition, and the Castle Saint Angelo."

"You are afraid? Very well, if you have learned to tremble, you should have learned also how to suffer. Why did you desert the banner of Nature? Why did you throw aside your ancestral spade to rule over men? When you priests leave the country, the vines cry after you, and the soil groans for you. Return, fugitive servants, to your ploughs and farms. The earth surpasses in love even the most affectionate of mothers; she feeds, clothes, and buries you—what more do you want, indiscreet men? Do you complain that Nature has disinherited you? It is false! Has the earth ever failed you? Where are buried the thousand generations that preceded you? In the earth. Has not Mother Nature destined for each one of you three cubic feet of earth, and to some even more? Does not this remark please you? The breviary weighs less than the hoe. You wish to enjoy here the heaven you promise to others above. Lazy men, you wish to eat without working the honey gathered by the bees! You shall not get one ducat from me. I have no money to aid your luxuries. I cannot pay the expenses of your vices, and you have more of them than Jacob's sons, although one of your vices costs more than three sons."

The poor priest stood like one who, far from any shelter, is surprised by a pouring rain in an open country, and bends his body ready to receive as much water as God is willing to send. But, struck by the abomination of the last reproof, he raised his eyes to heaven, and said:

"Your Excellency, as to Verdiana, the servant I have at home, I swear by Him who desires no man to swear, she is so old that she might have helped to bring the stones with which the Coliseum was built. But can you think, sir, that a man of my age and character would give a thought to such dishonest deeds?"

"Why not? Old bones, like dry wood, blaze the soonest, Petrarch said; and in love-affairs the canonical Petrarch was well versed, and more viciously, too, than the old sinner would have us believe, since he is of your profession."

The old priest, raising his hands and eyes, exclaimed: "Lord Jesus! what am I obliged to hear!"

Count Cenci suddenly made a horizontal line with his finger upon his forehead, as if he wished to change the tone of the conversation, and with milder voice continued:

"Oh, I did not apply this to you, my poor priest, who appear so reduced by want as to resemble Saint Basil. If I ever deign to speak about my own affairs to anyone, be assured I would confess to no one but you. But a truce to words, my dear curate. How much is needed to restore the church and parsonage, buy a new robe to repair Nero's mischief, and half a dozen napkins, to let the fur of Rodomonte rest?"

"I will tell you; Verdiana and I have made the calculation a thousand times, she upon a corner of the almanac, and I upon the margin of my breviary, and we never could agree; for she always makes it more and I less, but two hundred ducats might do, I should think."

"Two hundred ducats! Do you suppose they are plenty as prunes?"

"I do not see how it can be done with less," said the priest, crossing his hands over his breast; "and mark, your Excellency, to that I should have to add about forty ducats of my own which I keep in the desk at the head of my bed, and which cost me some forty thousand fasts not ordered by the Church."

"Listen to me, reverend father; I am not rich enough to presume to restore God's house. He is the master of good and bad weather; and if He is willing to have rain come into His house, it is certain He likes rain. I will give you a hundred ducats, but on one condition."

"What is it, your Excellency?"

"That you will use them, together with your forty, in restoring the parsonage, getting the necessary furniture, the napkins, and a robe for yourself, and a gown also for Verdiana."

"Oh no, never, your Excellency, never! I should like to repair the parsonage, to procure the furniture, and a gown for Verdiana, more than to replace my robe, but the Lord's business must be attended to before any private comfort. Verdiana and I agree upon this point, and we would never appropriate a penny to ourselves, if we could not first provide for the house of the Lord."

"What blasphemy are you uttering about God's house? Has He, like us, need of a house to shelter Him from the rains or the dews of night? The universe is the house of God; the stars, the sun and moon, and every earthly thing that lives, vegetates, or grows here below. God is all. He penetrates all, His divinity emanates from everything. God is to be worshiped in the magnificence of Nature, in the works of intellect, and in the innocence and sensibility of man."

"Count," replied the curate, placing his hand over his heart with dignified simplicity, "I am a man, poor in intellect; I believe what my fathers believed and seek no more. I know, too, that the human mind often rushes boldly on, till it reaches a certain point, and can go no farther, and then, between the doubts that torment a man and the faith that consoles him, the wisest course, it appears to me, would be to hold firmly to the faith."

These sincere words stung fiercely Count Cenci, who, endeavoring to conceal the wound under a multiplicity of wicked words, hastened to answer:

"You, of course, according to the fashion of sophists, run away from the subject. I did not dispute your belief, but the manner of believing. How can you think God dislikes rain in your church? If He did not, being the controller of it, He need not send it. He created water and fire also; when He is wet, if He wishes to be dry He has only to take one of the infinite number of suns in heaven, and put it in His fireplace. Look here; these are ducats, and new ones" (and taking a handful of ducats, he showed them to the priest); "these shall be yours on condition you will spend them for yourself and Verdiana. God is rich enough to pay His own expenses." And so saying, he thrust his tempting face forward, as the devil did to St. Anthony. The priest coveted the money with his eyes, and the cupidity of poverty was expressed in every fiber of his body. A terrible struggle was going on in his poor soul. The Count, seeing the poor priest waver, said quickly:

"And this last reason must convince you: if you do not accept my condition, I shall put the money back in my drawer."

"Your Excellency!"——

"But come; let us put aside the reasons which I have expressed to you; they do not please you, and I will insist no longer. Is it not true, however, that you must provide for two things: the church and the parsonage? You must confess, then, that if the church is holy, the parsonage is also a religious place. Now, tell me, do you not commit a gross error by beginning at the former instead of the latter? You will, at least, have done so much in the fulfilment of your duty. Do not be obstinate; remember that there are men so just that they perish on account of their justice, and this King Solomon said."

"Your Excellency—certainly—in such a light—it seems to me—and yet"——

"Come, come, then; accept, and promise to use it entirely for yourself. Think, if you please, of another reason; as God is, you and I believe, eternal, He cannot complain of waiting four or six years, and I might say even centuries. If you were different from what you are, I would say let us do as He does, who never thinks of us. Now, will you take them, or not?"

"Ah, sir! the temptation is great, but I fear to commit a very great sin."

"Will you take them, or not?"

"Let me reflect. It is no small matter to overcome

scruples for sinning, to a curate who has the charge of souls."

"Well, well; put it all to the debt of my soul; for I have a long account with Heaven."

"Ah! I will take them."

"Here is the money; now promise."

"I do promise."

"Now be careful not to fail. I will send, or I will come myself to see whether you have kept that promise: if I find otherwise, woe to you! My name is Francesco Cenci, and that is enough."

The curate, both happy and sad, pocketed the money, and returning humble thanks, with a number of vows, brought to a conclusion his ill-omened visit.

Marzio returned in company with Olimpio, and receiving the promised reward, retired by the Count's order to the ante room.

"Is there anything new, your Excellency?"

"There are a hundred and forty ducats more to put under your belt."

"Do you wish me to die of indigestion?"

"I thought a little while ago that you went off not well satisfied, and I have recalled you so as to give you some addition to good payment."

"This is really a deluge of affection to me!"

"A bad cavalier is he who takes no care of his horse; and there is no favor which I would not be ready and willing to do you to remove from your heart the little aversion which you may have conceived for me."

"Aversion—I? How can you think so, Lord Count. I have always liked you more than bread."

"Which one bites and swallows, eh? Come here, you funny fellow, for it is only a joke that I am now going to propose to you. The ducats I spoke of are already yours."

"Where are they?"

"Nothing is wanted, but that you go and take them. Don't make wry faces. Did you see that crow of a priest? well, I have given them to him for your sake. Now, you must know that this fellow is the curate of Saint Sabina, a small church, far from any habitation. In his house he keeps an old woman, a cat, and as I understand him, a donkey: an easy affair, and to be accomplished to-night. You will find the money within the kneeling-desk, on one side of the priest's bed."

"Why did you give them to him, if you intended to take them away so soon again from the poor devil?"

"When I attempted to teach you the way to enter the Falconieri palace, you said it was not becoming for me to enter into such affairs: do you remember? Use toward me, then, the same discretion that you wished me to show toward you."

"You are right; I shall not say another word. Do you wish anything more, Sir Count?"

"Ah, yes, another little service. Do you know the carpenter who lives near Ripetta; the one who rebuilt his house with my money?"

"The young man who was waiting in the hall a little while ago? Certainly, I know him, and where he lives; for when you gave the money to rebuild his house, I went to see it, to try to solve the riddle of your benevolence."

"What! am not I in the habit of doing good, then? and even now, am I not benefiting you? Do not add ingratitude to your other sins; for that is the one least liked by the guardian angel—to-morrow night."

"I cannot serve you; I am engaged with the Lord Duke; don't you remember?"

"I will excuse you to him."

"Excuse me; for the honor of the profession, I cannot fail."

"I will try to have him excuse you with his own mouth."

"Oh, very well, then."

"To-morrow night you will enter by some means the carpenter's shop; take his tools, and the wood you will find there, and make a pile of them; place underneath some bituminous matter (which I will prepare for you, and you may come to-morrow after the *Ave Maria*, by the back entrace, for it); light it, and then go away, after first bolting the door of the shop. You will receive for this pious work one hundred ducats. Serve me faithfully, for in a short time I will make you rich. And where, indeed, can I better employ my money than with you?—and you agree with me. Go now, by the garden gate, and mind that no one sees you either in going or returning."

Olimpio obeyed.

Francesco Cenci, being at last alone, rubbed his hands with deep satisfaction, and with half suppressed voice murmured:

"This morning is Easter for me! This is what I call living! A parricide plotted, an abduction contrived, a robbery and a fire prepared—the traitors afterward betrayed; and in addition, I have made a holy man fall. While I live in this world the devil may go and rusticate in a villa. I am the opposite of Titus. He mourned if he passed a day without doing good; I am in a fever if I do not commit a score of crimes. Titus! An impostor of humanity, a Jesuit of paganism! Judea shall speak for me, and the fire that was extinguished by a torrent of human blood; and the multitude of those crucified, for whom the ground failed to plant crosses, and crosses for bodies; the eleven thousand who died in prison by starvation, and the thousands thrown to the wild beasts for having courageously defended their country. Go, go, unfeeling nature, that knows neither how to love nor hate! I worship only force. Everything is false but force; it heats the iron, brands generations on their cheeks, and thus scourging, disperses them throughout the world!

"If I had been in the battle which the rebellious angels fought against God—God!—God! That word comes continually back to me like a tiresome gnat, vainly driven off. Who hath ever seen this Being? who hath spoken to Him? More than fifty years have now passed since I first offended Him with all kinds of outrages, and His curse fattens my fields. Why did He create me thus? And if He did not create me, why should he, Creator, suffer in peace others to rob Him and spoil His trade? *Anima mala;* are our souls wicked then? Be it so; was it not in His power to make me good or bad? Then, if He repented, it is a sign He had made a mistake; and if He mistook, why should we bear the penalty of His error? Where is, then, His omniscience? where is His omnipotence? where is His infinite love? Could He not destroy man and nature entirely, and begin again? Better to do so than lose Himself in that labyrinth of redemption, which, after all, has not redeemed anything. It was smoke; it has left the world as it found it—and if men went to perdition by gradual steps before, now they run to it. Hell! Let it be so; I will go there for the very reason that the sentence will be given by Him who is judge and party, and, what is more, without appeal. All wicked judges condemn without appeal. But God has made us, and not we ourselves. No matter; if the soul dies with the body, it is well; if it survives, with this even I am content, on condition that the faculty which I now possess of cursing shall not be taken from me."

CHAPTER V

THE DEVIL'S DOUBLE

NOT enough has been said of Francesco Cenci. So strange, rich, and monstrous appears his mind from what has been described, and from what shall be described in this history, that it is worth while to stop and think upon this man. I know not whether it be so now, but once such an intoxication was diffused through the very air of Rome that men seemed changed from the ordinary habits of human nature. Fate had ordained that for a time everyone should appear different from the accustomed manner of things, and rather immense than great. Who was more valorous than Cæsar? Who more virtuous than Cato? Who more of a politician than Augustus, more of a dissimulator than Tiberius, more cruel than Nero, more stupid than Claudius? And—but we will not enumerate too many names—who more magnanimous than the Antonines? The women themselves reach the summit of lust and of chastity, of perfidy and of truth. Lucrezia, Cornelia, Portia, Arria, Epponina were born in the same city that produced Livia, Poppæa, and Messalina. The buildings themselves, instead of being conquered by time, appear to conquer it. They stand; and in spite of the injuries of ages, and the more hurtful injuries of man, they have not been destroyed. Throughout Europe, Asia, and Africa still appear relics of this wonderful people, like the bones of a corpse of which the whole world is the sepulcher.

Francesco Cenci was a corrupt breath of ancient Roman genius; a Latin spark escaped from an uncovered sepulcher, but still a Latin one; he had an indominatable nature, a satirical talent, an implacable soul, and a love of the great, monstrous, and grotesque. Had he lived in the time of Junius Brutus he would not only have condemned his children, but, bringing violence against nature to its utmost, he would have decapitated them with his own hands. He was fond of science, which afterward, like Solomon, he despised, calling it vanity and labor of spirit; or he availed himself of it in the manner of the Sybarites, who used roses as an instrument of death. He had riches, and lavished them without being able to destroy them. With an immense power of sense, of thought, and of action, he saw before him the two roads of good and evil. That of the good seemed narrow on account of the age: some domestic affection, the power to found churches and monasteries, to alleviate poverty by alms, which perpetuates it; a quiet life, an obscure death; a memory as lasting as the echo of the voices of the monks who sing the *miserere* through the nave of the parish church. Nor was the age in which he lived such as to extend the wonderful powers of his mind to greater objects: those were days of agony for Italian intellect; our heaven bore the leaden cloak of Dante's hypocrites, which allowed those who vegetated under it to go barely an inch in a hundred years. Notwithstanding he endeavored to do great things, men and worldly affairs bound him like the garment of Nessus, so that after a time to do good wearied him, then seemed to him contemptible, and finally he hated it. He turned to do evil, and said, like the devil—"Be thou my good!" The Titan's part pleased him, and it seemed a magnificent boldness to him to raise his rebellious head against heaven and challenge it. Every desire he turned to evil; as a means of rising to fame, he loved it with the delirium of drunkenness, and with the obstinacy of a calculator; to exceed iniquities then known he imagined the column of Hercules transported by him and new worlds discovered; he joined family ties for the pleasure of wickedly tearing them asunder; he nourished the dearest affections to crush them either under the blow of cruel mockery, or less painfully with a dagger: he did not believe in God, but he felt Him like a nail in the middle of his heart; and then he brutally blasphemed Him, like the bear that bites the lance that has hurt him, thinking to heal the wound. In short, he was a horrid mixture of an Ajax, a Nero, a Don Giovanni, and a common bandit.

He was a torment to himself and to others; he hated and was hated in return; he fed himself on evil, and evil killed him. He died as perhaps he would have chosen to die; since his wicked passions had gone so far to stifle all feelings of nature we may be permitted to suppose that, knowing himself now burdened with years and his powers of injuring less strong, at least for a long time, his guilty soul exulted in the thought of the murder of his body, which would be able to send his whole family by a bloody path to their graves. I firmly believe it would have been a meritorious work not only to scatter his ashes to the four winds of heaven, but to condemn his memory to everlasting oblivion, if the Divine Council had not placed innocence by the side of crime, virtue by the side of vice, grief by that of pleasure, light by that of darkness: and had not his cruelty served to show how beautiful an angel of love was his daughter Beatrice—the most simple, the most courageous, and the most unhappy of Italian girls.

Since justice urges me to penetrate into this ancient sepulcher, I will uncover it, sure to find buried there a virgin as unspotted as the body of St. Cecilia, discovered in the Roman catacombs, clothed in a white robe, symbol of purity; in an attitude of deep repose, with a red ribbon round her swan-like neck: this red tape is the trace of the ax which severed a divine head from a divine body!

CHAPTER VI

NERO

BEATRICE CENCI was as beautiful as the thought of God, when he was moved to create the mother of all living.

Love with his rosy hands had delineated the soft curves of her delicate face, and pressing his finger on the chin to contemplate his lovely work, left there the dimple—true mark of love. Her mouth was like a flower freshly culled in Paradise, breathing a divine fragrance, and giving to her countenance an expression more than human; as the ancients sang, a fragrance of ambrosia revealed to mortals the presence of a God. Her eyes often sought heaven and fixed themselves there, as if with a desire either of looking upon her home, to which she was soon to return, or to discover there some mysterious signs revealed to her alone, or because the maternal spirit beckoned her to it. Certainly, between the eyes of this illustrious girl and our hemisphere, when it shines serenely, there seemed to be, I might say, almost a relationship, for both were of the deepest blue: both announced the glory of their Creator. When her eyes bent earthward, looking upon a person or any object, they would open so brilliantly and clearly that her soul seemed to expand with them; any one standing before her, if not most innocent of heart, would hastily carry his hand to his breast, doubting whether its covering of flesh would protect the bad thoughts there concealed; others would weep with tenderness; wherever she turned them, the air would become more pure, the heavens more joyous. Misfortune had certainly fanned her snow-white forehead with its wings; but had not courage enough to

THE BOY RESTED HIS HEAD ON HIS SISTER'S BOSOM, AND FIXED HIS MOTIONLESS EYES UPON HER

From an Original Drawing by R. E. Gould

leave there a disagreeable trace, and passed by. In the happy days, alas, too rare! of her life, she loved to unbind in youthful sport her mass of blond hair, and put it in the sunlight, as if she wished to establish a rivalry with its rays; but the sun shed such a loving splendor upon her, that people trembled with reverence and pleasure to look at her, deeming her a saint descended from heaven, and surrounded by a radiated halo.

Beatrice was seated upon a terrace of the Cenci palace, which overlooked the garden; she held in her lap a child who, from his eyes, hair, and general aspect seemed to be her brother; she lovingly smoothed his hair, and kissed him from time to time on the forehead. The boy rested his head on his sister's bosom, and fixed his motionless eyes upon her, but without speculation, like a person absorbed in the thought of something beyond this world. Sickness had withered the flower of his youth; his skin was light, and of so clear and pallid a white that the rays of the sun shone through his ears and fingers; often he would sigh, then open his mouth with a convulsive gasp; he looked like an angel in pain. Beatrice, disturbed, said to him:

"Of what are you thinking, my dear Virgilio?"

"I think it would have been a great charity never to let me come into the world!"

"Ah, Virgilio!"

"And as there is no remedy, it would be better to go out of it soon."

"To go out of it! and why?"

"Why should I stay in it? My heart has been dead for some time within me, and when the heart is dead, oh, how sad it is that the body should survive it!"

"You can hardly be said to have come to life, my brother, and yet you speak words of despair. This is not right; live and be happy—you do not know what roses fortune may have in store for you."

"Roses! Fortune! Death is now gathering the flowers for the garland of my coffin. Fortune left me the day that we lost our mother."

"But we cannot call ourselves quite orphans; has not the Lady Lucrezia always shown us a mother's love?"

"Yes; but she is not our mother."

"And, then, have you not me, who love you so much?"

"Yes, yes, good sister," replied the boy, throwing his arms around her neck, crying bitterly; "but even you are not my mother."

"And, besides me, have you not brothers? have you not a father?"

"A father—who?"

Beatrice, struck by the sudden change of the boy, at these words became silent. And only with hesitating voice, after a long silence, added:

"Is not Francesco Cenci your father—and mine?"

The boy leaned down his head, shut his eyes, crossed his arms, and with low voice replied:

"Sister, look at my forehead, near the roots of my hair; do you see the scar there? You do see it? Do you know who hurt me there? I never have told it, but now that I am so near dying I will tell you. Thinking to myself how Francesco Cenci despised me, and often looked angrily at me without a cause, I one day took courage to kneel at his feet and try to kiss his hand. He cried out, 'Go away, bastard!' and struck me so violently with his fist on the breast that he sent me furiously against the corner of a wardrobe which he has in his study. Francesco Cenci saw me fainting and covered with blood; he saw me, but did not raise me. Hence the wound, and hence the sickness that is killing me."

Beatrice shuddered, without being able to utter a word. The boy, with increasing warmth, loosed his sleeve and uncovering a thin arm showed it to his sister:

"Look," he added, "at the mark of this bite. Do you

know who did that? Nero; and hear how. One day, in the garden, I picked a fine peach, and said, 'I will give this to my father, perhaps it will please him.' With this idea I went to his room, opened the door, and saw he was reading. Fearful of disturbing him, I approached softly, when Nero jumped upon me and bit my arm; I screamed with pain; my father laughed."

The bosom of Beatrice beat, ready to burst.

"And if it had not been for Marzio, he would have let me be torn to pieces. Look here, also," and the boy, parting his hair from the top of his head, continued, "see this bare spot? A lock of hair is wanting. Do you know who pulled it out? My father! A little while after my fall against the wardrobe, with my head still bound up, overcome by a feeling of despair, I went resolutely to my father, and said, 'Father, how have I offended you? Why do you hate me? Bless me in the name of God—bless the child who loves you.' He, taking a lock of my hair in his fingers, answered me thus—listen, with these very words: 'If you had a head of sulphur and my words were fire, I would bless you to burn you. Go, viper, since I hate you, you must hate me. I do not know what to do with your love, bastard!' And he pulled my hair so hard it seemed as if the scalp would be torn off with the great pain; the lock remained in his hand, and the heartless man, infuriated, as if he, and not I, felt the pain, added, 'I curse you and your children, if ever you have any; may they all live in misery, be nourished with crime, and die on the scaffold!' Now, tell me, Beatrice, can I wish to live? My mother has left me; my father has cursed me; is it not better I should die? Am I not right, sister?" and the boy sighed convulsively.

His sorrows could not be consoled. Beatrice felt it, and was silent; her forehead was covered with perspiration, and the increasing drops fell fast as tears from weeping eyes. Having passed some time in painful silence,

Beatrice, repressing the feelings in her heart, endeavored to comfort him with soft voice:

"Calm yourself, Virgilio; perhaps you intruded at an unseasonable time."

"No; he was not busy."

"Perhaps he was disturbed by some secret care."

"No; he was joyful—after the dog had bitten me, he began to play with him—with the dog that had been ready to tear his child to pieces! Now I do not love him any longer. When I see him, I tremble all over; his voice makes my head ache. I often see, in my mind, a dark place, not very distant, whence issues a noise of blasphemies and wicked imprecations; and a restless voice whispers in my ear, 'That is the dwelling of hatred—you are expected there!' I don't wish to go; I don't want to hate anybody—much less my father. I would rather die."

Beatrice turned pale and felt as if she were about to faint; but her strong will subduing her nature, she conquered her feelings, and raising her eyes to heaven, she tried to speak, but could not; instead of a voice, a sigh escaped from her weary bosom. She waited awhile, and then, with a voice which she tried to render soft, said:

"My dear Virgilio, let us not despair; let us pray the Eternal Father to inspire milder feelings toward us in the mind of our father."

"Oh, Beatrice, do you think I have not prayed for him? How many times I have done it! The night before the day in which Francesco Cenci pushed me from him and hurt my head, I rose quietly from my bed in my night-clothes, and went barefooted to our chapel, and kneeling to the relics of Saint Felix, protector of our family, I prayed him with all my soul to soften our father's heart, and induce him to return with a little love the great affection we bear him. You see how the saint listened to me."

Pausing awhile, he then thoughtfully added:

"But I know that God listened to another prayer of mine, and it was when I rose a second time from my bed and knelt before the miraculous crucifix, and said: 'Have mercy, O Divine Redeemer, upon me, and either bestow upon me my father's love or call me to Thy peace.' At these words Jesus bowed his head, as if to answer, 'Your prayer will be granted.'"

"He will grant all our prayers, inspiring our father's heart with kindness."

"I am sure he has listened to my second prayer, though not to the first; for when I went to bed again a distinct voice called to me, 'Virgilio! Virgilio!' I got up, opened the door, but saw no one; I returned to my bed, again the voice cried, 'Virgilio! Virgilio!' Sure that I was not deceived, I answered, 'Who calls me?' And the voice replied, 'I call to you from heaven.' 'I am ready, my God;' but the voice said, 'No; your hour is not yet come—but it is approaching.'"

"These are fancies, caused by fever; come, cheer up, don't be conquered by sadness; I want to see you happy."

"Why do you call them fancies? Do you not read in the Holy Bible even, that the Lord caused his voice to be heard by Samuel? Last night, my eyes being open, I saw my room all at once filled with light; and a beautiful woman entered, dressed in blue and sparkling with gems; she came near my bed, bent her face to mine, kissed me on the forehead, and disappeared; her lips were like ice, and the chill struck to my brain. Do you wish to know, Beatrice, whom this lady looked like? She resembled the portrait of our mother which hangs in the great hall. Everything speaks to me of death. Do I not also feel that I gradually fail, like a candle burned to its socket? Life is going from all my pores. Look at these thin hands, white as marble; look at my nails of a bluish color; look, too, in the middle of my forehead, and see the distinct mark where death has imprinted his kiss." And he could say no more.

Just at this moment a bird lighted to rest his tired wing upon the railing of the *parterre;* he turned his head now here, now there, as if suspicious of harm; but taking courage, began to fly about and pick; finally, he seemed to gaze at the boy; then warbled a sweet note, spread his wings, and flew away.

"Oh!" said Virgilio, "how I wish I could follow him! he knows his father, and his mother, from an open branch, are looking anxiously for his return. Oh, my mother! Beatrice, tell me where our mother is now?"

"Our mother? she is above, in heaven."

"I know it, her soul lives with the just; but I should like to know where her body lies. Can you tell me, Beatrice? Count Cenci never would permit me to be carried to the grave of my mother."

Beatrice, endeavoring to turn the sad conversation to less sorrowful subjects, rose readily to satisfy the boy's desire, and seating him upon the parapet of the terrace, she leaned forward, saying:

"There, beyond those hills, is a rich estate, which our mother brought as a dowry to Don Francesco Cenci—a church is dedicated there to the holy apostles Peter and Paul. In this church, within a marble tomb, on the right hand of the entrance, by the wall, lies the body of our blessed mother."

And raising her arm, she pointed to the place; but leaning with all her body forward, it happened a letter and a picture fell from her bosom, and dropped into the garden.

"Oh, heaven, my secret!" cried the girl, with loud voice, and blushing.

Francesco Cenci, hidden behind a thicket of laurels, had stood a long time gazing so fixedly at these two beings that he seemed as if wishing to poison them with his gaze. Hardly did he see the picture and letter fall when he rushed in haste to pick them up; not so quickly, however, as his desire urged him, since his lameness impeded him. Beatrice, in great fright, saw him, and repeated:

"Oh, my secret, my secret! I would give my life to save it!"

The boy, turning from her who looked as pale as death, saw the old man. Then, resolutely and boldly, with a desperate effort, grasping the cornice of the terrace, he leaped into the garden, and quick as lightning recovered both letter and picture.

"Come here!" screamed the old man, in a rage. "Come here! bring me those things!"

And as Virgilio, pretending not to hear him, took his way to the terrace, the Count, more enraged, roared:

"Cursed viper! Bring me that paper, or, as soon as I reach you, I will tear your heart from your body with my own hands."

The boy urged faster his steps. The Count, blind with passion, cried:

"Nero, Nero! quick, at him!" and with both hands set the dog upon his son.

The dog rushed furiously after him, but in vain, for the boy, although he had run some distance, seemed already to feel the mastiff's teeth in his flesh, and had put wings to his feet—he did not run, but flew. He ascended two or three steps at a time, and panting for breath, his strength exhausted, fell, depositing the letter and picture at the feet of Beatrice. She put both quickly in her bosom.

A moment after, the dog rushed barking upon the terrace—his eyes like fire, his breath like smoke. Beatrice, hardly knowing what to do, turned her head round, and seeing within a niche a trophy of ancient weapons, placed there as an ornament to the terrace, she seized a sword and stood before her fallen brother. The mastiff, with head bent down, plunged on as if to tear him. The courageous girl, watching her chance, aimed such a powerful blow that, penetrating his flesh, it stabbed him to the heart. The dog, rolling in his own blood, expired with a painful yell.

A new and heavier danger now menaced them. Francesco Cenci advanced madly with a dagger in his hand: stammering with rage, he cried:

"Where is the cursed viper? Who killed my dog Nero? Who, I say?"

"I!"

"You also, then; but first of all, this viper!"

And he leaned toward his son as if to stab him. Beatrice, raising the bloody sword and pointing it at his breast, said, with an expression impossible to describe:

"Father, don't come near!"

"Wicked girl! Away, I say!" and he tried to reach the unfortunate child.

Beatrice, with a voice wonderfully composed, repeated:

"Father, do not come near!"

At this voice, which contained both a deep prayer and a menace, Francesco Cenci stood still to look at her.

Where is now the girl of so sweet a countenance? Her eyes dilated in a strange manner and seemed to send forth fire, her expanded nostrils quivered, her lips were compressed, her bosom heaved, her hair floated loosely on her shoulders, her left foot was planted firmly in an advancing attitude, her body straight, her left hand shut, and the right, by her side holding the sword pointed, as if to attack. Neither painter nor sculptor ever could figure this wonderful image, nor words describe her. Francesco Cenci was astonished; he stood looking at her as if in ecstasy, then let fall his hand, and threw away the dagger; his soul for the moment seemed quiet. Beatrice also threw away her sword. The old man stretched toward her his opened arms, exclaiming tenderly:

"How beautiful you are, my child! Oh, why do you not love me?"

"I? I will love you," and she threw her arms around his neck.

The father and daughter were bound in a holy embrace.

But good feelings lasted only like lightning in the breast of the wicked old man. He experienced in one feeling of humanity the same fear that others feel for remorse. Again appear the signs of crime; his eyes compressed, his eyelids trembled with that sinister smile which caused one to shudder; he smoothed her hair, pressed her by the shoulders, kissed and rekissed her, and, approaching his lips to her ear, whispered a single word.

Beatrice, with pale face, looked down, shook herself loose from her father's embrace, took to her bosom the prostrate boy, and in departing cast upon Francesco Cenci a long look—a thunderbolt of contempt, which had the power to freeze the blood in the veins of him who feared neither man nor God.

For a long time he stood immovable, buried in thought; a furious tempest was waging war within his soul. But the voice of sin conquered the roaring of the storm; the voice of virtue was desperate and lost, like that of a castaway. What thoughts revolved in his mind? Why did he doubt? What did he purpose to do? Who knows? Perhaps the devil himself, if he had seen the hell in the soul of Francesco Cenci, would have turned his face elsewhere, frightened. But it is to be believed that in that whirlwind of wicked thoughts he chose the worst; for striking with force his hand to his head, he murmured between his teeth:

"Now, how comes it that I find myself checked in my

path by less than a wisp of straw—by the will of a girl? Ah, miserable creature! Everything has as yet yielded to the grasp of my iron hand, and you, too, shall yield, or I will crush you body and soul."

CHAPTER VII

THE CHURCH OF SAN TOMMASO

THE Church of San Tommaso, the property of the Cenci, although changed from what it was, still exists. It is said to be a very ancient building and that Cinco, Bishop of Sabina, consecrated its altar in 1113, and that Julius III granted it in jurisdiction to Recco Cenci in 1554, with the obligation of restoring it, which he was not able to fulfil on account of his death; hence, Pius IV in 1565 sent again the Bull of investiture in favor of Francesco Cenci, son of Christopher, imposing on him the same charge, which he fulfilled, as the following inscription placed on the outer wall of the church testifies:

'Franciscus Cincius Christophori filius
Et Ecclesiæ patronus, Templum hoc
Rebus ad divinum cultum et ornatum,
Necessariis ad perpetuam
Rei memoriam exornari ac perfici,
Curavit. Anno Jubilei. 1575.

That inscription testified to the passers-by how great was the piety of Count Francesco Cenci! This church is almost square in form. It contains five chapels; its roof is like a cross, where even now may be seen the escutcheon of the Cenci.

This church on the 10th of August appeared all dressed in mourning; black cloth hung on the walls, garlands of flowers were seen mixed with cypress boughs: seven sepulchers of black marble awaited the dead, like open mouths greedy of water. All bore the same inscription, and it was this:

Mors parata, vita contempta.

The eighth sepulcher was conspicuous above the others, and of beautiful white marble, with the following inscription:

Si charitem, caritatemque quæris
Hic intus jacent.
Non ingratus herus
Neroni cani benemerentissimo,
Franciscus de Cinciis hoc titulum
Ponere curavit.

In the middle of the church was a catafalque covered with crimson velvet, embroidered with gold, and covered with fresh flowers. Around the catafalque burned six wax candles, in silver candlesticks worked with wonderful skill.

A chorus of priests, dressed in dalmatics of black damask, awaited the dead, in order to chant the funeral service. Presently measured steps were heard, and a moment later from the side door appeared a small bier carried by two men and two women.

Giacomo and Bernardino Cenci held the handles in front, Lucrezia Petroni, second wife of Count Cenci, and Beatrice held those behind.

The dead person was Virgilio. God had granted the second part of the unhappy boy's prayer: he slept in peace.

Several servants followed, dressed in magnificent mourning, and bearing lighted torches. One might observe, not without grief mixed with wonder, that the clothes of the servants were far better than those of Giacomo or Bernardino; Giacomo's, particularly, were so worn as to shame the poorest gentleman in Rome. His hair was disordered, his beard long, his sleeves and collar were soiled; he carried his head humbly bent, his forehead was wrinkled, his cheeks were pale and thin; he shed bitter tears, and one could see the beating of his heart outside his garment. Two contrary passions shone in his countenance: pity and ill-suppressed rage. Bernardino also wept, but as if from imitation, rather than from impulse: for he had become entirely stupid, his mind was so darkened by fear of his father and by the ignorance in which the latter chose to keep him. Lucrezia, although a stepmother, wept bitterly; but being more bigoted than devout, she was easily and readily resigned, bearing misfortune patiently, and attributing to the will of God every good or bad event of her life.

Francesco Cenci had married this woman because she was said to be very religious, and because she had exclaimed on a certain occasion after hearing of his wickedness, "Lord! I would rather marry the devil himself than Count Cenci!" After that, he began to pay court to her; feigned very exemplary habits; frequented churches, learned to bend his neck and raise his hands and eyes to heaven in a very touching manner; and above all, showed himself a generous benefactor to priests, the worthy doorkeepers of heaven. He knew how to tell stories of saints; he discussed the *gratia gratis data*, and the form and substance of the sacrament, better than the synodical definer of the Franciscan friars.

The lady began to believe he had been slandered. At least could he not be converted? Might not the Blessed Virgin have imparted to her the virtue to snatch his soul from the clutches of the devil? It is so sweet, so proud a triumph for a devout woman to gain a soul, in opposition to the devil, that, generally speaking, truly pious women are not contented with the first conversion, but work with praiseworthy zeal for the second, and this becomes an impulse for the third; and if the power lasted as long as the will, there is no doubt they would sacrifice their entire life in so great and meritorious a work. And for this reason, besides the advice of her relatives, and in consideration of the great wealth and nobility of the house of Cenci, the lady condescended to accept the Count for her second husband. Hardly had the Count brought the Lady Lucrezia to her new home, when he said to her, as if in jest: "You wished to marry the devil rather than me? I have married you to prove that you were right,"—and he kept his word. Every day he would stand near her desk where she prayed, and while she recited psalms and counted her beads, he sang obscene and wicked songs; she would open a prayer-book, and he the revolting prints of Marcantonio Raimondo, commented upon by Pietro Aretino. He tried to subvert her in all her ideas of religion and morals, to fill her mind with doubts and fears; but the Lady Lucrezia would never listen to these deviltries, and often paid no attention to them.

Sometimes, when her impious husband, tired of talking, would become silent, she would resume her prayers; and thus it often happened that Count Cenci, instead of tormenting others, was himself tormented; instead of urging her to desperation, he would bite his lips with spite, and was nearly mad with rage. This plan failing he chose another; he obliged her to listen to his daily crimes; as this did not irritate her, he filled his house with courtesans; he did not abstain from words and acts capable of offending her dignity as a woman and a wife; but she, with unruffled mildness would say: "May God reform you, and pardon as I have pardoned you."

Beatrice alone did not weep; her eyes were fixed on the

dead boy, and she followed the others mechanically. When they reached the catafalque, Beatrice lifted the boy in her arms, and with her own hands laid him upon it, parted his hair, placed a crucifix and a bunch of violets on his breast; then, pushing a little aside one of the candlesticks, with her face leaning on her hand, she rested her elbow on the corner of the catafalque, still gazing on the face of the child.

A servant looked fixedly at Beatrice, with eyes like fire, and sometimes he would start: it was Marzio.

Besides the four children mentioned, Count Cenci had three others: Christopher and Felix, whom he had sent to Salamanca to study, and a girl called Olimpia. She was very clever and bold, and not being able to endure the persecutions of her father any longer, she wrote a memorial in which she made serious charges against her father; and then, in spite of the domestic prison in which she was confined, she managed so well that the document reached the hands of His Holiness. She requested him to deign to place her in a convent until she could be provided for by an honest marriage. The careful girl revealed only the more credible and easily proved of her father's infamies, justly believing that enormities so much above the ordinary would obtain less credit; for the incredible, although true, might give discredit to the probable crimes. She thought, too, that a child appealing against her father for her own safety never should pass the limits of necessity; too warm a defence in this case might degenerate into open offence, and cause a suspicion that the accuser might be moved by an unnatural hatred against her own blood.

The Pope, admiring the moderation of the young girl, did not hesitate to aid her, and caused her to be removed from her father's house to a convent, and in a short time married her to Count Carlo Gabbrielli, a worthy gentleman of Gubbio, to whom the Pope obliged Count Cenci to pay a suitable dower. The records of that time relate that Count Cenci, maddened by her success, even went so far as to promise ten thousand crowns to anyone who would bring back to him his hated daughter, alive or dead; but the Pope was more powerful than he, and Cenci, for once, was compelled to swallow the bit.

The priests celebrated their holy office with the exactitude of soldiers when they load their guns in twelve movements. Beatrice heard nothing, saw nothing; only when the priest sprinkled the catafalque with holy water, a drop from the head of the dead boy flew up on her face. She shuddered, looked more gloomy, and sighed.

"I accept the omen!"

"To die? It is not your turn!"

These words suddenly fell upon the ears of Beatrice, as if they had come from the catafalque; she turned her head quickly, but no one was near. The crowd of servants and monks followed the priests from the church; then gradually the people from the neighborhood disappeared. The Cenci remained alone with the dead.

All were kneeling, with heads bent and hands clasped. Beatrice alone, who had not left her first position, suddenly raised her head, looked upon the afflicted ones, and with an imperious gesture exclaimed:

"Why do you weep? Rise! Do you know who has killed our brother? You know, yes; but you are afraid to think of his name even in your mind. That which you dare not think in secret, I will reveal in a loud voice: his father killed him; our father, Francesco Cenci."

Those kneeling moved not, only their sobbing was increased.

"Rise, I command you; we need something more than tears! We must provide for our own safety, and soon, if we would not have our father murder us all."

"Peace, my daughter, peace! it is wicked to allow ourselves to be conquered by anger," replied Lucrezia; "come and kneel, and submit yourself to the will of God."

"What do you say, Lady Lucrezia? You believe that you serve God, but you blaspheme. To listen to you, it seems that God created water to drown us, fire to burn us, and iron to wound us. Where have you read that the duty of parents is to torment their children, the duty of children to be tormented? Is there no limit beyond which opposition would be allowable? Is any rebellion unlawful? Has nature marked on the forehead of generations, 'Suffer and be silent?' Is there anything worse than murdering one's own child? Tell me, for I know many, but perhaps not all, the iniquities committed under the sun. Three things I know cannot be numbered: the stars in heaven, the wicked thoughts in the heart of man, and the agonies of the desperate; perhaps there are more; tell them to me. Lady Lucrezia, you loved poor Virgilio but little!"

"What! I did not love him? This poor child was as dear to me as if he had been my own."

"Truly? Those words are easily said, but they are not true. A mother's love cannot be imagined. If you had brought him forth, nursed him in your bosom, you would not weep now—you would rave. But what wonder if the voice of one's own blood is no longer heard among men, when it is not heard even in heaven? The cry of Abel would no more reach to-day the presence of the Avenger. Why is this? Has the Eternal Father grown weary and closed his ears, or has the cry of blood become more feeble? But if Heaven is of bronze, my heart is still flesh, and it groans, and raves, and beats, like the virgin hearts of our first parents. And you, Giacomo, who are a man, do not you feel anything here?" and the girl struck her left side.

"Oh, Beatrice!" answered a voice from the floor—it was that of Giacomo Cenci—"I am no more what I used to be; the better part of me is dead; I seem hardly a shadow—a memory of my former self. Look at me— is this the bearing of a young man of twenty-five? What can I do against fate? I have struggled more than you think, with the desperation of necessity. I have bitten it until my teeth have crumbled—if you could only understand it!"

"But the hand can find a club, and behold a lever capable of throwing down a tower! It can find iron also, and behold a hammer to break, a sword to clear the way before it! Besides, friendship multiplies heads and hands."

"Misfortune, my sister, is like a December night; it surrounds you with so much darkness, that you neither see others nor others you."

"Raise your voice in the darkness; relatives, at least, will recognize it. It is said the worst relative is worth the best friend."

"There are misfortunes, as there are diseases, which neither the virtue of wisdom nor of medicine can remedy. I do not deny piety, relationship, love—I deny nothing—but all these, in the hands of the powerful, are weapons wherewith to strike; in the hands of the weak, they become glass that cuts him. For see, sister, how great is the misery to which I am reduced. I have no clothes; I am in want even of linen; I have no means by which to keep my person clean, which, of all other trials, is most humiliating to a gentleman. This would be but a small grief, if it afflicted me alone; but I have four children, and am often in want of bread to sustain them. Of the two thousand ducats a year which my father is ordered to pay me by decree of the Pope, with great difficulty he gives me but an eighth part; he even denies me the interest of my wife's dowry; and often, on returning home, I find my children without clothes, my wife weeping, and asking for bread. 'Ah! what can I give you? Come, and eat my flesh!'"

"Why do you not have recourse to the Pope? Olimpia did so, and with success."

"Have I not had recourse to him? I threw myself at his feet; wet the floor with my tears; I prayed for my children, for you, and for myself; I exposed, one by one, the enormities of our father; I did not hide the most secret and infamous ones; I begged him, by that God whom he presumes to represent on earth, to bring a quick and efficacious remedy to it. The austere old man was not moved, he did not stir; I might have been praying to the bronze statue of Saint Peter, whose feet are worn thin by kisses but always cold. He listened to me with a stony face; he fixed his dull gray eyes on mine; then slowly pronounced these words, which fell on my soul like ice: 'Woe to the children who proclaim their father's shame! For this Cain was cursed. Shem and Japhet, who on the contrary were reverent to their father, were blessed, and their generations inhabited the tabernacles of Canaan. Is it anywhere read that Isaac murmured against Abraham? Did Jephtha's daughter go up to the mountains to curse her father? Fathers represent God on this earth. If you had reverently bent your head to worship him, you would not have seen your father's sins, and would not accuse him. Go in peace.' And so saying, he dismissed me from his presence. Now, you see clearly: Olimpia, adopting the same means, was able to find favor in the eyes of the Pope; I, instead, found indifference and disdain. It is fate that so wills it. What can man do against fate?"

"He can die."

"Yes! But you have no children, Beatrice; you have no husband, as I have a loving and beloved wife. Were I not a father, who knows how long ago my body might have been fished out at Ostia? But some day, too well

I see, this will be the only way to free myself from this daily and insupportable desperation. It seems as if I were swimming against the current of a river, the strength of my arms by degrees failing and my feet becoming more heavy. Oh! if you but knew how often, when I pass near the Tiber, the roaring of the water that breaks against the stones of the bridge seems to say, 'How long you delay!' But surely my life must end thus—even Beatrice advises me to it—in a watery grave!"

Beatrice, at Giacomo's words, changed color many times, an internal power seemed urging her strongly to speak; still she paused, until, regaining a sad tranquillity, she bent her head and extending her hand toward Giacomo, said quietly:

"Wickedness overflows the earth like the universal deluge! Brother, I have spoken foolish words—forgive and forget them. Arise now; be a man. In the impetuosity of my grief I distrusted the mercy of God. He has pardoned me, for I feel peace descending into my soul—forerunner of good counsel."

"Among altars and tombs do you conspire?"

A shudder ran through the veins of the Cenci; they turned their frightened faces and saw the old Count, as if he had risen from the pavement, his face livid, dressed in black, and upon his head the crimson hood the patrician Romans used to wear. The aspect of the fierce old man was calm with fearful tranquillity; impenetrable and sinister, like that of the Sphinx. His family pressed together and were silent, not daring to raise their eyes. Beatrice alone stood firm and resolute before him.

"The saints are witnesses how excellent children plot the death of their wicked father. Come on—who holds you back? Come! What do you fear? What resistance can a man, old, unarmed and alone, make to you? The place is suitable—God present--the altar prepared—

the victim ready. Where is your weapon, miserable ones?"

And as all, taken by surprise, were dumb, Count Cenci, with calm voice, continued:

"Ah! you dare not— my eyes frighten you! Not one of you has courage enough to look into my eyes! Poor children! Come, if you do not know, I will teach you the way to fulfil your design with entire safety, with all the cowardice of which you are capable. When the night is still, and your father—Francesco Cenci—sleeps—then my eyes will not frighten you—thrust hastily a well pointed knife—a dagger well sharpened by you between two rosaries—here—under the left breast—you see how easily it can penetrate. An old man's life is a thread, the hand of a child even—the claw of this spider—can cut it," and so saying, he raised the little hand of the dead child, and let it fall with infinite contempt.

And as some of them, horrified, hid their faces, the Count, with the same terrible irony, continued:

"I understand—even by your silence you let yourselves be understood. For you my death is not enough—you wish to enjoy the fruit of your crime. It is well; to me also the honor of our family is of consequence. Nor would I desire that my name should be stained; the crime is nothing. Hear me, then: we are among relatives—I see no one to betray us—give me a poisoned drink that will make me sleep; Nature's kingdom is fertile in plants that have such a virtue! I would not advise you to throw me down from the balconies, unless they were very high; for one thrown from there rarely dies at once, and the power of suffering might then draw from me a secret, which the heart would in vain strive to hide. You might imitate King Manfred, who, if he cannot be praised as a saint, can neither be called a demon, as Dante put him into purgatory; and this fact will explain it to you.

"Manfred was impatient to inherit the kingdom of

Sicily, and his father, the Emperor Frederic, was not at all impatient to die: what was to be done? Manfred was reading one night by the bedside of his father; the old man's eyes had become heavy; he fell into such a deep sleep that only a light breathing showed his life—a breath hardly enough to moisten a glass, or to move a feather. The father was wrong in keeping it; the son was not obliged to respect it—in short, a breath like mine. Manfred took a little pillow from under his father's head, and placed it upon his face—a thing, you see, of no importance; a movement, *a quo*, as grammarians would say—then he jumped on the bed, and with both his knees he pressed upon the old man's breast—and with both his hands upon his nostrils and mouth, and there he remained until he had lost a father for whom he cared nothing at all and acquired a crown for which he cared a great deal."

"Horrible! horrible!" exclaimed Beatrice.

"What! do you fear? You are afraid to burn your fingers with the coals of hell, yet presume to act the part of devils in this world? Do you not know that to be devils we must swim carelessly through a sea of fire, and laugh among torments? Then may man be called courageous, and be able to wash his hands in blood as he does his lips with wine, and say, even in presence of God: 'I have no sin.' Butterflies! You think to commit crimes by the flutter of your wings? Look at these seven sepulchers; I have prepared them for you, for Olimpia, Christopher, and Felix! You do not find mine there, as I mean to die after you. O God! whom I know not, neither do I know if Thou art—if Thou wishest one worshiper more, who would confess Thee, as Moses saw Thee, a powerful and jealous persecutor of the fourth and fifth generations of those that hate Thee, grant me the power of being able to assist in the agonies of these children of mine; to close their eyes and bury them in these tombs; and then I swear as a gentleman of honor to burn my palace, and make a bonfire of it. But if Thou canst not grant this to me, behold, I consent to die before them, on condition that power will be given me to stretch my hand from out my grave, and draw them to it by a bloody death. But Thou dost not listen, but sleepest on Thy celestial wings a golden sleep. I will provide for myself, and it is better so; since man while his breath lasts should confide the thoughts of his revenge to no one, not even to God. Go! free me from your hated presence! Go!"

And with his hand he waved his family from him; but suddenly changing his mind, he ran after Giacomo, and seizing him by the left arm, obliged him to turn back; then, looking at him and drawing nearer, he said:

"You complain that you have no linen, lazy fellow! Go to your mother's tomb, open it, take away the winding-sheet in which she is wrapped, and carry it to your wife to make shirts for your children. So may it, like that of Nessus, reduce them all to ashes! Tell her to spare two pieces, one to cover your face, when you have died by an evil death, and the other to dry her tears, if she should be so foolish as to shed any for so vile, so abject, so contemptible a man as you."

"For God's sake, let me go, Count!" cried Giacomo, trembling and shuddering, while with all his might he tried to loosen the grasp of the fierce old man.

"No, I will not let you go until I have taught you a way to procure what is necessary for your support. You want bread for your children? Carry home a handful of your mother's dust and fill their mouths. Snakes are fed on earth. Or rather, go and carry them my curse, of which I make them an irrevocable gift. *Inter vivos*—you will scatter it upon their youthful heads—be of good cheer, it will not fall upon stones, neither upon thorns. Do not turn your face—I tell you the truth: it is a custom in our family for the children to hate their father; from the devil we sprang, to the devil we return. The seed of the curse which you shall scatter shall be given back multiplied to you in the time of harvest. Between you and your wife let there be henceforth no other words than those of hatred and strife. May she repel you from her bed, and contaminate it. May your life be a torment, your death a relief."

And more he would have added had not Giacomo, by a violent effort, freed his arm and fled, covering his ears with his hands.

"Go, go!" continued the old man; "you shut your ears in vain; my words partake of the nature of the wounds of my seraphic patron, Saint Francesco; my words burn the flesh, pierce the bones—even after death their mark may still be distinguished."

Lucrezia and Bernardino ran trembling after Giacomo; Beatrice remained alone, immovable, at the head of the catafalque.

"And do you not tremble?" asked her father.

Beatrice, without answering, turned with devout air and clasped hands toward the altar, and said:

"Most Holy Crucified One, have mercy upon that poor soul."

"Fool! Why dost thou speak of Crucifix? Here is neither Christ nor God."

"Silence, old man! Know that in one moment you may appear before His tribunal; and He alone can pardon and save you."

The old man laughed; and his evil genius counseled him to say between his teeth:

"Do you wish a proof that neither a Christ nor a God exists? Behold it!"

Ascending the altar steps, he struck violently with his fist the marble tablet, exclaiming:

"Christ, if Thou art upon this altar, consecrated by a

holy bishop, as they say, but which I do not believe, before Thy table, in the presence of the wafer within which the stupidity of believers has confined Thee, I deny Thee ten times one hundred. I confess my sin of not having offended Thee enough until now, and I firmly intend, henceforth, to offend Thee in thoughts, deeds, and omissions; with all the faculties of my body, all the strength of my will, and all the powers of my soul. If Thou knowest how, and canst do it, turn me to ashes! I defy Thee to strike me with Thy thunderbolt."

Here he bent his head upon the altar, and, after a short pause, cried three times: "Dost Thou hear?"

At last he raised his wicked head boldly; his limbs trembled, but not his soul. He looked at his daughter. The half-closed eyes gradually contracted, and he smiled, the smile of a demon; he advanced menacingly toward her who awaited him without moving, and said:

"What is God? *Deus erat verbum:* God is a word—nothing but a word; and Saint John said it. This boy is not dead" (and with his hand he touched the corpse on the head). "Beings change their form, they are never destroyed. Matter existed before creation, and will endure after the destruction of the world. From this corpse will be born thousands of the living, and they, dying, will give birth to others. Perpetual change of life and death exists, and that is all. True wisdom, daughter of my heart, consists in deriving the greatest sum of pleasures in the form with which nature has at present gifted us. Come, Beatrice, I love you only—you are the splendor of my life—you"——

As if urged by some diabolical frenzy, the sinful old man approached her, had almost thrown his arms madly around her; the horrified girl started back, and pushing toward him the catafalque, exclaimed:

"Between you and me I place your murdered boy!"

The catafalque thus pushed, fell over, carrying with it

the garland of flowers, the little child, and several lighted candles, which, falling in a heap on Count Cenci, knocked him down upon the ground. The head of the corpse struck against the head of the old man; the cold lips of the one touched the lips of the other; the flaxen hair of the boy and the white hair of the old man were mingled. One of the lighted tapers set on fire the living and the dead hair; the spreading flame burned at the same moment the cheek and temple of Virgilio and those of the Count; from both arose the disagreeable odor of burned flesh; but one alone felt the pain. The old Count, shaking himself like a snake that has been trodden upon, screamed with inexpressible agony, "The dead burns me!"

With a desperate effort he freed himself from the body; succeeded in sitting up, and then with difficulty rose to his feet.

"Ah, Francesco Cenci!" he murmured, grinding his teeth; "you are afraid! Coward! you are afraid! A girl and a dead boy have frightened you—now I see that you have really become old!"

Beatrice had disappeared. The old man, staggering, retired to his own room, deep in thoughts of fear and crime.

CHAPTER VIII

DESPAIR

THE sirocco blew damp and heavy from the sea. Within a poor room, a husband and wife stood talking; between them was a rough, unpainted table, and on it was one candle, hardly bright enough to light the room, and yet enough to show their poverty. The man appeared sad and discouraged; the woman was reduced by suffering, but had a certain air of Roman fierceness, which was more apparent at that moment, since she seemed to have heard or suffered things that caused her to burn with anger. She said impetuously:

"No; you cannot make me believe such enormities—they are not possible—they would cause the sun to cease shining."

The man was Giacomo Cenci; the woman, Luisa Vellia, his wife. Giacomo was hardly twenty-six years old; he was naturally rather short and stout in person, but now was unusually thin. He had grown up in the school of paternal affliction, and, by the force of bad example, he might have been not unlike his father had not love inspired in his soul a sweet and powerful affection. He had fallen in love with Luisa Vellia, a pretty and amiable girl of plebeian though wealthy parentage, and she became attached to him, not because he was of a powerful family, but because he seemed to her very unhappy.

From the marriage of Luisa Vellia with Giacomo Cenci, four children were born, who were named Francesco, Felix, Christopher, and Angelo. They lived in the street of St. Lorenzo Panisperna, in a house certainly far removed from the splendor to which the high birth of Giacomo entitled him; still it had once been conveniently furnished with all the necessaries requisite for the support of a family; but Francesco Cenci, forgetting the order of Clement VIII, which directed him to pay an annuity of two thousand ducats to his son, and knowing that the Pope (although pretending severity) was of a different nature than Sixtus V, first began to delay it, then to diminish it, and, finally, gave him hardly anything; therefore the family lived in great poverty, wanting even the common means of support.

Although Luisa suffered, not so much for herself, as

may be easily imagined, as for her family, still she managed as well as she could; she was always cheerful to her husband, encouraged him to be of good spirits, saying that things would soon change for the better. The troubles of this courageous woman stood between God and herself; and she felt her heart breaking when she saw her noble husband not only poor in dress, but ragged, her children almost naked, and often hungry. By these constant strokes her soul had somewhat changed; a feeling of doubt would creep into her mind; not without effort she tried to stifle a voice of reproof, which would come, from time to time, to upbraid her for too much patience. Anyone observing her carefully might easily have seen, from the expression of her face, and by the tone in which she uttered the last few words, that she was beginning to repent of the suffered sacrifice.

But to Giacomo, overcome by sorrow, this was not manifest.

"My dear Luisa," he replied, in a mysterious voice, "many other crimes has this man committed. Listen—come nearer, that the children may not hear."

And as she, with a movement of repulse, did not approach, Giacomo drew nearer to her.

"You must know that my mother was as virtuous as she was beautiful. But, though she kept her heart always true to conjugal affection, she could not prevent others from falling in love with her. The Cavalier Gasparo Lansi was desperately in love with her; and, acting less discreetly than is consistent in a gentleman of honor, he spread abroad his passion by publishing an unfortunate sonnet. This sonnet may be forgiven as prompted by love, but it was not pardoned by my mother. The day after Signor Gasparo had sent those lines, printed on pink paper, he came as usual to pay her a visit, while Count Cenci was absent. My mother, as soon as she saw him, rose, and bowing politely, said:

'Signor Gasparo, after the publicity given to your verses, I hoped your lordship would comprehend that an honorable lady could no longer receive your visits; and as your good judgment seems to have erred, it is my duty to teach it to you.' Then, somewhat moved by the paleness of the gentleman, she added, in a milder tone: 'But why, Signor Gasparo, does your lordship offer me a love which, by the wife of another, could not be returned without guilt? whereas, if you would bestow it on some lady of your own rank, it would be precious, and would give her happiness. Look about you, and you will see that Rome is filled with girls of rare beauty and merit; address your affection to one of them, and be sure it will be willingly accepted, as it deserves.'"

"Signor Lansi, thus forbidden to enter the house again, went away humiliated; his voice denied its usual office, but his tears fell copiously. Yet, as love is fed on tears, sighs, and hope, he did not stop his usual habit of showing himself under the palace windows, pleased at least to gaze upon the dwelling of the woman he loved. One day, a little before dawn, I heard several voices under the window of my room crying, 'Mercy! help! murder!' I immediately descended to the street, my sword in one hand and a light in the other, and saw the body of Signor Gasparo pierced by a dagger, which passed from the right shoulder under the left breast.

"But this is not all. My mother, already worn out by grief, became more sad for the misfortune which had befallen Signor Gasparo, fearing, as indeed was evident, that on her account he had met with this awful death. Even before this bloody deed she rarely left the house; but now she never was seen out, as she lived very retired, shut up with her own afflictions. Thus oppressed by new and old sorrows, she failed so rapidly that it was clear to those who saw her she had but a little while longer to remain in this world; nay, news of her approaching death was spread with great care by Count Cenci, who had newly fallen, not so much in love with, as into a furious passion for, Lucrezia Petroni, our stepmother. One day, when the time seemed opportune, Count Cenci, watching the chance while my mother, sitting by my side at dinner, had turned her head to speak to a servant, threw a small quantity of powder into her glass. My mother drank, and as the draught was bitter, she reproved the servant. The Count asked for the bottle, tasted the wine with care, and assured her it was the most exquisite *Alicante* he ever had tasted. I was on the point of opening my mouth to speak of the powder, when the Count, with a threatening look, cut short the words already upon my tongue, and said, with a soft voice: 'Lady Virginia, do not mind it; when one is not well, the first thing that seems distasteful is wine.' And without saying another word he rose from the table. Three days after, at the same hour, my mother died. May God give her grace! Without embalming, on account of the sudden corruption, well closed within a triple coffin, she was hastily transported to a distant tomb."

Luisa had listened to this tale with a scornful face, as if incredulous. When he had finished speaking, she replied bitterly:

"I do not mean to say that the Count is a saint, God forbid! But such continual vituperation of your father has done you no good."

"How do I vituperate him!"

"Was it not for such accusations as this that His Holiness, believing you a heartless son and desirous of your father's death, dismissed you from his presence disconsolate!"

"The good luck of this devil is equal to his perversity."

"Shame! remember, you are talking of your father, and your children may hear you."

"And if they should hear, where is the wrong? It is

better that they should know how different is their grandfather from their father."

"You? ah! if what you tell of the Count were really true you would have, in common with him, the hatred of your children."

"The hatred of my children? Luisa, are you mad?" and Giacomo looked up bewildered.

"Yes, yes!" Throwing aside all restraint, Luisa burst forth with great passion. "The hatred of your blood! Look at your hungry children—you do not know how to feed them; see them naked—you do not try to clothe them; I do not speak of myself. The house once dear to you, you now hate; you come here seldom; you are sad; you go out immediately, and have not the least thought for us, who have been waiting for you whole nights in vain."

"Luisa, the soul which could, perhaps, bear your tears, is not able to sustain the spectacle of the silent grief of my family. I cannot bear the sight of so much misery. My dear wife, would you reproach me for too great affection?"

"Giacomo, does your absence benefit your children more? When they do not see you, do they weep the less? Does your absence feed them, clothe them, console them. Why do you leave me, a poor, desolate woman, without help? Were we not joined together in order to help each other? Why do you make me bear the cross alone?"

"Luisa, you are right; but cannot my tenderness, or my weakness, if you will, find pardon in you?"

"Cruel and deceitful man! Your tenderness! your weakness! and where do you spend your father's annuity?"

"What madness is this? Have I not told you a thousand times that he has stopped it, that now and then he throws me three or four ducats, as in charity to an unfortunate beggar?"

"Ah, yes! he has stopped your annuity and throws you three or four ducats in charity! And your mistresses, tell me, how do you support them? And the children of other women, how do you feed them?"

"Luisa, you are mad."

"Oh, for my own part, you see, I care nothing, because I can return to my parents' house; and although fortune has been against them, yet they will receive me with love, and I shall not be sorry to gain my livelihood by working. I will not reproach you for my faded beauty, my youth worn out with you. I shall certainly leave your house very different from what I entered it, but what does it matter? We women are flowers plucked for a passing fancy, then thrown away. I shall wish you no evil, God forbid! for I should wish it to the father of my children."

"My dear Luisa!—what new frenzy is this? Speak calmly to me—listen."

In vain; it would have been as possible to dam the overflowing Tiber with one's hands as to repress the torrent of passion.

"Go to the arms of another woman—go—you will never find another being that will love you as much as I have loved you. But these are woman's words, and you will not listen to them—but hear, I implore you, the others, which are those of a mother. Have pity on these unfortunate children—look them in the face—look in my face—and your heart will tell you they are your children—blood of your blood—at least, love them as much as the children you may have had from another woman; do not condemn them to starve. My little baby Angiolino, while I was able I nursed him myself—now, you see, I begin to fail—Oh, blessed Virgin!"

Giacomo stared around so wildly, and with such profound wonder, that he confirmed, rather than dissipated, his wife's suspicions. At last, in despair he exclaimed:

"Alas! who poisons the heart of my wife? who turns my wife's affection from me? What God has united, the wickedness of Count Cenci rends asunder. Francesco Cenci, I feel you here within! Your subtle breath penetrates through me, incurable as a pestilence—Luisa, tell me, who was the man that slandered me to your heart?"

"Slanders! How many sinners are there who strike their breasts saying, *peccavi?* Is the necklace you bought your mistress a slander? Slander also the dress of silver brocade to your illegitimate son? and is the house you rebuilt for her accommodating husband a slander too?"

"If you did not oppress my heart, you would truly make me laugh. Come, come, Luisa; these are lies."

"Lies, you call them? here then, read!" And taking a letter from her bosom, she threw it upon the table. Giacomo opened and read it. It was an anonymous letter, written in a coarse hand and a plebeian style, in which warning was given to Luisa of her husband's infidelity with the carpenter's wife at Ripetta, and the great sums of money he lavished upon this woman; it informed her also that Lord Cenci had rebuilt her house, and provided her husband with money for his business. It mentioned also the precious jewels and rich dresses given to this woman and besides this, the greatest wound of all to the heart of the poor mother was, that from this illicit union a son had been born, whom Giacomo loved more than anything in the world. The gift of the little dress of silver brocade was lengthily described with cunning complaisance.

Giacomo, with a languid and slow motion, returned the paper to his wife, and sadly shaking his head, said:

"How is it possible, my dear Luisa, that you, with the good judgment you possess, could put faith in such infamous and stupid writing?"

"Because it is true," she replied, petulantly, with a convulsive sob.

"Luisa, can you believe more in a calumniator who has not even the courage to sign his name—who certainly may have a thousand unjust ends to accomplish in acting thus treacherously, so as to alienate your heart from me, disturb my domestic peace, tear away from me the only blessing that is left me—your love—than in me, who love you, who honor you as the mother of my children? I affirm and swear to you upon my soul that these words are false."

"I believe more in the letter than in you, for the letter tells the truth, and you tell a lie."

"Luisa, I give you at a more proper time the instruction which you a short time ago gave me: remember that not only your children may hear you, but that they do hear, and that I am their father."

"I tell this to you purposely in their presence that they may learn to know you in time."

"Silence, Luisa, silence! All you are dreaming of is false; I swear it to you on my word as a gentleman of honor, and that is enough."

"Truly, you are a gentleman without reproach; you have only to be without fear to resemble the Chevalier Bayard! When you made me and my family believe that you had your father's consent to our marriage, did you not also swear to that upon your honor as a gentleman?"

Giacomo blushed to the very roots of his hair, then turned pale, and said bitterly:

"She for whose love I committed a fault certainly should not now so severely reproach me with it; at that time my passion for you took away my reason."

"And now, what does your passion take away?" Luisa insisted, unable to restrain her excitement.

Giacomo, exasperated, with a harsh voice commanded:

"Be silent!"

"Suppose I will not be silent?"

"I would find a way to make you—I"——

"You would find a way—perhaps you have already found it. When we place our heads upon the same pillow, who knows how many times you have thought to make mine leave it!"

"Luisa!"

"Now the snake has let his venom escape. Cruel man! is not the victim enough? You wish her to be silent also; not even to utter a sigh that may disturb the pleasure you feel at her death. Have at least the kindness of the ancient sacrifices—crown your victim with flowers and cover her with purple."

"Oh, be silent, for God's sake!"

"No, I will not be silent! No, I must speak—I must accuse you of your inquity before men and God—traitor! —liar!—hypocrite!"

Such scorn made passion boil in the breast of Giacomo, already exasperated by misfortune. He thrust his hand convulsively beneath his dress, but fortunately could not find his dagger. Turning his eyes about the room in a frenzy, he happened to see one of those long rapiers, sharp on four sides, called *verduchi*, he seized it, and blinded by his rage, rushed upon his wife.

Luisa, drawing her children about her in haste, placed the larger ones in front of her, and carried the little one to her bosom, then, falling on her knees before her husband, who was rushing upon her, she said boldly:

"Nurse him with my blood, since I have nothing to give him!"

Giacomo stopped; he tottered like one who had received a blow upon the head, threw the rapier away, and extended his arms toward his wife, who, turning her face from him, exclaimed:

"No—never!"

Giacomo despondingly turned to his children, and with a feeling of ineffable tenderness, said:

"Come, my dear children, persuade your mother that she is deceived; tell her I have always loved her, and do love her. You will at least come to my arms. Come to my bosom and console me, for my heart is full of infinite bitterness."

"No, you have made mother cry!"

"You wanted to strike mother—go away!"

"We don't love you any more; you are wicked!"

"Go away—go away!" cried all the children at once.

"Go away! it is well. My children repel me from their bosom—banish me from my house. I will go. But you, at least," added Giacomo, turning to the baby whom Luisa had replaced in its cradle, "innocent creature, whom men have not yet been able to poison—you must surely feel the cry of nature; receive my embrace, and keep it as the only inheritance your unhappy father can leave you."

The child, frightened by his agitated aspect and excited actions, raised both his little hands to shield his face and cried with fear. Giacomo stopped—looked at him—folded his arms upon his breast, and with agitated voice said:

"Behold; my father persecutes me to death—my wife denies me. Nature herself inverts her laws against me, and the little child abhors me as a thing which instinct teaches him is baneful. Man never should be brought to this pass, and I have suffered it to reach its last extremity! Like the trunk of a tree, I lie in the path of my children, a hateful and insidious encumbrance. Why, my sad soul, do you wait longer? Your departure is now useful to yourself and your children. I once educated them under my branches, now my shadow takes the sun away from them—the dew that falls from me is poisonous—I will go; shall I bless them, or not? I would, but dare not. No—lest my words, before descending upon their heads, be converted into a curse. A bitter life, a miserable death, a hated memory. O God! dost thou see these things—canst thou see them, and consent to them? Thou hast broken the bent reed, and I am conquered—alas! alas!"

Thus murmuring, with death in his thoughts, his hands thrust into his hair, groaning bitterly, he left the house. Whoever had seen him, though an enemy, would have said: "Lord have mercy on this unfortunate man!"

His wife, although the storm continued to disturb her mind, felt a milder sentiment arising in her heart, a forerunner of passionate tears, on account of the spontaneous burst of affection shown her by her children.

Luisa did not notice the departure of her husband, or, if she did, she cared little, satisfied with filial love. The warm caresses she received and returned, made her forget that the stronger tie of family was broken.

CHAPTER IX

THE FATHER-IN-LAW

"I WILL ascertain it personally," exclaimed Luisa resolutely. She arranged as well as she was able her humble attire; took a mantle of black silk for a covering; and, recommending her children to the only maid she had in the house, cautioning her repeatedly not to lose sight of them, she set out for the palace of her father-in-law.

Entering the ante-chamber, she noticed that the servants stared boldly at her, esteeming her a person of little consequence. They might have insulted her with some coarse epithet, if she had not cut short their looks and vulgar words by going directly toward them and saying with dignity:

"Announce to the Count Francesco Cenci that his daughter-in-law has come to pay him a visit, and is waiting in the ante-room."

The valets felt as if they had fallen from the frying-pan into the fire. They knew not whether to announce her or not; both ways were dangerous.

The older servants gathered to consult what was to be done; but their conference was short, for one of them, who had been butler to the convent of the Jesuits in Rome, winked toward a certain vain young valet who had been only a short time in the service of the Count, and said: "Praise the fool and make him run." So they said to him:

"Ciriaco—come now—it is your turn: we will give you a good chance to become acquainted with our master; besides, you are young, and courteous—we are old, and do not know what manners to use toward ladies of the present day; so that the presentation of this lady belongs by right to you."

The old servants spread the net through malice, the young one fell into it through vanity; perhaps with the secret thought of supplanting them one day in their master's favor.

"Your Excellency," said Ciriaco, bending his body like the first quarter of the moon, when he reached the presence of the Count; "there is a certain lady without who announces herself daughter-in-law of your Excellency, and desires an audience."

"Who did you say?" cried the Count, starting from his chair. He always addressed servants with a very severe aspect; but to-day he seemed frightful, as he had his face bound up in strips of linen, and felt severely the pain of the burn.

"The daughter-in-law of your Excellency."

The Count stared at the servant with so fierce a look that the youth felt a chill. But he bent lower to the ground, and added:

"Although it has not escaped my notice that your relatives, for a thousand reasons, each more plausible than the other, are not liked by your Excellency"——

"Have you noticed this?"

"This and other things; for it is my nature not to allow anything to pass unobserved in the wishes of my masters, in order to anticipate their desires. Nevertheless, I thought it improper to send her back, considering the respect due to the illustrious house whose illustrious name the lady affirms to bear."

Count Cenci smiled disdainfully, seeing how the blockhead, by his flattery, was endeavoring to ingratiate himself into his favor. So, after he had finished speaking, staring at him, he said:

"And what has given you reason to suspect that my relatives, and especially her ladyship Donna Luisa, my daughter-in-law, may be unwelcome to me? You spy upon the actions of your masters, and that is very bad; you interpret wrongly their motives, and that is worse. Go to my steward, make him pay you the whole year's wages, and take off my livery; to-night you must not sleep in my palace."

The servant would have knelt to sue, by words and signs, for mercy, but the Count, angry at his delaying after he had given his order, added:

"Go!"

"Ah! most noble and illustrious Lady Luisa," said the servant, "you see, in order that your ladyship might enter, I must go. I leave it to you whether it is right. I am turned into the street—I will not say on your account, God forbid!—but certainly to render you this service I must bear this misfortune. Try to remedy it: I recommend myself to you, on my conscience."

Luisa, to tell the truth, felt her heart sink for this sad chance, but more for the poor fellow; and was in doubt whether she should enter, or return home, as this seemed to her explanation enough, and perhaps a little too much. But the worse counsel prevailed, and she entered. The old servants crowded around their unfortunate companion, and slyly deriding him, tried to heal his wound with oil of vitriol.

Luisa, with a bearing neither humble nor proud, approached the desk where her father-in-law awaited her, standing. In order to honor him as a father, she was about to kneel before him; he would not allow it, but raised her quickly, with mild voice, saying:

"No, my daughter, my ears are not in my feet. Do not take it as a reproof, but human creatures never should kneel to any one but their God."

"Father, since you so kindly grant me the right of using this name, permit me before all to ask your pardon for not having presented myself to you before; but I had been assured that you would have turned me out of your house—this humiliation, you know, would have been insupportable to a Roman lady."

"Certainly, to become the wife of my first-born, upon whom I had placed all my tenderness as all my pride—without even asking my consent—rather, without my paternal blessing; but why do I say blessing and consent? without even saying to me a single word about it—seemed such a forgetfulness of every authority, such a contempt of all respect, that a father's heart could not help resenting it. As to turning you away from my presence, pardon me—but my daughter-in-law, as she feels she is a Roman lady, ought to know that a Roman baron never can fail in courtesy toward a lady, even should she be by chance disagreeable to him."

And as Luisa, stung by the slight allusion to her humble parentage, was about to answer with some warmth, the cunning old man, who had noticed the blush which passed over her cheeks, hastened to add with milder tone:

"And so much more so, since, as you were born of respectable parents, and called a very accomplished person, I could have found no reasonable cause of opposing your marriage. Nor would the moderate means of your family have been an obstacle, as my house has no need of it, for fortune does with riches as the sea with its waves, which flow to and from the shores without rest. Besides virtue without money always pleased me more than riches with pride, malice, or stupidity."

"Sir Count, I am sorry that in order to exculpate myself I must accuse others; but it is right that you should know how Giacomo, conquered by his passion, deceived me, swearing on his honor that you knew of and consented to our union, and only for some private reasons desired it should for a while be kept a secret."

"And see," exclaimed the Count, stamping his foot, "how the contempt of the first duty of a gentleman, loyalty, always leads to a miserable end. You, then, were deceived; I, betrayed. Perhaps I might reproach you for too much credulity; I might also call you and your parents indiscreet; but, however this may be, it is not the fault of your children."

"I come to you principally on their account, who are of your blood, and will continue your descent."

"And how many have you?"

"Four, all very handsome—angels of innocence and beauty," replied Luisa warmly, while her eyes sparkled with tears of maternal pride.

"How fruitful is the race of vipers!" thought Count Cenci; but with smiling lips he said:

"May God preserve them to you!"

"Father, your words encourage me. Hear me then,

for I have come on purpose to speak of your grandchildren. You see in me a sorrowful mother, truly a Mother of Tears. I am not here to speak of myself. Do not look at my humble dress, for which a little while ago I became the jest of your own servants—but my children, your grandchildren, have no clothes to wear—no bread to satisfy their hunger."

And the tears of pride were now turned into broken sobs and tears of grief.

"How can this be? I will not deny that I have always been rather parsimonious toward Giacomo; as experience had taught me that his no very praiseworthy habits had increased in proportion with the means which he possessed to indulge them. The task of the Danaïdes was a fable, but my son's extravagance is an irremediable vice. I always have refrained from contributing to render him worse than he is. A kind of remorse, and the fear of being called one day to render to God an account, has restrained me from showing myself too liberal. If our ancestors had not instituted an entail of the property, and if I did not intend to imitate them in this worthy practice, believe me, my dear lady and respected daughter-in-law, that I should be thoughtful, and really concerned about the fate of your children, and my grandchildren. Yet it has seemed to me that two thousand ducats a year might provide the necessaries and even comforts of life to your family."

"But Giacomo says that you withhold it from him, and that occasionally you throw him a few ducats, more as an insult than as aid to his family."

"He says this? Perhaps he swears it too, upon the same word of honor with which he assured you that I was cognizant of and consented to your marriage? I will not swear, for I have been taught that the language of a Christian should be 'Yea, yea,' or 'Nay, nay.' But look, and see for yourself, upon the family accounts" (and taking a book of records, he opened it, pointing out to her divers entries, which his daughter-in-law abstained from reading), "whether the promised annuity has been paid to him, or not. Since this unfortunate man reduces his father to the humiliation of justifying himself, the stones themselves would rise to testify against him. Slander—and always an unjust slander; yet that is not the worst fault for which I must reproach Giacomo! But my griefs shall be buried with me. Alas! Francesco Cenci, what a miserable father you are, and what an unhappy old man. Alas! alas!" and he covered his face with both hands.

Luisa felt moved at his venerable aspect and deep affliction; and the hypocrite continued with a lamenting voice:

"Would that I could find at least a heart wherein to pour the great bitterness of my soul!"

"My father—Lord Count—I also am an unhappy mother and wife—pour out your griefs to me—we will weep in secret—together."

"Excellent woman! My good daughter! No, no—the duty of the wife consists in remaining attached to the husband she has chosen as her companion for life; therefore I should abstain from words, and perhaps I have already said too many, which may make you love him less. Oh, Giacomo! what nights of agony you have shed upon the last years of your poor father! The faces of my grandchildren—proud boast of grandfathers—are unknown to me. We might all live under the same roof, united with the blessing of God! This palace is too large for me; I walk through it desolate and coldly; I, that should see myself reflected in the faces of my grandchildren—I that should be warmed with their caresses; between our hearts, which desire to come near to one another, an iron wall arises; and you, miserable Giacomo, you have built it!"

Luisa, observing the ashy hue of hatred that overspread the face of the Count, feared she might have aggravated the fate of her husband; hence she cautiously asked him, in a low tone:

"Do the faults of your son offend you so much, my dear father, that the hope of merited pardon may not enter your paternal heart?"

"I leave it to you to judge. I will remind you of a thing, which, being universally known, frees me from renewing the bitter grief of relating it. Who was it that induced Olimpia to write the wicked address to the Pope, by which my erring child was torn from my arms with so much grief to my heart, and injury to my reputation?—Giacomo. Who caused this infamous libel to reach the hands of His Holiness?—Giacomo? Who was it that knelt at the feet of Christ's Vicar, imploring him with sighs and tears for my death? Who? An enemy, perhaps? The heir of some whom I had murdered? No—Giacomo—the man who owes his life to me!"

"Oh, my dear father! Come, quiet yourself; perhaps they have reported to you more than Giacomo has ever said or done. Your good judgment knows the bad habit of servants to exaggerate the faults of the man fallen into the disgrace of their master, in order to ingratiate themselves into favor. And if the faults of your son were as heavy as you say, you must remember he is of your blood; you must remember our Saviour pardoned those who crucified Him, because they knew not what they were doing."

"But Giacomo knows too well what he is doing. Every day he increases in vice; every moment he labors to take away my reputation, and the little remnant of my unhappy life. My son wildly wonders at the slow approach of my death, whose wings he, with so much desire, hastens. Listen to me, my daughter, and if my passion leaps the boundaries and overflows, you must pardon it. But let me impress upon you that these horrors should be only with God, you, and me; above all, let your children never know them, that they may not learn to hate their father. Only a few days ago, he came here to pervert Beatrice and Bernardino, treacherously persuading them that I had caused the death of Virgilio; as if this unfortunate child, for his and my great misfortune, had not that incurable disease, consumption. And this is not all: down in the church of Saint Thomas, erected by the piety of our ancestors, and remodeled by me, while celebrating the solemn obsequies to the soul of my dead child, they were converting the catafalque into a seat of abomination, with no respect for the sanctity of the place, for the sacred altar, for the solemnity of the ceremony; in the presence of God, he was plotting with my other misguided children and my wife—my death. You shudder, good Luisa? suspend your horror, for you will have many other things yet to shudder for. Then, when I, a miserable father, went to weep over the body of the angelic creature, called before his time to a better world, I know not what new frenzy, or unheard-of rage, took possession of them—but they threw upon me the little dead boy—they struck me—they wounded me. See for yourself, my daughter; examine—I bear the proof upon my face—the marks of their unholy attempt."

Here he paused, as if overcome by the atrocious recollection; then, with tears, resumed:

"Henceforth, when my children approach me—Giacomo above all—do you know what I must do? See whether my coat of mail is well fastened—look to see whether I have forgotten my dagger. Place between them and me a faithful dog, who would defend my life from their fury. Yes, a dog; since my own blood is hostile to me. Suspicious of the human race, I must seek my defence among brutes. Indeed, I did have a dog—a faithful one—and they killed him by thrusting a sword in his heart—bloody forewarning of what they reserve for their father. For some time a thought has come to me—which, born upon my sad pillow, has already gained a mastery over me as a fixed thing—and it is, whether I should let them commit a parricide, or rather, with my own hands end this miserable existence and spare them the infamy and punishment of the crime—to myself, the insupportable burden of living. Ah! my God, how hard it is to think of losing their souls and mine!"

A soft knock was heard at the door. The Count, raising his head, with a loud voice said:

"Come in."

Marzio appeared, and after some hesitation on seeing the lady, said:

"Your Excellency—the notary"——

"Let him wait. Tell him to pass into the green-room, where he may wait at his ease."

"Your Excellency, he bade me say that very urgent business called him elsewhere."

"*Per Dio!* who is this fellow, that he dares to have a will different from mine, and in my own house, too? I feel almost tempted to treat him like Count Ugolino, and throw the keys into the Tiber. Go, and do not let him depart without my permission."

The ill suppressed rage with which the Count uttered these words might have shown, to anyone who should have paid the least attention to them, the hypocrisy which he had used in his previous conversation; but Luisa's thoughts were turned elsewhere, and she stood a long time with her eyes fixed on the ground, like a person wholly discouraged and unable to form a thought, or utter a word.

The Count looked at her suspiciously, but, reassured, continued:

"However, I will not depart from my intention that the children should not bear the penalty of paternal errors. This law, too severe a one, was mitigated by the doctrine of Christ, and I am a Christian. You have happened to come at the very time when I was about to put into execution this conviction of mine. I have arranged to institute your children heirs of all my personal property; as for the entail I am certain of its safety, for it cannot be either mortgaged or alienated; Giacomo can squander only the income of the entail, but he must, in spite of himself, render the principal untouched to the eldest son. I shall name you administratrix of my personal property; and I hope, after you have provided honorably for the family, there may be enough left to increase the patrimony."

Although Luisa, as a mother, could not but feel greatly pleased by the good disposition of the grandfather in favor of her children, still, as an honorable woman, she could not help saying:

"And Lady Beatrice and Don Bernardino?"

"Beatrice has her dowry already secured, sufficient for any great lady. Bernardino is to be educated for the Church, and the house of Cenci possesses the patronage of a large number of the highest prebands in Rome."

"And the other children?"

"What children?"

"Don Christopher and Don Felix."

"They? Oh! God be thanked, they are already provided for and have no need of anything," replied the Count, and his eyes contracted, and sent forth a most malicious smile.

"Sir Count, I am not moved by curiosity, but by a desire of not appearing in my own eyes too desirous of others' property. I insist, then, upon knowing how my brothers-in-law have been provided for."

"Each is married to a powerful lady, who will pay their expenses, and can also pay the expenses of others—of this, if you please, we will speak hereafter, and at our leisure."

"Sir Count, before leaving you"—and Lady Luisa hesitated a moment; but, motherly love conquering womanly pride, she took courage and continued: "I wish to tell you the reason that led me to seek you."

"Tell it."

"Should my prayers be answered by Heaven, you would live forever—but my children are in want of everything."

"Ah! fool that I am!" the Count began, touching his head lightly, as if talking to himself. "Poor woman! she is right. She cannot count upon the money of this miserable man, as he spends it out of the house on another woman whom he loves; upon other children, who are his delight more than his lawful ones."

"How! how!" exclaimed Luisa, seizing the arm of her father-in-law. "Then you know it also, Sir Count?"

"Lady Luisa," replied the Count, with severe countenance, "I would have you know that the heart of a father is no less jealous of his son's reputation than is the wife of her husband's affection; but in the wreck of every honest feeling in Giacomo, we all have lost—you, a husband—I, a son."

Luisa uttered a deep sigh.

"Now, hear me, Lady Luisa, I will willingly furnish you with the means necessary for your family; but on one condition, which you will swear solemnly to observe. I do not require you to promise blindly; no, I will state the condition, and my reason for it, so that finding, as I do not doubt you will, the former discreet, and the latter tending to the benefit of your children, you may promise it freely with your conscience."

"Sir Count, I am ready to hear."

"You, like all good women, wholly absorbed in one love alone, very quickly recover from the anger which excites you against the object of your lawful affections; you are like sails that fall at every slight lulling of the wind. Oh, I know what virtue lies in two little tears and a kiss, in calming the fiercest matrimonial quarrels. I see Giacomo already pardoned, and loved a thousand times more by his most affectionate wife. Then you will confide to him the money, and the means by which you obtained it from me; and he (let him alone for that!) will soon find a way to relieve you of it; and I, instead of supporting my grandchildren, shall see with grief, that it is gone to feed his vicious habits. I foresee also that in this very act he will take occasion for slandering me, and I do not want a benefit to cause me a new bitterness. Now, on no account do I wish you to tell him you have money, and much less to let him know from whom it came. Does this condition seem to you one to be refused?"

"Certainly not; you advise me for the best, and even without a condition I should have done just as you would have indicated to me."

"So much the better. See this holy relic."

And the Count took from his bosom a small gold cross, and giving it to his daughter-in-law, added:

"Swear upon this cross, blessed at the sepulcher of the Lord, by the salvation of your soul, by the life of your children, that you will keep the promise."

"There is no need of such solemn rites," replied Luisa smiling; "but I swear it."

"That is well; now take as much as you like." And so saying, he opened a drawer full of gold coins of different value; and as Luisa, somewhat abashed, blushed, the Count said insistingly: "Take some, take some. It would be very strange if between father and daughter there should be any ceremony. "Come, I will take some for you. And filling a purse, he gave it to her. Luisa thanked him with a motion of her head, blushing.

"Before you go, my dear daughter, listen to another word—because you understand very well how, in spite of the atrocious injuries with which Giacomo has offended me—and alas! will always continue to offend me—he is still my son. Leave no means untried to bring back the prodigal son to my heart—shut your eyes to his infidelity—suffer the insults—forget that he has other children besides yours; that while he causes his lawful children to want the necessaries of life, he lavishes his money upon his natural children, or rather the children of his sin, so that they may be clothed in dresses of gold and silver. Pardon him, convert him, and bring him back to me; my arms are always open to him, my heart is ever ready to forget everything in one sincere embrace. Try to give me back a son, and you will at once have recovered the father to your children, the husband to yourself."

"Sir Count, you have filled me with so much wonder, tenderness and gratitude, that I cannot express it to you in words. Let this kiss, which I impress with filial affection on your paternal hand, speak for me. But although I feel that I never can repay you for the many benefits which you have heaped upon me, still I beg of you to be kind enough to add another, which is, that you will deign to take back the servant whom you dismissed on my account."

"Excellent woman! not I, Luisa, but you, forgive the fault, since I had dismissed him for the want of respect he showed in speaking of you."

Then he rung his bell, and a valet appeared.

"Ciriaco."

Ciriaco came; his head bent toward the ground.

"Give thanks to Lady Luisa dei Cenci, my illustrious daughter-in-law, who permits you to remain, excusing your fault. Henceforth correct yourself, and be more respectful toward your superiors."

"My good lady," said Ciriaco, throwing himself at her feet, "may God reward you for me and my poor family, who without your charity would be forced to beg, and could have no bread."

Luisa smiled upon him. The Count accompanied her with great courtesy to the door, in spite of her prayer for him to be seated; and then, returning hastily, he placed his hand on the shoulder of Ciriaco, and with a fierce look fixed upon him, said:

"Not only must you leave my house this very instant, but Rome also, and even the Pontifical States, and quickly too. If to-morrow I know you to be here, I will myself see about your journey. Go without looking back—I have not the power of changing you into a pillar of salt; I can only change you into a dead man. Put a seal on your mouth, fear of me in your soul; if your feet fail you, walk on your hands and knees. You, who have had the dangerous curiosity of prying into the habits of your master, must have noticed that he never fails in doing what he promises. Go, and remember that God is not scrutinized but worshiped; and every master should be as a god to his servants and subjects."

These threats and the look threw so much fear into the heart of the servant that he left Rome without seeing his family.

"At your Excellency's orders," said the notary (with the servile familiarity of all barristers), on entering the room.

The Count, with the pride of a magnate, replied:

"I sent for you, sir, to consign to you my autograph will. Write the deed of receipt while I send for proper witnesses: do it well and quickly."

The witnesses came, and bowed; the deed was drawn up in proper form; the witnesses then departed as they came in, without uttering a word; impassible, seeming rather shadows than men. The notary, while collecting his papers, could hardly refrain from giving vent to his garrulity, a fault which he had in common with all his brothers of the bar.

"*Per Bacco*," he exclaimed, "I am aware your Excellency is not partial to observations, and therefore I hastened to serve you with all due forms: yet it seems to me that your Excellency is not of that age that such an act is necessary, and men change their wills even unto death; so one fulfils much better the duty of making a will, the longer he delays it. Such dispositions partake of the nature of melons, which, remaining a long time uneaten after being gathered, become at last rotten."

"Is man master of the morrow? Men at my age are like Jews at Easter, with the staff in their hands and sandals on their feet, ready to depart. I could have no rest until I was fully assured of the fate of my children and grandchildren."

The notary, who had a mouth and brain like a fox, fixed two little shining eyes upon him; and, pressing his lips, smiled as if he would say that such demonstrations of affection before him were not worth a straw.

"As to that, your Excellency," observed the cunning lawyer, "your paternal heart need have no uneasiness, since the law itself provides for all. Do you know, Count, how we lawyers, who understand such things, define a will? An illegitimate act, by which the father of a family takes the property from those to whom it belongs."

The Count cast a sharp look at him, but the notary had changed his expression, and looked as if he had made these remarks more from simplicity than malice. Count Cenci could do no better than to imitate him; so, with feigned simplicity, he replied:

"Only think! I may, after all, have done a useless act? But *utile per inutile non vitiatur*, as you lawyers say, and, even if it has not served me in any way, it has at least given me the pleasure of conversing with you, and you the pleasure of having gained some ducats."

And feeing him liberally, as he was wont, the Count

got rid of this importunate observer of his affairs, who went off wriggling like a snake, and saying, with his hands full of money:

"Too generous! always princely! God keep you healthy and prosperous."

The Count, alone, murmured to himself:

"Now, the Cenci can no more enjoy my free estates. I have disinherited all my children, in case any of them should survive me; but I shall try not to have this happen. The reason of the disinheritance is the principal one among the fourteen indicated by Justinian. My will shall be respected. *Per Dio!* if my grandchildren are not reduced to gnaw their fingers through hunger, I shall come to life again and strangle the judges who may decide in their favor. Besides, I have constituted as heirs, holy places, religious corporations, and such dead hands. The entail remains! An immense treasure! Now, how shall I be able to alienate and scatter it? I must come to some agreement with Cardinal Aldobrandini. But to take away from the wolves, I must throw to the hyenas—wild beasts against wild beasts—cruel necessity! but so be it; provided my children remain without clothing, let the devil himself wear my mantle. What a respectable figure the devil would make with my scarlet mantle embroidered with gold! Let no one dare to accuse me of not having left any property to my children and grandchildren, for it would be untrue. As Timon left to the Athenians the fig-tree of his field, so that they might hang themselves thereon at their ease, I leave as inheritance to my children the Tiber, in which to drown themselves."

CHAPTER X

THE BANQUET

FRANCESCO CENCI had prepared a sumptous banquet. The tables were in a spacious hall, the ceiling of which was painted by the best masters of that age, in which art was not entirely corrupted. Around the hall ran a white gilded cornice, supported at equal intervals by columns, also white, ornamented with gold arabesque. The spaces between the pillars were covered with mirrors more than eight cubits high; but as Venetian workmen were not then able to manufacture mirrors of such size in a single piece, they were covered, in order to hide the joints, with cupids, fruits, flowers, foliage, and various kinds of birds beautifully executed; eight doors were hung with curtains of white brocaded satin, the edges embroidered with golden flounces of raised work, and in the center the coat of arms, white and red.

Count Cenci received his guests with that politeness inherent in his noble house, and the courtesy that came from his own spirit. There were present several of the Colonna family, two of Santa Croce, Onofrio, Prince of Oriolo, and Don Paolo, of whom we spoke in the beginning of this history; there was my Lord Treasurer, and then came the Cardinals Sforza, Barberini, friends or rather relatives of the Cenci, and several others whom history does not mention; and last, by express orders of the Count, Lady Lucrezia, Lady Beatrice, and Don Bernardino. Beatrice was dressed in black. If she had not worn this dress as a kind of protest against the fearful joy of the paternal banquet, one might have suspected she had done it as a woman's artifice, to show the dazzling whiteness of her complexion. Her only ornament was a withered rose in her blond hair.

"Welcome, noble kindred and friends; welcome, most eminent cardinals, pillars of the Holy Mother Church, and splendor *urbis et orbis*. Could heaven bestow on me a hundred tongues of bronze, a hundred chests of iron, as Homer invoked, I could not consider them enough to give you thanks for the high honor which you do my family in favoring them with your presence."

"Count Cenci, your illustrious house is so distinguished that it needs no other ray in order to shine as the brightest star in the Roman heaven," replied, according to the custom of the times, Signor Curzio Colonna.

"You, in the fullness of your kindness, are too partial towards me, my honorable Don Curzio; however, I thank you greatly for your love. I, my lords, had almost become a stranger to you; I have feared that my appearance among you might cause you fear, as that of a man returned from the grotto of Trophonius; but what could I do? A great sadness troubled me—an evil disease! And I, who so well know how it penetrates to the very bones, have kept it carefully concealed in my breast, lest I should be like Pandora, when she incautiously opened the box, and poured, unwillingly, upon the world an infinite family of evils. But now that a ray of light shines obliquely into my mind to brighten it, I shake the ashes from my hair; I gather once more a rose—perhaps the last—to adorn it. Indeed, during winter one should not desire roses too often; nor will the gentle flower blossom among snows—but here, in loved Italy—and my daughter Beatrice gives you a proof of it—roses grow in all seasons; but if you cannot find them in your own garden, go to your neighbor's, and pluck or steal them. Yes, take them by force; what law will condemn an old man who, before dying, steals a rose in remembrance of his dead youth, and as a comfort to his dying life? It would be as well for

His Holiness to excommunicate a dying man for having given his last look to the light which is fast disappearing. And you, Beatrice, what strange fancy has taken you to put a withered rose in your hair? You fear, perhaps, a comparison between your cheeks and the fresh rose-leaves. Leave your fears, girl; you may provoke such comparisons, for you were born to conquer them all."

The girl darted a keen glance, like an arrow, upon him; he lowered his sparkling eyes.

Santa Croce replied:

"We have come, Count Cenci, as relatives and friends, to share your happiness, which I hope is great, for I have never seen you in such good humor; you may, indeed, emulate the good old man of Taos."

"I was wrong in not trying earlier to acquire this humor, Prince; and what is worse, I have tried too late. The Parcæ, you know—or rather you do not know—for you, most eminent cardinals, hold these stories as heresies. But 'tis said that the Parcæ spin for us days of black wool, mixed with a very few of a golden color; human wisdom consists in separating them; we weep during the sad days, laugh in the happy ones, or else we should turn our lives into an eternal funeral service for the dead."

The Lord Treasurer observed maliciously:

"This joviality of yours—perhaps excessive—is wont to manifest itself thus intemperately in persons whom it rarely visits; it has somewhat the nature of a fever; and this idea is confirmed when I think that a short time since death saddened your house."

"Ah, my lord, why recall it to my memory? Like King David, after his son's death, I said, 'While the child was yet alive, I fasted and wept: for who can tell whether God will be gracious to me, that the child may live? But now he is dead, wherefore should I fast? can I bring him back? I shall go to him, but he shall not return to me.' "

Beatrice, at this shameless hypocrisy, trembled painfully.

"But come," cried all the guests, "release us from our anxiety. We are impatient to share your happiness by the knowledge of it."

"Noble friends! if you had said we are impatient to satisfy our curiosity, which is excited, you would have spoken more truly, and more sincerely. But you labor in vain, for I do not intend to waste my good news on empty bodies. No, gentlemen; God sends his dew, morning and evening, upon the flowers ready to receive it, not at noon upon burning stones. First, prepare yourselves with the gifts of Ceres and Bacchus, as a poet-laureate would say, and then you shall hear my news—the gospel *secundum comitem Franciscum Cincium.* To dinner, then, noble friends, to dinner!"

"Lady Lucrezia," whispered Beatrice in the ear of her stepmother, "some dreadful misfortune is hanging over our heads! His eyes never before sparkled with so much malice. He laughed like a wolf when it seizes the hare by the throat to suck its blood."

"May God forgive me! I know not why, but I tremble too."

"Who has told you, mother, that I trembled? Neither my body nor my soul trembles."

And they seated themselves at the table. Count Cenci took the head, according to the custom then of giving the master of the house the most honorable place; at his side, right and left, sat his family, then followed the guests as the steward placed them, according to the rank and dignity of each. After the guests had satisfied the natural desire for food and drink, spurred by curiosity, they exclaimed with one voice:

"Is it not yet time to appease our anxiety? Come, Count Cenci, give us the reason for your happiness?"

"The time has come," said Count Cenci with a solemn

voice. "But my noble friends, I beg you first to answer this question. If I had ardently, earnestly implored of God one favor above all others—a prayer which I murmured as I dropped to sleep, and which was the first whisper of my waking lips—if God, who had heard this request repeated by holy priests during the sacrifice of the mass, by the chants of consecrated virgins, by the prayers of his poor; if God, I say, long after I had despaired of being heard, most suddenly, most unexpectedly, beyond my hope, had shown me His infinite mercy, and granted my desire to the full, should I not have reason to rejoice? And if so, exult with me—for I am indeed happy—happy in the fullest meaning of the word!"

"Beatrice—my daughter—support me—I am afraid."

"Help yourself as you can," replied Beatrice, "for I cannot—my head whirls around, and all the guests seem to me as if swimming in blood!"

"I suppose, noble friends and kinsmen, that you all know—and if any one is ignorant let him now learn"—continued the Count, "that I caused to be built in the church of Saint Thomas seven tombs of precious marble, and of exquisite workmanship, and I then prayed the Lord to grant me before dying the favor of burying within them all my children; and then I vowed to burn my palace, the church, the furniture and sacred vestments, in one joyous fire. If I were Nero, I should also have sworn to burn Rome a second time."

The guests gazed at one another more in astonishment than in terror; then looking at the Count, they thought, blushing for him, that he had been carried away by too much drinking. Beatrice kept her head bent; her face was as pale as the withered rose in her hair. But the Count with louder voice continued:

"One I have already buried; two others, through God's mercy, I am allowed to bury now: two are in my hand, which is almost as good as to have them lying in their tombs; we are drawing nearer to the end. God, who shows such manifest signs of his favor to me, will certainly, before I die, fulfil my prayers."

"Count, you should have chosen a less sad theme for jest than this."

"It is a very wicked pleasure to take delight in others' fear!"

"Do I jest? Read."

And taking several letters from his bosom, he threw them on the table.

"Read—examine them at your ease; inform yourself of all; I give them to you for that purpose. You will learn that two other of my detested children died at Salamanca —how did they die? It matters little to me—what I care most about is, they are dead, closed and nailed within two oaken coffins that I had ordered. Now I need spend but a few more ducats on them, and this I willingly do—two wax candles—two masses—if they were cartloads of quicklime, that their souls might be burned by it, I would order two thousand to be thrown into their tombs. Oh, Pope Clement! you who condemned me to pay them four thousand ducats yearly, will you oblige me to pay to them now?"

The Lord Treasurer, trembling with emotion, said:

"Alas! my noble lords, pay no attention to him, his reason is drowned in wine, or perhaps even a greater misfortune has befallen it. But a manifest sign that he utters a falsehood, Christian men, you have in this, that God could not receive thanks so against nature; and if what escapes from the lips of this madman were true, God would have made the roof of this house to fall upon his head."

"He has not done so on account of the painting, which would be lost; and also because you are here, most Reverend Cardinals, pillars of the Holy Church. You know

God does not always strike directly; and sometimes, hurling His thunderbolts at random, He kills the priest who is celebrating mass, and spares the thief who is stealing. Treasurer, Treasurer, you should be joyful that God minds my words no more than your hands. Pickpocket of the Holy Mother Church, if it is well for me that He is deaf, it is also well for you that He is blind. But even if He heard me, I have accustomed Him to hear worse things!"

The guests, in looking upon the Count, seemed to have experienced the effect produced by Medusa's head. Their wicked host, enjoying the terror he inspired, continued exultingly:

"For my own part, I am only glad that my sons are dead; but perhaps you would like to know how they died. Lend me your ears. Felix, who was a very pious youth, stood one evening reciting devoutly his prayers in the Church of the Madonna del Pilastro. The *Mater Misericordiæ*, to let him know his prayers were heard by her, let fall the principal beam from the roof upon his head, and gently broke his neck. The same evening, or rather at the same hour, as they write me, Christopher was killed with a knife, by a certain jealous husband, who mistook him for a lover who was at that very moment making love to his wife. For which circumstances, considering the time, the hour, the equal manner of their deaths, I declare that man an incurable heretic, and a fit subject for excommunication, who presumes boldly to deny that this could have happened without the express will of Providence."

Beatrice, as if her whole soul were concentrated in her eyes, looked at him; and Count Cenci from time to time would glance at her, and these glances, meeting, flashed like the swords of enemies. Bernardino, as if sleepy, hid his face in the bosom of Lady Lucrezia, who, with tearful eyes and outstretched arms, looked like the *Madonna dei Sette Dolori.* Of the guests, some, with clenched hands upon the table, menaced him with a fierce look; others pointed an accusing finger at him; some looked incredulous, others shut their ears; some looked fearfully up as if expecting a thunderbolt from heaven.

The Cardinals and the Treasurer were the first to rise, saying:

"Let us go! Save yourselves, for the wrath of God can no longer delay in falling on this wicked house!"

An unquiet murmur, increasing like the wind before the tempest, an ill-suppressed shuddering, spread throughout the hall; then all at once burst forth cries of shame and reproach, lamenting and groaning: finally, all, as if overcome by the same passion, thrust out their hands with a curse toward the Count.

"Stop!" he cried fiercely, "what are you doing? Here is no stage, here are no spectators, so that if you mean to act a tragedy, your labor is vain. Is it becoming in you, most holy Cardinals, to pretend a horror for blood? Tell me, why is your dress red? Is it not because the stain of blood may not be distinguished upon it? Away, you mountebanks, who sell your Christ like wine at a fair! Away, you Pharisees, who would make Christ himself, should he return to earth, fly to Mecca and become a Turk. And you, Prince Colonna, be not astonished; I advise you to be calm, for I lived long enough at Rocca Petrella to know all your words and actions; and if you do not know, I can tell you more of necromancy than you would like, having even the power to make the tombs and the dead speak. You understand me, Prince; and what I have learned of your affairs, I can whisper in your ears. To you I speak now, my illustrious Lord Treasurer: I advise you not to forget that I am the son of my father; and that my father was a treasurer, and in business accounts I feel competent to match the best accountants of the apostolic chamber. You are fortunate, Treasurer, that other business keeps me engaged—no matter what! I am a great wave, roaring and foaming—I may break against rocks on the shore, but first I overthrow and swallow everything that comes in my way. Respect your master, fall at my feet and worship me."

The guests, with signs of disgust, drew nearer the door, ready to leave the cursed house; but Count Cenci cried:

"Noble friends and kinsmen, you cannot go from my house without my taking leave of you. Come! be kind enough to grant me the favor of your company a moment longer."

Then taking a large glass of brilliant crystal, he filled it to the brim with Cyprus wine, and as he raised it against the light of the candles, it seemed as if filled with fire.

"Oh, blood of the vine, that grown in the sun's rays, sparkling and bubbling gayly in the light of the candles, as my soul leaped and exulted at the news of my sons' death—oh! were you their mingled blood, matured beneath the fire of my curse, and shed as a sacrifice to my vengeance, I would drink you as devoutly as the wine of the Eucharist; and toasting Satan, I would say: 'Angel of Evil, burst forth from hell! Mount with swift wings after the souls of Felix and Christopher, my sons, before they can approach the gate of Heaven, and drag them down to eternal woe, and torment them with the most atrocious agonies that your diabolical imagination can invent. And if you can not find enough, consult me: I trust to finding new tortures, to which your fancy cannot reach. O Satan! to your health I inebriate myself into an abyss of joy. Triumph in my triumph!' Now, noble friends and kinsmen, I have no longer need of your company; you are at liberty to go or stay."

"By the Holy Apostles, this man has become raving mad!"

"Ah, I always knew him wicked enough to make even angels weep."

"Say rather, to make devils gnash their teeth."

"At any rate, he is a fierce wild beast—it is best to tie him."

"Yes, chain him—let us chain him."

Count Cenci, after finishing his diabolical invocation, sat down quietly, and taking some confectionery, ate it with the utmost calmness. When some of the guests gathered around him menacingly, without even raising his head, he called:

"Olimpio!"

At this call appeared the bandit, whom the cunning old man had kept hidden, and with him twenty more desperate-looking men, armed like *bravi*. They surrounded the guests with drawn poniards, ready at the Count's order to shed their blood.

Cenci sat some time eating confectionery and watching the fear that paled all faces: then he rose, and walking among them with slow steps, and gazing maliciously at them, said with a sneer:

"You, who are learned, must remember the feast prepared by Domitian for the Senators. But be not afraid, I will not order them to *bring the dessert.** Indiscreet men! Do you not know that although the Cenci is no longer a red-hot iron as in his youth, he is still hot enough to burn? A man oftener burns himself with an iron half heated, than with one red-hot—beware! My revenge is like the sealed dispatches of kings—it surely contains a death, though the one upon whom, where, and when it will fall is not known. Leave me in peace, and as soon as you have passed the threshold forget everything. Let

* *Bring the dessert* in ancient times meant an order to murder treacherously. See the account of Friar Alberigo in Dante's Inferno, Canto xxxiii.

everything that has happened be like a dream, which a man hates to remember when he awakes. Mind, words are winged: like the raven of the ark, they never come back; but they stay away to feed upon corpses, and sometimes make them. But if your throats feel as if changing to a flute—then you may speak."

The guests, all frightened, and some stupid with horror, others with rage in their souls, were departing. Beatrice, shaking loose her hair upon her shoulders, furiously reproached them thus:

"Cowards! are you of Latin race? are you sons of the old Romans? yes, but only as worms are the children of the horse that lies dead in battle! An old man frightens you; a few ruffians freeze your blood! you depart—depart, and leave two weak women and a miserable boy in the hands of this man—three hearts beating in the vulture's claws. Did you hear? he does not hide it—he will make us die—and notwithstanding—alas! gentlemen, mark my words, and understand more than they can or ought to tell you—notwithstanding that, this is the least evil I fear from him. I do not speak to you, priests; but to you, knights: when you girded on your swords did not you swear to defend the widow and the orphan? We are worse than orphans—they have no father, and we have an executioner for one.—Remember your daughters, noble knights—remember your daughters, Christian fathers—and have pity on us—take us to your homes."

"Young girl, your grief makes us sad, but we can do nothing for you," said several of the guests.

"Wait and hope. Hope will yet bring forth roses of happiness for you," replied a cardinal.

"If prayers and vows can avail you, my dear daughter, we shall never cease from praying for you."

And the rest proffered similar words—cold and mournful, like drops of holy water sprinkled upon a bier. The guests departed, and did not breathe freely until they gained the open air outside the palace.

All left the hall; Count Cenci and Beatrice remained alone, except for Marzio, who, near a side table, seemed busied in collecting the silver dishes.

"Now are you satisfied?" Count Cenci said to Beatrice. "You know how the help of God tastes? do you think man's help is worth more? It is of no use to put a bandage on the eyes of Justice, that she may not be moved; leave them open—let her see—she will not be affected by the sight. Might is right; might and right were twin-born of the same birth and embraced each other. I know it; I have proved it, and every day I see and feel it more: might is right. Look around, girl, and you will see that no refuge is left you upon heaven or earth, except in my bosom: look there, and you will find the asylum which God and men, equally deaf and wicked, refuse you. That I love you greatly, you already know, since I hate everything in heaven or on earth except you. Throw yourself into my arms; you may in vain seek another man equal to me; I have inherited the gifts of all ages. The strength of youth has not yet left me; in me is the wisdom of mature age and the tenacity of old age. Love me then, Beatrice—beautiful—terrible girl—love me!"

"Father, should I say I hate you, or even fear you, I should not speak the truth. God has created in you a scourge like a famine, plague, or war, and this scourge he has thrown upon me. I bend, without murmuring, my head to His mysterious decrees; and the more hopeless I am of all human aid, the more I draw nearer to God, and trust my fate to His mercy. Father, for pity's sake, kill me!"

The desolate girl threw herself at the Count's feet with open arms, as if awaiting the stroke.

Why did Beatrice start suddenly to her feet, and throw

herself upon her father? Why with both hands did she screen his head? why did she utter that scream of terror, which echoed through the most remote rooms of the spacious palace—she, who feared nothing?

Marzio, who had remained unobserved in the hall, hearing the words which had openly revealed the infernal design of Count Cenci, had softly approached, holding in his hands a heavy silver vase, and was on the point of letting it fall with all his force upon the Count's head.

The Count, starting at her cry and motion, raised involuntarily his face towards heaven, and saw a flash dazzling his eyes—"Ah! may it not be the delayed thunderbolt of the wrath of God?" This idea flashed like lightning into his mind, but contained an eternity of torment for his wicked soul. But not for this did the old man start; and reassured, he turned his eye fiercely around the room and saw Marzio, who was replacing the vase upon the sideboard.

"Marzio—you here?"

"Your Excellency!"

"You here?"

"At the orders of your Excellency."

"Go!"

He bowed and went out, casting a look at Beatrice, as if to say: "Why did you prevent me?"

But Beatrice, in her impetuous passion, pressed with superhuman strength the Count's arm, as if to drag him away, exclaiming:

"Come, unfortunate old man, you have not a moment to lose. Death is covering you with his wings. Come, the measure of your sins hurls you to perdition. Put on sackcloth, cover your head with ashes; you have sinned enough. Penitence is a burning baptism; but fire purifies more and better than water. If your prayers cannot reach the throne of God, but threaten to fall back upon your head like hailstones of malediction, I will stand by your side, and add mine, too, and they shall both be heard; both accepted, or both rejected. And if justice requires a victim as expiation—behold, I willingly offer my life in redemption for your soul; but hasten, the edge of the grave is slippery—remember your eternal safety depends upon it."

Count Cenci stood listening and smiling. When she had finished, with mocking tone he replied:

"It is well, my beloved Beatrice; you alone can teach me the celestial joys of Paradise. I will come and find you to-night, and we will pray together."

Beatrice let fall her father's arm. The words and his malignant expression had the power of chilling all her enthusiasm, and brought her back to the stern reality of life. She departed with a dejected countenance, murmuring:

"Lost!—lost!—Oh, lost! without a hope!"

Count Cenci poured hastily another glass of wine, and swallowed it at one draught.

CHAPTER XI

THE FIRE

GREAT was the misfortune and grief that fell upon the poor carpenter and his family! Husband, wife, and child were all sleeping in a room over the shop.

They slept—but a fearful dream disturbed the wife: it seemed to her as if an enormous monster, with fiery eyes, a hairy body, and wings like a bat, pressed with his hind legs upon her body, and with his forelegs on her throat, as if to strangle her; she strived to move, and could not; endeavored to scream, but could not succeed. At last, by a desperate effort, she moved; her eyes were so heavy she could scarcely open them; yet two lights, now violet, now blue, like flame from alcohol, were visible. The whole room was full of smoke; an insupportable heat filled the air; little by little the floor cracked, and from the holes made by the falling of the bricks, tongues of flame burst forth, which in a few seconds increased to a horrible fire.

"Fire—fire!" screamed the woman, looking about in affright; and she leaped from her bed to seize upon her child in its cradle.

"Fire!" screamed the startled husband; and, undressed as he was, he ran toward the door, and opened it. This gave an ingress to the flames, which enveloped the room; the whole house was in a blaze; he retraced his steps, and grasped with one arm his wife, with the other his child, and rushed out to gain the stairs. On! on! if they can only reach the door of the house! They near it; one step more, and they will touch it; they have reached it—but, oh, woe! they cannot open it—they shake it—they beat upon it; in vain—it had been bolted on the outside.

Surrounded by a vortex of flames, the miserable father, his heart beating wildly, his breast panting, retakes his child in his arms—and leaves his wife—he is too weak for both. Raving, not knowing what to do, he turns and re-turns through the entrance, and then strives wildly to ascend the staircase.

The wife followed so closely that she placed her foot where he raised his; and the husband was invigorated by her breathing which he felt in the hot air on his shoulders —she always defending her child from the flames, and sometimes her husband.

He gained the room; but here his courage and his breath failed him—his eyes glittered in death, and he staggered and almost fell; but had just strength enough to replace the child in the arms of its mother before expiring—he could not utter a word—only with a look like a light before going out he expressed the desolation which lips cannot speak—a desolation which, if it could have been conveyed in words, would have uttered this: "I do not commend him to you, for you cannot save him!" Then, falling back five or six steps, he struck madly against the wall, attempting to grasp it with his hands.

It always happens, in cases of harsh necessity, both in the physical appetites and in the passions of the soul, that the more intense are lost in the less deep ones; hence the wife paid no further attention to the husband, who was so dear to her, but with all her force embraced the body of her child. She opened the window and looked out.

Groups of people in the street saw a figure delineated in black upon a field of fire, and had compassion and fear for her. They wished to help her, and consulted together; but the old men, with that great Roman calmness, projecting their under lips and crossing their arms, looked pitifully on the fire, saying: "We can do nothing for it: water would not be enough; and no one but a devil can pass through those flames. We can only see the fire go out by itself, and then say prayers for those poor souls, gone out of the world without sacrament."

Now, it had so happened that Luisa Cenci, a prey to jealousy, had wandered dressed in man's attire for several nights, and on this one also, about the carpenter's house to surprise her husband; but as yet her search had proved vain. Notwithstanding this, not a shadow of doubt crossed her mind that she might have been deceived; but instead, she wondered bitterly whether Giacomo visited her by night, or whether she met him elsewhere, or whether they had quarreled, and had a thousand other ways of tormenting herself with an error, instead of consoling herself with the plainer way of truth!

She ran, like the others, attracted by the screams and blaze of fire, about the house; and when she saw it, her heart exulted: "That which sin gave, justice has taken away," she thought.

Before the fire had reached ungovernable fury, some neighbors had gone in search of ladders and ropes, and were returning with a ladder, which they had found in a church close by. They placed it against the wall, raised their faces, but did not move, because the flames, breaking through above and below, showed it to be a desperate undertaking. But when the mother, appearing through the flames, supporting her child, and crying: "Save my son!" then one—yes, one alone—felt her heart moved, and this was Luisa Cenci. The woman was silent within her, but the mother spoke! Rushing to the foot of the ladder, she exclaimed hastily:

"Come; the distance is short, the undertaking not difficult: Romans, which of you will ascend to save them shall have one hundred golden ducats."

And as no one stirred, she called again: "Good Christians, courage! two hundred ducats to him who saves them."

Nor was this reward enough to move them; for the fear of the danger surpassed the desire for money. Luisa stood for a moment reflecting—she could dispose of only one hundred more, which spent, not one would remain for her own children, nor could she expect to obtain any more from her father-in-law. No matter, she thought a moment later, and then with louder voice, as if to recall lost time, she exclaimed:

"Three hundred ducats to him who saves them! three hundred golden ducats, I say—enough to marry two daughters! Romans! does no one dare? Clear the way for me, then—clear the way, I say! God help me!"

And light as a bird she ascended the ladder, while the

top, which was leaning against the wall, was already smoking. Reaching the window, she said:

"Give me"—and at the same time a voice said:

"Take the child."

They had understood each other. Both were mothers, and they knew the highest desire of a maternal heart is the safety of her child. She descended. A young man, ashamed that no one had attempted to move, ascended to the middle of the ladder, and receiving the child in his arms, carried it to a place of safety.

Luisa re-ascended, while tongues of flame darted about the ladder like vipers; being quenched wherever she put her hands, but kindling more vividly after she raised them. Arrived face to face with the woman who she supposed had taken from her her husband's love, she courageously stretched her arms to her who she believed had embraced the father of her children. The woman threw herself wildly into them. The mother of Christ, looking from Heaven upon this embrace, might be proud to be a woman. Certainly, neither human nor celestial eyes had witnessed for ages such an act of charity.

Luisa firmly grasped her rival by her waist, and descended.

Haste, Luisa, for the ladder is burning; haste, Luisa, for the charred rounds crack with the fire. Oh, Holy Virgin! why does she stop? One second may be fatal. Unmindful of herself, unmindful of the imminent danger, unmindful of everything, she cannot resist the great desire of looking upon her rival's face, and seeing by the light of the fire whether she surpassed her in beauty. Woman's heart! Although horribly distorted by grief and fear, with her hair scorched, her face spotted with burns, she looked, as she really was, most beautiful.

"Ah!" Luisa cried, "how beautiful she is!" and staggered upon the ladder.

She had come within three steps of the ground, when

the floor fell in with a terrible crash; the flames disappeared, clouds of smoke mixed with myriads of sparks surrounded the house, the ladder, and the women. A fearful cry echoed even to the shores of the Tiber, for they thought the two had been killed by the fire and the fall.

Then suddenly the fire, like pride humbled for a moment, blazed more terribly than before, and from the midst of the flames Luisa appeared with the woman in her arms unhurt.

Cries of joy, furious shouts rent the skies: "Who is the brave fellow?" "I do not know." "Did you ever see him before?" "Never." "He has no beard on his face, and seems too slender for such a deed of valor. Hurrah for the valiant youth; true Latin blood!" and the enthusiasm and applause grew louder and louder.

The Lord had mercy upon the wife of the carpenter, who, being beside herself, knew not the sad fate of her husband. Luisa, more fervid in her generosity, as the good always are, would not allow the woman to be carried to the hospital; but recollecting a certain widow of her acquaintance who would take care of her, thought to have her brought to her own house, so much the more, that, finding she had saved the three hundred ducats, which she had risked for this family, even should she now spend half, still some would be left for herself.

She then, in order to accomplish her design, had the woman placed upon a sheet, held at each corner by men who willingly offered to do this office. She carried the child on her own bosom, asking, at the same time, for some one to support her also, as her head was whirling, and she felt the ground receding from under her feet. From the crowd pressing about her, a stout, robust man appeared, his head, neck and face covered by a mass of hair and beard, dressed like one of the peasants of the Roman suburbs.

"Lean on me," he said, offering his arm with a voice more tender than his hard, bronzed face would have given hope for. "Lean upon it, for it would support even the Trajan column. I feel able, if it does not incommode you, to carry you and the child both."

"I believe it. May God reward you! This is enough. Now move on gently to the street of Saint Lorenzo Panisperna to the house of the Cenci."

"The house of the Cenci!" exclaimed the man, starting back.

"Why do you wonder at it? Perhaps you think my house so great a stranger to charity as to cause surprise. Pray, what gives you a right to think so, peasant?"

And as the man, without replying, merely shook his head, Lady Luisa, as if offended, added:

"If you wish to know who dared to ascend the ladder, while you men all remained immovable by fear, I will tell you—'twas a woman; and you see in me the wife of Don Giacomo Cenci, and daughter-in-law of Count Cenci."

The peasant staggered; he pressed his hand to his forehead, as if to prevent his thoughts and feelings from escaping.

The man was Olimpio, and the four supporters of the sheet that held the woman were his companions and accomplices in the horrible fire. Do not believe that any hypocritical feelings urged them to this act, or craftiness the better to screen themselves; for they had committed the crime with so much shrewdness as to leave no room for suspecting it had been done through malice rather than accident; but they were ennobled by the magnanimous daring of Luisa, and were really sincere.

The unfortunate woman was carried gently to the house of Luisa Cenci, who, with Olimpio, had preceded her; and with that thoughtfulness which women alone possess she had already a bed prepared, and wax, oil, cotton, and other remedies used for burns; she also sent for a surgeon and the widow. The latter fortunately lived in the same street, and came immediately.

The poor woman was delirious all night, sometimes weeping softly, then desperately, according as her excited fancy imagined things, pleasing or hideous. The day after she was no better, but on the next her mental faculties were somewhat restored, and she asked for her child. They told her he was near her, sleeping; she tried to move, but could not, and with feeble voice said:

"For God's sake, do not deceive me!" They reassured her and she wept. Then she asked for her husband, and, with a necessary deception, they said he was lying badly hurt at the hospital, but not without a hope of recovery.

Luisa, who, still disguised, watched by her, exhorted her to be of good cheer, and keep silent; since otherwise she would only add to her illness and delay the pleasure of embracing her child, and she then remained silent.

Luisa had become much attached to this lonely widow, which was not strange; since an offence given is a reason for offending, so one good act persuades to another; and we love others less for the good they bestow upon us, than for the cares they cost us.

It cannot be said how much inclined she felt to know the particulars of her husband's intercourse with her; but a thousand considerations detained her from satisfying it. In the first place, it did not seem honorable to take advantage of her weak state, to draw out her secret: neither Christian-like, nor consistent with the generosity she had been showing her to retard her recovery by making her talk; and finally, having conceived a doubt, although a very weak one, about the truth of her suspicions, she preferred rather to waver in uncertainty, than despair in the hated reality.

But no measure is so quickly filled as that of impatience. One day she was seated by the bed of the widow;

Angiolina, for this was her name, was looking devoutly in the face of Luisa, and whispered blessings and prayers. Luisa in her turn looked long at her; she noticed the hue of health gradually returning to her cheeks; the burns had left no scars, and she was becoming as handsome as ever. The heart of the jealous woman beat impetuously in her bosom, as with a bitter smile she asked:

"But am I really your only protector?"

"Who do you suppose would care for a poor woman like me, except you, with your charity?"

"Ah, yes — really—I am afraid your memory is not good just now."

"Ah! you say the truth," exclaimed Angiolina, blushing as if she had committed a fault. "Good Lord! how could I be so ungrateful?"

"Then you have another protector?"

"Another protector, as you say, who has been very kind to us."

"Indeed! and who is he?"

"He is the noble, generous Cenci."

"Cenci? Cenci, did you say? Cenci?" cried Luisa, as if stung by a viper, and she was silent. But Angiolina, as if to express her gratitude, and a desire of correcting her involuntary fault, added passionately:

"The kindest and best gentleman above all whom I have known, except you. He rebuilt our house, which had been ruined by the water, and now the fire has destroyed: he wanted me to buy fine clothes—pride of an hour; and reproved me for not asking him to be godfather to my child."

Luisa bit her lips until the blood came, and then with bitter voice interrupted her, saying:

"Enough!"

And while, in order not to betray herself, she hastily withdrew, overcome by different passions, she murmured:

"Insolent! Not even restrained from proclaiming her own shame! O God! do you really command us to nurse the snake that stings our hearts?"

CHAPTER XII

MARCO

VERDIANA had looked for the twentieth time out of the window, and as many times had numbered the steps that, according to her calculations, separated the parsonage from Rome. She went into the field, and although trembling on her legs, she bent her ear to the ground to hear whether any noise betokened the coming of the curate; nothing. She got up, sang the litanies, told her beads ten times over; then took her needles, upon which hung a half-finished stocking, and began to knit with great celerity: whoever had observed her would have easily noticed that while a sad thought was springing up in her mind two tears were slowly gathering in her eyes; the tears and the thought burst forth at the same moment, and throwing her needles down impatiently she exclaimed:

"Surely! if some misfortune has happened to the poor man, he will no longer need stockings or shoes. Well, why, after all, may he not need them? Do all accidents render stockings useless?"

She retook her needles and thrust them into the stitches.

"And dead or alive," she continued, "the stockings will be good for somebody." Then she replaced the ball of thread in her pocket: "Good for some poor man—or even for myself."

Suddenly the air resounded with the braying of Marco. Verdiana ran to the window, and from behind the hedge appeared at the same time the beloved heads of both the curate and the ass—not that she ever compared one with the other; God forbid!

"Here come the long expected ones!" exclaimed Verdiana, running hastily toward the curate and the ass. She threw her arms around Marco's neck, showing her affection like Sancho Panza; kissed the curate's hand, and assisted him to dismount.

"I suspect," said Verdiana, "that the promise of 'ask and it shall be given' has again failed; and brushing the dust off the curate, she continued: "the holy Gospel must mean grace given away and not ducats."

"Silence, Verdiana, it is a sin to murmur against Providence; I have knocked, and it was opened unto me; I have asked, and one hundred ducats were given to me."

"One hundred ducats! Then we may make a bonfire."

The curate sighed; went to supper; ate little, drank less, and replied in broken sentences to the questioning of Verdiana, who standing by him kept inquiring:

"Are you not well, reverend sir? Did any accident happen to you on the road? Have you been frightened? Blessed man, why don't you speak? Do you want me to make you some water-gruel with honey—or would you like a quince boiled in wine? Shall I bathe your temples with vinegar? Will you have a mustard poultice—a foot-bath?"

"Oh!" cried the curate: "do all these things for yourself, Verdiana, if you need them; I am very well, thank God! and here are the hundred ducats."

"Oh, how splendid! They that possess them do no wrong in holding them tight!"

"Listen, Verdiana; there are a hundred ducats; but

they are not enough by a good deal for the parsonage, the house furniture, and the church."

"Well, patience! we will restore the church in the first place, and God will provide for the rest."

"He will provide, certainly; but remember, Verdiana, if we do not take care of the parsonage, one of these days we shall be obliged to swim in the house."

"It is better for us to swim in the house, than for Christ in the church."

"Yes; but if His minister is drowned, the divine service will be interrupted, to the great detriment of His worshipers."

"Pooh! In the first place, the service will not be interrupted, for, as the proverb says, 'One pope dead, another is made'; and although it is true that it rains into the house, still we do not swim in it, nor drown, that I know."

"Yes; but the wise Hippocrates says: *principiis obsta, sero medicina paratur;* do you know what that means, Verdiana? It means if we do not mend things in time the hole will become a ditch. Besides, a ragged dress causes the wearer to be despised. For the fault of a dirty servant, a master has sometimes become contemptible."

"But it would be worse to hate the servant for the ingratitude he shows his master; and think for a moment what a master!"

The curate thought: "How the deuce did Verdiana get so much wisdom all at once!" But Verdiana continued:

"I said the ducats were splendid, because indeed they pleased me; but they are not more beautiful than conscience or duty, and much less beautiful than Jesus; and see how I would use them, if they could make me believe that you would do wrong?" and Verdiana took a handful of them, and made a sign of throwing them out of the window. "I would throw them as grain to chickens."

"Verdiana! Verdiana!" cried the curate, seizing her by the waist and pushing her back, "are you mad?"

How many and bitter were the words Verdiana spoke, and how keenly they stung the curate, need not be told; it is enough to know that he bent down his head and inwardly prayed that the bitter cup—that is, Verdiana—might pass away from him; he sighed, he repented, repeating the act of contrition ten times, and decided to return the money. Suddenly looking at the gold, he thought of Judas's thirty pieces of silver; and, remembering the end of this traitor, locked shudderingly at the fig-tree in the garden, and went away from the window. But while giving himself up to despair, an idea came to his mind; he felt as joyful as Archimedes when he discovered how to know whether copper had been mixed in the crown of gold. If he could have touched his own cheeks, he would have kissed himself; and raising his head, he said:

"Listen to me, Verdiana; you have talked much and badly, the Lord forgive you! Who taught you to think so ill of your neighbors—of a curate—of myself? Does it seem, as long as you have lived with me, that I have been a man to deserve such reproofs? And if I have not been, how could I change all at once from wine to vinegar? Listen now! We must rob Peter to pay Paul. Giannicchio and I will collect the unbroken tiles on the roof of the parsonage, and put them on the roof of the church, putting new ones on the parsonage. We will cut out six shirts somewhat long, and when a robe is needed for the church, we will add a strip of lace to one of them, and that will do perfectly. From the damask quilt we will make two copes—one yellow, and the other we will have dyed red. The lamps and vases can be used for both church and house; I will also have repaired the crucifix that hangs over my bed, and on festival days we will have it in the church."

The good priest had reasoned thus:

"The condition I made was not to spend a ducat on the church. Cursed be the condition! But if I remove the tiles from the parsonage, I shall prevent the rain from leaking into the church, and yet I keep my promise. True, in this way I shall have to make anew the roof of the parsonage; but I can safely say that I did not spend a cent for the church."

These subtle and false reasonings with which weak natures, although honest, are accustomed to quiet the conscience, were contrary to the common-sense of Verdiana, who said:

"Of what use is it to make this choice, and this change? What can you and Giannicchio do climbing upon the roofs like cats? For what purpose is this story of shirts and church garments? What partiality is this for mending the crucifix over your bed, and leaving the one in the church with its arms hanging down? What nonsense, what confusion, what deviltry is entering your head? No, sir; we must begin at the beginning—that is, at the church. If any money is left, very well; if not, patience! The ravens that brought bread in the desert to Saint John will come also to us."

"Verdiana, since that time it seems the ravens have given up the baker's business."

"And as to dress, have you not read to me a thousand times that passage in the Gospel which says: 'Why take ye thought for raiment? Consider the lilies of the field: Solomon in all his glory was not arrayed like one of these.'"

"Yes, Verdiana, yes; all this is true, it is in the Gospel; but we must not take metaphors to the letter. The dress of the lilies is a particular dress of their own. Have you ever seen a priest clothed in a tunic like a lily, or a lily like a priest?"

"*Misericordia Domini*! is it really yourself that speaks? You seem changed into a Lutheran!"

"Verdiana, I say!" exclaimed the curate, becoming impatient.

"I know the Evil One sometimes pounces upon religious people as he would at a village feast, but"——

"What are you about to do, Verdiana?" asked the curate, seeing her take the vase of holy water and put the sprinkler into it.

"Your words sound heretical—let me do it—one extra blessing spoils nothing; if there should be anything—you understand—the devil must go out of you."

The curate in vain cried: "Verdiana, stop! Don't make me angry!"

The pitiless servant sprinkled him with holy water from head to foot. But the curate was less vexed than he seemed; nay, in his heart he was glad of an opportunity to commune with himself, away from the logical persecution of Verdiana; so he said crossly:

"Give me a light, for I am going to bed;" and gathering the money, with a vexed look, he went to his room.

Verdiana followed him silently, but not appeased.

The curate opened his desk, and threw the money in topsy-turvy; and with a manner that would have shamed Agamemnon when he commanded Ægisthus—

"Go, let not the next sun see thee in Argo!"

he said to the servant:

"Good night!"

Verdiana knew from the tone that these words meant: "Go away immediately." She retired; but could not help replying through the half-closed door:

"Good night, reverend sir; but remember that the devil's flour is lost in the chaff; and mind lest the money of the devil does not spoil the money of God; for truly the ducats you brought home smell of brimstone a mile off."

The curate shut the door in her face, hastily undressed himself, and after he got into bed, he thought: "I should like to know who would blame me! I should not fail in keeping my promise, for I should not spend a ducat of Cenci in the church; but no one can forbid my giving to the church what belongs to the house. Perhaps it would have been better not to meddle in this bad business, and to refuse the money decidedly. But no; for if I had not accepted it I could not pull down the house to mend the church. When the sheet is short, the head or the feet must go bare. Consequently I have done well—very well!"

Satisfied with his arguments, he turned on the other side. But, curious circumstance! Here he found an entirely different opinion; a voice, which seemed to come from his pillow, reproached him thus: "Cheat, caviller, hypocrite, you want to serve half God and half Mammon! No, either all to God, or all to Mammon; there is no middle way. Are these the examples that the Prophet Elisha and Saint Peter have given you? Offerings presented with an impure heart are rejected by Heaven. You accepted the money with the express condition of not using it in God's service. Is this not worse than simony? He that does not worship God is already a servant of the Evil One. Get up—go to Verdiana, and ask her pardon; this woman has so much charity that she can spare some for you. Get up, and go to Rome, even in your nightclothes, return the money to Count Cenci, and say to him: Leave me my poverty with my innocence; for riches with sin do not please me."

"Ouff! how hot I am," exclaimed the curate; I cannot go to sleep;" and he turned on the other side. Here his bad genius awaited him, and whispered in his ears: "Console yourself, for the intention justifies the work, and in this world he that is wise rules himself according to the winds and tides. Should Verdiana again lecture you, you can quote the example of the Hebrews, who, before they went out of Egypt, borrowed the gold and silver vessels of the Egyptians, and very likely used them in the building of the Tabernacle. At any rate, the intention justifies the work; if not in men's eyes, at least in God's. Then I have done right, very right!" And he went to sleep.

Some time later he was startled by an unusual noise; he leaped into a sitting posture on the bed, and thought he heard a light footfall on the floor; supposing the cat had jumped down from some place, he stretched his hand out of the bed, and took one of his heavy iron-nailed shoes with silver buckles and threw it in the direction of the noise; the shoe struck against a closet, which sounded like a drum, for it was empty. Verdiana, awakened by the noise, screamed out from her room near by:

"Sir, reverend sir! evil money is that which disturbs sleep, and God sends it in an evil day and an evil year. When you were poorer you slept until morning; now, you neither sleep yourself, nor let others."

The curate hid his head under the sheets and stopped his ears with the quilt, in order not to hear her persecuting voice.

Next morning the curate, whom we will call Don Cirillo, when he rose, looked first to the heavens, then glanced at Verdiana; the former promised a fine day, the latter a stormy one. He began in a low tone to sing the matutinal hymn, and stirred about in order to provoke some friendly word, but did not succeed. At breakfast, in order to break the ice, he began to ask, with indifference, the price of this thing or that, and then bravely, with a cunning that would have thrown into the shade the sharpest diplomatist, suddenly observed that for so many things one hundred and fifty ducats did not seem enough. Verdiana, taken so by surprise on the subject of linens, in which every good housekeeper has so much pride, forgetting what the money was for, began to calculate with Don Cirillo. The latter, although a learned man, was a poor accountant, so the sum total never came right. Verdiana counted by touching her fingers to her lips, but she could not go far in arithmetic. The curate resolved then to take the money and divide it into as many heaps as there were things to be purchased.

Don Cirillo had reason to congratulate himself on this strategem, for he succeeded in appeasing the ill-humor of Verdiana and in cheering up his own mind; for the sight of money rejoices the eyes of man. He then, to execute his design, went to his room, followed by Verdiana, who said:

"You will see, by your calculation, a score or more will be wanting!"

"And I say there will be enough;" and he bent down to raise the cover of his desk; but, suddenly rising, he inquired:

"What did you say to me last night, Verdiana, about the devil's flour turning into chaff?"

"I said so because, in my youth, I was told by a priest that the devil made a bargain with a country fellow to buy his soul for many thousand ducats; having signed the paper and received the money, the countryman went home with his bag; the next morning he was found dead in his bed and the bag was full of coal; so he lost both his soul and the money."

"Rest easy, Verdiana; this money did not come from the devil, but from one of the noblest Roman gentlemen. But do you persist in saying a score or more will be wanted?"

"Yes; a score, and a little more."

"Now we shall see—I am certain there will be enough."

And he raised the lid—the money was gone.

Don Cirillo stood with his body bent, holding up the lid, his head turned toward Verdiana. Verdiana shut her eyes and put her hands to her head; both seemed seized by catalepsy. They stood a long time without uttering a word, without moving their eyes. A fearful commotion was raging in the breast of Don Cirillo while he was bending over the desk. In that warring of emotions, great was the grief for the loss of the money, great the wonder of how it had disappeared, but greater, indeed, the remorse of having accepted it with conditions surely not the best in the world. Don Cirillo, rising slowly, seemed to have lived ten years in a minute; but without any bitterness he said to his servant:

"Verdiana, you were a prophetess."

"Oh, poor me! I wish I had not said a word."

"And now, what is to be done?" asked the curate, striking his forehead with his hand.

"Resign yourself to God's will."

"Woman, you have said wisely. However, Verdiana, mark well, the devil has nothing at all to do with this business. The dirty foot-tracks through the house, the window that looks on the garden broken, and the noise that woke me last night, are clear proofs that some thief has robbed us. God forgive him, and may the money do him more good than me!"

But, alas! the grief of these unfortunate creatures reached its utmost limit when, on descending to the stable, Marco also could not be found! With what tears, what exclamations, did the parsonage resound! The neighboring hills reechoed with cries of "Marco! Marco!" Even Giannicchio joined the tearful chorus, and tried to console their great grief by putting on his neck the halter of the ass, and standing near the manger where Marco was always to be found, saying:

"Do not cry, Don Cirillo; Verdiana, wipe your eyes. I will take Marco's place; I will serve you like Marco. And when you wish to go to Rome, reverend sir, I will carry you on my shoulders as comfortably as Marco."

The thoughts of the priest finally rested upon Job: first of all he considered he had no wife, and this seemed a great cause for consolation; then he expected no friends, for if only one of Job's comforters, either the Temanite or Shuhite had come to comfort him, he would have thrown himself in despair into the well; and at last, his conscience being clear from any passion, and reasoning calmly and without prevarication, showed him he had committed a heavy sin against God and that he should thank Him with all his heart for punishing him only with this slight trial.

"God gave," sighed Don Cirillo, "and God has taken away; may his will be done: for the sin that I committed, Thy hand, O Lord, punishes me lightly."

Hardly had he finished uttering these words, when, as if Divine Justice, being appeased, wished again to open the founts of mercy, the hills and vales resounded with a glorious and triumphant braying, which sounded like Marco's. Nor had they time to say, "That is Marco," before he appeared crowned with green leaves; and leaping the hedge, he ran toward the curate. Don Cirillo joyfully relieved him of his saddle and bags, without noticing whether they were empty or full. Giannicchio first embraced and kissed him, then combed and washed him. Verdiana prepared fresh straw and grass; nay, turning her eyes about the garden, she saw one large cabbage. She reflected whether it were best to keep this for the curate's soup, or give it to Marco; but love for the latter conquered, and she resolutely plucked it and put it into Marco's manger. It was the return of the prodigal son, and she killed the fatted calf.

It may also be added that, for an ass, Marco had on this festive occasion the same honors as Pope Boniface VIII at his coronation banquet; for, as he was waited upon by two kings, the Hungarian and the Sicilian, in royal garments and crowns on their heads, so also the curate and Verdiana waited upon Marco. It is true, the curate had not on his cope, but in compensation Giannicchio acted as cup-bearer, and led him to the trough where once he had drunk the moon. At last, satiated, Marco felt the need of repose; he did not actually say "Good night" to any one; but he let it be understood by stretching himself on the straw, shutting his eyes, and hanging his head. On leaving the stable the curate took up the bags, and this time, not being excited, he noticed they were heavy, and put his hand in one. Worldly powers! Was he dreaming or was he awake? He touched money; he overturned the bags on the ground—ducats! ducats! and what a number! Don Cirillo and Verdiana sat themselves on the ground, and counted the money; it seemed as if there were four or five times the former amount. Counting and re-counting, they concluded there must be four or five hundred ducats.

"It seems to me, now, this money will be enough for everything," said Don Cirillo, but Verdiana answered warningly:

"Is this money ours? Let us be careful, reverend sir. God may have sent it to try us a second time."

"Verdiana, at first I thought as you, but now I am persuaded this money belongs to the thief that robbed me; he cannot be of the neighborhood, but one of the bandits that infest the country; so that to give it back to him would be a sin, and to the once robbed, impossible. I propose," and he said it with some hesitation, "that we spend for ourselves about a hundred and fifty ducats, the remainder for the church and the poor of the parish—and both crucifixes shall be restored, the one in the church and the other in the parsonage."

The proposal seemed to please Verdiana, for she added without objection:

"We can leave the damask quilt upon the bed, and buy copes of new damask."

"We need not change the shirts into church-garments."

"The tiles on the parsonage can remain, and those on the church also."

"It is right; render to Cæsar what is Cæsar's, to God what is God's."

"Yesterday you did not think so."

"Let us say no more about it. Come, God has forgiven; would you keep the bitter feeling? Would you be less merciful than God, Verdiana?"

"May the Holy Virgin forbid! You shall have two new tunics—one for summer, of camlet, the other for winter, of woolen cloth—and two new pairs of trousers—for yesterday, it seemed to me, eh—those you had were not in the best order."

"And two new gowns for you—one of cotton, the other of wool."

"And dishes."

"And napkins."

"Dishes are really necessary. Now that I can tell it without worrying you, you must know that for some time you have always eaten out of the same dish; when I went into the kitchen I washed it in a hurry, replacing it on the table so you might not notice it."

"And with napkins we can let the cat's fur rest."

"Oh, Lord! how poor we are. I never noticed it before as now, having money to spend, I think of the many things that are wanted."

"So it is; money is like the sun; it discovers poverty, and cheers it."

"But we have thought too much of ourselves."

"Giannicchio, for the first time in his life, shall have a coat made of one piece of cloth."

"And Marco a new bridle."

"By the way, what a good beast Marco is! and you,

Verdiana, are a blessed Christian—both of you give me a chance to do a pious work. Verdiana, the poor washer-woman has lost her donkey and is very sad, not knowing what to do about it. She cannot go to Rome after her clothes, and her boys cannot gain their living with the cart. Now then, give me a score of ducats. I will go without loss of time to console her, and at the same time I will bring her sons and the dog here with me, that they may keep watch here to-night. You see, Verdiana, if the robber came for my money, so much more eager he will be to return for mine and his also; and he may as well know that no good wind blows for him here."

And the good curate did as he said; nor was he wrong in being well prepared, for the next night the dog barked and growled continually; afterward he ceased.

CHAPTER XIII

TREACHERY

THE hour was late; Count Cenci had retired to his study, and was reading with great attention Aristotle's book upon the nature of animals; now and then he paused, as if thinking, and noted upon the margin the thoughts that entered his mind. Suddenly the clock struck two.

"I watch," said Count Cenci aloud, "but without profit. The mysteries of nature are sought in vain. Study, read, meditate—you are fortunate if you can again find the door by which you entered. I hold him that divided time into hours, minutes, and seconds, the worst genius the world ever produced. At the age to which I have come, it seems as if the hours escape more swiftly—like riders who ply harder the lash at the last round of the race: *motus in fine velocior.* One must attend with all one's mind—attend to what? Everything is in contrast, disorder and confusion in the world: we are at war with ourselves. I, who in my earliest youth embraced a certain course of life, and have since confirmed my choice by reflection and invariably adopted it in my actions—I, when I least expect it, feel within a spirit which disagrees, contradicts, and overpowers; which, either by flattery or force, tries to drag me where I do not care to go. Were it a rebellious eye, or hand, I could tear it out, or cut it off; but how can I lay my hands upon this rebellious spirit? If I cannot stifle it, I may at least conquer it. Beatrice thought to terrify me when she menaced that posterity would say of me: 'In the time of the prophet Nathan the scourges of God were three, afterwards they became four: famine, pestilence, war, and Count Cenci.' Would it were so! But posterity will not even know I have lived. Our terrible forefathers have devoured everything; they have even disinherited us from becoming infamous. O Tiberius!—O Nero!—O Domitian! you have taken from us the right of being called wicked. You plunged your lips in the rivers of lust and ferocity, until only a few drops remain for us to quench our thirst. Still I feel a heart and mind to outdo them; and if fortune had only given me an empire, or the Pontifical seat, I would have so reaped in your fields, most august emperors, as not to envy you your harvest. Gallop on, Sin; the way now is short—carry me to perdition at full speed."

A hasty knock at the secret door put an end to his wicked reflections. Supposing it was Marzio, who had come on account of some unlooked-for accident, he opened it quickly. Olimpio panting, his head bound with a bloody handkerchief, burst into the room, turning his head backward like a man who suspects he is pursued. He threw himself on a seat, wiping the perspiration from his forehead. Count Cenci, although very expert in dissimulating, could ill suppress his surprise and anger on seeing him; yet, feigning as well as he could, asked:

"What devil brings you here in this dress at this hour? you are wounded, too; what accident has happened?"

"Betrayed! Count Cenci, betrayed! But I swear to God, and the Apostles Peter and Paul, that before I die I will kill the miserable Judas the traitor, even were he mine own father."

"Betrayed! how can that be? But you are dropping blood!"

"Don't mind it; it is nothing—a mere pistol-shot—the ball only grazed my head, nothing more."

"Very well; now, Olimpio, sit comfortably, and tell me all that has happened to you."

"To-night was the one appointed for the undertaking of his Excellency the Duke of Altemps, from which a voice within tried to dissuade me, and had it not been for that cursed ass, I had decided to try whether, by using all my power, I might not succeed in again becoming an honest man; and just then, at the best moment, the bucket has fallen again into the well. The ass stands between me and heaven."

"Olimpio, you have been hurt on the head; you are raving, poor man!"

"*Per Dio!* I am not raving, Count Cenci; I am telling the truth. I had finished the carpenter's business, but with an addition to it that neither you nor I expected; it was the devil himself that made the unfortunate carpenter burn to death."

"Certainly it was the devil that bolted the door on the outside."

"I did that; but I swear to you, as an honest bandit, that I only meant to prevent him from running immediately out of the house, awaking the neighborhood to help him in extinguishing the flames; I did not suppose your combustible preparation burned so terribly; nor could I foresee that the carpenter would get confused and wander all over the burning house before opening the window. In short, I did not suppose so much trouble would come of it. Did you hear, Count Cenci, of the daring of your daughter-in-law, Lady Luisa? What a difference between us and her! True Latin blood!"

"This I also know. Certainly she is a courageous woman. Did I say courageous? Yes, and I will not retract my word; every creature has its virtues; and if I were not Francesco Cenci, I should wish to be Luisa Cenci; in our family the women are far superior to the men. If my sons had only resembled Olimpia, Beatrice, or Luisa; if this evil age had given me a chance to acquire fame by honest deeds, either by the hand or with the mind, perhaps then—who knows?—I might have taken a fancy to another path; but now, let us think no more about it."

"For me, it seemed as if my heart would break; I felt all my wicked nature falling away, and I cried like a child. I was deliberating upon changing my life, and I should not have hesitated; but in wanting to accomplish everything first, I spoiled all. I had done so much evil in the world, that it was necessary to atone for it with some little good; but the evil alone I could do; I could not do the good. I thought of getting the hundred and fifty ducats of the curate in order to have masses said for the soul of the carpenter and all whom I have killed. I did not think it a sin to steal them, because, as you said, you had only given them to him for a joke; and as for what the curate may have had himself, it is a well-known thing that the accessory follows the principal.

"I dressed myself like a beggar, examined the premises diligently, and at night slipped quietly into the house and took the money. In going away I went into a closet; the curate awoke, mistook me for the cat, and threw a shoe at me, but he did not hit me. I had observed the worthy curate owned a strong young ass, and I intended to borrow it, to ease me of walking. I went to the stable, unfastened him from his manger, put the saddle on him and led him into the open air. But when he saw I wanted to ride him, he began to kick, enough to break a mountain of iron. Finally I mounted him, and we started as good friends as if we never had quarreled. At dawn I saw the bags hanging from the saddle; and as the money I carried about me was rather heavy, I put the curate's money and my own within them, which in gold and silver amounted to about four hundred ducats, and more.

"Day coming, I went into a wood, intending to reach Rome about dark; I thought that now I might trust the ass, and so I let him go leisurely at his pleasure, little caring whether he ate the leaves of the trees or fed on the grass. We reached a rivulet, full of water on account of a dam to turn the mill. The ass plunged into it, I drew up my legs not to get wet; suddenly the ground gave way under us, the ass disappeared, and I found myself in the water up to my waist. This accident, the chill that ran over me, and more than all, the thoughts that occupied my mind, made me unable at that moment to take a course that might have helped me. Feeling the saddle under my feet, I jumped on it, and then gave a leap, which brought me upon the opposite bank. The cursed ass fell, on purpose to be rid of me, and as soon as he felt relieved of his load he turned and ran off like a deer. I forded the brook and ran after him, but could not catch him. The following night, imagining the ass had returned to his home, I tried again to get into the curate's house; but it was watched by dogs and peasants. And now, I said to myself, instead of gaining, I have lost, and have not a penny left to do either good or bad; and I found myself, as it were, with a knife at my throat, from being dragged into the enterprise of my Lord Duke. On one side it only appeared to me as a little trick—to abduct a girl!—Lord! they like to be stolen. On the other side, how can I benefit others without money? With the exception of this affair, I could think no way of procuring it. Some have been ruined for women, some for estates and titles, some for money: it was the fate of Olimpio to go to perdition for an ass!"

The Count looked intently at him, imagining from the absurdity of the story that Olimpio spoke in jest, but his appearance was so serious that he soon saw he was in earnest. Olimpio went on:

"There was no help for it; I went to the Duke to arrange matters. I had studied the house, the locality, the habits of the household; four companions, I making a fifth, went. The Duke waited in the street with his carriage. I entered the court-yard, said to the porter: 'My dear fellow, please call Lucrezia, and tell her to come down, for Giannicchio is here with a message from her mother—and here is a shilling for your trouble.' The porter went, and my companions entered the yard quickly, hiding behind the columns of the portico. The girl came down immediately, singing like a nightingale; in less time than I can tell it, we wrapped her in a cloak and carried her to the carriage of the Duke, who received her with open arms. I ordered the horses to start, and we followed; we went slowly, in order not to arouse suspicion, and met not a living soul. But as we turned the corner of a street, the police came upon us. The others got frightened. I, not fearing, cried: 'Turn, driver, and run for life.' Damnation! A storm of police rushed down on this side also. 'Boys, Master Alessandro has spread his net; if he don't want to be worsted, we must break it—out knives!' So said and done. The Duke himself descended from his carriage and bravely drew his sword. The police did not wait for us to approach, but sent us, from a distance, a discharge of musketry. The little hussy, pulling the handkerchief from her mouth, hung out of the window, crying: 'Help! Murder!' as if we were going to kill her. The police called out: 'Kill them! kill them!' and I backed against a wall, giving blows which gave no time for a sigh.

"At last I cleared my way, and ran as fast as my legs could carry me. Two policemen ran after me like hounds; the breathing of these fellows lifted the hair on the back of my head; they almost touched my clothes with their hands. I turned a corner, still running; I turned another and another; my breath began to grow faint; but they grew tired also, one more than the other, for their steps sounded no longer equal. Then I remembered the story of Horatius, the valiant Paladin; and thinking they had gone with me as far as was right, I stopped, turned suddenly round and said farewell to the one who stood nearest to me, by putting a pistol-shot in his heart. This fellow whirled about three or four times, like a dog running after his own tail, then fell to the ground. The other fellow understood that I meant to take leave of them, so, in his turn, before separating, paid a salute with an ounce of lead, which grazed my head above the left ear. Notwithstanding this, I did not stop running; after a grand race I paused awhile to speculate where I might be, and found myself, by chance, near your house. I resolved to profit by the opportunity that fortune had advisedly put in my way. I climbed the garden wall, and groping about, I have at last come upon you, following the same path that Marzio led me. Now, Sir Count, hide me until to-morrow evening; for, with God's help, I intend to go back to the woods."

Cenci, who had listened attentively, asked:

"You are sure no one saw you enter here?"

"No one. But as the police are on the watch, it is

better to avoid them; and, besides, here in Rome, I breathe a gallows air, which takes the skin from my throat."

"You assure me that no one knew you?"

"No one. Besides, don't you see, I am disguised as a gentleman?"

In fact, Olimpio had changed his usual dress.

"Cheer up, then; if, as you say, there is no danger. But we must act cautiously; the servants must not see you. I cannot trust them; they always have their eyes and ears open; we are surrounded by spies; they love their master as the wolf loves the lamb—to eat his flesh."

"Do you not even trust Marzio?"

"'Before breaking he was whole,' says the proverb. A little, but I have sent him into the country on business. You must remain hidden (and mind, more on your account than mine) a little while in the vaults of the palace."

"In the vaults?"

"Vaults—that is, the cellars; you will find yourself among honorable and agreeable companions—the wine casks. I give you leave to broach them and drink oblivion to your troubles as long as you please; on one condition however—that after drinking, you will replace the spigot."

"As I can get nothing better, I accept the room for the sake of the company."

"You will not live like a prince there, nor even like a bandit. You will find an abundance of straw; in less than half an hour I will bring you something to eat, a light, and a kind of ointment that will relieve the pain of your wounds. May I die an evil death, if in a short time you feel any more pain! Be comforted; not all undertakings are successful. The Romans, after the defeat of Cannæ, sold the ground occupied by the Carthagenian army, and at last took Carthage. Give me your arm—go softly, eh! —look out—go slowly."

And through the dark the Count led Olimpio to the cellars of the palace.

"Here, the devil himself could not find me."

"Oh, be sure of that, no one can find you!"

"Besides, no one knows I am here."

"Or ever will know it."

"It is enough for me—if the police don't find it out till the day after to-morrow, then I care nothing at all about it."

"Stoop down—be careful not to knock your head upon the lintel—here—this way—go in."

"Go in," said Olimpio, withdrawing his foot, while the cool, damp air blew in his face. Count Cenci asked smilingly:

"What is the matter—are you afraid?"

"I? No! I am thinking that when we enter a dark place, we always know it; but we never know when we shall go out."

"When? why, to-morrow night, you said."

"Suppose you should not come for me?"

"How would your death profit me? Where could I find another Olimpio to serve me with poison and knives?"

"But if you should not come?"

"You could halloo. These cellars are near the street, and the passers-by would hear you."

"A good exchange! To be carried from the Cenci cellars to the prison of Corte Savella."

"Remember that I should be obliged to go to the castle for having harbored such an old rogue as you."

"I find some truth in what you say; but at least leave the door open."

He went in; but the door swung on its hinges and shut tight.

"Count Cenci, how came the door to shut?"

"I hit against it."

"Bring a light soon, and open the door."

"I will go for the key, and return."

"Mind, don't forget the light."

"Light! Oh you will want no light, if the saying is true; *Et lux perpetua luceat eis;*" hummed Cenci in the tone of a requiem, retiring hastily.

"It seems incredible!" he added, after entering his room, "these fellows boast of having a sharp wit! What fox ever used greater cunning to escape the trap than this bandit? Wait for me, Olimpio: you may have to wait a long time; for unless the Archangel should take a fancy to open to you on the day of judgment, I certainly shall not. Farewell, Olimpio, good night! Sleep in peace, Olimpio; I too am sleepy: I wish you a sleep like that of an innocent man—like mine."

CHAPTER XIV

GUIDO GUERRA

BEATRICE, with pale face, clad in white, a lamp in her hand, resembled one of Eloisa's vestals, who went at night under the vaults of Paracleto to weep upon the tomb of her buried friend.

She put down her light, carefully opened a door, looked suspiciously around, and rushed into the garden.

Where is Beatrice Cenci going at this late hour?

She seeks a star that may guide her through a darkness more obscure than that of this night. She comes to look for a flower fallen from the heavenly gardens upon the human soul—Hope! It is a flower often withered upon its stalk, before it can diffuse any fragrance. Count Cenci's daughter goes to meet a trustful lover.

Her lover was worthy of her. Monsignore Guido Guerra, as the history of the times relates, was born of an illustrious house, was tall, handsome, and of noble bearing, and, like Beatrice, of fair complexion and blue eyes. The customs of the time were not outraged when prelates were inclined to love. Often did the great dignitaries of the Church take off their clerical robes and scale the walls where their loves dwelt. They wore cloaks and swords and often fought in battles..

Beatrice, so modest a girl, would certainly have repelled any love that was not really worthy; and although Monsignore Guerra was dressed in priestly robes, he was not bound to the Church by any vow or sacred orders; and by leaving off the dress, he could marry whomsoever he chose. He was very wealthy, and the only child of a widowed mother. Lady Lucrezia knew of this love and favored it all she could, for the great pity she felt toward the girl. She wished to save her from the infamously fierce persecution of her father, and to see her happy.

During the short intervals when Count Cenci was away from home, or from Rome, Guido, informed by trusty servants, would go to the palace and console the ladies as well as he could. Although he was pledged to Beatrice, he still enjoyed the favor of the Pope, and knowing him to be of severe temperament, and desirous that he should not leave the ecclesiastical state, in which he had been promised great promotion, he delayed from day to day the opportunity of revealing his intention to the Pontiff and receiving his consent without making him an enemy. But Count Cenci, probably informed by his spies of Monsignore Guerra's designs or perhaps only suspecting them, warned him to cease from visiting his family, and to give up any intentions he might have in regard to Beatrice, if his life were dear to him. The name of Count Cenci would have dissuaded even the boldest from getting into any quarrel with him, and whoever was at enmity with him never considered himself safe, even in his own bed. But it is to be supposed that Monsignore Guerra would have scorned his threats, had not the reputation of his lady, which is held dear to every ardent lover, withheld him from causing any scandal; therefore he saw her seldom, the ill-starred lovers expressing their wishes in letters.

To this state the lovers were reduced, when one evening Monsignore Guerra, disguised, passed beneath the windows of the palace. He looked up as he walked, to see whether a light shone in the room of Beatrice. As he drew near the arch whence, by stone steps, one can reach the Church of St. Thomas, he was knocked to one side by a man who was running. He almost fell, but regaining his feet, he seized the fellow by the neck, threatening him angrily. The other, as soon as he recognized him, said:

"Hush, for God's sake! Take this letter; it comes from Lady Beatrice;" and, shaking himself from him, fled.

Guido, heedless in his impatience, looked about for a light. At the foot of the arch he perceived a light burning before the image of the Madonna. Without thinking, he ran to it, opened the letter, but could hardly recognize in the trembling characters the writing of Beatrice. She begged him, by the love he bore to God, that very night to try, by one o'clock, to enter the garden, and wait for her in the laurel grove, and not to fail, if he did not wish to hear she was dead.

Carefully he concealed the letter, and went away. Reaching home, he took his sword and a hooked ladder, and at the appointed time went out alone. Arrived at the Cenci garden, he climbed over the wall and waited, concealed, in the appointed place.

Now and then the rustling of leaves would draw Guido

from his hiding-place; seeing no one, he would return with a sigh. The hour indicated passed. Could the misfortune, mysteriously hinted at in the letter, have happened without a remedy? He felt faint, and leaned against a tree for support.

A voice startled him—"Guido!"—"Beatrice!"—The agitated girl pressed the hand of her lover, who trembled like the leaves of the laurel against which he had leaned. Suddenly, Beatrice, as if startled by something that caused her great fear, forgetful of her maiden modesty, clasped him in her arms and cried wildly:

"Guido, my love, save me! Guido, take me away—immediately—without a moment's delay; the ground beneath me burns my feet—the air I breathe is poison. Guido, let us go!"

"Beatrice!"

"Not a word—let us go, I implore you, before the chance is gone. If you do not wish me for your wife, no matter—put me in a convent—any convent—even the Clarisse, where the door is walled up after one has entered—but save me, I entreat you, from this accursed place."

"My dearest, what frenzy is this? You are burning with fever."

"Here—within this place is death. Take me away from desperation—from eternal perdition—what frenzy do I feel! Imagine crimes that would cause men of blood to turn pale—crimes that would cause the hair of parricides to stand on end—that freeze the bones—make the teeth chatter as with the ague—that stifle the voice, and petrify the tears; imagine all the crimes ever told of the family of Atridæ—for which the Eternal Father might start from His immortal throne, and seize His thunderbolt—that would make even the cheeks of the devil himself burn with shame; imagine these—imagine more—and you will not find them equal to the infamies plotted and accomplished in Rome—here—in the palace of Count Cenci."

"You fill me with terror; but speak—tell me."

"Could I tell them, and you listen to them? If I should tell, you would see my blush break through the darkness which surrounds us—I should die of shame at your feet. But know this, that I, a maiden, and a Roman lady—I, from whose lips never escaped a word that was not modest—I, by whom a thought never was conceived that could not be confided to the Guardian Angel—I would rather live the infamous live of a courtesan, than stay one hour, one minute within that threshold, overflowing with the wrath of God—mysterious horrors, which ought not to, and cannot, be revealed."

"But how can you go with me thus? How can you scale the wall, encumbered with your dress? Wait until to-morrow."

"To-morrow! Alas! perhaps too late now! I will not leave you—I will bind myself to you. Go—go—run, for I will follow you."

"Be it then as you will; we will go, with God's help."

"Without taking leave of the master of the house? This is not courteous," cried a mocking voice, and at the same time a heavy blow with an ax was aimed at Guido. Fortunately, it missed him, for it would have cut him in two; but it struck with force against the laurel near the lovers, and cut it down like a reed; the tree fell, and in falling struck and separated the hands of Beatrice and Guido, which were joined. Unlucky omen of an unhappy love!

Guido, fiercely moved, but not frightened, groped in the dark to find Beatrice, when a strong hand pushed him many steps back, and at the same time a man close to him said in a low tone:

"Fool! Fly, or you are a dead man. I will appear to pursue you in order to save you;" and then with louder voice, he cried: "Ah! traitor, you shall not escape—here—take that, and that!"

Throughout the garden, mingled with the roaring of the wind, were heard terrible threats and confused voices. The hoarse voice of Count Cenci, like a bird of ill omen, screamed:

"Flesh! blood!—kill him—kill him like a dog!"

Guido ran, confused by this unforeseen attack; but, on a sudden, as if ashamed of having left Beatrice exposed to the rage of her terrible father, although unconscious how to help her, he turned quickly, and put his hand upon his sword; but before he was able to draw it, his pursuer, overtaking him, said:

"Why do you stop? For God's sake, fly!"

"And Beatrice?"

"There is one who will watch for her. Come—quick—you cannot save her, and will only lose yourself." And he pushed him toward the ladder, which he held firmly, in order that he might ascend; then struck his dagger volently against the wall, so that the blade was broken into the minutest particles, sending out sparks, adding at the same time oaths and cries enough to make the vault of heaven tremble.

Count Cenci arrived, panting heavily, and asked:

"Where is the dead man? Lights, bring lights, that I may see his wounds—lights, that I may tear his heart out of his breast and strike it upon his face. Where is he?"

"He has escaped," replied Marzio, sorrowfully.

"How, escaped? it is not true; he must be here, slain. Escaped! Ah! traitorous dogs! you have let him go. Whom shall I trust now? The right hand plays Judas with the left. Of you, Marzio, of you—I have been suspicious for a long time. Beware! my suspicions may change into steel points." Hardly had the words escaped him, before the Count thought how incautiously he had uttered them; he bit his lips as if to punish them for being so indiscreet; and, to repair the mischief, added immediately after, with milder accents: "For some time past you have been less diligent, Marzio, in serving me; I shall not keep you—although should you leave me, it would be like losing one of my hands; still I prefer to lose you rather than think you less attentive and faithful."

A word spoken and a stone thrown never return. The words of Cenci had struck the heart of Marzio like a stone hurled into the water; and he replied in a complaining tone:

"Say rather that your Excellency is tired of me. It is the common fate of servants. No ink can write their long and faithful services on the hearts of their masters. For any time that Fortune is against you, lo! ingratitude steps in with a sponge, and erases everything. Patience! to-morrow I shall take off your livery."

A common proverb says that in the skinner's shop is nothing but fox skins; and it is true; for presumptuous men, trusting too much in their own mind, strength and fortune, let themselves sometimes be caught by those whom they least suspect. Cenci trusted in having deceived Marzio, and Marzio, as we shall see, deceived him.

"Marzio, what are words uttered in a moment of passion? Wind that blows. I look upon you as the most loyal servant I ever had, and now I mean to prove it to you."

The Count, accompanied by several servants, who carried torches, went in search of Beatrice, and soon found her; for she had stood immovable, overwhelmed with what happened. When he saw her all his savage rage was again kindled, and seizing her by the arm, he shook her furiously, saying, with bitter sarcasm:

"And you are the modest maiden to whom the words of love and pleasure are incomprehensible, like voices in an unknown tongue! You, the chaste girl, who guards the lily that should increase the glories of paradise? Shameless! wicked! You a receiver of secret lovers—you a provoker of infamous pleasures—not sought, you seek! Tell me, who was this man with whom just now you stood embraced?"

Beatrice looked at him and was silent. The old man, stung by this calmness, which was stupor, continued:

"Tell me, unless you would have me kill you;" but as Beatrice persisted in her silence, he, mad with anger, thrust his hands into her hair, and tore it lock by lock; nor did he stop there, but cursed her with more atrocious curses than ever fell on guilty woman, and struck her on the breast, neck, and face. He threw her upon the ground, dragged her by the hair, trampled upon her—and she remained silent; only once from the bottom of her heart came these words:

"Oh, it is fatal!"

"Let every one go from this place," the Count commanded; "you, Marzio, remain and listen! I had thought to give her to you to watch, in proof of the trust which I replace in you—but it is better I should watch her myself, that she may not charm you. Go into my study; in my desk, in the first drawer, on the right hand, you will find a bunch of keys; and bring them here—hasten!—quick!—haven't you returned yet?"

Marzio, obliged to remain an unwilling spectator to this shocking scene, flew like lightning and returned with the keys; he lifted Beatrice, and, interposing himself between her and her father, feigned to push her roughly into the cellar.

Marzio had left Count Cenci some steps behind, when a groaning voice reached his ear, in these words:

"To die thus—without bread—and without sacrament—oh, treacherous Count!"

Marzio thought some other mysterious crimes, besides those now contemplated, were hidden in these subterranean passages, and turned his face in the direction whence the sound came. Count Cenci rejoined him panting just at this moment, and cast a glance of rage upon him.

"Did you hear groans?" asked the Count.

"A groan!"

"Yes, like a soul in pain?"

"It sounded to me like the moaning of the wind, which rushes through these passages."

"No, no—they are groans—for here my great-grandfather kept imprisoned an enemy of his, and made him starve to death; it was afterward said that ghosts were seen here; and I believe it."

"God help us! For my part I would not enter here even with the *Agnus Dei* in my pocket."

"You would do right. Open that door—there—the one to the right--the third one—that is it."

Marzio opened it, and the Count pushed Beatrice roughly in.

"Go, cursed girl! try how the bread of penitence and the water of grief taste."

Beatrice, thus harshly pushed, fell upon the pavement; and in her fall hit her face against a projecting stone. Overcome by pain, she fainted.

When she regained her senses, she rose from the ground, and found herself alone in the midst of darkness. She leaned against the wall, and said:

"God has abandoned me! No one living dares or can assist me. Destiny fells me like the vaults of Saint Peter. So much wind raised to break a reed; but since Thine, O God! are the treasures of the tempest, Thou wilt not condemn me if I bend to its fury. Guido, alas! he is dead surely—perhaps at this moment talking with Virgilio—and both are waiting for me. Alas! Guido, do not accuse me of your death, now that I can speak to you without shame, I can confess how great, how infinite was my love for you. But why, God forgive you! why did you wish to unite your destiny with mine? Did I not tell you that my days flowed like the waters of desolation, which, wherever they flow, carry death? Did I not tell you? can you deny it? Oh, why am I alive? Why cannot I die? They say we must not destroy ourselves! The soul must feel, suffer, and not will. I would cheerfully bear my fate, did I not know myself to be a seed of misfortune born to ripen into harvest of tears to all those who love me. I do not accuse thee, O God! On the back of Thine only Son, Thou didst put the cross of wood, and He fell beneath it three times. Thou hast given me one of lead—I cannot bear it, and I throw it down. Whoever will may have my desolate soul—the covenant of my life is too hard, and I break it."

So saying, with the desire to kill herself deliberately, with death depicted on her face, her soul overflowing with desperation, she rushed with all her strength at the wall, and struck her head against it. Alas! she staggered, opened her arms, and fell rigidly at the foot of it.

CHAPTER XV

THE STORY OF ANNETTA

WHEN at last Beatrice regained her senses, she raised herself with difficulty into a sitting posture, remembering neither the place where she was nor how she came to it. She pressed her hands to her head, which pained her greatly, though she knew not why. She heard her name called: listened anxiously and heard it again; then she remembered what Virgilio had said about his mother calling him; and the voice she now heard seemed to her that of both her mother and her brother. She thought that at their intercession Divine mercy had saved her from eternal perdition, and the idea was so consoling that she started joyfully to her feet; and clasping her hands, exclaimed, "Thanks, thanks, dear mother! thanks, Virgilio, my love! come to me, come!—let me see you—open your arms—I will clasp you in an eternal embrace. Why is not Guido with you? He has died young! But if he comes here—with you—to me who am his bride, he will not be grieved at having died; and now I may kiss him, may I not, mother, even in your presence, for he is my husband?"

But the voice, coming nearer, again said:

"Lady Beatrice, rouse yourself; do not lose courage. Oh, Lady Beatrice, courage! it is I—it is Marzio who calls."

"Marzio! This in the world below was the name of a servant who was friendly to me; it was he who meant to crush the head of Count Cenci on the day of the feast; it was a crime, but pity for me had induced him. Let us all pray God to pardon him; let Him put this sin to my account, and may I atone for it in purgatory."

"Oh, my lady! I fear God will punish me, but only because I did not send him out of the world."

"And now, what is Marzio doing? Is he dead too? Has he too proved that the fatality which comes from me is contagious? Has he too learned, poor man, how mortally my glance wounds?"

"Lady Beatrice, for God's sake do not rave so; come here—listen! The wicked old man, Count Cenci, now sleeps—do you wish he may never awake?"

"What do you say, Marzio? I did not understand, I am bewildered."

"He who begat you to torture you; he who calls himself your father; he who, if he lives, will kill you; do you wish him to die—to-night—in five minutes? His life hangs on the point of my knife."

"No, no!" suddenly exclaimed Beatrice, at once recovering her senses. "Marzio, do not, for the love of God; I should hate you, I would accuse you. Let him live and repent; he will repent one day, perhaps."

"He repent! Have wolves ever been seen at confession? I have told you, should he live, he will make you die."

"What matters it? Have I not attempted to die? Oh! how great a woe it is to return to life! Marzio, my faithful servant, I have no more breath. I should like to quench my thirst in death. Have you never heard of those ancient people who kept a friend or affectionate servant, so that if necessity required them to leave this world, they might inflict the kindly blow? Marzio, I do not ask so much of you—only bring me the juice of some herb which has the virtue of closing the eyes to a peace which I have never enjoyed in this world."

"No, by the soul of Anna Riparella! if I can help it, you shall live. Unfortunate lady; do not become desperate. In a little while I will come back to you; now I must return to your wicked father; should he awake and surprise us, there would be no way of escape." And he went away weeping, to think of the miserable state to which Beatrice was reduced. Deep in this thought he was about to leave the place, when he remembered the groans he had heard the night before. He retraced his steps, but could hear nothing; then he began softly to shake all the doors that he could see, and at one door the groans became more audible and painful than ever.

"Alas! I am dying of hunger—of thirst; it should not have been thus—to be hanged at the proper time would have been well; I was prepared for that—having confessed and taken the sacrament; with the priest at my side and with all things as they should be."

"Who are you? Answer quickly."

"Oh, your Excellency, don't you know who I am? Open the door for charity! I am hungry enough to eat my flesh."

"Answer quickly, I say, or I shall leave you."

"I am a man who has an open account with justice, but truly for boyish frolics; for the rest I am an honest bandit, and above all faithful: my name is Olimpio. Count Cenci shut me in here two days ago, I believe, but I cannot say, for here I see neither when the sun rises nor sets; he promised to return, and I am still expecting him. Oh, if you are a Christian, for the love of God, give me a little water—a little bread—a little light—for mercy's sake!"

"Horrible! to let a human being die of hunger, and without sacrament! This villain's soul is like hell, to which there is no bottom. Olimpio, I cannot help you now; be patient, I will soon return to you, but now I have no key."

"And who are you?"

"I am Marzio."

"Did you come here to enjoy my agony?"

"I never have betrayed any one; keep up your courage—farewell!"

"Once, among ourselves, we never betrayed each other—I will wait—I will hope—I will suffer in silence; but oh, Marzio! return quickly if you wish to find me alive—I am hungry—cold—thirst is killing me."

His recent violent excitement had so swollen Count Cenci's lame leg that he could not move from a lying posture. He had closed his eyes to an unquiet sleep; when he awoke he tried to rise, but intense pain prevented him. He ground his teeth in rage, and exclaimed with an oath:

"And I must trust this traitor!" Then he called Marzio, who entered immediately and silently.

"Marzio, see how I trust you: take the key of Beatrice's prison, and carry bread and water to her."

"Anything else?"

"No, but take some holy relic with you, to expel the evil spirits, in case any should appear to you. If you hear a voice, don't mind it; it is a deception of the devil; and avoid above all others the passage on the left—it was there my great-grandfather's enemy died by starvation."

"Your Excellency, why do we not go together?"

"Don't you see—curses on it—that I cannot move?"

"If your daughter is bruised, must I not dress her wounds?"

"No. But do you suppose she is injured?"

"It seemed so to me; and her beauty might be spoiled by it."

"I do not want her—that is, at present—to lose her beauty. In that closet there is some ointment and medicine; if it should prove necessary, attend to her."

Marzio seized dexterously the other keys, for he had taken away the one belonging to Beatrice's prison while the Count slept, and he returned to the vaults.

"Lady Beatrice," said Marzio, bitterly, when he saw her, "see the gifts your father sends you;" and raising his lantern he looked upon that angelic face, stained with blood. He repressed a groan of anguish, and added, as well as he could, in milder tones:

"Come here, and let me bathe your face."

And he gently bathed the wounds and applied the ointment and bandages.

"O God!" he repeated from time to time, "dost Thou see these iniquities? And if Thou dost, how canst Thou permit them?"

The work accomplished, he said:

"Young lady, see the gifts which he, whom you call

father, sends you—bread and water. I, against his express commands, have added other food; but I certainly cannot comfort you in prolonging a life which imposes the most cruel torments; and what pains me more than all is, that from this time I can help you no longer, for"—and here his voice sounded harsher—"I intend to-day to leave your house."

Beatrice bent her head, like one so overpowered with grief that no new trouble could be felt.

"Guido is dead, and now you leave me?"

"And who told you he is dead?"

"Does he live, then?"

"He lives, and is safe."

Beatrice leaned her face upon Marzio's shoulder, and remained a long time in that position, then, in a low voice, said:

"Guido lives, and you abandon me?"

"But it is you who abandon yourself. Listen: I will confess to you that which I would not tell my own father, should he rise from the dead. I entered Count Cenci's house to fulfil a vow. Would you know that vow? It was to kill him. His daily crimes have only strengthened me in my design; besides, taking him out of the world not only would satisfy my revenge, but it would acquire a merit in the eyes of man and God. But as this event will cause you sorrow, I will not commit it under your eyes; more do not ask of me—do not weary yourself in talking—no one can dissuade me from it—no one; what is to be fulfilled, must be; by the sword he has killed, by the sword he must die—these are Christ's own words."

"And in what way has the Count harmed you? When you came into the house, you were, I thought, entirely unknown to him."

"But I knew him. If he had harmed me, wounded me, I could have forgiven him. Certainly, I am a great sinner—but once I had a Christian heart. He has killed my soul, and spared my life; now I am dead to all things but one, and this I have told you. Hear me! If I knew Count Cenci before entering his house, this would not prove him more wicked; for in him, one crime more or less matters nothing; but it may, perhaps, stay the curses against his murderer upon your lips. I have not much learning; I will narrate as my heart prompts, and you can believe it as it were the Gospel. I was born in Tagliacozzo; my father died when I was a child, and left me farms and flocks; my mother fell ill, so that she could take no care of me. I grew up; fell in with bad companions; I was wrapped in all manner of vices as in a cloak; and at last, partly by gambling, partly through usury, I squandered all my property: with the last glass of wine drunk in my house, my friends drank oblivion to me; they vanished with the smoke of the last dish; but at their disappearance others appeared; they were creditors; they despoiled me of everything—turned me out of the house. In the daytime, I was forced to carry my mother in my arms to the hospital; malicious boys jeered at me in the streets; one threw a stone at me and my sick mother. Nor did the trouble cease here: before reaching the hospital the police came after me, took my mother from my arms, laid her in the middle of the street, and bore me off to prison. My creditors, not satisfied with taking my property, even wished to drink my very blood. I heard smothered groans—it was my mother who wept. I turned to comfort her, but could not see her, my eyes were so full of tears. I tried to speak—not even that—it was well.

"I broke from the prison; betook myself to the woods; I revenged myself on everybody. The boy who threw the stone at my mother—I broke his head upon a stone; it was well. Henceforth, I signed my calendar with the point of my knife—every day was a stream of blood; my flesh burned; blood intoxicates more than wine. God will judge whether I could resist the devil, who took possession of my soul; I will not add any excuse; if I deserve pity, let Him pardon me; if not, let Him condemn me. But of what I have done, of what I shall do, I know not how to repent—the work which revenge has put in death's hands is not yet accomplished; to my list one head is yet wanting—your father's. The air of the Neapolitan kingdom was not good for me; I entered the territory of the Church, and enlisted in the band of Marco Sciarra.

"What I committed as a bandit there is no need for you to know; let not the Eternal Justice know! One Saturday, about sunset, I was sitting upon a stone near the edge of the forest, my elbows leaning on my gun, my gun upon my knees, and my face resting upon my closed hands. I was waiting for my companions near the oak of Rocca Odonisi to say our evening prayers before the image of the Madonna of the Oaks, and to make our plans for the morrow. I had a horror of myself! 'Am I afraid?' I murmured; 'why am I alone? Oh, if I only had the company of a living being, to free me from my terror!' I turned at the moment, and saw before me an angel's face, Lady Beatrice—a Madonna, stepped from her frame to gladden the earth! and then—hear me—do not be offended—except being a little burned by the sun, and much larger, she resembled you: she carried a pitcher on her head, and came to draw water from a neighboring spring. She did not stop upon seeing me (although I was dressed as a bandit, and armed), or seem to have any fear. Indeed, what could she fear? Her poverty defended her from robbery, a heart like Lucrezia's and a poniard, which held the tresses of her hair, against violence; she pursued her walk, and when she passed before me, with a voice like fresh leaves blown by the early breeze of spring, she said: 'May the Blessed Virgin save you!' I did not raise my head, I did not answer; I only followed her with my eyes, until I could see her no longer. Then, thinking of the manner and the moment when she appeared, I exclaimed: 'The Lord has taken pity upon me!'

"But, remembering the history of my crimes committed against heaven and earth, which seemed painted in blood, laughing at myself, I added: 'Yes, truly, Christ has nothing else to do but to take care of me!' And here the same voice suddenly descended again into my heart, repeating: 'May the Blessed Virgin save you.' It was the girl who, having filled her pitcher, returned home by the same way. The next evening I went again to the Oaks, and the girl consoled me with the usual salutation; and so on the next, and the next. A whole month passed, without the girl or I ever missing, through storm or wind, to come every evening to the Oaks; and in all this time she had never said more to me, than: 'May the Virgin save you!' and I to her: 'God reward you, Annetta!'

"She was Annetta Riparella, daughter of a shepherd belonging to Vittana. One evening, without rising from the stone where I was seated, I called to her with humble voice: 'Annetta, put down your pitcher, if you please, and come and sit by me.' She put her pitcher down, looking intently in my eyes, and with hers led mine to the holy Image of the Oaks. By that I understood she meant to say: 'I place myself under the protection of the Madonna.' Then I arose, took her by the hand, and led her before the holy image, saying: 'Annetta, where are we going? Is it not a long time that we have walked without knowing where we shall come at last? Strangers dwell in the house of my father; in the fields which were mine, others sow and reap. I can offer you nothing good, therefore I offer you nothing. On the contrary, hear me attentively, for I do not wish to deceive you: a reward is placed upon my head; all the water you have drawn from the spring would not be enough to wash my hands—do not look at them, you can discover nothing; the blood with which they are stained only my eyes and God's can see. Should you unite your life to mine, days of danger will await you, nights of fear, years of suffering, and a life of shame. To our children, should misfortune ever give them to us, do you know what inheritance I could leave them? A bloody garment. To you, what widow's dowry? The name of the wife of the man who was hanged. If I listened to my heart, I should wish you to take me for a husband; if to my judgment, I would have you refuse me; therefore I neither pray you, nor advise you: I have thrown the dice, and accept the fate that destiny sends me; open your heart freely, and do not fear to offend me —for, by the Holy Virgin who hears us, if you wish to remain free, I swear from this moment you will never see my face again.'

"'Marzio,' replied the girl, resolutely, 'I know your misdeeds and yourself; that I have loved you for some time, my eyes must have told you; better grief with Marzio, than joy with another. What matters it to me, if a reward is offered for your head? should justice seek you, we will hide together; if it finds us, we will defend ourselves; if taken, we will die together. But it is not of this justice that my heart is afraid; there is a justice that finds without seeking; an eye that never shuts its lids upon sin; it is this justice, Marzio, that you must appease; what all the water in the river cannot do, one tear can—the tear of penitence.'

"So spoke Annetta, a simple girl, whose only education was drawn from the ardent love she bore the Mother of God. I felt as if a stone had broken in the middle of my heart, and humbly I replied: 'Annetta, I bind myself by an oath to abandon my present companions as soon as I can, for should I leave them suddenly, they would suspect treachery, and my death would soon follow the suspicion.

They are many and powerful. Meanwhile I swear to abstain from any wicked deed, and also swear to take you as my lawful wife and love you always.' So saying, I drew from my finger a ring, which had belonged to my mother; and putting it near the face of the Holy Image as if to consecrate it, I placed it on her finger, adding: 'You are my wife.' 'I don't own rings,' said Annetta, 'but take a lock of my hair as a pledge that I will marry you.' I drew out my knife, and she bent her head; I cut a lock, but my hand trembled so that the hair fell, and the wind carried it off. It was a bad omen! She looked up, and smiling said: 'Cut another—what does it matter? If fortune will be kind, we will thank God; if otherwise, it is all the same; have I not told you to be ready for everything?'

"A few days later, by means of our faithful spies, news came to Signor Marco that from the kingdom of Naples and the States of the Church a large band of armed men were coming to surround us, and then capture us easily. Signor Marco, who, although by adverse fortune forced to the condition of chief of the bandits, amply possessed all those qualities requisite for a good general, sent me without delay into the Abruzzi, to keep an eye on the police force of Naples, in order to surprise them in some ambush. He gave me minute instructions about places, and the means to be used; and, thanks to the skill of our excellent captain, the undertaking was successful, and not one policeman remained to carry home the news of their defeat. Aften ten days of absence, I returned. I found Annetta at the foot of the Oaks—I found her—but murdered!

"Her hair had been torn from her head, her limbs and clothes also were torn; on her face I saw the impress of feet that had trampled on her; a knife had been thrust in her bosom, the point coming out between her shoulders. and sticking into the ground.

"I bought a scarlet cloak; I had a coffin of gilded wood made; I put her into it with my own hands; I covered the black marks and wounds with flowers—how lovely she looked, even after death!—and accompanied by all the country people, in the midst of universal tears, I myself buried my beloved. In lowering her into the grave, my eyes grew dim, and I fell into it. When I regained my senses, I found myself seated on the ground; the grave was filled, the priest supported me, weeping, and some good women tried to console me. I got up, and went away without uttering a word.

"Afterward I learned that for several days Count Cenci had been residing in Rocca Petrella, which we also call Rocca Ribalda—the tracks of this man were marked with blood. A voice within me said: 'He is the murderer!' I began to inquire more particularly into the affair, and from a little shepherd boy I learned that Annetta used to go every evening to the Oaks of the Virgin, and would remain there a long time, kneeling and praying before the Image. One evening the boy saw a man pass by on horseback who seemed to him, by his dress and bearing, to be a great lord. He stopped his horse, and stood looking at the girl until she had finished her prayer; then, going up to her, seemed to try to enter into conversation with her, but she saluted him and went on her way. The next evening the boy, being in the same place feeding his sheep, saw two ruffians come out of the forest, who, taking the girl unawares, bandaged her eyes and mouth, and, in spite of her struggles, carried her away.

"The boy had been silent through fear, he now spoke for gain; so that with care I derived minute information in regard to the dress and appearance of the man. I kept a lookout on the castle; I wandered near its walls in the night; in the daytime I hid among the bushes, or the branches of the trees. The castle was always closely shut, like a miser's chest. But one day the gate opened and a man came out, whom, by his dress, I recognized for one of the ruffians seen by the boy; he walked cautiously, and carried, as we say, his head over his shoulders; but I fell on him like a falcon; he was lying under my knees, and I had my hand to his throat, before he could escape. 'I will spare your life,' I cried, 'if you will confess to me how you killed the girl of the Oaks.' Livid with fear, he told me that his master, Count Cenci, having seen the girl and finding her handsome, conceived a desire to possess her; therefore, he had commanded another servant and himself to take her by force and bring her to the castle, esteeming her an easy conquest; but finding his flatteries were of no avail with the girl, and his threats still less, and believing he had already done too much honor to a peasant, he had recourse to violence, to which the girl had replied by using her hands courageously. Then the Count seized her by the neck, and she him, and they both fell on the ground, striking each other. Finally, the girl, more active, rose to her feet first, and kicking the Count in the face, exclaimed: 'Take that, you old villain! If I had my poniard you would be dead by this time; but a kick is better for you; in a few days my husband will return, and, by the Blessed Virgin, I will give him no peace until he brings me your ears for a present.'

"Count Cenci rose in haste, without saying a word, and before the unfortunate girl was able to defend herself, he gave her such a fierce blow with his knife that it passed out between her shoulders, and she fell without having time to say even, 'Jesus!' or 'Maria!' A groan, and she was dead. He then kicked her, in revenge for the ignominious kick she had given him. In the night he commanded his men to carry her body to the Oaks of the Virgin, and they did so; for they who eat the bread of others must obey. The Count followed with a lantern; and when they had laid the body on the ground, he drew his knife, replaced it in the wound, and pushing it with force, fixed it fast in the ground. 'When your husband returns,' exclaimed the Count, 'you can tell him this also.'

"When I heard this, I was so overpowered with fury—always an enemy to well conceived designs—that I cried to the fellow: 'Go, then, and inform your master that the husband of Annetta Riparella has returned, and to-night will visit him at his house, as it is his duty.' And I did not fail in my promise; for, aided by the most daring of my companions, I assailed the castle, sacked and burned the palace. I burned the den, but the fox was saved. The Count, having no force to resist us, went off hastily; and so great was his hurry to get away that I found in his room, on his table, a half-written letter. If you should ever go to that castle, you can see the marks of my revenge impressed with fire on the walls. What remained to me in the world, and what remains now? To revenge myself, and die. Having related the whole affair to Signor Marco, he praised me for the deed I had done, and counseled me to persevere in it, and made me most generous offers. Then I asked for my leave, and he, with great regret, gave it to me. I cut my hair, shaved my beard, changed my clothes, and came to Rome swearing by the soul of my dead wife to temper my indiscreet fury with prudence.

"I was revolving in my mind how to enter your house, when fortune favored me by a singular accident. Walking in the Piazza di Spagna one day, I heard a noise behind me, a confused number of voices crying: 'Take care for your life—mind your life!' I turned, and saw a carriage dragged by two powerful horses, that had broken the traces and were running away. The driver had been knocked off his seat, his head had struck against a post, and he lay senseless on the ground. Some fled, some looked out of the windows or from the doorway of their shops, without giving aid or even thinking of doing so. I rushed at the bit of one of the horses; and although he dragged me furiously a little way, I succeeded in stopping him. Then a gentleman of mature age, putting his mild and tranquil face out of the carriage window, commended my courage, and requested me to present myself during the day at the palace of Count Cenci!

"So it was; without knowing it, I had saved the life of my atrocious enemy. I was not sorry for it—on the contrary, I rejoiced; since, if he had died in any other way than by my sword and my hands, it would have seemed to me as if my revenge were lost.

"The Count received me with the affability becoming a nobleman; inquired about me, and hearing I was idle in Rome, himself proposed to employ me in his house. It was the very thing I had sought with so much eagerness: never pilgrim kissed more devoutly the Madonna in the Holy House of Loretto than I touched the threshold of his palace, with the intention of surrounding Cenci with solitude and desolation. To disinherit him of all affection, surviving his own children, whom I designed to kill with various deaths, to orphan him in heart as he had bereft me—when life had become a torment to him, death a relief, to keep him until his pulses felt pains of agony; and when his benumbed soul had become accustomed to sorrow to hurl him by a bloody death into the bloody tomb of his children.

"By showing myself ready to execute any order, by subtle counsels, by always proposing new schemes, I acquired by degrees his confidence, inasmuch as he can trust who always mistrusts both himself and others. You may conceive how great was my surprise to find I could afford him no better pleasure than to kill his children! His unnatural hatred conquered mine, and even had I continued to hate you because born of him, could I torment you worse than your father? For hate, then, was substituted profound pity toward you all, and particularly for you, Lady Beatrice—because for you, poor girl, I feel such an affection—such dear love, that I am reminded of the good soul of my dead Annetta, and in spite of myself it forces me to tears."

Overcome by grief, Marzio was about to kneel before Beatrice; but she with gentle hand prevented him, saying:

"Rise, Marzio, rise; dust should never bow down to dust, and we are all dust;" and then added: "Marzio, I advise you to take heed to what escapes your lips;" but with so sweet and supplicating a voice that Marzio was not mortified.

"Gentle lady, why should you forbid me to kneel to you? Sacred things are worshiped on our knees, and misfortune has already consecrated you; no being in this world ever resembled the weeping Madonna more than you. Do not doubt; never will you hear from my lips a word that could offend your modest ears—I was about to say, that a father might not say to a daughter, but the example of Count Cenci has stayed the comparison upon my lips.

"I know you are beloved by Monsignore Guido Guerra, and I esteem him highly, for he has placed his love on a worthy maiden. Marzio has favored your love more than you think. Incautious ones! How many times the malicious old man would have surprised you had it not been for me! This last time, if I was not able to forewarn Monsignore Guerra on account of the suddenness of the event, I obliged him to fly, and thus saved his life, for he would not abandon you. I showed him how he would lose himself, and not save you either; and I also promised him to take care of you, and I would keep my promise, if you did not prevent me. Because of this I have resolved to leave the house to-morrow. I entered it to accomplish my revenge, and now I must leave it if I wish to fulfil it. On one hand you do not wish me to rid you of this wicked old man; and although I cannot renounce my vow of revenge, still, that I may bring less sorrow upon you, I will not kill him under your own eyes; on the other hand, I am afraid that should this death occur in the house, suspicion would rest upon the innocent; therefore the best way is to quit the house, for if I stay I can do you no good, and should only ruin myself. Lady Beatrice, if I should beg you to remember a man who had no other feeling than one of good-will and reverence toward you—if I should ask you not to hate me entirely—should I be too presumptuous?"

"I shall remember that you wished to kill my father; when you are gone I shall think that you could have defended me, and that you have abandoned me. Ah, let the Count live! his years are many—do not hasten him to God's judgment; wait until He calls him."

"Your voice is powerful, but it cannot conquer the one that rages in my breast. Impossible! Do you not see expressed in it the will of God, since my design in appeasing the vengeance of the woman I loved brings safety also to you, unfortunate girl?"

"God's finger, Marzio, does not write His counsels in blood!"

"Why not? In Egypt the destroying angel wrote in letters of blood the decree of God upon the thresholds; so, at least, I have heard our priests say."

"I know nothing of priests; I know Christ reproved the law which says an eye for an eye and a tooth for a tooth, and wishes us to love as brothers all those who do evil unto us. Marzio, leave to God his judgment; that which in God would be justice, in you would be crime."

"But how can I let him live?" exclaimed Marzio, striking his forehead, as if he suddenly remembered a forgotten thing; "do you not know that he breathes death?

Hear me! if I should stay here, an unfortunate man would die of starvation."

"What! of starvation?"

"Alas, poor me! talking with you one might even forget paradise. Poor Olimpio! while I delay, you count the moments with the anguish of your starving body."

So saying, he took in haste the lantern, the bunch of keys, and the basket, and with swift steps went to the other side of the vault.

Beatrice, hardly able to move, followed his steps with difficulty, curious to learn the cruel mystery that seemed hidden in Marzio's words.

CHAPTER XVI

THE ADDRESS

BEATRICE followed Marzio, who, reaching Olimpio's door, called him; receiving no answer, with anxiety he again cried:

"Olimpio! Olimpio!"

A weak voice replied:

"Go, wicked traitor—free me from temptation—let me commend myself to God, as best I can, so that I may die in peace."

Marzio opened the door; and to such a state of weakness was the bandit reduced by the fasting and the darkness, that the feeble light of the lantern dazzled his eyes painfully, and made him stagger. Marzio supported him, and prevailed upon him to drink some cordial. After a few moments of relief, hunger and thirst again raged in Olimpio; he rushed like a wild beast upon the basket, nor could Marzio have stopped him if he had not been so weak. Marzio warned him that unless he were careful, he would escape starvation only to die of eating.

Revived by a discreet allowance of food and drink, he began to speak, in spite of the groans that issued from his lips:

"Renegade! Traitorous dog! Fiend! To starve me to death, eh? To confess without torture is not right—the dead, resuscitated, kills the living—no matter—I must speak—I must give vent to my rage. Rascally old man!—you wished to make me silent—I understood it—I have killed five men on your account—four by the knife, and the last, the carpenter, burned to death—poor young man!—burned like a mole drenched in vitriol. The Count thought: 'This man is sought by justice; and should he be put to the torture, he might injure me in his confession; when he is dead, he can no longer speak.' Marzio, give me some water. Is not Count Cenci a very obliging gentleman? Yes, by the Holy Virgin! Sir Count, if this is the hospitality you show your friends and servants, in faith, your income will never diminish—some drink."

"Olimpio, do not worry, be silent; eat at your ease—rest yourself—regain your strength—in a few hours I shall come to take you out."

"No; you will not shut me up again; now I am thirsty and greedy for air; I feel as if I had the Church of Saint Peter on my breast. Saint Peter! Did I say Saint Peter? Well, I do not even trust him who holds the keys in his hands, for he practises the same trade, and uses them more to shut than to open."

"Olimpio, be easy; you see I have not betrayed you yet."

"Is the minute that passes a guaranty for the next? Once, among twelve apostles, one could hardly find a Judas; and now, among twelve men, eleven are traitors, and the twelfth is uncertain. If I must die, let me drink another glass of wine, and I will go; but as heroes and Roman banditti should die—in the open air."

"Fool! does this seem to you the face of a traitor?" said Marzio, uncovering his head. "I have promised to save you, and I will; do you not see that you stagger like a drunken man, and your knees knock together? The wine has got into your head. Now they would discover all, and kill both of us."

"But who is that woman with you? Is she not his daughter? What business has she here?" said Olimpio, rubbing his eyes.

"It is, indeed, Lady Beatrice; but be assured she did not come here to do you harm."

Then Beatrice spoke:

"Marzio will save you, do not doubt it; and I, as a reward for it, ask of you something which you can give me very easily, and in giving which the profit will be wholly yours. Promise me that, this danger escaped, you will change your way of life."

"Can one change his life as he can his dress? I have learned nothing else than to use my steel, and steel is made to wound."

"Steel is not made to wound the hearts of brothers, by which death comes; but to till the ground, which is a source of life. Change your weapon into a spade, and God's mercy will reach even you."

Beatrice said this to the bandit so calmly, without irritation, and with so mild a voice, that Olimpio, accustomed to bow to others' counsels, felt within his breast something which he did not know whether to attribute to the words he heard or to the fasting he had suffered.

Marzio, reentering the prison of Beatrice, said:

"Your father is a mine of crimes; the more you dig the more you find. I, who am not easily frightened, looking into that desperate abyss, am horror-struck, and can understand nothing. But you will not consent to his death! Better so. Keep your soul pure, like a white rose; although it is my opinion, should it be stained red with wicked blood, it would not lose its merit with men or with God But be cheerful; your slavery will be less long than you may fear."

"God forbid it! for I know to what a ransom I should owe liberty; and, Marzio, if you loved me truly, as you say, if my miseries had touched your heart, you would not persist in rendering me the most unhappy woman in the world by your design of killing my father."

"Say rather, your executioner."

"My father—since by him I had life, and through him I live and breathe."

"He gave you life only to contaminate it, and to take it away."

"Be it so; but if he forgets a father's duty, should I forget a daughter's?"

"No! Then everyone to his duty: for myself, that of avenger. Cease—I repeat to you, lady—you strive in vain; you could more easily transport with your hands the obelisks of Pope Sixtus from Rome than stir me from my purpose."

"I am not your mistress, but I am mistress of myself."

"Nor do I object to it."

"Then beware, for I am ready to warn the Count so that he may be prepared."

"Warn him. I am not a fox to set a snare for the chicken: before falling upon him, I will roar, so that he may know the lion is coming."

"But should he kill you?"

"I have heard it said that, anciently, in the duels called judgments of God, one coffin alone was carried; one of the two combatants had to fill it. If Providence judges of human affairs, does it seem to you that I ought to fill it? A few more hours shall I stay in your house: have you anything more to say to me, Lady Beatrice?

I by myself am nothing; but a small copper, given with a kind heart to the poor, is rewarded by one of those prayers which go straight to heaven."

"I warn you still, I will prevent you all I can."

"You?"

"Even the ant saved the pigeon by stinging the foot of the archer. And now, Marzio, that I have said all this, are you not angry with me?"

"Not at all. Did I not say before, that every man must spin the thread fate puts in his hands? Who knows? If I had found you different from what you are, I might have esteemed you of greater wisdom, but perhaps loved you less."

"Marzio, as a last favor, I ask you to leave me the lantern for a little while, and bring me writing materials. I do not wish to omit attempting every means for safety, more that I may not reproach myself with negligence than any hope I have of it. I will write an address to His Holiness, begging him to provide for me as he did for Olimpia. This appears to me the best plan. I now repent of the flight I would have taken with Guido, which I, excited by passion, contemplated. I know it would have created a scandal; the wrong would have been mine; and the world, ignorant of the causes that instigated me, would have confounded my determination with the vulgar fancy of a shameless girl, who lets her will overcome her reason. And besides, on my account, every plan of Guido's would have been spoiled: for he does not wish to displease the Pope, and it is enough for a discreet girl to respect his wish. The last means of safety must be this: Guido must try to cause this address to reach the hands of the Pope soon, and obtain the desired resolution. You must then, in order to persuade Guido not to delay, tell him that which I should die of shame to repeat to my own mother. No, no—ah me! Say nothing to him—promise me, Marzio, that you will say nothing to him."

"I will do as you wish. Lady Beatrice, listen! I fear nothing for myself now, for I am ready to leave here in a few hours, and your father, cunning as he is, cannot surpass me. He even suspects me. The confidence he placed in me this morning is feigned in order to deceive me: but I am not afraid. But you, weak, unarmed, and powerless, should fear more than I. I wish to make you a present, which may be of service to you in any extremity; it is worth as much as we wish it—it is a dagger."

"I thank you; when no other escape is left me, death with this will be more certain and less painful."

"In a few moments I will bring you some writing materials; go immediately to work. I will pretend to clean my pistols in the garden; should Count Cenci come near the vaults to surprise you, I will fire the pistol, as if it went off by accident. You will, thus warned, extinguish the lantern and hide everything before he comes."

"I will do so. Farewell!"

When Marzio returned to the Count's room he found him still in bed, and pretending to be in intense pain. Marzio saw, and not without surprise, on either side of the bed two Dominican friars, with not particularly angelic or seraphic countenances, which they themselves did not seem to think possessed an air of sanctity, as they kept their hoods drawn down over their eyes. The Count ordered Marzio to leave the keys and withdraw. After his departure the Count smilingly said:

"Reverend Fathers, did you notice him well? Tomorrow he will start for Rocca Petrella; your Reverences will wait for him in the place you deem most appropriate, and you will send him to hell, or heaven (I care little which) with two balls in his body—and even four would not be amiss: then you may celebrate two masses for his soul. Meanwhile take this alms;" and he gave them a purse of gold.

"Sleep in peace, your Excellency, for we will serve you according to your deserts," said one of the friars.

"Predestined souls! But, in order not to mistake, look at this scarlet mantle; you will see it either upon your man or on the saddle."

"Oh, there is no need of that, for I know him."

"Indeed! And how?"

"I will tell your Excellency another time, for here in Rome I seem to be walking on burning lava—it burns my shoes."

"Marzio, accompany their Reverences. Fathers, I commend myself to your prayers."

"Peace be with you!"

"Amen!"

Marzio accompanied these friars, whose aspect was so strange as to make one shudder; he attempted to look under their hoods, but could not recognize them. When they were about to go out, one of them, turning round, in order to salute with the usual phrase, "Peace be with you," let fall a large knife, which was immediately picked up by Marzio, who, with an humble gesture, presented it to the worthy brother.

"Reverend father, see, you have dropped your rosary."

"My son, the Lord does not forbid us to defend our lives from the attacks of the wicked; even saints have done it."

"Of course! Because, to become saints, there is no need of being martyrs also. On the contrary, father, instead of scandalizing me, you have edified me, and I devoutly beg your Reverence to listen to the confession of a certain sin which weighs upon my soul."

"In this place? Now?"

"Is not every moment good to save a Christian? Did Jesus reply to those who had recourse to him, 'Come to-morrow?' Father, do not send me away disconsolate; you will see that it is only an affair of a few moments; enter this lower room, and all will be right."

And so saying, he took him forcibly by the arm, as if to lead him in. The friar did not make any resistance, and, asking his companion to await him a moment, entered with Marzio into the lower room.

"Oh, Grimo, I recognized you, you see," said Marzio, boldly pulling down the friar's hood.

"And I you, Marzio—how you have degraded yourself! Who would have thought you capable of being reduced to the office of a valet."

"And you a friar? What business have you here?"

"I will tell you. But how came you a servant in the house of the Cenci?"

"To kill the Count, the assassin of Annetta Riparella, the girl of Vittana."

"And I to kill, to-morrow, a certain Marzio, who, I think, must be some relative of yours."

"Me?"

"How right you have guessed! But I always said that you had great wit in your cranium."

"And you will do it?"

"I have received the price; and you know the duty of an honorable assassin."

"In that case, it is but just that I kill you first."

"Not at all; there is a way to arrange everything. We were old companions in the band of Signor Marco, where we always had honorable examples of virtue; a dog never eats dog's flesh; sometimes, in a moment of passion, a blow more or less, which we give each other, does not spoil our friendship; but we never do it by treachery. This we undertake on account of gentlemen against gentlemen, for they are old enemies of ours.

However, when one has received the price of the homicide it is necessary to fulfil the agreement; otherwise our trade, as you know as well as I do, would lose credit and customers. I have promised to wait to-morrow upon the road of Rocca Petrella for a man who will wear a scarlet mantle or have it on the saddle, and I must kill him. I wait; he does not go by; my obligation is fulfilled, and I can return with a good conscience to the forest. How do you like that?"

"Eh! it is not bad. And your companion, who is he?"

"He is the son of Trofino, the miller. Just think how big he is grown! He was in love; found his *innamorata* talking with a young man of Rieti, and he happened to kill both of them—mere boyish affair. It is about six months since he came upon the highway, and he promises well. Now let me go, and keep a sharp eye, for the old fellow is a hound of a good breed."

"We will try, brother Grimo; if for nothing else than not to wrong the reputation of our company."

The old companions separated better friends than ever. Marzio returned to the room of the Count, who, after demanding certain little services, which Marzio fulfilled with his accustomed diligence, said in a kind tone:

"Marzio, if I hate, it is because others hate me; nor is it an easy thing to bear this life, for, excepting you, all try to ensnare my life, all greedily desire my property. I am alone against all; but I have not, like Horatius, a bridge on my shoulders. My children hate me more than any one else; instigated to this by the two most powerful motives among men: longing for revenge and desire of property. One thing troubles me: my strength fails, my vigorous body grows weak. It is useless to attempt to hide it; years begin to weigh heavily; I do not wish to be reduced like the lion, and be obliged to bear even kicks from the ass. It is more prudent to leave the theater before the lights are put out. I have, therefore, decided to retire to Rocca Petrella—an estate which I possess upon the confines of the State. Do you know the way?"

"I think so."

"To-morrow, then, you will set out on horseback, with my letters to the castle-keeper, and you will start for that place. There, as an able and experienced hand, you will superintend the works which I have planned to put the castle in order; you will have new bolts put on the doors; prepare some rooms for me, and try to make the traces of the fire disappear."

"Fire! you say? Did the castle get on fire?"

"The bandits, while it was badly guarded, sacked and burned it. At that time the band of Signor Marco Sciarra was hiding in the neighboring wood, and wherever his band passed grass never grew again."

"But I never heard that the band of Signor Marco ever burned or destroyed."

"I got into a quarrel with one of his men for some nonsense, which wasn't worth the while. Once I took a fancy to a certain peasant girl, a shepherdess, or something of that kind. Would you believe it, Marzio? this girl had the courage to resist me, and to threaten me with the revenge of her husband. As she was a devout worshiper of the Blessed Virgin of Tears, I made her entirely like to her holy advocate by planting a knife in her heart. The husband, or lover, whatever he might have been, took the joke in a serious light, and, aided by his companions, played me the trick of burning my castle."

"In truth he was wrong. What a fool not to understand the honor which the Count did him by falling in love with his peasant girl."

"But so it was—they would not understand it. Now, let us throw aside old stories. There is no need that you should take any money with you; the castle-keeper must, by this time, have received the payment of the tenants; only, for my sake, I would have you take this mantle which I give you—it will shield you from the night dews, of which we must be very careful."

"Does your Excellency's scarlet mantle, trimmed with gold, seem a suitable dress for a poor servant like me? I should look like one of the kings of the East."

"He who gives considers his generosity, not the humility of him who receives. Then, either to-night or to-morrow, you will saddle the black colt, which is the strongest among my horses, and start; I will follow you in five or six days. In the mean while, give me the keys of the subterranean passages; I will provide myself for my rebellious daughter."

Marzio gave them to him without hesitation, but in handing them to him thought, "Rascally old man! you don't know that an old bird like me cannot be caught by chaff?" He thought this because he had lost no time, and with some instruments had altered other keys, so as to fit the locks of the vaults.

He took leave, pretending to prepare himself for the journey; then, in order to watch the lower rooms, he went into the corridor that led to the gate of the vaults. Here he took his valise, examined the bridle, the straps, the saddle, and the weapons, and, as if he had found the latter rusty for want of use, began to polish them with oil and emery, being always on the watch.

Cenci, when he thought it time, persuaded that he should surprise Beatrice with some paper written by her or received by means of Marzio, cautiously and stealthily, like a cat, moving his body carefully on account of his lameness, endeavored to enter unobserved the prison of Beatrice. Hardly did Marzio see him appear at a distance before he snapped the pistol, which caused a great noise in those close places. The keen Count understood the plot at once; rage was in his heart, but he did not change color, he did not even move an eyelid; by this sign Beatrice was warned, and the surprise was in vain. He drew near to Marzio, and said in a hypocritical tone: "Be careful, my boy, another time, for you might wound your hand."

"Oh, it was a mere accident. I should not wish to be mutilated for life. Allow me to congratulate you, seeing your leg is so much better as to let you leave your bed."

"Those good religious men, whom you saw, brought me a relic able to work this and other miracles; but I did not permit them to disturb the saints in heaven: I stand modestly by my mallows plaster. I feel far from well, however. The need of taking a little air, the insupportable *ennui* of keeping my room, induced me to come so far. Marzio, give me your arm, that I may take some fresh air in the garden."

Marzio gave him his arm, and one would have thought them to be the most affectionate master and servant that ever were seen.

The Count, after a short walk, complained of his lame foot and desired to be reconducted to his room; Marzio accompanied him and helped him with affectionate care.

During the night, when it seemed to Marzio that all slept in the palace, with hasty steps he descended into the garden; here he made fast a ladder to the enclosure, then opening with his false keys the gates of the vaults, he liberated Olimpio. The latter, with food and rest, had recovered all his strength, and with it the keen desire of revenge; and he had planned to set fire to the Cenci palace before abandoning it. Marzio had as much as he could do to prevent him, telling him to be quiet now; that he too was more desirous of revenge and that in a few days he would have an easier and a sure way of killing the Count, and also that it was wrong to injure so many innocent ones on account of one wicked person.

Then he went to the prison of Beatrice, and advised her to fly with him, but found her firm in her design of bearing all that Providence should send her. Failing to persuade her, he took the letter, comforted her as well as he could, and tried to leave her. He returned; he felt his heart breaking in abandoning her. Finally, he kissed her hands affectionately (she always conjuring him for God's sake to give up his design of revenge against her father), and departed.

Olimpio saved himself by means of the ladder in the garden; Marzio went out of the palace courtyard, mounted upon the black colt, and carrying upon the saddle a red mantle trimmed with gold.

CHAPTER XVII

FATHER TIBER

FOR several days the home of Giacomo Cenci in vain awaited its master. Luisa, though still excited by passion, felt the force of her anger against him decline. Pride governed this Roman lady; but she was not able to hide the great affection she felt for her husband. The treacherously generous words of Count Cenci, that a good wife should, with all her power, try to reconduct to the right path the truant husband, against his expectations, came into her mind as rules of duty, and as a reproach. Then she thought that either Giacomo had let pass from his heart all affection for her and for their children, or that some great misfortune had happened to him. To divert her grief she took extraordinary care of her children; she hardly ever left them; the baby she would often carry to her bosom and cover him with such impetuous kisses, that, frightened, he would cry. But too often the caresses of the elder ones, their smiles, and even the tears of her infant, caused her mind to turn elsewhere, and sometimes, also, involuntary tears bathed her cheeks. Although she persisted in believing Angiolina the first cause of the evil which oppressed her, nevertheless, through her generous nature, she did not at all relax her charity toward her. While these conflicting thoughts agitated her, one evening the door opened softly, and Giacomo suddenly appeared.

He did not utter a word, saluted no one; he sat at the farther end of the table opposite his wife, covering his face with both hands. We have already seen him miserable, and badly clothed; and yet now, how changed from what he was! His beard and hair were in disorder; his hat was stained with mud; his eyes were bloodshot, and a circle of an ashy color surrounded them. Luisa felt at the same time frightened and compassionate.

She took up the little child and carried it to her bosom. But this did not attract the attention of Giacomo; who, believing himself betrayed, wept over his buried hopes, happiness and love. Starting suddenly, and grasping his hair with his hands, he exclaimed:

"Why have I come here? Would that one could cast out from his heart his affections, like the cargo of a ship, to save it from shipwreck; but if he cannot cast them out, he may uproot from his breast both his affection and heart." He made a movement to go.

Luisa, with a voice neither soft nor severe, said:

"Will the father go away from his children without kissing them?"

"Where are they, and who are my children? Which of these children can say that he is born from me? All is founded upon faith—a fragile thing! How can I trust to the tongue of a deceitful woman, whose words are snares set to lead to vileness and death?"

Luisa knew not what to understand from these words, and stared as if out of her mind. Giacomo, with a bitter smile, added:

"I understand that a man like myself, incapable of providing for the subsistence of his own family, must inspire contempt—and I understand also that contempt kills love and begets hatred. But why should one justify misdeeds with audacity? Why convert one's own fault into a stone to throw at the innocent? It would have been enough, I think, to insult me, to cover me with shame, without perfidiously scattering a storm of reproaches which blinded my eyes like dust, and prevented me from seeing your guilt."

"Giacomo, to whom are you speaking?"

"Be quiet! I have not come here to curse you, but only to tell you that you have put desperation into my soul, but have not deceived me. These words are enough —now that they are expanded like the smoke of an extinguished flame—all has been said between us," and again he made a motion to depart.

"Giacomo, do not go; by the faith of an honorable man, do not go! When words carry in their obscurity the destruction of a person's reputation it is necessary to explain them. Do you suppose that the secret is yours alone, when you have given me to understand that it concerns my dishonor?"

"It seems to me that you have no right to say so, for my words may sound obscure to every one but you. Do you wish a comment to my text? Very well! How did this furniture come to you? Who provides this abundance of provisions? In this house I left misery, and I find abundance; but I left also another thing, which I seek in vain—my honor. Should not the poverty or wealth of his family come from the father? Whose is the treasury whence you took the money? Certainly it was not your husband's. What is the name of him who provides for your need, and that of these children? Where is the courteous gentleman hidden who takes better care of you than I? Why is the friend of my family afraid to show his face to me?"

"Giacomo, for your honor's sake, remember that you are insulting the mother in the presence of her children."

"But they—what are they but witnesses, who criminate you more than my words?"

"A relative of yours—and mine—helped me. I cannot tell his name, because I promised to be silent. I am strong enough to see my children starve to death rather than fed by shame. These suspicions do not touch me, and I wish you to know, Giacomo, that I am as pure as your mother in heaven."

"But tell me, what could you have alleged against the faith of your husband except the perfidious calumny of a person who concealed his name? Nevertheless you refused belief to my oaths and tears? Now, how can you expect that I should give credit to your bare assertion?

"Giacomo—of that with which I reproach you I have manifest proofs in my hands; proofs which it is impossible to doubt. But your suspicions are infamous—go!"

"Very well. I have neither the heart nor the breath to quarrel with you."

After saying this, he approached her without menace, asking in a low voice:

"Will you tell me truly whether any one of them is my child?"

"Giacomo, you are mad! All are your children."

"Yes, certainly, so it is said. *Pater est quem justæ nuptiæ demonstrant;* thus, at least, is declared by the civil law, which was invented here in Rome; and the court would condemn me to pay for their support. I am a father, but only by a presumption of right; I am a father, but am good only to be given to the wild beasts. 'Tis pity that the spectacles of the Flavian theater are no longer in fashion. No matter! beams, trees, wells, rivers, are found everywhere." His voice became more animated and he continued:

"I could revenge myself! But did revenge ever have the virtue of restoring lost happiness? Being miserable, I could render you so—that is all. No, I do not wish to revenge myself—I will rather remove myself from your life so that you may go where your heart calls you. I do not ask you to remember me, because I do not care; nor shall I ask you to forget me, because I care even less about that; and this you can easily do by yourself. But I have loved these sweet beings; I have believed them part of myself, and it grieves me now to be obliged to tear them from my affection—I recommend them to you, Lady Luisa—if I cannot consider them my own, remember that they are yours. Certainly, in this last hour, it would have been a great comfort to me to touch my lips to a forehead that was of my own blood. Farewell! I desire that your years may pass without remorse, and with a new husband worthy of your fidelity."

Luisa had not dared to embitter the raving of Giacomo with words of dispute or rebuke. Now, observing how weak his voice was, she said tearfully:

"Oh, my children! embrace him—make him feel that he is your father!"

The children obeyed at once. One seized the hem of his garment, and tried to draw him toward their mother; another embraced his knees, and another strove to ascend a chair to be able to embrace his neck. Giacomo, somewhat soothed, broke from them, exclaiming:

"Go to your mother, unhappy ones! Do you not know

that the Cenci poison with their breath? Farewell forever!"

And he disappeared. Luisa rushed to the balcony, and with a most lamentable voice called:

"Giacomo! Giacomo!"

Again and again she cried; but Giacomo fled in the power of the fierce passion which took possession of him. Then, in the courageous woman, love conquered every other feeling, and she ran from her house in search of her husband. She had traversed several streets, when her breath failed, and she was obliged to stop and lean against the wall of a palace. Looking around, she knew this to be the dwelling of Monsignore Guido Guerra. Knowing that this youth was familiar with the Cenci family, and very intimate with Giacomo, it seemed to her that Providence had led her there. She ascended the steps, and following the valet, without waiting to be announced, entered a room, and found Monsignore in company with two men. The face of one seemed familiar to her, although, at that moment, she could not remember where she had met him; she hesitated a minute; then, urged by fear, she said:

"Oh, Monsignore, you who are such a friend of Giacomo, my husband, for the sake of Christ, send somebody to seek him through Rome, for he left our house in a great passion, and I fear with evil intentions."

"Against whom, Lady Luisa?"

"Against himself; and I fear that he has taken the way to the Tiber."

"*Cielo!* Come, Marzio, let us go—you, with some of my servants, on the left of the river; I, with some others, on the right. Olimpio, you must accompany Lady Luisa."

Omitting any leave-taking, Guido, Marzio, and the servants rushed out of the house in search of Giacomo. Lady Luisa, taking the arm of Olimpio, said to him:

"Your face is not new to me, but my brain is so disturbed that my memory wanders—Ah, yes!—I remember now—you were at the fire of the house of the poor carpenter."

"I?"

"Yes, and were among those who worked to help the powerless ones."

"I have done nothing but evil! To you, illustrious lady, all the merit is due; you are a saint, God bless you! If the question is not impertinent, will you tell me why you were disguised on that cursed night? Why did you run such a desperate risk?"

"I will tell you as we go. The woman I saved has wounded my heart; she has filled my family with mourning. It was not very happy before, but not so desolate; for where love rules hope never leaves. In short, she has stolen my husband; and on that night I wandered there with the intention of the wolf around the barnyard. I longed to drink her blood, and it seemed to me that this alone could have quenched my rage. Desperate cries reached me; the woman appeared with the child in her arms at the window; I saw no longer the hated rival, I saw only the mother. I thought of my own children, and rushed to save her, because Christ spoke within my heart, and said: 'Pardon!'"

Olimpio, hearing Lady Luisa speak thus, turned red and pale. He searched within his soul to see whether any hope was left for mercy, but could find none. Then he groaned from the depth of his heart. "If I could hope that absolution could save me," he said falteringly, "I would confess my sins to none but you, revered lady, and between God and myself I would not desire to place a better mediator. But I have so filled the book of my life with crimes that the Guardian Angel could not find so much blank space left as to write the word *mercy* even with the finest feather of his wings. Nevertheless, I will confess, because if my confession cannot avail me it will you. Do you know who burned that house? I!"

"You!"

"Do you know who brought to your noble husband the calumniating and perfidious letter which, perhaps, dragged him to despair? I! Do you know who has conceived all this, in order that you and your husband should hate each other?—Count Francesco Cenci. He rubbed his hands joyfully and said: 'It would be easier for a rock split by the thunderbolt to join again, than for my daughter-in-law to return to her love for Giacomo. I have sown hatred; they will reap desolation.'"

Lady Luisa let go the arm of Olimpio, and ran so swiftly that she might have outstripped a deer. Reaching home, she rushed into the room where Angiolina still lay ill, and, approaching her bed breathlessly asked: "Woman, by the love you bear your God, beware of telling a lie! Do you know Count Cenci!"

Angiolina, frightened at seeing her, and not recognizing her on account of the change in her clothes, for she had always appeared before her in man's dress, said:

"Who are you? What do you wish of me?"

"I do not answer; I ask," imperiously added Lady Luisa, "tell me whether you know Count Cenci?"

"You are, perhaps, the sister of my benefactor?"

"What matters that to you?" exclaimed Lady Luisa, striking impatiently one foot upon the ground; "man, woman, or demon, do not question the being who saved your life. Answer—answer!"

Angiolina, as if under the influence of a troubled dream, said:

"Yes, I know him."

"You know him, eh? miserable one! and is this the son of your loves?"

And, so saying, she thrust her hand into the hair of the little child, who, feeling pain, began to scream.

"Don't touch him! In what has this poor child offended you?" And in order to protect him she half-raised herself in her bed.

"This is the child of sin, and you had him from Cenci."

"From Cenci, Madame?" continued Angiolina, bursting into tears, "is it becoming in a lady thus to tear the reputation of a poor sick woman? Yes, I know an old nobleman who is called Count Francesco Cenci; it was he who was the benefactor of my poor dead husband, who took me once to thank him; he wished to give me money, which I unwillingly accepted, because, in spite of his white hair and mild words, something in his eyes frightened me. I never saw him more than once."

"Not of him—I am not asking of him, but of his son, Giacomo."

"I have heard that Count Cenci had children, but I never saw them, nor do I know how they are named," and she gave this answer with such simple tranquillity that even the doubting apostle himself would have believed her.

"Never saw him? You know not his name? Swear it before your God! Swear it on your soul and conscience; swear it on this Redeemer, who, were you a perjurer, would lift His hand from the cross to curse you forever!"

Taking a crucifix from the bed, she placed it before the woman's eyes. Angiolina took it, kissed it devoutly, then returned it with a gesture full of sweetness, saying:

"Are you a mother, Madame?"

"Had I not been a mother, should I have had the courage to rush into the flames to save you and your son?"

"You? And what is your name?"

"Lady Luisa."

"Wife?"

"Of Giacomo Cenci."

"Ah, Madame! although I am a woman of little understanding, still I comprehend that wicked tongues must have invented some scandal about me. Now, listen to me. Holy is the name of God, that of the Redeemer is holy, our souls and consciences are holy things, but I will not swear upon those." Placing her hand on the breast of her beloved child, who lay in a cradle beside her bed, she continued: "If I have spoken words of falsehood, may this heart of my heart cease to beat!"

Luisa, as if beside herself, exclaimed: "I believe you —ah! I believe you;" and leaning over Angiolina, she took her face between her hands, and kissed her on her hair, cheeks, and neck.

Giacomo Cenci, his first fury passed, strode slowly toward the Tiber. He had come to the decision of destroying himself, not by the impetus of passion, but by cool deliberation. He reached the bank, and, with his head and shoulders bent, he fixed his eyes upon the stream.

Just as he was about to take the fatal leap, he felt himself seized by two hands, and a familiar voice cried:

"Madman! what would you do?"

Giacomo, astonished, raised his head. Then his mind, which had rushed even to the extreme limit of the infinite, returned with abhorrence to the usual routine of life, and he recognized his friend Guido Guerra.

"Oh, Guido!"

"Miserable man!" continued Monsignore Guerra, between pity and reproach, "what of your children?"

Giacomo shrugged his shoulders, and answered not a word; he allowed himself to be led away like a man without will. When he noticed that he was placing his foot on the threshold of his house, he turned to Monsignore Guerra and said:

"Guido, if you suppose that I ought to thank you, you

deceive yourself. No, I cannot thank you, even at the risk of appearing ungrateful."

On entering the house, he saw a strange sight. A man of sinister appearance, cradling in his arms the youngest of Giacomo's children, held him suppliantly toward him. Then he earnestly confessed to Giacomo all the crimes he had committed by order of Count Cenci for the purpose of destroying their domestic peace. The child from time to time raised his little hands and smiled sweetly, so that Giacomo could not show anger toward Olimpio; who finally placed the child in the arms of the father, adding:

"Now, since with your son I have restored your peace, for the sake of this innocent being, who intercedes for me, I pray you, sir, pardon me!"

Giacomo was silent, and glanced around suspiciously, still disquieted. Lady Luisa, guessing the meaning of that dumb language, drew Olimpio aside and kneeling before her husband, said:

"My husband, we have doubted each other. Now that I know the wicked end at which Count Cenci aimed, and considering the hypocritical and wicked arguments urged by him, I feel myself free from my sworn promise, and I declare to you that, moved by despair, I went to him, exposed the state of our family, and prayed him to help my desolate children, who were of his blood. His words and acts were those of a loving father; he narrated to me, credulous with jealous passion, a long story of your loves, and of your money lavished in dissipation, denied to our children. He gave me affectionately three hundred ducats, on condition that I should never reveal whence they came; thus, with perfidious design, he made me believe you lost in extravagant vices; and you, that with the reward of shame I had procured comforts for myself and for our children."

Until now the lady had spoken with such vehemence

and rapidity that Giacomo had not been able to interrupt her. Here, however, he cut short her words, saying:

"This position is not becoming the wife of Giacomo Cenci. Rise, Luisa, your place is here, on my heart, on the heart of your Giacomo, who has loved you, and who loves you so much."

The children joyfully grouped themselves around their father and mother. Monsignore Guerra and Marzio, although pressed by the urgent need of putting into execution a certain scheme of their own, dared not disturb the sanctity of the domestic affections. Olimpio, seated with his back to the wall, had again taken possession of the beautiful little child, and fondly caressed him.

CHAPTER XVIII

THE DEPARTURE

IACOMO CENCI, having been invited to dinner by Monsignore Guerra, returned home late the following night; but if his long delay troubled Lady Luisa, his arrival did not console her; for he appeared pensive and sad and he refused to see the children. In bed tormenting dreams afflicted him, and he was heard to cry in his sleep: "He is dead! he is dead!" He awoke, suddenly frightened, casting uneasy glances around, and seeing his wife by his side clasped her in a warm embrace, and exclaimed with tears:

"How much better it would have been, if I had ceased to live!"

"You repent, then, of having returned to the bosom of your family, which adores you!" replied his wife, affectionately.

"No, Luisa, no; God forbid. Yet, believe me, it would have been better if I were dead—and you will see the reason why."

Luisa, like a discreet woman, was silent, attributing this anxious trouble to past emotions; and she trusted that time, her cares, and the caresses of the children would restore peace to his agitated mind.

On that same night, Marzio and Olimpio departed from Rome provided with much money. They rode two powerful horses; and although they traveled without suspicion of meeting any impediment in their way they were furnished with firearms.

A few days later, Count Cenci, being in better health and his foot sufficiently recovered, one morning at dawn awoke all his family suddenly, and ordered that, dressed as they were, they should set out on a journey. In the courtyard Beatrice saw horses already harnessed, a carriage and guides in readiness—manifest indications of a long journey. Where their father would take them, how long he would remain from Rome, neither she nor any of the family dared to ask.

Cenci had provided for everything with his usual care. As it did not appear safe for him to venture with his family alone through the dangerous roads that led from Rome to Rocca Petrella, he had hired for several days a band of rural guards, in order to protect him on the road. Formerly he had traveled over the fifty-eight miles, which lay between the city and his estate, in a single day; but now he could not depend upon doing it, considering the weight of the carriage, the roads thick with dust or broken with hills, and the great heat of the season.

Beatrice, the first to enter the carriage, turning to the Count, said:

"My lord and father, I must speak to you."

"Silence!"

And Beatrice, raising her hands entreatingly toward him, exclaimed again:

"Father, hear me, for the love of God—your life is"——

But Count Cenci, thinking these were mad attempts to free herself from the hated journey, pushed her into the carriage, locked the door, and ordered the curtains to be pulled down.

Having given the signal for departure, Count Cenci mounted with the others on horseback, and all set off without saying a word. They went out of the gate of St. Lorenzo, and keeping always to the Tiburtina road, they reached Tivoli.

From Tivoli, following the Valerian road, they arrived at Vicovaro, where, on account of the intense heat and hard roads, they were obliged to stop; with what rage on the part of the Count, who vainly tried to urge them forward, cannot be described. The tired horses would obey neither whip nor spur. In the afternoon they resumed their journey, and reached the inn of Ferrata, where it was necessary to leave the carriages and ascend the mountain upon horses or mules. Count Cenci dismounted, called the innkeeper, and asked him whether mules had been sent from Rocca Petrella to carry them.

"I have seen no mules," replied the host, with an ill-natured look.

"But has not my servant named Marzio stopped here in passing?"

"I know nothing of Marzio."

Count Cenci had artfully put this question to find out whether Marzio had been murdered, and to feign in every respect ignorance of the homicide; but since the innkeeper knew nothing, he thought it best to pretend great anger, and he cursed Marzio, and the carelessness of servants generally in fulfilling the orders of their masters, seeming perplexed how to procure means for traveling. The host observed to him crossly:

"Your Excellency, what is the use of getting angry? When you have cursed all the saints in Heaven, have you made horses and mules come? Probably your servant has not found them; he may have fallen sick at the castle; he may not have thought that you would arrive so soon; the bandits may have murdered him by the way, and I know not what else may have detained him! So many accidents happen in this world! Every evil has its remedy. Leave me to act. You know that host comes from *hospes;* and if Fortune had not looked askance at me, I would lodge people according to the commands of the Apostles."

"I thought," replied the Count, smiling, "that host was derived from another word."

"From what?"

"From *hostis*, which, in the Latin language, means enemy; but perhaps I am mistaken. Now, let us hear what you intend to do, my host."

"We will send a boy up into the woods where the coalmen are. At this hour the coal-pits must have been made; so that the workmen, partly out of courtesy to me, and partly to gain a few crowns, will be willing to come down here, and carry you to Rocca Petrella. It will be necessary for you to travel all night, because it is a good distance; it must be nearly thirty miles."

"The road is like that to Heaven, which should be made wider to accommodate us poor sinners. At all events, the moon rises late, and will facilitate the ascent and descent."

"But why do you not wait till to-morrow? Here I can find means to accommodate you all—remember we have only one neck to break!"

"No, I must get there immediately."

"And besides, to-morrow early you will have norses that will suit you."

"No, send for the mules of the coalmen."

"I will do as you please, your Excellency; even mules can carry one home."

CHAPTER XIX

THE NIGHT OF CRIME

WITHIN a room in the castle of Rocca Petrella is Beatrice, kneeling, with her blond hair loosened, her forehead turned towards heaven, her arms hanging down. In beauty and attitude she resembled the famous statue of Faith, by Lorenzo Bertolini.

The room is a prison. So far her life has been a toilsome road, of which imprisonments have been milestones to distinguish the spaces. The aspect of the room was strange to look at: splendid was the bed, with wide curtains of damask and gilded cornices; the floor was covered with a carpet representing Æneas listening to the malignant forebodings of the Harpy Celæno; upon a rough wooden table were placed vases and basins of silver; the walls were dreary, and here and there traced with words of sorrow.

Beatrice, with her eyes raised to heaven, neither prays nor reproaches; she seems rather to ask: "God! hast thou forsaken me?"

A long while did the girl remain kneeling, absorbed in deep and painful thoughts; when she rose, weariness overcame her and she let herself fall on the bed. Sleep was a better friend to her than watching.

A slight touch pushes the door; it moves silently on its hinges; the head—then the chest—finally, all the person of a white-haired old man appears, wrapped in a large cloak with a red hood on the head. It is Count Cenci, dragged there by fate. He stops—and listens to the breath of Beatrice. He leans all his body on one foot, cautiously moves the other, advancing quietly, and reaches the head of the bed.

Beatrice has shut her eyes in a troubled sleep, and moving restlessly, has caused her hair to fall in disorder over her neck.

He looks long at her. The sight of a veiled form so divinely beautiful would rejoice the soul; for a rose and a woman, the less they show of themselves the more beautiful they appear.

The fierce old man stretches his lean arms and draws very cautiously the covering toward him. The beauties of her form are revealed to him—of such a form that Love himself would have veiled with his own wings the eyes of a lover.

Softly—softly the door of the room moves again on its hinges; another man enters, and stops—is astonished—and in the feeble light does not recognize the Count. The latter trembles; his eyes quiver like those of a viper; the blood reddens his cheeks; he lets the cloak fall from his shoulders, bends one knee upon the extreme edge of the bed, and deliriously extends his hands.

A tempest of rage shakes the soul of Guido—for the new comer is he. Unconsciously he finds his poniard in his hand. The Count hears a groan behind him, and turns his head. Guido darts in the eyes of the old man a glance of lightning, which means death. The Count, terrified, lets the covering fall, but Guido rushes with one leap upon him, and grasps him by that hair whitened in crime. The Count opens his mouth with a convulsive gasp—in vain; the steel, penetrates so deep into his breast that he is not able to utter a word. He staggers—falls—strikes heavily on the pavement, shedding fountains of blood.

Beatrice, uttering a groan, languidly opens her eyes—God of heaven! is it not an illusion?—she fixes them on the face of her beloved Guido. Love, with his rosy hands, opens her lips in the sweetest of smiles; but it fell upon the soul of her lover as upon a bronze statue—he looks fiercely at her, and with his dripping poniard points to the fallen man.

The smile dies upon the lips of Beatrice, like the kiss which, in the moment of our waking, we send to the vision of our dream. Still the girl does not know all the mysteries of this accursed night. Who is that fallen man, and what does he here? He has his face turned to the ground, does not breathe, and the light of the lamp can hardly reach there. Beatrice already moves her lips to ask; Guido notices this movement, and fears it; he motions with his eyes to the dying man; she follows with her eyes the glance of Guido on him; then turns to look on her lover—he is gone!

A terrible idea flashes into the mind of Beatrice. Unmindful of her maiden modesty, she leaps from the bed, and does not shudder, nor notice that her foot is bathed in the blood with which the floor is inundated. She grasps the hair of the dying man and turns his head—it is her father!

He slowly moves his mouth in the last agony; his eyes stare horribly in the immobility of death. Beatrice springs to her feet, with her arms stretched out, her body inclined, petrified with fright; she seems struck with madness. The eyes of the Count open wider—brighten—give one long look—then become of the color of lead—extinguished. Count Cenci is no more!

Beatrice stood stupefied and immovable, without thought and without feeling. Guido, in fury, descended the stairs hastily, and entered the room where Lady Lucrezia, Bernardino, Olimpio, and Marzio were. Throwing far from him the bloody poniard, he exclaimed:

"He is dead! He is dead!"

"Why did you not leave us the care of settling our old accounts with Cenci?" asked Olimpio.

And Marzio, coldly, added:

"This is an event of which we must be assured;" and he went to the prison.

Singular human nature! Marzio, capable of killing the Count with the same devotion with which he would have recited his beads, as soon as he perceived the girl undressed, retired modestly, and spoke in a low tone to Lady Lucrezia, who, overcoming her fear, entered the room. She approached Beatrice; called her; shook her; and not obtaining any answer, covered her with the cloak that had fallen from the Count, and taking her by the wrist led her way.

Marzio, according to his ferocious design, entered the room, followed by Olimpio; he shook the corpse by the hair, and drawing out his *stiletto* thrust it into his left eye:

"Now I am sure he is dead!"

"There was no need of this," observed Olimpio, placing his finger in the wound of the Count; "see what a hole! The soul might have gone out in a carriage from here. Now let us think a moment, what we must do with this man;" and he kicked the corpse.

"Let us carry him into the garden and bury him under ground."

"You have lost all your judgment; it is not enough to bury him; he must die first, in a manner which may have some sense in it. Come here; take him by the feet; I will take him by the head, and let us carry him upon the terrace which looks upon the garden; I know that this terrace leads to the ante-chamber, and in some places the parapet is destroyed. The poor gentleman, getting up for something during the night, was groping without a light—think what an imprudent thing! Perhaps he had eaten too much supper, and certainly he drank more wine than usual. What an accident! Unfortunately, he missed his footing and fell!"

"Pooh! pooh! it is very well that a man falling from a height should break his neck or his head, but he is never wounded by a sharp and acute steel."

"And even for this there is a remedy; we will throw him upon the trees; then we will stick the points of the branches into the wounds, and that will be enough. Do you suppose, Marzio, that they will be so particular about it? Who is dead is dead, and a health to the living!"

"Sometimes the dead come back, but the idea is good."

And all was done as Olimpio suggested.

Lady Lucrezia, by means of a window on the lower floor of the castle, the iron grates of which were wanting, had admitted Guido, Marzio, and Olimpio in the dead of night, when the family were all in bed, so that they were seen by no living person; and they intended to go out by the same way from which they had entered. Guido, who had come to consult about the manner of freeing Beatrice from prison, having chanced to kill the Count, decided to start for Rome immediately. Marzio and Olimpio departed the same night for the confines of the Neapolitan state, to sail for Sicily or for Venice; they received two thousand sequins for a present, besides the promise of future favors.

Guido arrived at the inn of Ferrata and ordered his horse to be saddled immediately. When this was done, the innkeeper, who had scrutinized him keenly with his malicious eyes, holding his stirrup, said:

"Oh, sir! day before yesterday you told me you were going up to Rocca Petrella to pass the month of September; have you eaten the whole month in two dinners? *Cielo!* what an appetite!"

"Man proposes, and God disposes!"

"I should rather say that you went to enact a tragedy; you have performed your part, and now return home."

"What do you mean?"

"Nothing; except that your sleeve is stained with blood."

Guido looked bewildered at the sleeve and saw that the innkeeper had told the truth; and turning to him, with cross tone, said:

"Are you the rural police?"

"I am astonished at you, sir. I am a friend of a certain Marzio, whom I imagine you must know a little; and I am almost like a father to these poor children of the wood; I am a natural enemy of poverty, but honest. I have said this so that, in case you should have need, you may count upon the innkeeper of Ferrata."

The next day Rocca Petrella resounded with wailings and lamentations, which echoed more noisily than sincerely. The inhabitants of the place, and the peasants around, gathered in crowds to see the spectacle. The corpse of the Count, not without design, was left for a long time hanging upon the branches of an alder-tree.

Presently arrived a number of men with the curate at their head, and all speculated how this body could have happened to be thus hanging in the air; but these importunate speculations were interrupted by a servant who, on the part of her Excellency the Countess, invited them all to enter the palace. They went, and found Lady Lucrezia inconsolable, according to the custom of all widows. After she had spoken for some time, interrupted now and then by her tears and sighs, of the unfortunate accident, she ordered the curate to prepare a most magnificent funeral, becoming the nobility and splendor of the Cenci family; she invited the mountaineers to come and assist at it, promising very large alms in relief of the poor families, that they might pray for peace to the poor soul. They departed edified by the piety of her Excellency, and did not cease to magnify her mildness and benevolence. When they returned to take down the body of the Count, they found it not only already removed from the tree, but shut and nailed within a double oaken coffin.

CHAPTER XX

THE RED MANTLE

"THE game is lost; shuffle the cards again."

"But, Don Olimpio," observed the gamester, "remember that you began to play before twilight, and now it is near morning. Every minute that passes, I seem to be on the grate of Saint Lorenzo."

"When you opened your mouth before, and I shut it with a ducat, you stopped barking, ugly dog. *Per Dio!* I have lost this also. Hand the cards to me."

"I wished you would go home more than I wished your money—on my word."

"Pah! what is your word worth?"

"The Viceroy has decreed that the game should stop at midnight, and now it is already seven hours past. If the police, who have an old spite against me, should find me in fault, I might as well take a stone and throw myself into the gulf."

"Judas Iscariot!" cried Olimpio, striking his fist on the table, "you cast a spell upon my cards; this also is lost! I am losing everything."

The gamester had lied as usual, for he and the police were united like fingers on the same hand—always ready to shut in order to grasp.

"Broke!" roared out Olimpio.

"Courage, Don Olimpio; you may regain it tomorrow."

"By the Apostles Peter and Paul! a long time have I said the same; but fortune caresses me with a hatchel."

"Perseverance will conquer; and that you are persevering we have proof, for you return every day furnished with balls and powder."

"Marzio keeps continually grumbling that my share is ended, and that his thousand sequins are very near the end."

"A thousand and a thousand make two thousand. But do you know," observed the gamester, "that here, with two thousand sequins, one can buy a dukedom? What did you do to gain so much money?"

The question was too direct not to make Olimpio avoid it. He looked somewhat cunningly at the gamester, and answered:

"They came to me from plunders when we were fighting for the faith."

"For what faith?" continued the other; "for, by your leave, it seems to me you must have found yourself oftener with the Turks than with the Christians; and in what sea have you fought, Don Olimpio?"

"Oh, in many seas."

"Still, in which one?"

Olimpio, besieged by questions, would have easily blundered had not one of the gamblers casually helped him out by asking:

"Why do you not bring with you your friend and companĩon, Don Marzio?"

"Oh, Marzio moves in higher circles; he plays with gentlemen and cuts like a duke, as if we had not lived together in the forests of Luco."

"In the forest, then," remarked the sneering gamester, placing his finger upon the table, "in the forest, then, and not on the sea, you won your plunder?"

"Either the forest or the sea, what matters it to you,

ugly Judas? Ah! do you wish to spy upon me?" replied Olimpio, savagely.

The following evening Olimpio did not sit as usual before the gambling-table, but at the end of the room, with his arms folded and a pipe in his mouth, puffing continually. His face, usually savage, now shadowed by this dense fog, looked more savage still.

"Has not the galley of Peru arrived this evening?"

"Why did you not bring your companion, Don Marzio?"

These questions, like two arrows, struck on the same target; so that Olimpio, feeling stung, after cursing this saint and that, said in a rage:

"Because he has got on his back a red mantle, he thinks that he is Count Cenci himself, from whom he stole it."

"Here, console yourself," said the gamester, placing a flask of wine before him.

Olimpio emptied it in a moment, and, sighing, replaced it on the table.

"You don't like me," continued the gamester, "and you do wrong. To prove it to you, if you want a dozen ducats, to play with and regain your losses, I will lend them to you."

"And who has said that I don't like you? I like you as I like bread."

"And Marzio, whom you honor as your superior, maltreats you and denies you money?"

"True! Do you know what he told me when I said that I had no more money?—'If you are poor, hang yourself.'"

"Did he?"

"Yes; and said I must tell him where I intended to go; for if I went west, he would go east."

"*Per Bacco!* it would make even stones cry out;" and the gamester sipped the wine, and then offered the flask to Olimpio, who drank the contents without taking breath. "The ungratefulness of men: while they have need of you they promise everything; after the feast they remove the flowers, and who has had it keeps it. Now, what can you do? If I can help you, you may rely on me; and you will see that for my friends I would throw myself into the fire. True friends are known only in need. Come, let us drink."

"Let us drink," replied Olimpio. Having drunk, he continued:

"If I could send secretly a letter to Rome, to the Cenci family, I am certain that aid would not fail me, because it would be necessary for them to help me."

"Yes—eh?" said the gamester, keeping his ears stretched eagerly.

The truth was, Marzio had not said offensive words to Olimpio; on the contrary, he had very mildly told him that for several days his share of one thousand sequins was gone, and that, as it was urgent both should leave the country, he could not consent that the money necessary for the voyage should be stolen in gambling houses or wasted in taverns. But Olimpio lied purposely, and feigned a wrong to believe himself in the right.

Nevertheless, Marzio thought he had not acted wisely, and that it was dangerous to contend with the brutal passions of Olimpio, greatly increased by the corruption of a large city; therefore he decided to find him and quiet him until he could take him out of the kingdom. Knowing to what gambling house he was accustomed to go in the evening, he went there.

"Would it be necessary?" continued the gamester. "What! are the Cenci your bankers, Olimpio?"

"You may think—that they are."

"I understand," added the gamester. "You have, perhaps, sent some enemy of the house to sleep?"

"Pensions are not given nowadays for such business;

for even here, as there, I suppose marplots have ruined everything."

"What then?"

'It is worse—worse than that—the secret is here within—and in order that the safe be locked, they must put on a silver cover."

"Truly? And can you trust me with this secret?"

"I know who killed Count Cenci!"

"Oh!" exclaimed in chorus the gamblers, on seeing appear among them at this moment a man of polite bearing, wrapped in a magnificent red mantle embroidered with gold. "Welcome, Don Marzio."

Marzio wondered not a little at hearing himself called by name; and turning his eyes around, fixed them on Olimpio, who slightly moved his head, and then restored it to its first position, without looking up, and grumbling with rage.

"I am glad not to be unknown to these gentlemen."

"Don Marzio," said the gamester, moving towards him, "will you lay aside your cloak? By my faith! it deserves to be well taken care of, for it looks as if it might be a gift from some Prince, Marquis, or, at least, *Count*"

Marzio looked at Olimpio a second time, but the latter remained immovable. Marzio then laid his cloak carefully aside, and sat down to play. Having remained a sufficient space of time, pretending he would continue to visit the place, took his cloak and went away, leaving Olimpio deceived in his momentary expectation of being asked to make peace, and accept a dozen ducats for that evening. Marzio, considering the wild nature of this fellow, had been offended at it, and had resolved to spare himself the mortification of trying to mollify him; he thought to reach his home, pack his things, and start next day from Naples.

Olimpio, who kept angry as long as he hoped to be asked to make peace, was discouraged when he saw himself neglected; he then left the gambling house, hastening to rejoin Marzio. The gamester did not stay behind, but rushed after them.

Marzio, hearing the hasty steps of some one behind him, placed his hand under his cloak to seize his poniard, and stopping suddenly, asked loudly:

"Who goes there?"

"It is I, Marzio."

"What do you want?"

"Don't get angry; let us go on further, if you please; we can talk more freely."

And they continued their way, the gamester still following them.

"Does it seem to you right," began Olimpio, "to leave me without a penny to buy a pipe? You saved me from dying of starvation to die of thirst."

"Olimpio, I have told you a thousand times that when you like you may come to my house, where there is plenty to eat and drink; but I never will consent to your spending my few ducats in wine, gambling, and worse things. You have had your share; I have made the settlements with you, and proved that I am your creditor by more than two hundred ducats; nor can you deny it. Now, what right have you over my money?"

"You taught me that the want of right in bandits, soldiers, and great lords even, is no reason for preventing them, when they can, from taking the property of others."

"And that is right; but I spoke of right, and not of force; for I have as much force as you. Now, when forces are equal, the best thing is to put our hands in our pockets, and let our tongues quarrel."

"You know, Marzio, that desperation often makes men worse than dolphins—it makes them sharks."

"I understand," thought Marzio; and then, with milder voice, added:

"Olimpio! Olimpio! certain words which I heard from

the gamester make me strongly fear that you have committed some great imprudence; and then we should both be ruined."

"Yes, truly! Do you suppose I am a child?"

"Do not dissemble, Olimpio; for it may be our secret is no longer ours; I have always been obliged to mend your imprudences; think that it is a question of life and death."

Olimpio made a little examination in a moment, and knew too well that Marzio was right; and beginning to fear very much lest something might happen, said, with hesitating tone:

"Now I remember rightly—truly—my dear Marzio—you must try to remedy this—but what could I do? I was so mad! I am afraid—that something—might have escaped from my mouth—which may make them believe—suspect—that we killed Count Cenci."

"Are you in jest? Then we are lost."

"No—I am in earnest—but those who heard me seemed to be good sort of people. Still, if I had not spoken—if there was any means to make them forget—or at least if they would no longer speak."

"How? Letters are sealed with wax; mouths must be sealed with lead, like the bulls of the Pope!"

"Eh! that would be the shortest way—and even steel would answer."

"So I think," said Marzio, and looked stealthily at Olimpio. They had just reached a shrine of the Madonna, where two lamps were burning. Olimpio, who was walking on the left of Marzio, raised his right hand to remove his hat before the Image; and Marzio, taking this chance, turned suddenly upon his left side, and thrust his poniard, even to the hilt, in his breast. Olimpio fell, crying:

"Marzio, what are you doing? Oh, Holy Virgin, help me!"

And Marzio leaned over him, saying:

"You condemned yourself, Olimpio, when you agreed that an open mouth should have an iron seal; and would to God that this would be enough!" and while he said this he continued to despatch Olimpio with other blows. Thinking he was about to expire, he wiped the dagger on his clothes, and made the sign of the cross before the Madonna, saying:

"Of this blood I must render an account some day; but thou, Mother of God, knowest if I shed it for myself. Had I not done it he would have ruined whole families, and a maiden who in her grief and beauty resembles thee, if not in glory."

Upon reaching his lodgings he packed his clothes, money, and everything carefully into a bag; and later in the night, leaving the money for his lodging upon the table, went off to sleep somewhere else, with the intention of embarking at dawn the next day upon any vessel that might leave the port. The gamester, who from a distance had seen the affray, rushed to Olimpio and found him dying.

"Don Olimpio, did Don Marzio kill you, eh? for fear you might reveal to the police that affair of the Cenci, eh?" He bent over him with eager curiosity.

With a strong effort, Olimpio opened his eyes, heavy with death, and seeing the face of the gamester, shut them, groaning. The gamester said, quickly:

"Revenge! Revenge! If you wish to revenge yourself upon Don Marzio, reveal to me everything, for I am acquainted with the chief of police; and I promise that before your soul reaches the other world, you will see that of Marzio following after."

Olimpio could see no longer, but he could hear; so that recovering somewhat his senses, he knew the evil he had done, and acknowledged that Marzio was right. He moved his lips, and muttered a few words. The gamester kneeling, with both his hands resting on the pavement of the street, greedily inclined his ear to the mouth of the dying man to hear his words. He was able to hear them, and they were these:

"Ugly—Judas—Iscariot!"

In the meanwhile the gamester, in order to hear better, had inserted the edge of his ear within the mouth of Olimpio, who, shutting it hastily, bit it. Olimpio expired, the gamester screamed; and they remained, one in the act of confiding the secret, and the other of receiving it. Having recovered his ear from the teeth of the dead man, the gamester began to rub it to allay the pain; then ran so swiftly that he hardly seemed to touch the earth, to a certain dark lane in the midst of the city; and here, without using any caution, for the night, being very dark, did not permit any person to see him, he knocked in a particular way at the secret door of the back of a palace. The door opened and shut carefully and quietly.

Next morning before dawn Marzio was on the wharf; and not finding any other vessel ready to sail, except a felucca bound to Trapani, he soon made an arrangement with the master, and was about to mount on the deck of the vessel, and would have been saved, if his red mantle had not fallen overboard. It was necessary that some seamen should lower their hooks to fish it out; not being able to catch it at first, they tried several times. While they were thus fatally losing time, in the distance, a crowd of policemen appeared running straight toward the vessel. Marzio, with his sharp eyes, had already perceived the gamester; and the latter, no less sharp-sighted, perceived the red mantle, and him who wore it. Marzio hastened to cry out to let the mantle go, and to weigh anchor without delay; but it was too late.

"Stop that vessel, by order of the Viceroy!"

The vessel was stopped, and the policemen, jumping on

board, arrived in time to seize Marzio by the clothes at the moment he was about to throw himself into the sea.

"God wills it!" exclaimed Marzio, and allowed himself to be bound without resistance. In order not to have a crowd assemble and make a disturbance at this early hour, the policemen, according to their usual custom of doing things quietly, threw over him the red mantle, having drained it of water, covering his fettered hands.

The chief remained behind on the wharf, and cried:

"Ship ahoy! you can now go on your voyage."

"Your Excellency! the police have returned with the prisoner."

Thus a servant announced, who, in his face and motions, had something of the policeman and the priest. These words, whispered through the crack of a door, awoke the Criminal Judge; he dressed in haste, and entered his office. Having seated himself gravely in a high chair, he immediately rang the bell.

The captain of police entered with Marzio, handcuffed, and covered with the red mantle.

"Captain Gaetanino," said the judge, gravely, "conduct this man into the trial-room, and prepare the instruments according to law." The captain obeyed, the judge followed, and sat in a solemn attitude before a long table, having at his side two notaries, and before him all the instruments of torture prepared. The executioner and two assistants were there, awaiting his orders.

Marzio stood impassible.

A notary began to interrogate him concerning his name and the circumstances of the crime of which he was accused. After the questions, the judge read the following charges to him:

"Marzio Sposito, you are accused: *First*, that, in company with your accomplice, Olimpio Geraco, you murdered barbarously, and with premeditation, the illustrious

Count Don Francesco Cenci, a Roman nobleman, in Rocca Petrella, situated on the confines of this kingdom. *Secondly*, that you received the commission to kill him by *all* or by *by some one* of the Cenci family. *Thirdly*, that as a price for the murder, two thousand sequins were paid to you; of which one thousand were for yourself, and the other thousand for the aforesaid Olimpio. *Fourthly*, that you are also guilty of theft, by stealing from the murdered Count Cenci a red mantle embroidered with gold, which was found on your person at the time of the arrest. *Fifthly*, that in the past night you treacherously murdered your accomplice, Olimpio Geraco, with a sharp and pointed instrument called a poniard, striking four blows, which caused the almost instantaneous death of the aforesaid Geraco. Upon these five charges, which I have read to you in a clear voice, and which, at your request, may be read anew, you are ordered to tell the truth in confessing them, after taking the oath; and this, not because justice has any need of other proofs, but for your good both in this life and the next, and to fulfil the orders of the law, which desires such admonitions. The notary of the court will now swear you."

The notary, who sat upon the left, took a crucifix with such irreverence that it seemed as if he might have been one of those who crucified our Saviour, and began the formula of the oath, saying:

"Marzio Sposito, swear by this image of our crucified Jesus."

"I will not swear."

"Why not swear? Everyone swears."

"And all falsely. Does it seem natural to you that I should willingly swear my ruin and death?"

"But you will avoid the torture," observed the notary.

"You have no right to interfere," interrupted the judge; "he has the right to choose. Master Giacinto, execute your duty."

With the same accuracy with which an artisan gets ready to begin a delicate work, Master Giacinto, who was the executioner, assisted by his aids, undressed the poor man in an instant, tied him by the arms, and swung him in the air.

Marzio suffered these atrocious torments without uttering a moan; only when they gently lowered him to the ground, his evil genius whispered in his ear: "Why do you live any longer?" His memory presented before his mind, as through a mirror, all the vicissitudes of his life. Betrayed by his friends, persecuted by men in his dearest affections, these were changed into scourges to his soul; his passions bore the aspect of love. Filial love had made him a bandit; the love for a woman, perfidious and dissimulating; the love for Beatrice, a murderer.

The judge, as soon as Marzio was placed in a seat, ordered:

"Master Giacinto, in fifteen minutes you will repeat it; in the meanwhile, if he wishes to drink, give him water and vinegar;" and so saying, was about to depart.

"Your Honor!" called Marzio with a feeble voice, "if I would confess, could I rely upon a favor?"

"I will do what I can," said the Judge; "our Viceroy is very generous and magnanimous. Sir Notary, register that the accused has proposed to confess; *ergo*, the charges are true. This is a step acquired for the trial—go on."

"The favor which I would ask, is not, perhaps, what you imagine."

"What is it, then?"

"That as soon as I shall have confessed my sins, I may be executed."

"I will ask this of His Highness the Viceroy. Come, then, confess your crimes."

"How! so soon? Where is the priest?"

"This is not a sacramental confession, but judicial."

"And what do you wish me to confess?"

"What I read to you before; do you wish that I should read it again?"

"Oh, no; it is right; I deserve death."

"Then you confess, and certify in full the charges against you?"

"Yes; as you wish, provided you take my life quickly."

The judge then ordered the act of accusation to be closed with the necessary formalities; he signed it first himself, followed by the two notaries, and put it into his pocket.

The judge presented himself at the palace of Don Pedro Girone, Duke of Ossuna, Viceroy in Naples for Philip III, King of Spain. He was introduced into the room of his secretary, and told him that he wished to speak to His Highness the Viceroy. The secretary reported that important business prevented His Highness from giving an audience. The judge then related the motive of his coming to the secretary, who listened to him carelessly; and, before he had done, took away the papers from his hands, and went away, saying, "I understand!"

This is the important business with which His Highness the Duke of Ossuna was occupied. His Eminence, the Cardinal Zappata, had sent to him from Madrid a magnificent parrot, and he was playing with him. The secretary entered suddenly, and surprised the Viceroy teaching his parrot—what was he teaching him? A Spanish word that no gentleman would proffer, and no lady listen to—although, pronounced by the parrot, it would excite the merriment of the ladies, and sometimes the blush, so that they would hide their faces.

The Viceroy, displeased at being surprised at that moment, turned with an angry face to the secretary, who knew not what to do. He thought best to approach the parrot, but it was frightened, and bit his finger. The secretary murmured in an undertone:

"Curse him!" and said in a loud voice, " A magnificent —a beautiful parrot!"

But the Viceroy, angry, asked him with a severe voice:

"Inigo, who has called you?"

"Your Highness, the Criminal Judge wished to see you. I, knowing that you did not wish to be disturbed, took his papers, and came to bring them to you."

"We know too well," said the Viceroy, with lordly haughtiness taking the papers, "that we are denied what every one else has in plenty—a moment of rest. Don Inigo, say on."

"Your Highness, a bandit of the Roman State treacherously killed last night a companion of his, near the image of the Madonna of Buonconsiglio. This morning, being arrested, he confessed during the torture. The judge, considering the spontaneous confession, is of opinion that he be condemned to death without further trial."

The Viceroy, taking a pen, was about to sign the sentence; but he stopped.

"By Saint Jago! is it nothing to sign a sentence of death? There must be some difference between signing it and suffering it. To pass at once from one world where the splendor of the sun shines so luminously, into another, where the clearest thing which I comprehend is an eternal darkness—it seems to me a truly ugly passage;" and here he dipped his pen into the ink. "I think," he added, "that it must be more easy to weigh the anchor of this life on a January day at Stockholm, than at Naples in an April day."

These thoughts escaped from the brain of the Duke, not from his heart; he spoke them so as to make his secretary forget the bad word he was teaching to the parrot. Meanwhile, the parrot, to increase his confusion and rage, repeated with loud voice the bad word learned, and seemed wishing to mock at him and his pretended philosophy. Then he sat down again in haste, and, to free himself from the importunate witness, was about to sign. "For, if this rascal deserves dismissal," thought he, "come, let us send him into eternity."

But the parrot, either struck by the novelty of the thing, or cross because he was no longer petted, with his bill snatched the pen from the hands of the Viceroy.

"Montezuma does not wish that he should die; or, rather, Montezuma reproaches the Viceroy for signing sentences of death without even examining the papers of the trial. The parrot is right—the Viceroy wrong. Montezuma, thanks for your advice. If I were a king, who knows but, in reward for your long and honorable services, I would present you with a cross of honor? But being only a viceroy, I will give you a whole sweet biscuit."

Don Pedro then began to read with attention the papers handed to him; and after perusing them carefully, and considering for some time what would be necessary to do, said:

"Don Inigo, Montezuma, with your permission, showed himself a great deal wiser than you in persuading me to read papers which you have not read, and which you should have read. This is an affair hardly begun, and we should only cut the thread and lose all traces of it. I don't see what prudence this would have been. It would be better to send this man to Rome, accompanied with a good escort, and with letters to conciliate His Holiness towards us. You will observe that although this is a crime committed within our jurisdiction, it seems to have been long before premeditated by persons of high rank residing in Rome. Send these orders to the judge; and I hope that fortune may always be as good to us as to-day, in which she has spared us the signing of a sentence of death, and given us an opportunity of securing the encomiums and good will of the Holy Pontiff, of which wise kings have always need, so long as they wish to rule their subjects with absolute power."

And all this because the Duke of Ossuna had been surprised teaching a bad word to the parrot! The secretary went out humbled, and gave the proper orders to the judge, who had them immediately executed, sending Marzio, with a good escort, to the Governor of Rome.

CHAPTER XXI

THE ARREST

BEATRICE loved the sun of autumn, the rays of twilight, and the long shadows of the west. Often, in company with her sister-in-law, Lady Luisa, whom she now loved like a sister and revered as a mother, she used to walk around Rome accompanied by two or more servants, according to the custom of the Roman noble ladies. One day, walking as usual, they entered the Plaza Farnese; continuing in the street of Corte Savella, they arrived at last in the Julian Way. In the middle of this street, Beatrice suddenly stopped to gaze on a building of mournful appearance—black, very large, without windows or any other openings, except the gate, which was so low that no one could enter without bending his body.

Heavy clouds darkened the heavens, and the damp fog arising from the Tiber covered the whole building; so that every projecting point was dripping. Beatrice stopped to look at this sad edifice; and learning that it was the prison of Corte Savella, pressing the arm of her sister-in-law, saying:

"Does it not seem to you that it weeps?"

"Who?"

"This prison."

"Certainly many must be the tears that are wept within it; and if they had succeeded in piercing through the walls, I should not be surprised."

"And those greenish mosses, which thrust themselves through the cracks of the stones and have found means to burst forth, do they not seem to be prayers of prisoners that escape from these walls?"

"Too much they seem so! And as those herbs remain attached to the walls of the prison, to be blown by the wind or burnt by the sun, likewise the prayers are turned in vain to the passer-by to remind him of those who groan within, so that he may feel pity for them."

Thus sadly conversing, they returned home.

Don Giacomo, with his family, had come back to live in the ancient Cenci palace, and under this roof they all dwelt, some securely, some timidly, and Beatrice desolate in her heart, and fearing some impending misfortune, although she did not show it.

The evenings in the house of the Cenci never were passed without a number of relatives and friends, because of the many relatives of the family and its reputation for courtesy; but on this evening it happened that no one had yet come, although it was already late. The assembled family endeavored to keep up the conversation, but it often happened that a question remained unanswered, and the painful dialogues were cut short; everyone wished to be alone and commune with his own mind. At last Lady Luisa said:

"I notice that this evening the silent mood rules over us; let us take Ariosto, and try to cheer our spirits with some of his wonderful fancies."

"I, for my part, do not like him, on account of his style, rather mild than smooth," observed Beatrice; "and what is more, he is so light; let us read Tasso instead, if you like."

"I like that better," added Don Giacomo, briefly.

"But you did not always think so; for my part, I never change, and as I once thought I think now of Ariosto; fancies, strange things, loves, battles, good and bad passions, tears, smiles, earth, heaven and hell, all did that great author sing; whose genius, like his, so resembles nature, always varying and always beautiful?"

"You may be right," observed Beatrice, "but I do not like him. The story of Olindo and Sofronia moves me to tears as if the fact had really happened; while the stories of Ariosto seem to me only fine imaginations; and, besides, I am always fearful lest all at once they may make me laugh. But come, let us read of Ginevra, if you wish."

Lady Luisa, somewhat proud of her victory, went to seek the volume; and opening it, placed it before Don Giacomo, saying:

"You must begin."

Don Giacomo had barely glanced at it when he turned pale, and said, quickly:

"No—no—it belongs first to you."

"I will begin, then; but I have mistaken; the story does not begin at the sixth canto, but the fifth." Turning several leaves of the book, she began in a fine style to declaim from the verse, *Tutti gli altri animai che sono in terra*, until she reached the following:

> *"Quel, dopo molti preghi, dalle chiome*
> *Si levò l'elmo, e fe palese e certo*
> *Quel che nell' altro canto ho da seguire,*
> *Se grato vi sara la storia udire."*

"Now I have read enough," said Lady Luisa, pausing; "let some one else continue."

At this moment, a handsome young man with blue eyes

and blond hair opened the door of the room without being announced. He was dressed in a prelate's robe; he did not bow, but stood still and silently admired the family group.

Donna Luisa, not noticing the new arrival, continued to read. The prelate was about to retire unnoticed as he had come, but it would have looked improper in him to do so, and Don Giacomo gave him no time for it; raising his head, he saw him, and cried:

"Ah! welcome, our Guido!"

"You are having a literary club here; but be careful, for in Rome literary meetings never end well."

"There is no danger," continued Don Giacomo; "we have here a family circle, and by your addition we remain such, I hope."

"I hope so with all my heart; and since it is so, be kind enough, Lady Luisa, to continue your reading."

Indeed, Monsignore Guido Guerra was considered as being one of the Cenci family, because betrothed to Beatrice; this news was soon spread among the young Roman noblemen, and they called him a fortunate man, and envied his happy state. Even at Court it was known, but the Pope was much incensed at it, both because he had selected him, knowing him to be very capable and of refined manners, to send as ambassador to some foreign court, and because he had not first asked his consent, or at least consulted him; and it displeased him the more to hear him proclaimed as the *fiancé* while seeing him still in priestly garments, since one of the points most strongly contested among the Roman Catholics and has been, and still is, the celibacy of priests. Maffeo Barberini, a Cardinal of great influence, and very intimate with Guido, gave him warning of what was talked at Court concerning him, in order that he might govern himself accordingly; Guido then, having inquired if the address of Beatrice to the Pope had been presented, and learning that it had not, was cautious enough to withdraw it from the office, fearing lest, coming to the knowledge of Clement, it would only excite a nature already too suspicious.

Guido, with easy familiarity, approached Beatrice to take her hand and kiss it; but she, instead of giving it to him, resolutely rose, asking him to follow her. She led him into the alcove of the window, so that the ample curtains hid them completely.

They remained there only an instant, and then came out one after the other, with such an expression in their faces as to make one believe thay instead of having tied the chain of love they had broken it violently and forever. In fact, both of them felt their hearts bound; both of them dragged a part of the chain, but still the links had been broken irreparably. A word of Beatrice had broken it as by a blow of an ax; by accepting the hand of the murderer of her father would she not be an accomplice of the homicide? This she thought, and this was the word she had spoken to her lover.

Guido, oppressed by sad emotions, stayed only a short time, then, making the excuse that business called him elsewhere, he left. Lady Luisa, noticing his confusion, and attributing it to one of those quarrels which increase love, said, playfully:

"Beatrice, do not be so hasty in throwing down the king of hearts; remember that a card badly played often makes one lose the game."

Monsignore Guido had hardly turned the corner of the street, when he met one of his valets coming hastily to find him. As soon as the servant saw him, he said:

"My Lord, His Eminence the Cardinal Barberini has sent a servant of the governor to the palace to find you immediately, and give you this pair of spurs."

"Spurs! And did he say nothing else?"

"Yes; he said that His Eminence, having returned from the country, had found Monsignore Taverna awaiting him in his palace; and after being closeted a long time with him, His Eminence had opened the door of the room, and, giving the spurs to the servant, saying, 'Immediately to Monsignore Guerra;' had reentered."

Guido stopped a little to think; then, as if struck by a sudden idea, exclaimed:

"I understand!"

In the Cenci house, after conversing for some time sadly, the group became silent. Suddenly a distant noise was heard—it increased—one could easily distinguish the tramping of a large number of men, mingled with the rattle of weapons. Don Giacomo, rising with wonder and fear, went toward the door to see what was the matter. Hardly had he halfway reached it when the doors were thrown roughly open, and a crowd of police filled not only the room where the Cenci family were, but the whole house. Some remained at the entrance with drawn swords, to forbid any one to pass.

"You are arrested by order of Monsignore Taverna!"

"Why?" asked Don Giacomo, with a voice which he endeavored in vain to render firm.

"That you will know at the proper time, in the examination. I am here only to execute orders. The Lady Luisa may remain; I have no order to arrest her."

In the courtyard the Cenci found several carriages ready, with the steps let down; they entered them by the uncertain light of the dark lanterns, and set out for their destination, surrounded by a crowd of police.

Guido saw the mournful procession pass; and on being told what had happened, overcome by passion, he was about to rush forward himself, if his good servant, holding him by the arm, had not said:

"Monsignore, you would lose yourself, and would not save them—while if you remain free you may be of use both to them and to yourself."

Guido exclaimed, groaning:

"Let us see where Fortune will lead us;" and walked toward his home. Arrived within a short distance, he sent his servant ahead with caution to see if any police were near. The servant returned and said there were none; he then entered his room, wrote an affectionate letter to his mother, in which he gave her notice of the impending danger, saying that it was necessary for him to hide himself from the hands of justice without losing time. Then, changing his clothes, and taking with him as much gold as he could carry, he went out of the secret door of his palace, designing to leave the city. He had not gone far before he met a band of police going toward his palace. They passed near him, but in the dress in which he was disguised they did not recognize him. He saw, however, that the affair was becoming serious; he dismissed his servant, and cautiously approached the Angelica Gate, but he retired hastily, noticing that several policemen near the gate examined minutely every one that went out. He wandered about the streets meditating various designs without concluding upon any. Presently he perceived a light in the cellars of a palace. Looking through the grating, he saw around a table a group of coalmen, who passed their time, as their fathers had done before them, in drinking and playing.

Guido, recollecting the innkeeper of Ferrata and the watchword he had given him, descended into the cellar. The coalmen were astonished, but Guido reassured them, saying:

"Long live Saint Tebaldo, and he that honors him!"

The coalmen looked one another in the face irresolutely. Then one of them, who was pleased with the aspect of Guido, said:

"Praised be he! but the labor of the coalman is great, the gain small."

"Saint Nicholas protects the coalman, and his gains multiply."

"The coalman lives in the woods, and is surrounded by wolves."

"When the coalman joins in a league with the wolves, they can descend into plains where the flocks feed and take the dwellings of the shepherds."

"Give me the sign."

"Here is the sign." And it was three kisses: one on the forehead, one on the mouth, the third on the breast.

"Good! You are one of us; there can be no mistake about it. Still, it seems strange, since our society is made up of desperate people bound together by poverty and by the need of defending themselves from the impositions of the powerful. But, perhaps you also are one of the persecuted ones. What do you wish? But before speaking further, follow me into a more secret place."

Guido thought he had misunderstood him, for he could not see a hole big enough to enter anywhere. He was soon enlightened, for the coalmen, clearing the heaps of coal and raising a stone from the pavement, opened the entrance to a lower passage. The coalman and Guido descended by a ladder, and immediately he heard the stone replaced and the coal heaped on the top again. In that room were collected goods and silver utensils of all kinds. The coalmen had been, from time immemorial, in league with the bandits of the country, and served them as brokers in the city; some of them exercised both trades.

Guido related to his new friend the danger he was in, and asked advice and help. It was the custom of the coalmen to move twice a week; when one caravan came into the city with a load, the other set out for the country. The coalman talking with Guido had arrived that very morning, and would depart from Rome in three days, toward evening. So he said:

"To-morrow I will send out of Rome one of our companions to see whether there is any news. You must shave your beard, cut your hair, and dress in some of our clothes, of the worst kind; we will dye your skin with a certain herb and blacken your face with coal-dust, so that you will not even recognize yourself. We have among us a companion who limps; he will teach you to imitate him in voice and motions. To-morrow, at daylight, you must go with two donkeys to sell coal about the city; if they call to buy of you, a few words are enough, because the bags contain just two hundred pounds, and the price is fixed at half a ducat a bag. You may also put a little stone in your mouth, and pretend to be chewing; in this way your cheeks will swell out, and so you will be better disguised. The people will mistake you for the lame fellow; at any rate, they will soon get accustomed to the sight of you, and thus I hope to get you safely out of Rome."

As among such people deeds are more than words, in a short time Guido was transformed by the coalman in the way he had described; and the next morning, one of the handsomest among the young noblemen of Rome might be seen changed into a coalman selling coal.

When the appointed day came, the coalmen left Rome without detention, and Guido with them.

CHAPTER XXII

THE FIRST VICTIM

THE carriages containing the Cenci family stopped. The door of the one in which Beatrice was, opened, and she was ordered to alight. While obeying the command, her foot on the steps, by the red light of the lanterns that the jailer and his assistants carried, she met, face to face, the marble image of the Saviour that she had noticed a few hours before over the gate of the prison Corte Savella. The afflicted girl stretched her arms toward it, exclaiming in a transport of grief:

"O God, have mercy upon me!"

Alighting, she bent her body to enter the gate of the prison. When she turned her head to see her friends, they were already far from her, and between them was a sea of armed men.

They made Beatrice pass through long galleries, ascend and descend stairs; then, at the end of a vaulted room, they opened a door and pushed her in; the door was immediately shut, the bolts drawn, and she found herself in a cold, dark, damp room; a true hell for the living. She did not move a step; she knew not where to turn; she recalled certain stories told of traps, by which, in those times less hypocritical but not less wicked than our own, they used to make away with those whom they dared not condemn. She was afraid, and stood firmly near the wall.

Suddenly the door opened, and a throng of rough men broke in, bringing water and some coarse utensils for the first necessaries of life. They offered her no consolation—said not a word; jailers and assistants returned as they had come, noisily shutting the door.

Beatrice noted the situation of the rough bed; she groped her way to it, and sat on the extreme edge. After a time the door of her prison was again opened, and the same men entered, bringing a straw bed, a woolen coverlet, and other articles, and went out as they had come, fiercely and savagely. Beatrice lay down upon the straw bed without a desire for anything, exhausted, stupidly impassible; she shut her eyes, but could not sleep; her heart was oppressed, but she could find no way of giving vent to her feelings, although the tears escaped from her eyelids. like a spring of water that starts out from under a stone.

At daybreak, when she rose to a sitting posture on her bed, she looked around the chamber in which she had been confined; it was a cell six or seven feet square, with a lofty ceiling, the middle of which ascended into a sharp point; in the upper part of this a hole was visible, grated with large iron bars, but whence the sky could not be seen, for it opened into a window which received its light from another. In this slaughter-house, an August noon seemed like a December evening, and an evening of December like one of the evenings of the far North.

A little later, they brought to her some coarse bread, sour wine, and a disagreeable soup, upon which floated pieces of fat meat and herbs. She tried once more to look on the faces of her jailers. One of them looked like an Egyptian hieroglyph, which presents a human form and a vulture's head; the other was more hideous still. Half an hour after these men had disappeared, a man very finely dressed entered the prison, preceded by the usual unbolting. He had large ears, a flat nose, and projecting lips, like those of a monkey. He examined the walls, the pavement, and the window diligently, and cast a glance on Beatrice also; he alone showing her a ray of compassion. Just as he was leaving the cell, she heard him say:

"This prison certainly cannot be called healthful, and besides, it is too dark; you will transport number one hundred and two to number nine, and furnish the room with suitable articles; for food, give her everything she may desire, within the limits of temperance, of course—do you understand? Neglecting this, you shall be punished with two blows of the rope, or more. Do you hear?"

Thus humanity itself assumed the appearance of ferocity and contumely. Beatrice thought that this person, whom afterward she found to be the superintendent of the prison, had given these orders in a loud voice so that they might reach her ear and comfort her; she therefore recommended him to God, having no other means of expressing her gratitude.

The removal took place as had been commanded, and Beatrice had in her new cell a piece of white bread and a ray of pure sunlight; with these human creatures can at least live, or wait until the ax or affliction shall kill them.

For three days Beatrice was left in peace, if it could be called peace; the fourth day, toward nine o'clock, new intruders appeared. These were two men dressed in black; one remained a little distance behind, and Beatrice hardly saw him; he seemed of savage mien; the other, of light complexion, with a forehead like porcelain and half-shut eyes, appeared a compassionate man—at least by his frequent sighing and the crossing of the fingers of one hand upon the other, as if praying. This man introduced himself as the physician of the prison; he questioned her particularly about her health, looked at her attentively, examined her pulse and her tongue; then he congratulated her on her good constitution, offered her snuff from a box, upon the cover of which was represented a beautiful miniature of the Heart of Jesus; exhorted her to be of good cheer, for her sorrows would soon cease; and also added that she might ask of him anything she wished; then, after recommending her to the great Mother of God, he went out.

"This gentleman also seems kind," said Beatrice, consoled.

"Although at first sight," said the doctor, in the corridor, to the criminal notary, for such was his companion, "I was fully convinced there was no need of a careful examination, still, I wished to make it, for, you understand, humanity precedes all things—and the soul is of importance."

"Yes, I understand!—the soul, and the body also—of course!—and you can assure her, eh?"

"Certainly, she is able to sustain the torture. Her pulse beats regularly, and gives no indication of weakness."

"Of course; but for the sake of formality, you will be kind enough, most excellent doctor, to give me the usual little certificate, in order to file it in the process, that we may proceed with all legal forms prescribed by the reigning laws."

"Willingly most illustrious Sir Notary; these scruples honor you; we must consider that one day posterity will read this trial, and it is important that they should see with how much regularity and regard we worked for the sacred rights of humanity."

"And justice," added the notary; "thank God, we do not live in barbarous ages!"

Even these men thought they were civilized, and boasted of it. The notary, with the certificate of the doctor in his hand, went into the room of examination.

This was a vast hall, which perhaps had once been an oratory; at one end, over a platform of wood, stood the bench of the judges, covered with black cloth; the leather of the high chairs was black also; behind the head of the presiding judge hung from the walls a large black crucifix, carved in wood.

As none of the judges had yet made their appearance, the good notary began to arrange things in order; he placed the big chairs with symmetry; laid upon the table before the President the certificate of the most humane doctor, and the hour-glass.

A short distance from the bench, a strong balustrade of iron separated this space from the remaining hall; and here might have been seen another man, also preparing the instruments of his profession, as by virtue of sympathy; and this was Master Alessandro, the celebrated executioner of Rome. Master Alessandro was powerfully proportioned; his lips were thin and compressed, partly by nature and partly by the long habit of being silent. On the whole, his face showed harshness, rather than brutality; it was of a degenerate type, but still a Roman one.

In the room were several poles, with a transversal arm, and on the ends of the latter hung blocks with bronze wheels, and ropes adapted to draw up weights; on the ground lead weights were scattered, which were fastened to the feet to give the torture of the rope with a hard shake; and many other instruments of torture. Master Alessandro passed them all in review before him and put them in proper order. The notary and the executioner, each on his side, prepared to celebrate becomingly the judicial solemnity.

In the meanwhile, another notary and two judges arrived; who exchanged the usual salutations and spoke at length of the weather, the season, their health and that of their families. One of them, Cesare Luciani, a very ugly man, with a head that looked like a basket and a face of greenish hue, said that the chill air had increased his gout and cough; and the notary, Ribaldella, who considered him as a protector, cautioned him to have a care of his precious life. He, grumblingly, answered:

"We will try to—we will try to, Giacomino;" and we cannot say whether he said this through wonder, fear, or satisfaction that a human being lived who felt, or feigned to feel, an affection for him.

Another judge (and this one had the reputation of being very kind-hearted), with staring round eyes, and so red in his face that he looked like a pitcher of wine left through carelessness upon the table of Lady Justice, interrupted the conversation by narrating how he had been obliged to sit up all night on account of his sick dog.

"What can I do?" he added; "this is all my own fault; I am tender-hearted; I really was not born to be a criminal judge."

And the flatterer Ribaldella:

Your Honor, he who does not love animals does not love men."

"Certainly, Giacomino; last night," Judge Luciani said, between one cough and another, "last night four murders and six robberies were committed. We are upon the tracks of certain witches; and if we put our hands upon them, I can tell you that we will make a famous trial of it. These trials, thank God, grow more common every day, and soon we shall have another Giordano Bruno sent to the flames."

"It seems impossible! You know everything, you are informed of everything—one cannot tell how you do it! Eh! such energetic men as you never will be born again," cunningly observed Ribaldella. And Luciani:

"It is a passion that I had even from a boy; but you see, I pay for my curiosity with the gout."

"Will you take some snuff?" interrupted the notary, whose name was Bambagino Grifi, vainly displaying a magnificent snuff-box.

"Beautiful! Splendid!" exclaimed the bystanders. "This is a new one. How many have you collected, now?"

"I only need a dozen more to make three hundred and sixty-six, when I shall stop. And this one—whose work do you suppose it is? Listen! no less a person than Benvenuto Cellini."

"Master Alessandro, have you oiled the rope?" asked Judge Luciani of the executioner, who nodded.

"His Honor the Lord Chief Justice!" cried an usher, opening the door; and all, stopping their conversation, turned toward the newly arrived.

Ulisse Moscati advanced with heavy and slow steps. His manner did not come from vain pride; in spite of the long exercise of his unfortunate profession, whenever he approached the judges' bench he had always felt a sort of shudder. By nature he was inclined to compassion; family reasons had obliged him to exercise an office from which he revolted; and thus, between doing a thing and abhorring it, he had reached that part of life where, the vigor of mind extinguished, habit takes the place of the will; now he failed in strength to discard his old habit, and, like most tired men, allowed himself to be carried by the current of external events. He had the reputation of eminent legal wisdom in his time, and he deserved it; since, at that time, everywhere, and particularly in Rome, a knowledge of scholastic sophistries was called science.

Judge Moscati, having saluted his colleagues and minor officers courteously, took his seat on the bench, where the first thing his eyes fell upon was the certificate of the physician regarding the state of Beatrice's health; he read it twice, then said, quietly:

"It seems, then, that should there be any need of it, we can, without scruples of conscience, subject this unfortunate girl to the torture."

"Certainly," replied Judge Luciani; "precisely so."

"I doubt, however, whether it may be applied to her legally, because the accused is but little over fifteen. Upon which I desire to learn your opinions, gentlemen."

"For my part, I am fully convinced," began Luciani, "and have no doubt at all. I will say, however, in all conscience, and in conviction of what I feel to be the truth, if we consider the right, by common consent we find it established that age is of no account in cases *atrocioribus;* and since parricide is a most atrocious and dreadful crime, in full conscience we can then omit in this trial the rules of an ordinary process. Besides, gentlemen, malice in woman is shown earlier than in man, like puberty; in fact, the law considers a woman of age at eleven years, man at fourteen; nor is the question of malice to be solved according to the age, or by abstract presumption, but according to the proof of the facts. For these reasons the solemn judges of the ancient Areopagus wisely condemned to death the boy thief of the golden crown of the temple of Minerva, for having known how to distinguish the leaves of the true laurel from the leaves of gold. And so, I think, and you all, my honorable colleagues, will be persuaded, that a greater depravity than that shown by these most wicked children, in the murder of their father, would be difficult not only to find, but even to imagine. If, then, we wish to abide by the law, a number of instances can be shown in which the age was no obstacle; among which I am pleased to record one which gave occasion to Sixtus Fifth, a truly great Pontiff, to proffer golden words. Monsignore, the Governor of Rome, caused the Pope to consider, with due respect, that the Florentine boy guilty of resisting the police of Trastevere could not be condemned to death because he was not of the age established by law. 'If he needs nothing but years,' said the blessed Sixtus Fifth, 'you may let him be executed, for we can give him ten of our own.'"

Chief Justice Moscati could not find any good reason to oppose; so, looking down, he ordered:

"Bring in the prisoner Beatrice Cenci."

And she was brought in. Surrounded by guards and immediately turned toward the bench of the judges, she did not perceive the instruments with which the hall was hung. Those present fixed their eyes eagerly upon her; and, struck by her divine appearance, wondered how so much depravity of mind could be accompanied by such beauty of form. All thought so, except two alone, who had the courage to think her innocent; these were Judge Moscati and the executioner Alessandro.

The notary Ribaldella soon began to question her, and she replied neither timidly nor boldly; but properly, like one who felt the dignity of her own innocence.

"Swear her!" ordered the chief justice.

Ribaldella, seizing the crucifix in such a manner that he appeared rather to wish to strike her than to present it to her to fulfil a solemn rite, said:

"Swear!"

Beatrice, extending her soft white hand, said:

"I swear upon the image of the Divine Redeemer, who was crucified for me, to tell the truth, because I know it and can say it; if I could not, or would not, I should have abstained from swearing."

"And this justice expects from you. Beatrice Cenci," the chief justice began, "you are accused, and the proofs in the trial show it sufficiently, of having premeditated the murder of your father, Francesco dei Cenci, with the connivance of your stepmother and brothers. What have you to answer?"

"It is not true."

She pronounced these words with such sincere simplicity, that St. Thomas himself would have been satisfied; but Judge Luciani growled:

"It is not true, eh?"

"You are accused, and the proofs in the trial show it sufficiently, of having, in company with your relatives, conferred a commission on the bandits Olimpio and Marzio to kill Count Cenci, with the promise of a reward of eight thousand golden ducats; of which one half should be paid upon the spot and the other half after fulfilling the crime."

"It is not true."

"Wait a minute, and we shall see whether it is true or not," murmured Luciani.

"You are charged, and from the trial it is sufficiently proved, with having given to Marzio, in addition to the prize, a red mantle embroidered with gold, which had belonged to the deceased Count Francesco Cenci."

"It is not true. My father gave that mantle to Marzio before he started from Rome for Rocca Petrella."

"You are charged, and from the trial it appears sufficiently proved, with having caused the paternal murder to be committed at Rocca Petrella on the ninth day of September in the year one thousand five hundred and ninety-eight, and this by express command of Lucrezia Petroni, your stepmother, who prevented its being committed on the eighth day on account of its being the festival of the Blessed Virgin. Olimpio and Marzio entered the room where Count Francesco Cenci slept, to whom had been given wine with opium; and you, in company with Lucrezia Petroni, Giacomo and Bernardino Cenci, awaited in the anteroom the consummation of the crime. The ruffians, returning to you, frightened, you asked them what was the matter, to which question they replied that they did not feel courage enough to kill a man while asleep. You then reproached them with these words: 'What! if, prepared, you are not able to kill my father sleeping, imagine whether you would dare even to look in his face if he were awake! And to come to this conclusion you have already received four thousand ducats? Since your cowardice is so great, I myself with my own hands will kill my father, but you will not live long.' Upon which reproach and menace, the ruffians re-entered the room where Count Francesco Cenci lay, one of them put a great nail over his eye and the other drove it first into his head and then into his neck, which caused the death of the said Count. The assassins, having received the remainder of their price, departed; and you, in company with your brothers and stepmother, dragged the body of your dead father over a parterre, whence you threw it into an alder tree. What can you answer?"

"My lords! I reply that charges of such horrible atrocities might more properly be made against a pack of wolves than me. I deny them with all the power of my soul."

"You are accused, and the trial shows it, that you consigned to Laurenza Cortese, nicknamed La Mancina, a sheet drenched with blood in order that she might wash it; and you are accused also of having caused Olimpio to be killed by the bandit Marzio, for fear that the former might reveal the crime to justice. Answer!"

"Am I allowed to speak?"

"Rather it is imposed upon you to do so; speak openly all that may be of use to enlighten justice and defend yourself from the accusation."

"My lords! That I was not educated to such horrors there is no need of my saying; I will speak to you sincerely, as my heart dictates, and you will excuse my insufficiency. I am only sixteen years of age; I was educated by my most pious mother, Lady Virginia Santacroce and by Lady Lucrezia Petroni, well known for her piety; neither my years nor the teachings of others could persuade anyone to suspect me guilty of the atrocious crimes which could hardly be equaled by the Locustes, and other famous criminals, who were hardened to crime by degrees. Granting even that nature wished to create in me a prodigy of wickedness, consider, if you please, that so atrocious a disposition could not have been so concealed but that it must in some measure have appeared, as a novice at least, before it was deeply rooted in the path of wickedness. What I may have been, and how I have lived, it will be easy for you to ascertain by asking any of the friends, relatives, and servants of the house. My life is a book composed of only a few pages; turn them over, read them attentively, and wholly. If I am not mistaken, it seems to me that in order to judge human actions with discretion it is necessary to find out the causes that may have induced them. For what end, then, do you imagine I was urged to commit so enormous a crime? For desire of money? The greater part of the property of the Cenci family is entailed, and goes to the eldest. The benefices, prebends, and such other offices cannot be inherited by women. It was unknown to me that my deceased father had disposed by will of his free estates in favor of pious places; as he died a violent and sudden death I must have supposed him intestate; and from this property likewise, as a woman, the laws would have excluded me. My property comes to me from my mother, and my father could not take it away; and, between dowry and overdowry, I have heard that it amounts to about forty thousand ducats: thus you see that avarice could not have prompted me. I do not deny —I rather confess—that my father made me pass days full of bitterness, and—but religion forbids children to look at the paternal tomb to curse it; therefore I abstain from saying too many and unworthy words about this. Be this enough: if I wished to escape from daily torments and procure a less sad life, among bad counsels that of parricide seems to be the worst; for besides eternal perdition to the soul in the next world, it would have been full of remorse, dangers and fear in this. Domestic examples were not wanting of plans well contrived which would teach me a way of defending myself from paternal persecutions. Olimpia, my elder sister, had recourse to the benignity of His Holiness, and by means of a humble address obtained honorable marriage with Count Gabbrielli of Agobbio: and, following her example, I wrote a supplication and intrusted it to Marzio, hoping he would be able to present it at the office of the memorials."

"Do you know whether your supplication was presented?"

"Sir, I recommended it to Marzio to have it delivered."

"And why did you trust Marzio with a commission so important?"

"My father kept me shut up; so that, excepting Marzio, in whom alone my father trusted, I was not allowed to speak to any other person."

"Continue!"

"And—supposing that nature had given me the brutality, my father the motive, and the devil the occasion to commit the crime—tell me, can you imagine a more absurd manner to accomplish it than that which the accusation depicts? Why use an iron nail? With eight thousand ducats one could easily buy poisons which kill like apoplexy, or destroy like consumption, without leaving any traces to the investigations of justice. But what do I say of poisons? The accusation says that I did procure them; and not only procured, but administered them. But if I gave my father wine and opium to make him sleep for one night, it would have been easy enough to increase the dose in order that he might never awake in this world. What need was there of so many dangerous operations? What need of assassins? And above all, what need was there to call into the secret of the plot Bernardino, a boy twelve years old? What aid could he have been to us, or rather, in how many ways might we not expect him to be of injury to us? If in the house of Cenci there might have been an infant, the accusation would probably have held him also as an accomplice; as if, tired of maternal nourishment, with cries and plaints he desired to be nourished with his father's blood! These accusations seem to me, and are, absurdities. Don Giacomo, when the sad accident happened, was in Rome, and he can give sufficient proof of this. I have explained in regard to the mantle. Of the sheet it may be so; I heard it talked about at the time, but I will add that the washerwoman merely confessed that a woman of about thirty years consigned it to her. Now am I neither thirty years old, nor do I look so—at least I did not look so before having gone through so many sorrows—and the place that the washerwoman asserted was spotted excludes the suspicion that the stain came from the head of a person lying down. My lords! you are able men, and versed in these matters; therefore I do not doubt you will refuse to believe such knavery. What need was there of the nail and hammer? Assassins always go fully armed with knives and pistols; imagine, then, whether they would have left them behind when they came purposely to commit a homicide. It is true that the nail was used to kill Sisera; but Jael was not an assassin, nor did she await the enemy in her tent. Why should we have dragged the corpse, while we were surrounded by strong men? Perhaps you will say an instinct of brutality induced us to it! Things out of the natural order must not be supposed; and the thought of wife and daughter dragging the body of husband and father, as two wolves would drag a rabbit, would have moved the assassins themselves to smile and shudder. If here you have hearts," and with one hand she touched her side, "if here wisdom," and with the other her forehead, "not only will you cease to afflict my disconsolate soul with such accusations, but you will take care not to confuse my mind with the thought of so many monstrosities."

Beatrice spoke fluently, with a beautiful intonation of voice, and noble manner. The bystanders, with their arms leaning on the benches, their bodies inclined, and their heads stretched forward, stood in admiration; even the notary Ribaldella, with his left hand firm on the papers and his right suspended on high, had remained without writing; even Judge Luciani had exclaimed wonderingly:

"How quick one learns in the devil's school!"

"I warn you," began the Chief Justice Moscati, "to maintain your promise of confessing the truth, and to observe the sacredness of the oath, since your accomplices have already revealed the crime and ratified the confession by the trial of the torture."

"What! Then, because of the pains of the torture, they did not abstain from adding a sin to their souls, and have made themselves infamous forever! Ah! the torture does not prove the truth!"

"What! the torture does not prove the truth?" broke forth Luciani furiously, unable to contain himself any longer; half rising from his seat and leaning his hands upon the arms of the chair to support his trembling body. "The torture does not prove the truth, when all legal authorities proclaim it to be the best of proofs? You will soon see whether it has the virtue to make one confess the truth."

Beatrice shook her head, as if an evil wind had covered it with dust, then continued:

"Lady Lucrezia, already advanced in age, educated in luxury, of a weak mind, not foreseeing future evil, for the sake of avoiding the present may have been easily induced to confess falsely. With Bernardino, a boy, there was no need of torture to make him confess whatever was wished of him—a little confectionery would have been enough. Giacomo, too, has for a long time been tired of life, and at other times has attempted to throw it away, as a load too heavy for him. Such have been those whom you have tried with the torture, and you presume to have discovered the truth!"

"Not these alone were your accomplices," added Moscati, "others also have confessed."

"Who?"

"Marzio."

"Very well; let Marzio come before me, and let us see whether he dares to sustain it to my face. Although I may suppose this man capable of the most horrible deeds, if I do not hear him myself I refuse to believe so much iniquity."

"Very well; you will be assured of it."

"Alas!"

And this seemed a sigh that would have broken the heart of him who uttered it. Beatrice had turned her eyes and seen what she had not before perceived—the preparations of the infernal instruments, and she shuddered from head to foot. Under one of the scaffolds stood Marzio, or rather his shadow; excepting his glassy eyes, every other part of the body seemed dead. He endeavored to throw himself at the feet of Beatrice, but was not able to move a step, and fell with his face to the earth. Beatrice stood a moment staring at him with a wild look; her foot advanced as if to spurn him; but immediately her anger changed to pity, and she stretched her arm to help him rise. Then with a hardly audible voice Marzio murmured:

"My sweet lady, am I still worthy of your pity? O Lady Beatrice, have compassion upon me for the love of God; for I am miserable."

"Marzio, why did you accuse me? What had I done to you that you should have conspired with the others to take away my reputation?"

"Ah! I know only too late the divine hand that chastises me; late—for innocence alone can give us happiness. I took another course, and I have caused with my own hand the ruin of others. I killed Olimpio fearing that the shameless wickedness of that man might have offended you, and the contrary has happened. But I swear, by that God who is soon to judge me, that I never had the intention of harming you. Tired of life, worn out by disease, gnawed by the remorse of crimes committed, benumbed by torments, I heard nothing of what they read to me, and made me affirm; I confessed all that they wished, on condition that they would put me to death, and immediately; they did not keep the promise, and have converted my words into poniards to thrust them into the hearts of innocent beings."

"Your Honor," interrupted Judge Luciana, "I hope you have not called us here to listen to the recitations of eclogues between Amaryllis and Melibœus."

"Be patient," Chief Justice Moscati mildly admonished him, "and remember that we have not come here for amusement; and since we have the terrible power of cutting short words with an ax, let us allow these unfortunate ones the free vent of tears."

"But the State certainly does not pay us in order to have us waste our time in words," said Luciani, "and if we are to continue in this manner, I must ask permission to go and attend to other business of greater importance."

"Sir, you may go—and God be with you!"

But the judge did not avail himself of the leave of the chief justice; he rather seemed to sit with greater ease upon his chair. Meanwhile, Moscati turning to Marzio said:

"Prisoner, answer briefly: do you ratify, or not, your deposition in regard to this accused person?"

"My Lords Judges! the harm which you can do me may be great, but short. You may shorten the thread of this life, but not lengthen it. Learn the truth as He knows it who shall judge me and you also. Who Francesco Cenci was, many among you ought to know, for you must have been present to try and judge him for his shocking crimes. The days of his calendar were crimes each more atrocious than another; his sport was to trample upon all laws, human and divine. Such was Count Cenci: and who among you is ignorant of it? One day this devil robbed me of my bride, beautiful, fresh, and full of life; he restored her to me—yes, he restored her to me—but a disfigured corpse, with a dagger in her breast which passed from one side to the other. I assailed his castle, and not finding him there, I destroyed his house and burned everything that fell under my hands. I left the country, swearing to revenge myself by the blood of his family and his own. I came to Rome, endeavored to enter into his service, and succeeded: I succeeded also in gaining his confidence; by what means it is not necessary to tell—it will be enough to say that they were deeds to frighten even the devil. There, while I was planning how to fulfil my revenge, I discovered the inexpressible affliction of his family. He hated his children as enemies; he besought God and the angels to grant him, before dying, the favor of seeing them all killed. Go to the Church of San Tommaso and you will find the sepulchers he had caused to be prepared for his children, whom he desired to bury there.

"Only one creature he loved. Did I say he loved? I have said wrong, and still I cannot express myself differently. I fear to have said little, but I could say no more without covering my face for shame—but I cannot raise my hand to my face, for you have broken my arms with tortures. He loved Beatrice. Prisons, hunger, beatings, and worse — corruptions, flatteries and abominable images—all did this infamous old man use to contaminate this angel of purity. Then compassion for the unhappy family which I had sworn to exterminate conquered me, and in one day alone I prevented more crimes than you perhaps have judged in one year. When news arrived of the death of his sons Felix and Christopher, he had the courage to prepare a banquet for his relatives and friends, where for what he said and did it seemed a miracle that Rome did not fall upon him. When the guests, urged by terror, left the hall deserted, he, more intoxicated with impiety than wine, dared to lift his wicked hands upon Beatrice. That would have been his last day—for I behind him raised a vase of silver to crush his head—if this innocent girl, screaming, and protecting him with her arms, had not saved him. I was moved by her ardent prayers not to attempt the life of her father, but I did not wish to give up my revenge. I resolved to leave the house, and surprise him elsewhere. But the malicious old man had begun to suspect me; and, pretending friendship, sent me to Rocca Petrella to prepare his rooms.

His rooms!—He had already commissioned some assassins to murder me on the road, and meanwhile he cautiously gave me the red mantle embroidered with gold; and although I refused to accept it, as it seemed unbecoming to my state, he wished I should take it to preserve myself from the influence of the malaria in the Campagna of Rome—so he said; but he intended the red mantle should serve as a signal for the assassins. I saved myself from his snare and planned one for him.

"I did not give up my fierce idea but still thirsted for revenge; and one night, having first well reconnoitered the place, taking with me two companions, I entered the castle of Rocca Petrella through a window in the lower floor, breaking through the iron grating: there we separated to look around the house; one of my companions saw a form cross the room; he hid himself in the dark, and then followed it in the distance: the form ascended the stairs of the tower, opened a room, and entered: my companion hastened after it; he touched the door, it yielded; either because the man wished not, or forgot, to shut it, considering himself safe. In this place Count Cenci kept his daughter Beatrice imprisoned. Ought I to say what drove the wicked old man there? No—you are all fathers—it would make your flesh and bones creep with horror!—my companion rushed upon him, killed him with a knife, less for the sake of my revenge than to revenge nature. He did right, and any one of you that would affirm he would not have done the same, I declare him here, in the presence of Christ, more a traitor than he that struck him. We dragged the accursed corpse out; we hurled him down from the terrace upon the tree.

"Lady Beatrice was awakened by the noise of his fall on the pavement. The sheet remained spotted with the Count's blood: but she neither saw it, nor gave it to the washerwoman, because she fainted in her prison; and removed thence more dead than alive, she lay many days in bed afflicted with the fiercest convulsions. I killed Olimpio—how and why I told you before. At Naples I confessed what they wished, on account of the tortures; but what I say now is the truth—everything else is false. Now do what you will with me. Meanwhile concluding, I thank God with all my heart, for having given me breath enough to finish—for I could not begin again." And saying this, he would have fallen again to the ground, if Master Alessandro had not quickly supported him.

"Tell me, your Honor, is there not some danger that she may have bewitched him?" whispered Luciani, with an air of mystery, in the ear of Moscati; and as the latter shrugged his shoulders without answering, Luciani continued to grumble: "Well, well—you do not believe such things; they seem to you nonsense—be careful not to allow yourself to be dazzled by the obscure light of the age, for I can tell you that scepticism clears one path alone, and it is that which leads to hell."

The petulance of Luciani displeased Moscati; still, hearing his faith doubted, since in those times to believe in witches was an article of faith, as he was a very pious man he started, and resolutely asked Luciani:

"Sir, what reason have you to doubt of my believing in witchcraft? I do certainly believe in it; but it seems to me that this is not a case of it. Then you persist in retracting your confession, prisoner?"

Marzio nodded his head.

"Definite torture—there is no remedy," observed Luciani, readily; and Valentino Turchi repeated loudly:

"There is no remedy; definite torture."

Moscati, taking out his handkerchief, wiped the perspiration from his brow; then turning to the notary he said:

"Sir Notary, warn the accused not to insist on his retraction; warn him that otherwise the law requires that he should be exposed to definite torture—warn him what definite torture means—and in case he should persist, draw up the decree."

The good man spoke these sentences sighing, and the notary in clear language repeated them to Marzio; explaining besides that definite meant to subject him to torments even unto death. Marzio assented even to this with his head, because his swollen tongue now prevented him from speaking. The decree being drawn up, read, and subscribed, Notary Ribaldella, turning first toward Luciani, who winked pleasantly at him, said to the executioner:

"Do your duty."

Master Alessandro took the arms of Marzio; drew them behind his back; placed one over the other, bound them with a cross tie; shook the rope to be assured that it ran smoothly in the block, and then, taking his cap off, asked:

"Your Honors, with the shock, or without it?"

"The devil! with the shock, of course, and a good one," replied Luciani, who could not contain himself.

The others nodded their heads.

Master Alessandro, assisted by one of his aids, pulled up Marzio very slowly. Beatrice bowed her face upon her breast in order not to see; but forced by an internal motion she raised it: "Horrible! horrible!" Screaming, she covered her eyes with both her hands. The executioner let go the rope. Marzio fell heavily to within four inches of the pavement; tremendous was the shock, and a hoarse groan issued from his throat. In truth it had been one of the most famous shocks that Master Alessandro had given in his life; if he was pleased or sorry could not have been divined; he stood hardened and silent, gazing at his work.

"Come, Master Alessandro, well done—give him another shock," insisted Judge Luciani.

"It will not matter, your Honor; for death has given him the last shock."

"What? What? Is he dead?" indignantly cried Luciani. "Why did you let him die? Why did this fellow dare to die before annulling his retraction?"

Then he turned to the dead man as if to reproach him:

"Ah, you have escaped, ruffian! You died to cheat justice of the confession, and Master Alessandro of thirty ducats' fee for hanging you." Returning to the bench, with angry voice and gestures he cried to Moscati:

"Come, your Honor, let us strike the iron while it is hot; let us profit by the fear which terror must have infused into the mind of the accused; let us hear in what note she will sing with the sound of the rope," and he darted his eyes upon Beatrice like the tongue of a viper.

"Enough!" ordered Moscati severely; "I rule the trial; the sitting is closed;" and he moved to depart.

Beatrice, white as a winding-sheet, staggered as if falling, her lips turned black, and her eyes stared wildly; shortly after she shook her head, and raised herself again like a tree bent by the passing gust of wind; then courageously she walked toward the corpse of Marzio, stood before it, and looking fixedly at it murmured:

"Unfortunate man! You have not been able to save me; but I forgive you, and will pray to God to forgive you also. You have sinned much; but have loved and suffered much. You did not live for virtue, but have died for truth. I envy you—for my life is such that I envy the dead." She turned to the keepers, and with a firm voice added, "Now let us return to prison."

But the trembling of her flesh showed the tremendous emotion of her mind; her limbs quivered, and at every step she staggered. Master Alessandro, taking his cap from his head and keeping himself at a distance with dutiful respect, said to her:

"Lady, I know that you cannot touch me, and may it

please God that I may never touch you; but you have need of some one to support you; if you allow me, I will call such a person, upon whom you can rest without fear; she was born of an evil stock, and in prison; yet, nevertheless, she is a flower that could be presented to the Madonna—she is my daughter."

He called with a prolonged whistle; in a few moments appeared a girl, beautiful indeed, but white as wax.

"Virginia," said her father to her, "give your arm to this lady—she is as unfortunate as you."

Beatrice, looking the girl in the face, felt well disposed toward her; when she heard she was named like her mother, she smiled sadly upon her, and leaning on her arm walked toward her prison.

Master Alessandro purposely gave that terrible shock with the rope to Marzio, in order to let him die under the blow; and he succeeded as he had wished, considering the miserable state to which that unfortunate man was reduced—not, however, through cruelty; on the contrary, through pity. In order that the man might die soon, and with less suffering, the executioner threw away the thirty ducats he would have received for hanging him, which, for an executioner, was much.

CHAPTER XXIII

THE JUDGES

MISFORTUNE has an ill wind that runs before it and is called a presentiment; peaceful minds foresee it through a thousand indications, as birds feel the approaching storm; but others, continually excited by the changes of daily events, do not notice it, and misfortune falls upon them suddenly and unprovided for.

In vain did Judge Moscati shut his ears to the internal voice which continually said: "You throw away your trouble." The voice came back to discourage him, and through his mind thoughts passed like specters, which partly hid and partly showed their awful aspect; he dared not question them, and feared lest they should show themselves to him more openly; still, heaving a deep sigh, and begging heaven for a look of pity, he went to the palace of the Vatican. Having requested to be announced, he waited patiently full two hours, until the chamberlain of the Pope told him to enter, and, accompanied by him, he found himself in the presence of the Supreme Pontiff.

Either on account of the Pope's sight, or some other cause, the chandelier was surrrouned by a circle of green silk, in such a manner that the face of Clement VIII could not be seen, nor could be seen either Cinzio Passero or Pietro Aldobrandino, Cardinals, nephews of the Pope, who stood behind the back of his chair.

Clement was clothed with his cope of crimson velvet trimmed with ermine, and a garment of magnificent lace; the hood also was of crimson velvet; the toga, stockings and shoes were of white silk, and on the latter the golden cross was embroidered.

The old man with simple frankness opened his mind to the Pope in regard to the trials of the Cenci; he made manifest the uncertainty of the accusation, exposed the unlikelihood of the depositions, the youth of several of the accused, the facts not only discordant, but contrary to one another; and although he added several things of his own, he repeated the observations of Beatrice; and even dared to hint at the doubtful proofs which, according to his opinion, were derived from the tortures; since Marzio had confessed under the torture, but had also retracted his confession, and had died under it, in testimony that he had at last said the truth. The Cenci, then, excepting the girl, had confessed some things, and denied others, declaring they had accused themselves because obliged by the force of the pain. Wonderful, he added, was the simplicity of Beatrice, her language very powerful, her means of persuasion irresistible; so that for himself he judged her entirely innocent. These things he wished, as a duty of conscience, to signify to His Holiness, so that in his infallible judgment, he should advise what would be for the best. Bernardino, a boy twelve years old, he had tried with the torture, and he felt in his heart an unspeakable remorse and affliction. Beatrice he had not tortured, it seeming to him to be a mortal sin.

The Pope, in a milder voice than usual, praised Moscati for his good judgment; he promised to give full consideration to the thing reported to him, and, requesting him with kind words to return the next day at the same hour, dismissed him. Moscati, notwithstanding the singular demonstrations of benevolence, went away with a more despairing heart than when he had come. An internal voice, more pertinacious than ever, admonished him that he had thrown away his work and steps; educated in the school of experience, he knew well that the more men promise the less they fulfil.

Notwithstanding his presentiment, the good man went at the appointed hour next day, supplicating God that at least his good intentions might be accepted. He was received by the chamberlains with unusual obsequiousness; they signified to him that his Eminence the Cardinal of St. George, nephew of His Holiness, awaited him. The Cardinal Cinzio, educated early in state affairs, was famous in the knowledge of courtly address, so it is not necessary to say that he received Moscati with exquisite urbanity: he made him sit beside him, not without begging him at first to sit in his own chair, and said:

"I am happy, my lord Chief Justice, to be able to assure you, that your wise considerations about the trial of the Cenci have been very acceptable to His Holiness; they were a proof not only of your good heart, but also of your excellent judgment; and if he before had a great faith in you, his affection and esteem have increased a thousand-fold. The blessed Father wishes to avoid the asperities, though proper, of the glorious memory of Sixtus Fifth but he disapproves at the same time of the too great benignity of Gregory: he has seen with inexpressible bitterness that the evil plants, on account of the little care used during the war with Ferrara, have budded forth oftener and more malignant than ever in the bosom of his States: this his religion, and the duty which he owes toward God, forbid him to allow. Still it cannot be doubted, without offence to the lofty piety of the most blessed Father, that the experiments which in his supreme wisdom he has been pleased to adopt may not be akin to justice." Here suddenly changing his subject, with a more benign voice he continued: "The paternal heart of the Supreme Pontiff was deeply moved in considering the notable failing of the health of such a zealous servant, and so well deserving as your Honor; he has known with profound regret that misfortune has visited your house, and he desires, as much as can be granted to mortal hands, to alleviate your Honor's grief. He desires me to signify this to you: he is greatly edified by your zeal, my lord; but charity and justice do not consent to accept this more than human sacrifice."

"Ah! there are afflictions here within," replied Moscati—upon whom the mildly cruel words of the Cardinal had the same effect as the touch of a hand that undertakes to unbind a wound in order to see, not to cure it—"which men cannot console, but embitter. Only God can, and perhaps with that only remedy for all evils—death!"

"I believe it; hence I wonder so much the more how

you, oppressed by so much domestic grief, have strength enough to fulfil the duties of your office, which, laborious and by their own nature melancholy, instead of alleviating must keep sad thoughts in your mind."

"It is true; but I persevere because I have always believed, and do still believe, that in duty there is no difference between a soldier and a magistrate."

"This, which should be esteemed and commended as estimable goodness in the subject, would be a reproach and harshness in the Prince, who should not suffer a faithful magistrate to wear himself out in his work. Even the Romans, who were so active, when they arrived to that part of life distinguished by them with the name of *senior*, were allowed without shame to abandon public service. Toward evening every animal that lives upon earth ceases his work."

"And even I, your Eminence, desire to follow the usual tenor of the life of all creatures; not indeed to rest myself, for as to rest we shall have time enough for that in the grave; but rather to prepare myself with the meditation of divine things to that end, common to all of us, and desired by me more than any other mortal; but I would wish to carry my white hair to the grave without reproach."

"I advise you, in the first place, my dear brother in Christ, to give a listening ear to the call from above; besides, I assure you, that instead of blame, you cannot but receive praise from good men, and ample approbation from the most blessed Father, in the name of whom I proffer to you all those favors that you may desire as most fit to accomplish your worthy intention."

"Since your Eminence is pleased to console my afflicted heart with so much benignity, I declare that I feel a desire to give myself up to God in some convent of monks famous not only for sanctity but for useful works to their brothers in tribulation."

"And of these convents, my dear sir, the Catholic Church is so abundant, that there is no other trouble but that of choosing."

"May the Lord reward you for having instructed me! Shortly, if your Eminence will grant me, I will place in your hands a petition in order that His Holiness may dismiss me from my present office; and in presenting it, I beg your Eminence to explain to him the reasons that move me to this step, so that there may still be continued upon me the approval of the Father of the Faithful."

"Do not leave for to-morrow what you can do to-day, says a very old proverb. You have before you, my dear sir, all that is necessary for writing; there is no need of delay—be assured of my good depositions, and doubt not of the good intentions of the Holy Father toward you."

The judge, persuaded by this extreme haste, wrote the petition and consigned it into the hands of the Cardinal St. George, who received it with a smile; perhaps it was a smile of satisfaction, perhaps of scorn—it may have been both.

The Cardinal of St. George presented that same evening the petition to the Pope, who, placing it upon the table, pressed it down with his closed hand; and then said briefly to the nephew of his choice:

"Now, Cinzio, keep an eye on the other."

If, on the plains of Africa or Asia it happens that an animal dies, hardly does the first faint effluvia of corruption come from the carcass when, if you raise your head, you will see a black cloud appear, which at once spreading around you, shows to your astonished eye a flock of vultures, which are attracted to the foul banquet. Likewise cunning men, without fear of being deceived, discern their kind from afar; they soon recognize each other and help each other.

So Cardinal Cinzio Passero, wishing to bring out from the mean herd of magistracy a malignant beast, raised his nostrils, and detected Judge Luciani. He sent for him, and with his accustomed courtesy said to him that the Holy Father, his most glorious uncle, was never wearied of speaking with great respect of him, for his great learning, and particularly for the ready and salutary severity with which he accomplished business; he knew that Pope Sixtus, of holy memory, had held him in high estimation. As a sign of confidence in him, His Holiness wished to trust to him the trial of the Cenci, scandalously protracted, while, as was the general opinion, the proofs of the guilt of the accused were many and powerful. He must proceed, then, without delay, for he would do a deed acceptable to the Roman people and the Holy Pontiff; and thus merit the name of restorer of justice.

"Even owls sometimes are caught," says the proverb; and the Cardinal, extremely desirous of accomplishing his design, had used more fuel than was necessary. The eyes of Luciani sparkled like those of the wild beast before leaping upon his prey; and his words issuing forth impetuously impeded his speech.

"Certainly," stammered he, "certainly, your Eminence, with Lord Moscati there was no way of drawing out a spider from its hole; he had so many scruples and fears, that even I myself knew not what he was about. I found him even unwilling to apply to Beatrice Cenci the preparatory torture *monentibus indiciis*, while (God forbid that I should make a rash judgment!) it seems to me that there is proof enough to have her hanged (I beg pardon for the *lapsus linguæ*, she being a noble lady)—to have her beheaded, ten times."

"To think of it!" exclaimed the Cardinal, in astonishment, and raising both hands.

"And when I thought she may have been a witch, considering her shrewd talents and her eloquence of speech, not at all natural in a simple girl, he shrugged his shoulders as if I had uttered a heresy. Your Eminence knows that the devil when he enters the body of a person gives him the gift of language."

His Eminence, on the contrary, knew by the second chapter of the Acts of the Apostles, that the gift of language came from the Holy Ghost; still, it not being for his interest to contradict the judge, he approved by closing his lips and nodding his head.

"Repose upon me," continued Luciani, "as upon two pillows; I am accustomed to act quickly and well. When Pope Sixtus sent me to Bologna on the business of Count Peppoli, I had the honor of despatching the affair in less than a week."

"Well, your Honor may go now, and attend to this business, which I in the name of His Holiness recommend to you."

The new Chief Justice Luciani, bowing to the earth, renewed his alliance with dust, and took leave. In going home the coward trembled in his anticipated joy of being able to torment human beings, creatures of God, at will. If I affirmed that in his fierce and vile nature no desire existed for advantage to himself, with promotions and money, it would not be true; but such passion was secondary to that of tormenting.

Next morning, when it was hardly daylight, Luciani might have been seen entering the prison of Corte Savella accompanied by two old women, or rather furies, and going straight to the prison of Beatrice.

The sad girl lay absorbed in many thoughts, all of which ended in afflicting conclusions; she therefore, wearied and tired of life, continually prayed God to call her in pity from this martyrdom to His holy peace. Suddenly the door of the prison opened noisily, and the cruel faces of Luciani and his companions appeared before her.

He with short and bitter voice apprised her that they had come to see whether she had any witches' marks about her; therefore she must with good grace submit herself to the examination. He then went to a corner of the room, and thence, with his face turned toward the wall, ordered the two Megæræ to perform their office.

Beatrice, burning with anger and shame, wrapped herself in her blankets, and, binding them tightly to her body, refused to undergo the humiliating search. The two bigoted executioners did not stop for this, but, using their bony hands, tore the blankets and sheets away by force. The beautiful angel of love love fell naked into the power of those women.

"*Piscis a capite fœtit*," said Luciani from his corner; "so begin to examine her head: divide first her hair, look carefully at the skin.—Dorothea, clean your spectacles—I repeat to you for the twentieth time—you will find there a small livid or black spot little larger than a lentil—have you found it?"

"I find nothing," replied Dorothea, "except a mass of hair sufficient to make a wig for both of us, and some left."

"There would be enough for all three," observed the other.

"Look down now look on the neck, the chest, the shoulders."

"Nothing."

"What, nothing? It is impossible!"

"It is so. It would be easier for a buffalo to pass unobserved over the snow that a single hair over her white skin."

In this manner Beatrice was searched minutely, without their being able to discover the indicated sign.

"Truly," Luciani grumbled from his corner, "the masters of the art tell us that the devil usually impresses his mark on the bosom, or over the left leg; nevertheless, as he is not bound by any law, search with great care upon her back."

"Here is—we find"—

"What do you find, eh?" asked Luciani, hardly able to contain himself.

"We find on her side a mole surrounded by some fine hair of a golden color."

"Well! very well—although the masters of the art say that the mark must appear livid or black, it is well known that the Evil One, being a despiser of all laws, cannot subject himself to any fixed rule: especially as now having to do with me he must have understood it was a fight between Greek and Greek. Dorothea, take a pin, and put it first into the holy water."

The bigot, pulling out a long steel pin, put it, murmuring I know not what prayers, within a case of holy water. Luciani asked impatiently:

"Well, have you done?"

"Yes, sir."

"Now then, courage! thrust it softly in the infernal mark."

Beatrice wept with rage seeing herself reduced to such ignominy, and fiercely defending herself, struck first one, then the other of the women away from her; but they fell upon her more strongly than before. Feeling her flesh pierced with a pin, she broke forth in a fury, asking with agitated voice what foolishness this was; and added that she was a Christian like them, and a better one, too, and that they should be ashamed of tormenting a poor girl, who might have been their daughter, with such contemptible superstitions.

"Most Holy Virgin!" bleated Dorothea, still using her bold hands, "we wish no sort of evil to you, my dear sister in Mary; no, truly, we do it for your good—for the safety of your soul."

The examination finished, Luciani, recalling the women, without even turning a look upon Beatrice, went out with them from the prison reasoning seriously and learnedly about the power of the devil, to whom, according to his idea, the mercy of God had left too much power; then, giving a ducat to each, he begged them to pray for him to St. Gaetano, and beg him the favor of accomplishing successfully the important business which he had on hand. The two women went directly to the church, and prayed to St. Gaetano that he would deign to grant to the most holy brother in Christ, Chief Justice Luciani, the favor of being able to send legally to the scaffold all the Cenci family, not one excepted.

While the good Luciani stood in expectation of Divine favors, he did not leave untried earthly ones; for he appointed next morning that the other judges should meet him very early in the prison of Corte Savella; where he ordered the girl to be brought before him.

In the place remaining vacant by the promotion of Judge Luciani, they had appointed a certain person, more stupid than a post; he was neither good nor bad as a man; but bad enough as a judge, for, excepting for drawing his salary when due, he had never given himself the trouble to think of anything else; he always bent his will, like the sunflower to the sun's rays, to the part indicated him by his superiors.

Beatrice came before Chief Justice Luciani.

"Prisoner," began Luciani, with a plebeian manner, which he meant to render solemn, "you heard once before the charges against you; do you desire them to be again read to you?"

"There is no need of it; they are things which once read are never forgotten."

"Especially when one has committed them. Now, I warn you that by the confession of your accomplices you are fully proved guilty of your crime; so that justice, lawfully, could do very well without your confession."

"Then why do you so pertinaciously ask it of me?"

"I ask it for the safety of your soul; because, as a Christian and a Catholic, although an unworthy one, you ought to know that dying without confession you will be infallibly lost."

"What, sir! the care which you should take for the safety of your own soul gives you also time to think of mine! Leave every one to provide for the safety of his own as best he can. These are matters between the Lord and His creatures, and you have nothing to do with them. You, if you are convinced of my guilt, can condemn me, and that is enough."

"Prisoner! be on your guard, and remember that your bold manners before your judges can have no other effect than that of injuring your condition, already dangerous enough; and as for myself, they have no effect, for, besides having exorcised you according to the prescribed rules, I always carry about me a potent remedy against witchcraft and enchantments, had there remained any power in you to use them against me. Now, for the second time I ask you, will you confess, or not?"

"That which holy truth made it my duty to confess, I have already confessed; the falsehood you seek, with the help of God, in whose arms I trust myself, neither your torments nor your flatteries can draw from me."

"This is what we shall see. In the mean while I wish you to know that better heads than yours I have been able to set right. Notary Ribaldella, write: The most Holy name of God invoked, Amen. We decree, etc., before passing to ulterior trials, the torture of the *watch*, in the usual way, according to law, for forty hours, to which the prisoner, Beatrice Cenci, is to be submitted in place of the torture *ad quæstionem*, etc.; charging to assist in the above sad experiment, the notary Jacomo Ribaldella, for the first four hours; the notary Bertino Grifi for the second four hours; the notary Sandrello Bambagino for the third four hours; and in this way to begin again, succeeding each other, until the time decreed shall have expired or the confession of the accused occurs. Sign it."

Thus Chief Justice Luciani commanded, after signing the paper, which the notary gave him, and then passing it to the other judges; these signed it obediently, as if Luciani thought, felt, and deliberated for all three.

The watch was a wooden stool about a cubit and half high, with the seat sharpened diamond shape, about a foot square; the back likewise.

My history will not stop to narrate those things which the Vicars of Christ allowed, and not only allowed, but granted and promoted; the pen abhors to write them and the ink in tracing them would become red through shame. My history will rather speak of the superhuman courage and constancy of the glorious girl, who, in spite of the greatness of her martyrdom, remained firm in her purpose to die amid the tortures rather than contaminate her fame by the confession of a crime which she had not committed. Removing her, almost dying, from the torture, they took her back into her prison and replaced her in her bed.

There she was left two days. Her senses, brightening, would shine upon the past anguish; but the other, alas! more bitter, which remained yet to be passed, would darken all surrounding her with wavering uncertainty, like the light of a ship in a stormy night appearing and disappearing, alternately, upon the top or in the abyss of the waves, a fatal sign of approaching shipwreck to him who breathlessly contemplates it from the shore; only the sense of pain lasted, which with its pangs strengthened that firm soul not to yield, but to die in silence.

The third day the officers came for her whom Luciani called to new torments. By this time fully resigned to her destiny, she did not refuse to go; only begged them, with a soft voice, to be kind enough to wait until she could dress; and as the ruffians understood that undressed as she was they could not present her before the tribunal, they replied they would wait; however, she must hasten, since the judges were already on the bench, and it was not becoming in the prisoner to let them wait. While Beatrice, helped by the daughter of the executioner, dressed herself, she said:

"Listen, my dear Virginia! Since they call me, you know they do it in order to torture me; now, I strongly doubt but that I may die under the torture, as I saw it happen to poor Marzio; therefore, I intend not to recompense you for your charity, my dear Virginia, but to leave you a recollection of me. You will take all my linen and dresses that I have with me in prison—and here—take also this cross, which belonged to Lady Virginia, my mother, on condition that if I return alive from the torture, and can otherwise leave you a reminiscence of myself, you will restore it to me; since I desire it should be buried with me. Of these violets, alas! watered by my tears, and grown in the rays of the sun which penetrate but lightly and sadly through the grating of the window, you will, as long as they last, make every day a bouquet, and offer it to the image of the Holy Virgin which I keep at the head of my bed. Also—listen, Virginia," and here she blushed, and spoke in a lower tone, "you must know that I have—oh! no—I had a noble lover, handsome and good; I loved him—and he loved me, and I still believe that he loves me exceedingly—but we can never be joined on the earth—and I much doubt whether even in heaven we can—alas! it is not my fault! You will take this image, and endeavor to present yourself to Cardinal Maffeo Barberini, and tell him that I sent it to him in order that he might give it to his friend, and let him know, at the same time, that I often prayed before it for the safety of his soul; remember, bear it well in mind, so that you may not forget. And add, also"——

"Oh! do you suppose you are going to a ball? We have waited nearly an hour—come as you are."

Beatrice went; nor could Virginia answer her a word, for the haste of the officers prevented her and grief choked her; she accompanied her, weeping, to the door, and here, after kissing her, she stayed. Beatrice turned her head upon the threshold, and saw that the good girl had gone to kneel before the image of the Madonna, hanging under it the little cross of diamonds which had belonged to her mother, Virginia Cenci.

Chief Justice Luciani, with both his arms stretched out upon the table, like a dog when he rests, was reasoning thus to his honorable colleagues:

"It seems impossible! If I had not caused her to be searched diligently, I may say almost under my own eyes, since *honestatis causa*, I held my face turned to the wall, I could not persuade myself that she was not bewitched."

"But," observed Valentino Turchi, gravely, with ostensible humility, "permit me to observe that her hair was not shaved."

Luciani, turned suddenly his head towards Judge Turchi, like a dog bitten by a fly, with bitter voice answered:

"I did not have her shaved, because Del Rio, Bodino, and other most famous writers on necromancy, do not mention hair as a part upon which the devil generally exercises his power."

"Generally; and it is right," added Turchi; "but I have many times considered, on one hand God placed the great power of Samson in his hair, and on the other, that the devil always likes to imitate, and turn to evil what the Lord does for good; so, against the opinion, only a negative one, of the alleged authors, I have always been of the opinion that the hair can very well be chosen by the devil as a place for his abominable witchery; and finally, *utile per inutile non vitiatur;* and in such grave business the shaving of the head, with your permission, is never useless."

"Your doubt," replied Luciani, leaning his head as if convinced, and with a voice, wh' h ill-concealed his internal rage, "is not certainly without foundation, and"——

But here the notary Ribaldella, who was as an echo of the soul of his patron Luciani, aiding him in this difficulty, wrote upon a piece of paper, and with a humble bow passed it to him while he was about to end his speech. Luciani read it and his eyes flashed with ferocity and pride; he raised his head, but first turned it to his faithful servant with a look, that seemed wishing to bite him, but only meant for a smile; then to Judge Turchi, and continued: "and would deserve praise if it did not prevent us from trying the torture *capillorum*, which I intended to apply this morning: and you are too well versed in the practice of criminal trials not to know that this trial always produces the best effects.

Notary Ribaldella upon the scrap of paper had written: "And the torture *capillorum?*"

Judge Turchi in his turn bent his head confused; Luciani continued:

"For my part I am rather of the opinion that we should this morning begin by the torture *capillorum*, and according to what comes from it we will rule ourselves."

At the appearance of Beatrice, pale, with a suffering air, her eyes burning within a blue circle, Luciani, still in the position of a tired dog, endeavoring as much as it was possible for him to appear mild in his rough aspect and harsh voice, said:

"Gentle maid! how much my heart has grieved in being obliged to subject you to torture, God may tell you for me, for I could not express it in suitable words. I am a father of girls by age, if not by beauty, equal to you; and in seeing you tortured, not without fear I have asked myself: Luciani, what mind, what heart would yours be, if your own blood should be tormented thus? The duty of a magistrate, a feeling of humanity, the piety of a Christian persuades me to advise you to take compassion on yourself. Alas! have pity on your own youth. Of what use is your obstinate pride? I have told you, and repeat it now: the proofs in the process are enough to convict you as guilty; the confession of your own accomplices condemns you. Try to deserve with a sincere confession the mercy of the most blessed Father. Do not force me, Lady Beatrice, to use rigor; consider that the torments suffered by you are as pleasures compared with the atrocious tortures" (and here he gave free vent to his harsh voice) "which justice reserves for the stubborn."

"Why do you tempt me?" replied Beatrice calmly. "Is not the power which you have to lacerate my body enough—why do you strive to humble my soul? These are the qualities of the devil, not of a judge, or at least they should not be. My body is yours; a wild force places it in your power—torment it as you will; the soul my Creator gave me, and this, instead of being frightened by your menaces or deceived by your flatteries, comforts me to sustain more than you will be able to inflict."

The eyebrows of Luciani compressed like pincers; and striking with his open hands upon the table, he cried furiously:

"*Ad torturam capillorum!* Where is Master Alessandro? He must always be present before the tribunal when I preside."

"He has gone to Bassano on professional business, by superior orders; and left word that he would return during the day."

"When I most need, everybody leaves me alone. To you then, Carlino, I know you to be a well-deserving youth; do yourself honor now."

These words Luciani addressed to the executioner's aid, who answered ingeniously, rubbing his hands:

"Eh! we will try."

The truth was that Master Alessandro, taking the occasion which chance presented him, had gone from Rome. Two ruffians now fell upon Beatrice, unbound her beautiful blond hair, twisted, and tied it around a bunch of ropes as quickly as, beyond all imagination, horrible; and then they raised her from the ground! Chief Justice Luciani, without moving an eyelid, at every contortion barked out:

"Confess the crime!"

"My God!—my God!"

"Confess your crime, I tell you!"

"I am innocent!"

"Here—quick, the fine ropes—the torture of the fine ropes."

This was an infamous order; the bystanders were wearied of the spectacle, the executioners themselves tired of the labor; Beatrice gave no sign of life.

"The fine ropes, I tell you—the fine ropes!" roared Luciani.

The executioner's assistants stood motionless, and rage choked Luciani, who now only stammered indistinct sounds. The former in fact could not imagine the Chief Justice to be in his right senses; since the torture of the fine ropes consisted of an infinite number of small, thin and cutting ropes, with which they bound the tortured one in such a manner that, cutting the nerves, the flesh and veins, the body would become one wound; and it seemed evident that it could not have been applied to the victim without despatching her entirely.

Upon the threshold of the door, opposite the bench of the judges, appeared the livid face of Master Alessandro: he stopped awhile, turned a sad look upon the scene, and he seemed, although an executioner, to feel something, for in attempting to button his red dress his hand shook from one buttonhole to the other without being able to accomplish it: except this indication there was nothing manifest which could give one an idea of emotion: he coolly approached the patient, looked fixedly at her, and felt her pulse; this done, with that expression which could make not only the condemned but even the judges shudder, turning to Luciani, he said:

"Your Honor, let us understand plainly; do you wish the patient to confess or to die?"

"Die now?—God forbid! She must confess first."

"Then for to-day she cannot bear any more tortures."

"Master Alessandro," broke forth Luciani, maddened, "I think I know as much as you do of your profession, and"——

Notary Ribaldella, who hung to the fortunes of Luciani as to his anchor of hope, fearing some imminent scandal, with a hypocritical expression cut short his words, saying:

"Your Honor, who is such a famous master of proverbs, must remember what you have told me so many times, that, 'a bow long bent at last waxeth weak:' if your Honor allows me I would suggest"——

"Come, speak!" answered Luciani crossly.

Then Ribadella rose hastily from his seat, and approaching the ear of Luciani whispered his idea. It must have been a truly infernal one; since Luciani, who had listened with a disturbed expression, calmed himself at once, and almost smiling said to him:

"Giacomo, you will be sure to succeed." Then turning to the executioner, he continued: "Master Alessandro, you may suspend the tortures, comfort the patient, and endeavor to revive her. You, my honorable colleagues, be kind enough to await me a few moments on your benches." Saying this he disappeared.

About twenty minutes after, a sound of chains was heard from the corridor where Luciani had gone, and soon the door opened, and Giacomo and Bernardino Cenci with Lucrezia Petroni appeared, emaciated like persons who had suffered a great deal and had not yet recovered from the torments. Luciani followed them as a driver that follows the herd going to slaughter.

After the night of the arrest Giacomo and Bernardino had never seen each other, nor Lucrezia Petroni. Suddenly they heard the doors of their prison open, and found themselves, without knowing why or how, in each other's arms.

Luciani then notified them of what he termed the invincible obstinacy of Beatrice. This obstinacy of hers, added he, was a great obstacle to the conclusion of the trial, and consequently delayed the mercy of the Pontiff; they must aid in conquering her obstinate mind; he, as a friend and a Christian, not as a judge, begged them to induce her to confess; they must be assured that they had no better advocate to influence His Holiness in their favor than himself.

It is an easy thing to deceive those who trust! It is very pleasant to believe that which one desires! So much had these unfortunates desire of consolation that the brothers Cenci and Lady Lucrezia abandoned themselves entirely to the hands of Luciani; who, having become very mild, promised them they should not be separated again.

When the two Cenci and Lady Petroni saw the merciless outrage of the divine body of Beatrice, and herself like a dead person, they broke forth into unrestrained weeping, and kneeled around her, kissing the hem of her garments. Thus they remained a long time; when Beatrice revived, long before opening her eyes a sorrowful groaning smote her ears, so that she imagined she was where human souls become purged of their sins and worthy of ascending to heaven; which idea was the more confirmed when, regaining the sense of sight, she saw herself surrounded by the dear but emaciated faces of her beloved relatives: at which she, as if pleased, exclaimed:

"Finally then, thank God, I am dead!"

She shut her eyes again; but the sharp pain which tormented her too well told her she was still alive. She reopened her eyes, and said:—

"Alas! my beloved, in what a state do I see you again?"

"And we you, Beatrice? Alas! alas!"

After a little while Don Giacomo rose to his feet, and the noise of the chains around his body served as a mournful exordium to the following language, which he addressed to his sister:

"Sister, I beg you, by the cross of our Lord Jesus, not to allow such ill usage of yourself. Confess what they have made us confess. What can we do? I see no other way of escape; and, if nothing else, this pretended confession of ours will save us from tortures which have no end, and with one blow will cut short torments and life. The wrath of God walks over our heads: can we pretend to oppose that terrible power which uproots the mountains from their granite foundations, and blows them as the wind the grains of sand? I bend to the lash with which God scourges me, before whom I bow; and since to contend is of no avail, I endeavor to mitigate the rigor of my destiny with prayers, humility, and tears."

Bernardino sighing and raising his little hands imploringly, continued also:

"Do, Beatrice, confess for my sake; say everything these gentlemen wish, for then the Lord Justice has promised to let me be unbound, and to send all of us into the country for the harvest."

Lady Lucrezia, resigned, in her turn said:

"Trust in the Holy Madonna of Sorrows, my dear daughter; she alone is the consoler of the afflicted: and beside, who among us can boast of being spotless? We all are sinners."

Beatrice, as they begged her, by degrees turned her eyes around threateningly. By chance they happened to meet those of Luciani, which sparkled with malignant exultation—now almost sure of the success of his plan to entrap them. Anger, contempt, and above all, an infinite sense of disgust agitated the mind of Beatrice. Then resolutely and courageously she began to admonish her relatives in the following words:

"That you were not able to resist the trial of the torture, and bent to the first assaults of pain, and threw away your good fame, as the soldier abandons his sword in the day of battle, I have heard with infinite bitterness of soul; but I abstain from reproaching you: only allow me to turn severely to you, and ask why you wish me to share your shame? Two were to be queens of sorrows: one in heaven, the other on earth; and I am the earthly one. Do not envy, I beg of you, my crown of martyrdom, since I wear it more gloriously than if it were of gems. Listen! Holy men have taught us that we cannot turn murderous hands against our bodies, which are God's work, without doing violence to His supreme will: now, how much more sinful must it be in us to destroy with our own venomous tongues our reputation, which is the life of the soul! Pagan Rome saw a courtesan endure with great constancy unheard-of tortures, and biting out her tongue with her teeth she threw it in the faces of her executioners rather than disclose the conspiracy in which she had participated; and I, an honest and Christian maiden, shall I not be able to support torments in testimony of my innocence? Unfortunates! What do you hope to obtain by your cowardice? Perhaps to preserve your life? Do you not see that they wish it extinguished, not as an end, but as a means to lead to an intent already established; nor is our death enough to this intent, which they would have already given us, but it requires also our infamy? Now, have you thought what this intent may be? Who can look into the abyss of iniquity of the Roman court, and perceive all the dark designs that are planned therein? In my late agony a phantom crossed the darkness of my mind, and a thousand voices cried after it: 'Avarice! avarice!' The wolf having already tasted the property of the Cenci and finding it good, its hunger has increased. You will lose all; the spotless fame, which no one in the world could have taken from you, you have yourself thrown away; life and property, frail things and in the power of others, they will take from you when they think fit. I cannot prevent them from cutting short my days, and with my life stealing also my property, and even if willing, I could not prevent it; but my good name is in my own hand—they will not be able to steal this from me. While all that which belongs to earth has left me, behold two angels bind themselves closer to my spirit: the one who has the keeping of innocence, and the other who rewards constancy; I feel their power, dear ones, to be great over me, since not only they sustain me in the midst of the anguish of my torments, but they promise me as soon as these are ended to raise me kneeling upon their holy wings toward my Creator. Farewell, earth! farewell, crowd of malignant atoms, who call yourself men! farewell, time, briefest mark on the face of Eternity! A ray of celestial joy falls upon me and removes every pain. How happy I feel! I am satisfied! How sweet it is to die!"

And she fainted again.

No one dared to breathe. Luciani was astounded, having surprised his soul in the act of softening: abhorred compassion had for a moment caused in him the same effect which the Gentiles attributed to the head of Medusa. Ribaldella, with his face leaning over the bench, held a kind of pious truce with his perfidious thoughts; and notary Grifo, not to commit himself, mended the pens, but could not see to cut, because a tear loitered in the corner of his eye.

Beatrice with a sigh returned to life, and her relatives, kneeling before her, excited by admiration, pity, and shame, exclaimed sobbing:

"Beatrice!—holy angel!—oh, point to us the path to which we should keep to imitate you."

Beatrice rose a little, and, gathering her utmost strength, said in a loud voice:

"Know how to die!"

"And we will die," cried Don Giacomo, starting to his feet and shaking in the face of the judges the chains with which he was bound. "We are innocent! We neither killed nor caused our father to be killed. We confessed through pain of the torture, and by means of the snares prepared for our inexperience."

Beatrice, almost changed in face by her internal ecstasy, with a sweet voice like a mother's blessing, concluded:

"Martyrdom upon earth is called a glory in heaven: persevere, and die as the faithful of Christ died."

Chief Justice Luciani had easily got rid of the unusual sting of humanity as a temptation of the devil; seeing that in his new experiment, instead of having gained, as he had supposed, he had lost not a little, his rage re-kindled again, and burst forth noisy and foaming:

"We shall try you again, and see whether you will maintain yourselves as strong by deeds as in words. Master Alessandro, apply to the prisoner the torture of the *taxillo*."

"Have I heard right, your Honor? Did you say the *taxillo?*"

"Yes, the *taxillo:* what of it?"

"Nothing," replied Master Alessandro, shrugging his shoulders; "I thought I didn't hear rightly."

The *taxillo* was a small, fine wedge, large in its base, sharp on the point, and soaked with turpentine and pitch.

The brothers Cenci and Lady Lucrezia, benumbed, stared upon what happened. Master Alessandro, bringing the small wedge, undressed the left foot of Beatrice. Short, smooth and round, it seemed the work of a Greek chisel in pink alabaster. They saw him insert the sharp point of the wedge betwixt the flesh and nails of the toes: they shuddered at the sight, but what new form of torment it was they could not well understand. Master Alessandro took a taper and lighted it at the candle which burned before the holy image of the Redeemer; then approached it to the wedge, which immediately took fire. The flame rapidly approached the foot, and rushed like a tongue, as if greedy of flesh and blood.

Most horrible was the pain which came from this torture; human nature could not resist it, how much the less when we consider the sufferings already borne by the poor girl. Nevertheless, Beatrice fearing on the one hand to discourage her relatives, and on the other designing to give them an example of how one should suffer, conquered her anguish, and was silent. She was silent, truly; and taking the flesh of her cheek between her teeth she pressed it so as to fill her mouth with blood, to divert one pain with another, but she had no power to withhold a cry desperately shrill, in which it seemed that her life was cut short, while her head drooped like that of a dead person.

Even the hare, reduced to desperation, forgets his natural timidity and bites. Don Giacomo did not fear to approach with his face the burning wedge, and to seize it with his teeth, trying to detach it; but he derived no other advantage than that of burning his face. Then all of them, not even excepting the mild Lady Lucrezia, urged by a spontaneous instinct, rushed against Luciani, showing a desire to tear him with their teeth. They roared like wild animals, nor did their faces seem any longer human. Although this was impotent rage, since they had their hands chained, and the balustrade would prevent their approach to the judges, still Luciani was frightened, and starting to his feet, made a shelter for himself with the back of a chair; behind which, as from a bulwark, he barked:

"Take care lest they untie themselves! Hold them! They are of the Cenci race, and tear to pieces!"

Master Alessandro, availing himself of the confusion, had let the *taxillo* fall from the foot of Beatrice.

The Cenci were easily held. Luciani was agitated, and seeing his colleagues and the other assistants, although through different causes, more frightened than himself, thought it advisable to suspend such tortures, which in those times had the name of examinations.

"Take them back!" roared Luciani, standing upon the threshold of the door, "take them back to prison; separate one from the other; give them the food of penitence—let them drink torments—let them eat despair."

Beatrice, fainting, was carried back on a chair to her prison, and there intrusted to the care of the physician; who between one sigh and another observed, that the prisoner could not be subjected efficaciously to the torments before an entire week.

CHAPTER XXIV

THE SACRIFICE

"INTRODUCE him immediately."

Thus commanded Cinzio Passero, Cardinal of St. George, to his chamberlain, who had entered to announce that his Honor, Chief Justice Luciani, very earnestly desired to speak to his Eminence. Luciani moved a few steps, and stopped in the middle of the room, bowing profoundly, and in this attitude he remained without uttering a word.

The Cardinal, casting down his eyes in order to hide his satisfaction, asked in a slow voice and with pretended indifference—a forerunner of approaching ingratitude:

"Well, where are we now? Is this great trial finally finished?"

"Your Eminence," replied Luciani, with his head hanging, "sees in me renewed the case of Sisyphus."

The Cardinal, less from the words than from the aspect of Luciani, suspecting the cause, threw aside his feigned indifference as a wearisome mask, and angrily added:

"What does this mean? Speak without metaphors, for I am already tired of these."

"Your Eminence, it means that we have not been able to obtain from the prisoner Beatrice a confession of any kind; and the other Cenci, moved by her example, have retracted theirs."

"But you—did you allow yourself to be affected by pity, too?"

"I!" exclaimed Luciani, as if he had heard a serious mistake: "eh, not exactly! Ropes, your Eminence, torture *capillorum*, torture *vigilæ*, *cannubioribus*, *rudentium*, *taxilli*, all I have used, and without any interval of time, so that I was astonished myself. If we had only continued the torture of the prisoner a little longer, by this time she would have been despatched, with incalculable injury to the trial. In fact, she remained three whole hours in a fainting-fit."

"And did she not confess with the *taxillo?*

"Not even with the *taxillo*."

"But do you make them of butter now?"

"No, your Eminence, we make them of pine wood, sharpened and covered with pitch as usual; and I commanded all her tortures to be redoubled, until Master

Alessandro himself advised us to suspend them, for she was in imminent danger of her life."

"Who is this Master Alessandro?"

"The executioner, your Eminence."

There are, in all languages, some words of such a sound, that they have the power bitterly to stir human nerves; and the word "executioner" is without doubt one of these. The Cardinal shook his head disdainfully, as if to say, "What has the executioner to do with us?"

"When you saw," said the Cardinal, "that severity availed nothing, why did you not have recourse to mildness?"

"Um! I have done everything, your Eminence. I even dared to promise (well understood on my part, however, so that your Eminence and his Holiness could take it back if you wished) pardon to all of them. I made those who had confessed see the girl when most likely weakened by torture, and beg her with tears and prayers to confess, at the same time assuring her that I had told them this would be their only means of safety. All breath thrown away! The girl, beyond all belief, obstinately despised both flattery and tortures; and after suffering more than human nature seemed able to bear, in the midst of the torture from the *taxillo* she begged her relatives to imitate her courage and retract their confession. How it happened I cannot say, for I am almost doubtful in what world I am; they listened to her, revoked their confession, and again denied it.

"You cannot persuade me that in this business you have used the care which my wishes should have enjoined."

"Indeed you suspect me wrongly. Consider, fearing the prisoner might have some witchery about her, I ordered (and directed the examination myself) that she should be carefully examined, to search for the diabolical spot indicated by necromancers."

The Cardinal shrugged his shoulders in contempt; and

Luciani thought within himself, "A Cardinal of the Holy Mother Church does not believe in the devil! If he is dead, what will become of sinners?"

"Then," asked the Cardinal, "what do you propose to do?"

"Oh, I came here on purpose to learn the wise opinion of your Eminence, who, as all the world knows, is so learned in such matters."

They exchanged glances; already they hated each other. Avarice and cruelty make an infernal contract, which tenaciously binds the souls of the wicked until the consummation of a crime; when this is done, the accomplices share at the same time plunder, hatred, and remorse.

A light knock came at the door, a chamberlain entered, notifying his Eminence that the lawyer Prospero Farinaccio was awaiting an audience.

"Farinaccio!" exclaimed the Cardinal and Luciani, astonished. The Cardinal paused a moment, then said to the chamberlain:

"Let him come in. And you, Sir Luciani, be kind enough to await our orders in the anteroom."

A greater sting to Luciani's pride could not have been given. What! He to give place to a lawyer? He to await the closing of an audience in the anteroom? He, accustomed to treat his equals with arrogance, his inferiors with pride! What would the servants think, while he awaited the conference of Farinaccio with the Cardinal? And he to risk the salvation of his soul for such ungrateful men!

The great haste of Farinaccio to appear before the Cardinal and the preoccupation of Luciani in going out of the room, caused these two gentlemen to stumble against each other upon the threshold. The lawyer being stout and strong, and Luciani weak and lame with the gout, the latter would have reentered the room like a crab, had he not clung with both hands to the lawyer's robe. Farinaccio was not disposed to laugh at the accident; on the contrary, wishing to correct with his tongue the involuntary fault of his body, he saluted Luciani politely, saying:

"Your Honor's most obedient servant. I beg your lordship's pardon;" and Luciani, considering the credit that so obsequious a greeting from so great a lawyer might procure him among the servants, softened a little, and answered less fiercely than usual:

"Good morning, sir."

"Your Eminence," began Farinaccio, having bowed to the Cardinal with the usual frank and sincere manner which so well became him, "I will tell you plainly the reason which induced me to come with so much haste to pay my respects to your Eminence. I came to beg you to procure permission for me to assume the defence of the accused Cenci, in company with some of my learned colleagues."

"Sir Advocate," replied the Cardinal scowling, "what is this you ask? Do you think those depraved people deserve the honor of your defence? The enormity of their crime forbids it; and it would be a strange thing to grant it, now the trial is finished."

"Your Eminence, defence is a divine right. The Lord granted it to Cain, and none knew him to be guilty more than the Lord himself."

"That is true; but human prudence has decreed nowadays that to atrocious crimes should be forbidden such benefits; and among these parricide must be considered the greatest. Tell me, Sir Advocate, did these cruel children grant their father time for a defence? Or did they—and this seems more enormous still—give him time to reconcile himself to God, and save his soul?"

"I do not deny this, your Eminence; but allow me humbly to observe that for this very reason, being an exceptional case, we must not go by common laws, where all is given up to the discretion of a judge."

"Certainly, but by all that belongs to the greatest rigor; for were it different (and this cannot escape your wisdom), the benefit would increase in proportion to the depravity of the crime. Does this seem good logic?"

"But in the world something more powerful than logic rules, and it is propriety. I will not remind your Eminence by how many favors I feel bound to the sacred person of His Holiness and yourself, nor with what zeal I have always studied, and still study to promote, according to my weak powers, the exaltation of your most noble house—I fulfil in this way a duty of gratitude, that is all. I have taken the liberty briefly to mention this, that your Eminence may be persuaded that if you can find a more authoritative counsel, you cannot find so easily a more devoted one. Your Eminence must know, then, that for several days a rumor has spread through Rome that says it is incredible to think that Bernardino, a boy of only twelve, of mild disposition, could have participated in this parricide; much less could the girl" (this however was not true, nay, the contrary opinion was prevailing), "whose wonderful beauty, and the courage with which she underwent the most rigid experiments of justice, have obtained for her a deep compassion. Calumny whispers in a low tone from ear to ear that it is purposed to entangle the Cenci in the same accusation, and consequently to the same condemnation, in order to ensnare the property of this wealthy family; it has caused extraordinary rancor among the nobility to see threatened with entire destruction an illustrious race, which they affirm to be sprung from the most ancient Romans. I believe, and many with me think so, that in order to remove every ground for slander it will be best to grant the accused a defence, and counsel, and all the forensic aid of the bar. They say: 'How can a boy, and an inexperienced girl defend themselves from these old foxes of the bar, frightened by threats, encompassed with snares?'"

Cardinal Cinzio was startled by these words; but accustomed as he was to subdue the impetuosity of his temper, and to dissimulate, he had kindly assented to all the advocate said, and even smiled upon him. But here the Cardinal could no longer refrain, and exclaimed with ill suppressed rage:

"How dare you suspect such horrible things?"

"Eh! It is not I who suspects; it is calumny, which says all this, and also adds that confession extracted by means of most atrocious tortures can not be relied on; and it would have been a much shorter way to let them die within some trap at night."

The Cardinal, to restrain his anger, chewed some paper. Farinaccio, a very cunning man, knew he had struck the hardest blow, and now sought to flatter the purpled priest; so he added:

"It grieves me, your Eminence, really pains me, to hear science and the reputation of others thus assaulted: for in my writings I have always proclaimed torture to be the queen of proofs: nor would I have come here did I not know how this atrocious crime happened, and did not flatter myself to draw from the accused a sincere confession, which will not only confound all slander, but will also offer a way for the appearance of the Blessed Father's innate clemency, the rays of which have so often spread throughout the world."

"And do you really flatter yourself you can make them confess?" asked the Cardinal more calmly.

"I hope so?"

"All of them?"

"All!"

"Sir Farinaccio, you assume a load too heavy for your shoulders; at least I fear so, for they show an obstinacy equal to their depravity: and you know that the gates of mercy may open to the humble prayer of the repentant, and not to the haughty knocking of the obstinate. The trial besides contains proofs enough to conquer a Pyrrhus. We are not in the habit of minding the people's murmurs."

"Oh! I mentioned this myself," Farinaccio hastened to reply, who began to fear he had gone too far, and now thought of making an honorable retreat; "nor did I hesitate to make it understood as it deserves; nay, moved by the knowledge of your great magnanimity and famous judgment, I concluded to tell it all openly to you, so that everything may be done quietly, without noise, and without scandal, in the way most suitable to the wishes and justice of your Eminence. And for this very reason, to all those who seemed anxious to inform your Eminence of the humors of these Roman brains, I said: 'What do you fear? ignorant people! you do not know how much goodness there is in the heart of the Cardinal Saint George; how much love, how much zeal for all that which is proper and decorous to the Holy Catholic Seat, and to the dignity of his illustrious house.' And to confirm my words by deeds, I resolved to come and speak to you about it; hence I now humbly beg you to take my proceeding in good part; and to pay more attention to the reason which induced me to speak than to the words, and to pardon those which unintentionally may have seemed too free or bold."

Farinaccio's words seemed unaccountable to the Cardinal: he could not understand his motives; and, accustomed as he was to suspect even good intentions, he was puzzled about this mysterious visit. He neither granted nor refused the quest of Farinaccio; he took time to think of it, and the pretext of being obliged to confer with His Holiness furnished him with a very good excuse for delay. They took leave of each other rather satisfied than otherwise; Farinaccio, because he hoped to succeed in his desire of speaking with the prisoners, and counseling and directing them in their defence: the Cardinal, because he relied upon the insinuation of Farinaccio in obtaining the confession from the prisoners and obviating in this way the suspicions which he felt he too well deserved. Both were aware that their game was equal; both felt they were deceiving each other; and yet both knew that one was necessary to the other for the purpose of accomplishing their common design.

Farinaccio on turning the corner of the street opened the door of a carriage that stood awaiting him, and, speaking to some person within, said:

"The plot works well, your Eminences. Do not lose a single moment of time, but strike while the iron is hot. Fear has him by the hair: should she leave him, we never shall catch him again."

Farinaccio was at the same time both right and wrong in his reasoning; he rightly guessed that fear ruled the soul of the Cardinal, but he wrongly imagined that this rendered him more mild towards the prisoners; since, having need of their confession to proceed with a firm foot and erect head to the cruel conclusion of his purpose, and having in his conversation with Luciani despaired of obtaining it by torture, he seized upon Farinaccio as a lever to move the stone that was an obstacle in his path.

Before continuing, it is necessary to say a few words about Prospero Farinaccio, who is to take so prominent a part in the events of this history, and tell who he was; and the reason why he so warmly undertook the defence of the Cenci.

Farinaccio was born of humble parents, but they were not so unprovided with Fortune's gifts as to prevent their educating him in the liberal studies; he was sent to the University of Padua and studied law, in which he succeeded wonderfully. Returning home, he soon distinguished himself as a man of superior talents, and easily acquired the reputation of being one of the greatest lawyers of the Roman bar. Restless and insinuating, by great industry he was often able successfully to conduct defences that were looked upon as desperate; and this gained for him a great reputation for learning, even by those judges who had yielded to his importunity rather than to his arguments, for they preferred to confess themselves conquered by science, rather than overcome by weariness. Vitality was superabundant in him, and not finding sufficient labor in the exercise of his profession —since the age in which he lived did not allow him to attend to public affairs—he had been led into dissipation.

Such was his temperament that, having spent the whole night in gambling and revelry, the next morning found him more than ever ready and prepared for his work.

As he was liberal in giving, so he was ready in taking; he contracted as many debts as he could, sometimes through necessity, but oftener through a natural taste; esteeming the ties of friendship little, and not knowing those of relationship, he used to say that according to his ideas, the strongest tie that could keep men bound together was the one of debt, for three ropes kept the knot fast: the benevolence of the creditor for the debtor, the hope of deriving a large profit from him, and the fear of losing both interest and principal; and he firmly declared that even the sword of Alexander would have been powerless had it tried to cut it. Notwithstanding all this, under that heap of vice was hidden the best of hearts, open to generous acts, provided they took little time; and to sacrifices, on condition they would not take him too much from his predominating passions.

One morning toward the end of the month of August, a coalman, leaving at the door of a lawyer's office four mules loaded with bags of coal, boldly entered the anteroom with both hands in his pockets, and his hat cocked on one side like a duke's. The clerks, glancing at him, did not move, but continued writing without raising their heads.

"Oh, there! is the lawyer in?"

"Here? no—he may be at home."

"I ask you whether he is here, not at home."

"Suppose he is? do you think he is going to buy coal in his office? Do you believe we roast our clients?"

"God forbid! I have only heard that you sometimes skin them. But no matter for that—I do not wish to sell him coal, only to speak to him on business."

"You?—You indeed?"

"I—exactly so—I. Is there anything strange in that? Cannot we speak to the Pope, who has his ears in his feet? Why not, then, to the lawyer Prospero Farinaccio, who wears them on his head, I suppose?"

"But do you know who the famous lawyer Farinaccio is?"

"Of course I do! He is a man, as I am; is he son of the Coliseum, or does he boast of being cousin to King Porsenna? Come, you may as well announce me, for I know he is in his room."

"What an obstinate blockhead he is!" murmured the head clerk in a low tone; then in a louder voice he added:

"He is engaged."

"Then I will wait."

A little later, the door opened and revealed Farinaccio, who, on dismissing some person that had been closeted with him, observed the coalman, and with a courteous manner asked him in, saying:

"How can I serve you? Speak, and sit down if you please."

"I will speak standing. Tell me, have you heard the trial of the Cenci talked of?"

"I? How would it be possible not to hear of it? It is the only thing that gives Rome any excitement."

"And have you not heard a voice in your heart, speaking in behalf of these unfortunate people?"

"I have, indeed! And even now I feel compassion for them;—nay, to speak plainly, I will tell you that the secrecy of the trial, the unusual preparations, the dismissal of Chief Justice Moscati—a compassionate and worthy man—and the appointment of Luciani, a man more cruel than torture itself, the age of the accused, the probable incompetency of all, or the greater part of them, to defend themselves, and many other things upon which I ought to be silent, oppress my mind and cause me to suspect some abominable plot."

"Then tell me why you, whose defence never was refused to the most infamous culprits, should now show yourself so chary of it toward these betrayed people?"

"Because, having duly considered the affair, I have concluded, should I work in this ground, I should only break my spade. I have already told you that I fear in this a secret persecution and a powerful one, too; I fear that this is not to be a judgment, but a juridical assassination. I see, or fancy I see, justice armed, not with the sword of the law but with the dagger of the assassin, and"—

"Continue, Sir Advocate," said the coalman with trembling voice, seeing him hesitate.

Farinaccio rose from his chair, and went to the door to see whether it was shut; returning, he continued:

"There is a rumor, although I doubt it, that the Cenci being very wealthy, and the Pope's nephews poor and avaricious, a pretext is sought to make this wealth revert to the Apostolic See, and then by some means or other, which can easily be found at court, to transfer it to this herd of starving nobles."

"How? By the murder of four innocent beings? But have you not the right of defending the widow and the orphan? Is not a lawyer's profession considered a most glorious one, for the very reason of the great danger it runs in defending the cause of innocence cruelly persecuted?"

"True, and that is the reason why this calling is preferred to the more learned ones—but, coalman, I should have asked you before—pray, who are you?"

"Alas, Sir Advocate, do not seek to know! I am one —and let this touch you—who has not his equal in misery in this world."

"No—confidence for confidence. How can you expect me to open my mind to you if you intend to keep your identity secret from me?"

"We are not on equal terms. I do not doubt your discretion, still less your honor; neither am I deterred by fear, for no greater evil can befall me than the one I now bear; and yet I beg you to let me preserve my secret."

This entreaty contained so much humility and went so mildly to the heart of Farinaccio, that it seemed rudeness in him to insist, and he only said:

"Well, so be it, then; I will tell you" (and he spoke in lower tones) "that I believe the public rumors are but too true; and how can I, believing so, without a certainty of success, take upon my shoulders so heavy and dangerous a load?"

"Then you have the heart to let these creatures, as innocent as our Saviour, perish without a defence?"

"You must know, in the first place, that the defence of parricides is not a right, but sometimes is granted as a favor; in the second place, tell me how can you prove they are innocent?"

"I?—I *can* prove it, because—because it was I—who killed Count Cenci."

"You? Pray, who are you?"

"I am he whom you, through courtesy, allowed to remain unknown. I killed him with these very hands, and would do it again, at the very moment when he was about to outrage nature."

He then explained all the particulars of the affair, confiding every secret of the family, and the deeds, words, and habits of the murdered Count, and also the virtue and wonderful courage of his daughter Beatrice.

Farinaccio endeavored, while he was speaking, to recognize him; and not succeeding, the idea that he might be Monsignore Guido Guerra passed through his mind; but having known him very well, he did not think the coalman's features, face, gestures, or even his voice resembled his.

At the conclusion of his words, the coalman raised his eyes to Farinaccio to see their effect; but the latter kept his face bent thoughtfully. After a long pause he said:

"If I should say to you, go and present yourself to justice as the murderer, would you do it?"

"This very moment, if it would save them."

"No—no, you would only be one victim more—you could not take the lamb from the wolf's mouth. Love is as fatal to this unhappy girl as hatred. People charge her with the murder of her father, to give her a crown of glory; she is accused of parricide in order that her property may be seized. A hard fate!"

"Ah, Sir Farinaccio, do not abandon them, for pity's sake."

"I am not a favorite at court," continued Farinaccio, "and I fear that if they should get a chance now, they would hack and cut me like a piece of cloth."

"At court, I know people who would surely aid you, and I am sure you would find the Cardinals Sforza and Barberini very ready to second you."

"That would be something. But how can I present myself to these great people?"

"Go boldly; you will find them informed of everything."

One could read in Farinaccio's face that he was unbecided, but the coalman with sad voice said:

"Now that you know all, can you let them perish without help?"

"But if I should be lost too?"

"A benefit that is calculated is no benefit."

This dialogue had been carried on with so much passion on both sides, that Guido Guerra, forgetting himself spoke in his natural voice: and Farinaccio could not help exclaiming:

"You are Monsignore Guido Guerra!"

"I—yes, I was."

"*Heu quantum mutatus ab illo!*" exclaimed Farinaccio, giving him his hand, which the other pressed affectionately, saying:

"Now that you know my misery, now that my misfortunes force you to weep, will you let me become desperate?"

"Well, I will do as you wish. But I pass the Rubicon with a greater weight on my heart than I ever felt before. I am afraid I may take such steps that, instead of leading to a good result, I may involve them in ruin. I know the Cenci family can hardly fall into a worse condition than their present one; but I do not wish to be the one to give them a final push. But be not discouraged, for I will not act slowly or irresolutely on account of this. Now go; and rest assured that as much as my brains can work or my mouth can say, I will use for the safety of your friends."

"For this I came to you; but in case of failure, some other plans may be of use. You will see her—you will see Lady Beatrice, I mean. Do not speak to her of me at all; or rather, yes, speak to her and give her this ring, which will at once gain her confidence in you. Her father's blood stands between us—it is just, but I shed it for her. I love her, and she cannot cease to love me;

always bound to each other, and yet forever divided, our love is a flower which death will gather."

Farinaccio when left alone stood meditating for some time upon the singularity of the affair, and the misfortunes which oppressed the unhappy Cenci family. Then he immediately revolved in his mind how to carry out his plan of defence, which he soon decided upon; it was uncertain and truly dangerous, but it was the only one that he deemed might prove successful. He set out for the palaces of the Cardinals Sforza and Barberini, whom he found favorable to his undertaking and kindly disposed to aid him with their influence. He arranged with them the interview with the Cardinal's nephew, Cinzio Passero, and the means to be used in this delicate business; and they, very ready to assist the Cenci, offered themselves to wait in the place above mentioned, within a carriage without escutcheon, for the termination of the visit, and to plan then according to the turn of events.

Chief Justice Luciani, tired of waiting in the anteroom, grumbled like a chained dog, but suddenly he heard his name called by a chamberlain, who said:

"Your Honor, his Eminence dismisses you, and commands all proceedings to be suspended for the present until further orders."

The chamberlain said this very haughtily, for servants usually possess the sense of smelling more acutely than bloodhounds, and know how to distinguish when one is blooming, when mature, and when about to fall from his master's favor. Luciani, offended at his dismissal, and still more by the manner of the chamberlain, looked at him, as if to say:

"Be careful to keep at a distance, for should you fall into my claws I will show you that a dog never bites me without my answering in a like manner." He then departed silently.

The Cardinals Barberini and Sforza presented themselves in the anteroom to pay their respects to his Eminence of St. George. They were immediately announced and introduced in the midst of a great raising of hats and profound bows. Afterwards from each side came the usual salutations; and after the visitors had repeatedly assured the Cardinal visited that they had come only to pay their respects to him, he began to sound them upon the news then in Rome.

The Cardinals Sforza and Barberini kept him in suspense, and pretended ignorance of anything new; so that Cardinal Cinzio was obliged to speak more openly. They, pretending to enter unwillingly upon a subject which they had already agreed upon and committed to memory, riveted the nail already driven by Farinaccio, adding a few inventions of their own, which they said only showed how unjust public judgments were, and induced a necessity, for the reputation of the Pontificate, to deny them solemnly; especially as these were dangerous times for the Church, and heretics, not only in France but even in Italy, were too ready to receive and give credit to all such calumnies.

It is not necessary to relate all the discussions upon this topic held by these purple-robed men. It is enough to know that the Cardinals Barberini and Sforza played their parts so well that they left Cardinal Passero very thoughtful, and almost persuaded to be lavish in concessions of defence to the Cenci; for he hoped by this to reap more fruit than by severity. At last Farinaccio, flattered with a thousand caresses, had the satisfaction of hearing from the very lips of the Cardinal's nephews, Pietro Aldobrandino and Cinzio Passero, that for *his* sake the Pope had granted his request. From this first advantage Farinaccio drew a good omen, and rejoiced.

Farinaccio, thanking them with all his heart, went to find the advocates De Angelis and Altieri, to persuade them to compose with him the board of defence; and after some difficulty he induced them to be his colleagues in this case.

In their united conferences Farinaccio explained his design; it appeared to them, as it really was, one full of danger; but he with his eloquence, and many reasons, persuaded them that the case offered no better way; that they should treat it as surgeons treat hopeless cases. The lawyers, understanding the gravity of the affair, almost repented of the charge they had assumed; and, could they have done it honorably, would have retracted their word, when Farinaccio lightly reproached them, saying that heaven belonged to eagles and earth to snails, and had it been a common case he should not have had recourse to them, the pride and light of the Roman bar.

This was such open and excessive flattery that it should not have deceived men so skilled in the usages of the world. But they drank it all in, and were now disposed to aid their colleague with all their power.

Farinaccio ended all this business when it was late at night, for that day he had worked enough.

But hardly had he opened his eyes on the following morning before he found his new anxiety upon his pillow, and throwing aside all other business, he gave his whole attention to the Cenci case. Dressing in haste, he went to the prison of Corte Cavella at the moment when they were opening the doors. Farinaccio, being well known in these places, met with smiling faces; for, either as prisoner or visitor, he had long since tamed the Cerberuses of such hells, and kept them continually friendly to himself. He was furnished with a permission from Monsignor Taverna, Governor of Rome, which he showed to the superintendent, who declined to read it, alleging he had too much respect for the eminent advocate to require any other proof than his honorable word. The notaries showed him the process, which he learned quickly, because it treated of the usual things that he had studied all his life. After finishing this business, he asked leave to confer with the prisoners Giacomo and Bernardino Cenci, and Lucrezia Petroni, which was immediately granted.

Beatrice in her solitary prison, lying in bed, had not a limb that did not pain her keenly, and yet her mind was more troubled with the sorrows of her heart. She was thinking of her lover. The bolt of destiny had struck them and torn them asunder like a riven rock; the sea gurgles whirling and foaming between that broken cliff whose summits are to unite no more; yet, standing opposite each other, they recall the mutual calamity, and testify that nature created them one. Her life now wanted an aim; existence to her was useless: whether she died or lived, Guido could not even stretch out his hand to save her from falling into an abyss—how, then, could he become her husband? Nevertheless, if it pleased God, so be it.

"Lady Beatrice," said Virginia, entering the prison, "the lawyer, Prospero Farinaccio, wishes to speak with you."

"With me? What business can I have with the lawyer? I know him not. But admit him—so many have come that he may also."

Farinaccio advanced a few steps within the room, and then stopped, astonished. Although he had heard wonderful stories of Beatrice's beauty, the reality seemed to him far more than the report. Her divine face, sad in consequence of the pains she suffered, her pure beauty in this hour of anguish, made her seem like one of those angels that assisted our Redeemer in his hours of passion. The lawyer's boldness failed, and an unusual hesitation took possession of him; so that silently, and affected by a feeling of ineffable reverence, he approached the bed of Beatrice.

"What do you wish?" she said with gentle voice, as she saw that Farinaccio had lost his power of speech. He hesitatingly answered:

"I come, gentle maiden, urged by your misfortunes, and still more by the prayers of one who weeps most bitter tears—one whom you perhaps hate, and love at the same time—one who never was so worthy of being yours as at that moment when he lost you forever. Your heart may have already told you with its beatings who is he that sent me."

"He?—And does he weep?"

"He does, and says to you that he shall die of despair if you do not try to save yourself. In order that you may put absolute and entire confidence in me, he has requested me to give you this ring."

Beatrice took the ring, and looking at it said:

"Has he told you all?"

"All."

"What, everything?" and as Farinaccio nodded, she continued: "Then what do you think of it, sir? do you not think my marriage resembles that of the Doge of Venice when, throwing a ring into the sea, he marries the abyss."

Farinaccio did not answer immediately; when he had recovered from his emotion, he begged Beatrice to listen to him attentively, for the matter was of great importance. He then told her what we already know, spoke of the state of the trial, and finally concluded:

"Now, for the sake of your relatives and yourself, after the mature deliberation which the case requires, I see no other way of safety than this: that you freely confess your father was killed by your own hand."

Beatrice interrupted him with a cry of surprise, and gazed at him bewildered. If this were jesting, the time, the place, and her condition rendered it too cruel; if advice, it seemed so monstrously strange that she really thought the lawyer or herself had lost all sense. Farinaccio seeing her astonishment added:

"I fully understand that my advice must seem very singular to you, still I am ready to enlighten you upon all your doubts."

"Is it possible," said Beatrice, "that after I have suffered so many tortures to save my good name, I should myself defame it, leaving it as a byword of horror to posterity, when I wished to leave it one of compassion and sorrow?"

"Let me say to you, gentle girl, an incredible, but a true thing. Everybody believes you did kill the man that cannot be called your father without outraging nature. Some believe so for a particular reason of their own, and in my opinion it consists less in hatred toward your person than in a greedy desire of your property. Others believe it because they love you, and it pleases their imagination to look upon you as a wonderful being, and to hail you as more virtuous than Lucretia, more strong than Virginia. The people have placed you first in a trinity of courageous Roman women, and worship their invention: should any one endeavor to undeceive them now, they would not only disbelieve him, but they would detest him. Should I take my course of defence upon this presumption, I should at the same time lose myself and not save you. Meanwhile, you by denying it will not succeed in persuading anyone that you did not murder your father, neither would you save your own life nor his who, through loving so much, lost you; for the judges consider the proofs gathered in the process sufficient for your condemnation as a parricide, and the laws of our tribunals grant the power, taking into consideration the confession of the accomplices, of subjecting the refractory to the trial by torture until death ensues."

"Amen! It seems to me they have reduced me to such a condition that the path now left for me to tread is very short. After all, it is not so painful to die as men generally think. I can assure you of the truth of it—I, to whom it has more than once been granted to touch the gates of eternity."

"No, dear lady, you must not die, and although among the Gentiles your resolution might appear magnanimous, among Christians it is sinful; since God is equally offended with him who does not strive to save his life and with him who lays violent hands upon himself."

"Shall I then consent to live, and see fathers shudder at my approach? Shall I live to see people, curious and frightened, fix their eyes upon my face as if to read there the word 'parricide.' Ah, no! May it please God to let me disappear from this earth, and blot out even my memory!"

"But do you suppose that from the belief of your having murdered your father, you have awakened any hatred or horror? If you believe so, you are deceived. So long as men have hearts to beat at the name of virtue, will they despise, instead of exalting, the name of the noble girl who, becoming a heroine for her virtue, defended it with an act piously cruel? The stronger the tie, so much more the offence, and it gave you a legitimate right to resist. Recall ancient and modern history to your memory, and see whether children were thought infamous and depraved who for a just revenge killed their parents."

"But tell me, sir, would you like to have your son marry a parricide?"

"My answer cannot satisfy this question, for your case is unusual; but soon, I hope, it will be as clear to others as to me. Justice is not a fruit of all seasons; it should be, but is not; neither is truth; both need to bloom and mature, and he who plucks them when unripe injures them and himself. At the proper time, the astonished people shall know how a girl of sixteen, after suffering tortures which no patience or human strength is able to endure, did not at last hesitate to compromise her life and fame, out of love for her family. I cannot find a person who ever made so solemn a sacrifice, and derived from it, not only praise, but affectionate veneration, except one only—and He was God, not a man."

Thus speaking, he took from the head of the bed a small crucifix, and placing it upon the counterpane, said:

"He, with his silence, teaches you what sacrifice is more than my words can; He, for the redemption of those who had offended Him, who then offended Him, and would do so still, accepted the unmerited execution; He gave to Eternal Justice an eternal ransom with His precious blood—an everlasting baptism falling upon our heads like a deluge of mercy which never has an end."

"Yes; but Christ did not die infamous."

"Who was more vilified than He? Who more overwhelmed with scorn and ignominy? Whom did they prefer to Him in the pardon which was accorded? Barabbas, a robber! They gave, for His companions upon the cross, Cismos and Dismos, two thieves! He had foretold this, as it says in the Gospel: 'You will be reviled of all people for my name's sake; but take my cross and follow me; whosoever is ashamed of me is not worthy of me.' "

"Must I, then, take this God of truth as a witness to a falsehood?"

"That is no objection; in the first place, it is against nature to oblige the accused to swear, thus putting him to the necessity of feigning, or doing injury to himself. But, putting this aside, how is it possible that Divine laws can allow us to take the life of another to defend our own, and not give us the right of defending it by affirming the false for a holy end? Is not homicide worse than perjury? Certainly; and were they even equal, if it is permitted to us, by universal consent, to defend one's own life by the first, why should it not be so with the second?"

"Sir Advocate, you puzzle, but do not convince me; my mind is not competent to confute yours; still I feel—here, within my heart—that truth is not on your side."

Hardly had she spoken these words, when her prison door opened again, revealing the sad faces of her mother and brothers, who surrounded her bed. They did not speak or even make a motion, and yet a prayer seemed to emanate from each. The lawyer's eloquence had been nearly exhausted; more words would have injured instead of availing, and he was almost in despair of succeeding in his design. The silence was long, and Beatrice kept her eyes fixed upon the crucifix lying by her side. Suddenly she took it up, and kissing it fervently, with a mournful voice, as if chanting a psalm for the dead, said:

"Since you wish it, let it be so. O Lord, Thou seest and knowest these things; if they are wicked, forgive them, for they are done with a good intention; if good, reward them as they deserve. For my own part, I know there is no other hope for the desperate than that of hoping nothing. The fate that pursues us will cease its persecutions only upon our tombstones; it will turn its steps elsewhere when it sees written upon them: 'Here lie all the Cenci, beheaded for their crimes.' However, I will not take from you the last ray of hope; and as it is a great comfort to the dying to gaze with their last look at the fading light, so it will not seem to me that I am a useless victim. If I could suffer the penalty for you all, and be accepted as an expiation, or appease the relentless fate that persecutes our family, I would do it; not being able, behold, I sacrifice myself uselessly; I wished to warn you of this, in pity for the grief you will feel when you shall fall into the depths of despair."

Farinaccio tried to speak words of hope, but they expired on his lips. The Cenci wept, and the lawyer's face was bathed in tears; he covered his eyes with both hands, and leaning upon the bed, tried to think whether he could contrive any other plan less dangerous than the one he had devised to save these unfortunate people, and not finding any he groaned. Other cases pressing upon him, he took leave of them with a silent salutation and his mind, bold when he entered the prison, was now discouraged as it never had been before.

"Now," said Luciani, with a scornful voice, "what have you been able to obtain from that strong-willed girl?"

"She confesses," replied Farinaccio, oppressed, "she confesses that to defend herself she was forced to kill Count Cenci."

"Indeed! You work miracles, my dear Sir Advocate. If you remain at the bar, I shall burn all the instruments of torture, both ordinary and extraordinary."

Farinaccio, displeased at the joy of this cruel man, replied in a reproachful tone:

"Sir, remember that the Greeks (and they were pagans) when they gained a victory over Greeks, instead of exulting, ordered public expiation."

"Oh! You are a very literary man, walking in the lofty paths of learning; I, who walk through the lower ones, know that the peasant gives eggs to the hunter who has killed the fox. Eh! there is no nonsense with me; and that little *Ave Maria* face has not deceived me at all. *Cara de angel, corazon de demonio*, as the Spaniards say."

Farinaccio, moved by an enthusiasm so much the more fervent in him as it was rare, took Luciani by the arm, and dragging him to the balcony, pointed to the sun shining in the fullness of its rays, saying:

"If you could take away those rays and make a crown of them, it would not be worthy of the virtue of that divine girl."

Luciani, not looking at the sun but at the face of Farinaccio, shook his head, and replied very gravely:

"My dear sir, I look upon this wretch with very different eyes than yours; and for two reasons, one better than the other: the first is this" (and taking off his hat he showed him his white hair); "the second is this" (and unbuttoning his coat, he showed an amulet against witches hanging about his neck).

Farinaccio, disgusted, saw that he was throwing pearls before swine, and cut short the conversation, recommending him to receive the girl's confession as she would give it, and went away.

Luciani, after vainly attempting to make Beatrice appear before his tribunal, proceeded in company with his colleagues and notaries to her prison, and received her confession; in which she, exculpating in every particular her mother and brothers, took all the crime upon herself, declaring there was nothing premeditated in it, but that all had happened from a sudden passion of her soul, moved by the horror of her father's attempt; and, substituting herself for Guido Guerra, she gave the particulars of the case very nearly the same as they really happened. To Luciani's question concerning the means by which she procured the dagger, she hesitated, somewhat embarrassed; then replied that she had for a long time been accustomed to carry it about her person, with the intention of killing herself before suffering violence; but at Luciani's cross-questioning she contradicted herself, and it was natural; for if he had been eager in seeking for the truth, which he hated, as he was satisfied with the false, which pleased him, Beatrice would not have been able to sustain the story that had been suggested to her. This not being the aim of Luciani, he swallowed all, and thought it useless to seek further, since what he had obtained was in his opinion sufficient to condemn the whole family. In the hope of seeing all the Cenci executed, Luciani forgot, or at least made a truce with, the hatred he bore the Cardinal of St. George; and, taking the papers of the process, he went to the Cardinal's palace, like a wild beast carrying his prey into his den to share it with his family. Entering the room, he did not wait to be questioned but exclaimed, panting:

"We have—we have got at last the desired confession!"

Cardinal Cinzio, looking at the dogged face of Luciani, thought involuntarily of the wild men that had lately been sent to him from America, and started back two or three steps. Being a man of good judgment, however, after reading all the particulars of the process, he immediately saw the untruthfulness of the depositions and the contradiction of the circumstances; he entertained a doubt also whether the lawyer pleaders could not destroy this ill-constructed edifice, like the witches' kettle which, when broken, disperses all enchantments. But Luciani solved every doubt. "Particular circumstances," said he, "were not to be considered; only one thing was to be retained, and this was the confession of the accused of having taken part in the crime, either consenting to it, or committing it; that it would be impossible for all the contradictions and lies to agree, which the guilty, in endeavoring to escape the just vengeance of the law, are accustomed to invent; there was no necessity of being too particular in these cases; and when the crime was so evident as this was, and confessed by all, there could be no need of a process, much less of a defence."

Cardinal Cinzio had no need of a spur, and, as the evil loquacity of Luciani flattered his passion, it seemed to him that the new Chief Justice never before had spoken with so much wisdom and eloquence.

These doings were not kept so secret but that the rumor of them ran through Rome very swiftly; the people were greatly excited about it, and in the squares, at the crossings of the streets, and at every corner was anxious questioning among those who met. People came out of their shops to learn more news; women stood on the balconies, eager to obtain the lightest whispering; I believe the Hebrews, who stood upon Mount Sinai waiting eagerly for the voice of God, showed no more anxiety than did these Romans with their minds turned toward the Vatican in expectation of the word which was to decide the destiny of the Cenci; and this word was heard in the midst of darkness preceded by lightning, a sign of blood:

"They shall all be tied to the tails of wild horses, dragged through the streets until dead, and their bodies then thrown into the Tiber."

A shudder ran through the veins of the Romans. They seemed to hear the tolling of the bell that knelled the funeral of Rome. Many refused to believe such unheard-of cruelty. The news reached Farinaccio's ears; he ran quickly to confer with the Cardinal Protectors, and with others of the sacred college, who, although they took but an indifferent part in this affair, were easily persuaded that the command was an atrocious barbarity.

The Cardinals, to whom the reputation of the Apostolic Seat was dear, went to the Vatican to try to divert the Pope from so imprudent a step. Farinaccio, who felt he had been deceived, went to find Cardinal Cinzio; and when the servants told him he had gone to visit the Spanish ambassador, he threw himself upon a bench in the anteroom, saying:

"I will wait." From his expression, he seemed determined to stay there all night without moving. But in a short time, overcome by his emotions, he began to walk to and fro, gesticulating and murmuring. Often he would look at the door, but more often wiped the perspiration that streamed from his face by the horror and pain of the unexpected announcement.

After a time, the servants told Farinaccio he could see the Cardinal. He did not wait for the summons to be repeated; and hastening in an excited state found his Eminence seated and as tranquil in appearance as if about to receive a strange visitor. He was obliged to throw off his feigned impassibility, for Farinaccio, trembling with emotion, went boldly to him, and casting aside all respect, exclaimed:

"Is this priestly faith, your Eminence?"

The Cardinal, arguing from the preface what the discourse might be, cut short his words with a dignified but excited voice, saying:

"Sir Advocate, I could say that my promise of the defence was made *sub modo;* that is, provided the confession of the accused was not so clear and explicit as to render any defence useless. I could also say that I honor those lofty intellects who, as lights sent from God to illumine us in the darkness of our doubts and errors, come to lead us in the path of rectitude; but on the other hand I greatly despise those advocates who, abusing their intellects, which certainly never were given them for such a use, torture with their sophisms what is right, rendering entangled, by caviling, that which is plain, and disturbing the clear waters that they may fish in them."

"Do the proofs of the crime appear plain to you? How long since that part of a complicated confession which declares the guilt must be accepted, and the other, which justifies it, rejected? These are snares."

"I have nothing to say about that; I will only declare what your own good judgment might have suggested to you. My promise was given, and it could not have been otherwise, upon the condition that the Pope should consent; and this condition, you know very well, in an inferior, whose will is subject to others, although not expressed, must always be virtually understood. Now if the Supreme Pontiff, the fountain of all wisdom, your master and mine, found it well not to approve of my doing, with what justice you can complain of it I leave to your wise understanding to consider."

"I was born in Rome, educated at the Roman bar, and you ought to understand, most Eminent Sir, that all these subterfuges are perfectly useless with me—I know them. You promised; if you had not the power to keep it, you should not have exposed yourself. But no; you promised, and ought, and can keep that promise. Does not the whole world know that you are the mind of the pontifical thoughts, that your august uncle prefers you to Cardinal Aldobrandino, and that he never refuses anything to his beloved nephew? I obtained the confession on condition of the defence, trusting to certain arguments, which I now know by proof were most unfortunate. Grant, I beg of you, a defence to the accused; otherwise, do you know what will be said in Rome? That the innocent were betrayed, and that in this capital Judas found a companion."

"Sir Farinaccio, you——"

"I am that one."

"Your mind is unusually excited—calm yourself—this excitement may be injurious to you—calm yourself."

Farinaccio was in no state to listen to this advice, or to the hidden menace concealed in these words; if he were, it was like a spur to an unruly horse; and boiling with indignation he said:

"How can I be calm? The times in which we live and the universal corruption have dragged me into the path of ungovernable pleasures, which I have run through without shame, it is true, but at least without depravity; but within my breast I keep a secret place where the voice of God can sometimes be heard, and which commands me to proclaim to you Lady Petroni and all the Cenci innocent! Lady Beatrice confessed at my request, through the prayers of her relatives, and by the virtue of that same love which induced Christ to sacrifice himself for the human race. Notwithstanding the confession of the murder of that wretch whom nature herself is ashamed to call a father, I trust no Christian judge would ever condemn the maid who courageously defended her virtue. Should I not obtain this, I—yes, I—shall have placed her head upon the block; if I do not succeed, your Eminence, my garments, my hands, will be indelibly stained with innocent blood; there will be no more quiet or peace for me; nor could I ever shed tears enough to clear myself of the remorse—and I swear to you upon the Gospel that, in expiation of my involuntary crime, I will dress in sackcloth like a pilgrim, and from Estremadura to Palestine, from Jerusalem to Loretto, I will not leave a city, town, or village behind me, where I shall not have preached the innocence of the Cenci family, and the deplorable error of which they were the victims."

"Pray be calm, Sir Farinaccio. You lay too much stress on this affair, allow me to say. You cannot be ignorant of the great esteem in which you are held at court, and how agreeable it would be to please you, if possible. I can secretly trust you with this, that His Holiness has not yet sent an order for the execution of the sentence to the Governor of Rome. In the meantime, I will endeavor to speak with him, and humbly beg him to allow the defence to take place, telling him that I had engaged my word in the fulfillment of it. Go, and be assured not a leaf will be moved without your knowing it. Now, as a friend, let me advise you that, it having been a long time decided at court to promote you to some conspicuous office, and avail ourselves of your great legal talents for the benefit of the State, you do not break the design with your own hands. I shall soon have the pleasure of seeing you again."

And they separated.

The Cardinal's words gave some uneasiness to Farinaccio; but he shook it off, and proceeding indefatigably in his assumed charge, he met his colleagues and warned them of the threatened treachery, inciting them to present themselves before the Pope in order to make their reasons prevail. Indeed, he was not obliged to expend many words to make them undertake it, for the lawyers Altieri and De Angelis, although of mild nature, were very partial to what was just. They agreed to go to the Vatican; and since a rumor had spread that the Pope refused to allow any one who came in behalf of the Cenci to be admitted to his presence, they decided that De Angelis alone should present himself, as the advocate of the poor, hoping the Pontiff, ignorant of the part he had assumed in the defence of the Cenci, would receive him; and then, watching their opportunity, his colleagues would follow him, and all kneeling at the feet of His Holiness, endeavor to make him confirm the grant of the defence, already promised by his nephew, the Cardinal of St. George.

They set out for the Vatican, but on the way they saw the carriages of the principal prelates and Roman barons returning, and observed that some appeared dejected, while others gesticulated with excited looks and words. It was a bad omen. Made more cautious by necessity, they determined to present themselves separately in the antechamber, and mix with the crowd of those who were waiting for an audience; thus removing the suspicion that they had come on the same business. The plan succeeded—De Angelis obtained leave to present himself; and the door being opened by the chamberlain, before he had time to prevent it, Altieri and Farinaccio followed, and all together knelt before the Pontiff, who asked, in an angry voice:

"What is this? What do you want of me, gentlemen?"

"Your Holiness," replied De Angelis, raising his hands,

"we shall not rise from your most holy feet if the permission is not granted, already promised by the most Eminent Cardinal Saint George, to defend the cause of the unhappy Cenci."

Clement VIII, thus urged against his will, said in a low voice:

"Am I destined, then, by Providence to see that Rome not only produces wretches that kill their own father, but lawyers that do not refrain from defending parricides?"

De Angelis, astonished, let his arms fall, not daring to open his mouth.

Altieri, to whom the Pope's words sounded strange, was about to give a suitable answer; when Farinaccio prevented him by saying boldly and frankly:

"Most blessed Father, it is new to hear one who was the pride and light of the Roman bar stigmatize the counsel for the defence as champions of the crime. We did not come here to defend parricides, but to beg the fulfilment of a promise, which is sacred; we trust by means of the defence to show that some of the accused are innocent, others excusable; but all deserving of the mercy of Your Holiness. You believe them guilty, most blessed Father, and we bow down to your conviction; we hold them innocent, and beg, as a right, that our belief may be respected; the voice of conscience comes from God, and in the scales of Eternal Justice the consciences of all men weigh equally."

The Pope, surprised, and not able to find an answer immediately, to gain time said:

"Rise!" Then, looking suspiciously at Farinaccio, he asked: "Are you the advocate Prospero Farinaccio?"

"I am; and a most unworthy son and subject of Your Holiness."

"So His Eminence, Cardinal Saint George, promised you the defence of the Cenci?"

"Yes, to me, most blessed Father."

"Cardinal Saint George shall keep his promise. Go in peace!"

Altieri was fearful of having injured himself in the Pope's estimation, and his colleagues had hardly passed the threshold of the door, before he returned and threw himself again before the Pope, saying:

"Most blessed Father, deign to consider that I, being inscribed in the board of the advocates for the poor, cannot deny the office of defence to whomsoever asks it of me."

The Pope, having entirely recovered his impassibility, replied mildly and softly:

"We do not wonder at you, but at the others: but in thinking it over, I feel that they also are deserving men, and zealous in their noble office."

When Altieri rejoined his colleagues he found them in close conversation with Cardinal St. George, whom they had met and approached without any ceremony, telling him that they were just returning from a conversation with His Holiness, and were convinced, by indubitable proofs, of his good intentions; it being his wish that, since His Eminence had given his word, he should keep it. Would he be pleased to go, and fulfil it? They would wait in the anteroom the termination of the colloquy.

"Do you not think you sin by over-confidence?" observed the Cardinal to Farinaccio, smiling.

"*More Romano*, your Eminence, *more Romano*. Our forefathers derived the word *pegno*, pledge, from *pugno*, fist, not reputing themselves safe unless they had the pledge in their hands; they did not even trust to summons, but dragged the witness by the ear to judgment."

The Cardinal entered the room of the Pope. He remained there as long as he thought proper, and then came out feigning great joy for having, by his humble supplications, obtained from the Pontiff the power of keeping his promise, anc a reprieve of twenty-five days, in order that the advocates might have time to prepare their defence.

CHAPTER XXV

THE JUDGMENT

THIS is the hall that displays the paintings of Raphael, and listens to the consultations of the priests. This is the hall where were discussed, and sometimes even decided, the destinies of the kings of the earth; since power, before being itself extinguished, consigned its torch to cunning, who hastened to set the four corners of the earth in a blaze.

The Pope was seated high above all, under a canopy of crimson velvet trimmed with golden fringe. A step lower, sat four Cardinals upon stools: on one side Cinzio Passero, Cardinal of St. George, his nephew by his sister Giulia, and Francesco Sforza, Cardinal of St. Gregory of Velatro; on the other, Pietro Aldobrandino, Cardinal of St. Nicholas, nephew by his brother Peter, and Cesare Baronio, Cardinal of the Saints Nereo and Achilleo, wrapped in their magnificent purple robes. In a larger circle, upon splendid chairs, sat cardinals, bishops and prelates of all ranks, conspicuous in their purple and vermilion robes.

In the middle, on the right of the throne, was a bench covered with black cloth, where sat the judges of the palace and of the sacred criminal Rota, presided over by a special Chief Justice, Luciani being ill; on the opposite side was another bench for the attorney of the government, and several chancellors and notaries; across these was a third for the advocates of the defence.

German soldiers, with iron helmet and cuirass, the halberd over their shoulders, guarded the hall and pushed back the curious; ancient pride and humiliation at the same time of our Italian princes, who are obliged to call from the North those wild beasts with human faces to exercise brutal force.

Everyone was seated in his proper place. Silence having been enforced as usual by the ushers, the Chief Justice, having first asked leave from the Supreme Pontiff, gave a sign with his hand to the Government Attorney that he might begin.

He arose. While he wipes his face with his handkerchief and arranges his hair, let us stop to look at him.

His complexion was like the ancient images of Christ in ivory. His eyes were dull and lifeless, like those of a dead fish: his straight hair hung down on one side of his face like a willow, weeping over his heart and brains long since dead: he moved his arms like a windmill; now he would shrink and then leap up, like a snake springing from a box. To see him one would have said that at his birth petulance, presumption and stupidity had endowed him in his cradle.

The attorney with great solemnity affirmed that he had used all diligence in the examination of the process, and had invoked the aid of Him who never denies it to one who prays for it with all his heart. He then narrated how, urged by the persuasions of the devil and by an abominable avarice, certain persons, neither enemies nor strangers, but relatives—wife and children—had planned the murder of Count Francesco Cenci, a man famous for his piety, illustrious for his lineage, and renowned for his learning. He told of the commission given to the assassins Olimpio and Marzio; of the treacherous sleep, of the postponed parricide on account of the festivity of the Blessed Virgin: he depicted the horror of the assassins, the savage threats of the girl to conquer their repugnance; the nail driven into the eye; the corpse dragged by the hair along the floor, and then with barbarous cruelty thrown from the balcony. He spoke of the proof, which, thanks to the salutary torture, appeared most clearly from the unanimous confession of the criminals; it was already spread over the world, horror-struck at hearing that in Rome, in the great seat of the most holy religion, near the throne of the best among the vicars of Christ, such enormities were committed. Finally, apostrophising the crucifix hanging from the wall, he called upon the judges to remember His divine precepts, when He commanded that the tree incapable of bearing good fruit should be cut down and burned. "It is intended," he added, "to excite your sympathy, gentlemen of the holy Rota, by asking you to consider the youth of some of the parties, as if this, instead of diminishing the crime, did not furnish a plausible foundation for proceeding with greater severity. If the accused had not as yet reached the age of puberty, or had just attained it, it showed, if capable of such abominations now, what might be expected of them when they shall have become adults." He concluded with a hypothesis elaborately arranged, in which he described the soul of the illustrious Lord Count Cenci sent by violence out of this world, without the comfort of the sacrament and condemned, perchance, to eternal fire, standing upon the threshold of hell, shaking his white hair drenched with blood, and, raising his hands toward the judges, crying desperately: "Revenge! Revenge!"

The first of the advocates to plead (for Lady Lucrezia Petroni) was Altieri, who with mild gravity thus began: "I congratulate myself and my office greatly for not being obliged to frighten the judges with images drawn from hell; it is my duty rather to beg them to look upon a pious and mild matron, and to raise a cry—not of revenge, everywhere disapproved before an assembly of

Christians, but more abominable before the Vicar of Christ the Redeemer, and such pious judges—a cry which alone can be worthily raised in tribunals—that of 'Justice! Justice.'"

After reviewing the causes that might have led to the crime, he said: "None of those mentioned by the attorney were applicable to Lucrezia Petroni. Not the desire of gain, since she had nothing to hope from the death of her husband, Count Cenci; for the wife would inherit her husband's property only if he should die intestate, with the exception of the entail; in this case, it was well known by all that Count Cenci had made a will, by which he disinherited every one of his relatives; hence, had she conceived the idea of murder to satisfy the impious desire of her avarice, the heir of the entail and her husband's will were contrary to it. Nor could she have been induced to it by spite, since she had borne many injuries and insults from her cruel husband, but not having resented them while she was young and handsome, when she must have felt the sting in proportion to the right which she must have believed herself to possess of not submitting to them, it is not only unlikely but absurd that she should desire to avenge them after such a long space of time, when they had ceased, and when, old age approaching, the blood runs more languidly in the veins, and the mind, even in passionate natures, assumes milder counsels—especially to avenge them by means so atrocious, and at the same time dangerous. If the cruelties (I leave aside the offences to conjugal faith) had lasted, Lady Lucrezia, having recourse to the tribunals, could have obtained a separation from her husband, which, although not allowed by religion, so far as the tie is concerned, still is granted so far as dwelling apart; nor was she wanting in help from powerful relatives; nor, being provided with a large dowry, would she have been obliged to remain with her husband for want of means of support. Much less should it be supposed that she yielded to the temptations of the devil, for although we are all subject to be tempted by the Evil One, yet our religion teaches that souls zealous of piety are either exempt from them or conquer them. Now, what woman ever showed herself more devout than Lady Lucrezia? The attorney himself, although he uses it as an argument against her, gives her credit of piety, when he asserts that the murder of Count Cenci was postponed out of respect to the festivity of the Blessed Virgin; but I desire the attorney to remember that a woman possessing so much zeal for religion will never offend, not only against the day of the festivity, but the Mother of all mercies, the Mediatrix of all pardons."

Continuing, he examined, act by act, the whole process; endeavoring, with subtle industry, to show its irregularities, the contradictions of the depositions, the weakness of the proofs. Finally, he concluded by appealing to the conscience of the judges, not to consent that a matron so universally esteemed, so beneficent to the poor, should be dragged by a path of infamy and shame to the tomb. Now that her mortal breath was so near its end, they should not raise so great a blast to extinguish it.

De Angelis now opened his argument in favor of Don Giacomo, and he also endeavored to exclude the cause of the crime asserted by the attorney, saying: "He could not have been instigated to it by actual want, since his father, by a just command of the Supreme Pontiff, paid him a decent allowance, and he, moreover, enjoyed the interest of his wife's dowry, which, with his own, was not so limited but to suffice for domestic expenses; much less could he have been moved to commit the atrocious parricide in hopes of inheriting the entire patrimonial property, since it was well known that Count Cenci himself openly boasted that he had disinherited him from all the free estates, although he could not have deprived him of the entails. Count Cenci was old, and had already reached that time of life when any slight cause might send him to the grave; therefore, Giacomo Cenci must have been not only wicked, but insane, if, with so much depravity and danger, he could have hastened that event which shortly, with safety and without remorse, nature would have brought about for him. Now, how is it probable that this son could have shown himself so patient as to wait, when his father was in the vigor of his health, and entering into a green old age, and afterward impatient of delay, when he had become decrepit and in ill-health? Don Giacomo, a stranger to intemperate pleasures, a guiltless gentleman, a good husband, a good father, how could he all at once show such a ferocious disposition, which surpasses that of the most cruel of wild beasts? How is it possible that *he* should become a monster of crime, and with one single step run over the whole career? Nature does not consent to this; and all that which is opposed to the eternal laws of truth should either be entirely rejected, or at least admitted with difficulty. But here," the advocate continued with more vehemence, "I observe, with bitterness in my soul, that a course entirely opposed to reason is followed. The more the circumstances of a crime are contrary to nature, so much more readily are they admitted; the more adverse to the rules of humanity and right, so much the more easily believed. This is not just. Don Giacomo was not at Rocca Petrella when the crime was perpetrated, but staying in Rome. Hence it is clear that he could not have participated with his presence in the murder. If, then, the attorney suspects that he shared in it by means of letters or messages, why does he not bring them forth? He does not even mention them. And certainly he must know that it is his duty to produce the *proofs*, as to us belongs the *defence*. The foundation of the charge consists in the confession of the accused.

"I, for my part, think that the confession of the accused should not weigh anything in the scales of justice, being unworthy of belief and contrary to nature. Indeed, with what charity or wisdom can we oblige a man to confess? A man who does harm to himself was always considered as deprived of sound intellect, and if the Church allows Christian burial to the unfortunate being who has raised a violent hand against himself, it is because she believes he had lost his mind. Now, I ask if one accuses oneself of a capital crime, should it not have the same effect? Certainly it should; and the tongue may kill as well as, and even better than, the hand. Here will be objected: we have not a spontaneous confession, but one extorted by means of the torture. An excellent answer, indeed! A day will come in which posterity shall wonder how we, their forefathers, were so stupid or so barbarous as to accept as an evidence of truth that which by its own nature is a manifest sign of brutality and error."

A murmur of disapprobation spread throughout the hall, and Farinaccio, pulling the gown of his companion, warned him in a low tone to touch lightly upon that subject. Cardinal Baronio, who was a very learned man for that time, leaning toward Cardinal Aldobrandino, who appeared to be highly displeased, whispered:

"These lawyers, once started, come out with blunders enough to astonish heaven and earth!"

"Without the torture," replied the other, "I wish they would show me how we are to find out the truth? What is the use of granting these talkers the liberty of thus boldly outraging the wisdom of great doctors? Continuing in this manner, I ask your Eminence, what is to become of all authority? Why do not the judges impose silence upon him?"

"Your Eminence, let them speak as long as they let us act; when they shall presume to cut our wings, *on aviscra*, as the French kings say when the parliaments refuse to register their edicts."

The advocate De Angelis changed his subject, and, like Altieri, began with sharp logic to demolish the ill-formed edifice of the process, entangling himself in numberless observations, which wearied the minds of his listeners, and somewhat injured the efficacy of the argument. Finally he ended the defence, calling to mind the antiquity of the ancestry and nobility of the Cenci blood, and then, with better judgment, the desolate wife and children of Don Giacomo. "Let the judges proceed cautiously," he said, "in impressing such a mark of infamy upon so noble a house; they should remember that to the son of the parricide no maiden would ever give her hand; to him no one would open his heart; having become, without any fault of his, an object rather of dread than of pity upon this earth, it will not seem a crime but a duty to cover him with shame; no one would ask him to his table; in the church they would shun him. And to you, supreme and best Father of the universal faithful, grant that I may represent the misery of a wife, the mourning of children: in the hands which I supplicatingly raise to your most august throne, be pleased to see the hands of four children and a woman; in my voice to hear the cries of five innocent beings, who, with tears and sobs, hope and expect mercy from you, after God."

"Here, your Eminence," said Cardinal Sforza to Cardinal Cinzio, "is your handkerchief, which I picked up from the floor; you will need it to wipe your tears."

"I? I am not weeping."

"The plea of the advocate De Angelis, however, seemed to me very conclusive; the peroration a very happy one without doubt."

"Eh! according to tastes, your Eminence. But silence!

Farinaccio is rising. Let us see how this racer will run; the prize is four heads. What will you bet that he will lose it?"

"When *you* say so, your Eminence, there is no need of betting; how could I have a conviction different from yours?"

Cardinal Cinzio looked suspiciously at Cardinal Sforza, but the latter, an old adept of courts, showed a physiognomy as open as a miser's box.

Farinaccio rose, tossing his head; and, throwing a look of inexpressible contempt upon the Government Attorney, with a loud voice began:

"May God assist me! I know not, in beginning this oration, whether wonder or grief oppresses me most; both weigh upon me heavily; for, before exercising the office of defence, I find myself obliged to call to mind the nature of the charge. The Government Attorney, if ancient doctrine has not failed to-day, as a defender of the law predetermined for the security of this civil fellowship, should proceed to his conclusions strictly, but without bitterness; carefully, but without passion; subtly, but without perfidy; and whoever does otherwise, I say it boldly to his face, usurps the office of an executioner, and perhaps even worse. How can I have recognized a defender of the law in the magistrate raving like the pythoness upon the tripod, overcome by the demon that agitated her? How can I recognize him, when he draws from the facts consequences maliciously sophistical? How could I recognize him, when I heard him distort the facts, alter them, and as if this were not enough, imagine false, and assert others that were untrue. Do not move, Sir Attorney, for what I say I mean to prove.

"You dared to describe Count Cenci as a model left by the mercy of God upon the earth to bear witness of the golden age, and stripped the classics to gather gems for weaving a diadem of virtue, to place it upon the head of your hero! Francesco Cenci a religious man! He was certainly a procurer of holy images, but only to curse them; a builder and restorer of temples, but only to profane them; a preparer of tombs, but planned to bury in them, as he used daily impiously to beg of God to allow him, all his children before dying himself. Was Francesco Cenci pious? He prepared a banquet on the day the news of the cruel death of his sons reached him; and appealing to God with his glass full of wine, he proclaimed that were it the blood of his sons he would drink it with greater devotion than the wine of the holy Eucharist! You all knew him, and knew what and how many crimes were charged to him. Perhaps some of ·ou condemned him; for this pious man, as the attorney says, received several condemnations, but had his penalty annulled by the Apostolic Chamber by paying very large sums of money. Come with me, your Honors, and let us ask how many volumes, the fruits of sleepless nights, has this man, *famous for his learning*, left to edify and teach posterity. Behold them—the book of his ephemerides, where he, I know not whether with more immodesty than iniquity, noted his crimes day after day. Nor were his bloody crimes the worst. He had all those ties that the human heart desires in this earthly pilgrimage for his comfort in life—but he was a friend in order to become a traitor; he feigned himself a lover the better to seduce innocence, and to leave his victim in the power of despair; he became a husband to commit adultery, a father to commit incest. It was reserved for Cenci to show to men that the cruelties of Caligula, of Nero, of Domitian, of Caracalla, and all other monsters, whom God in his wrath sent to scourge the earth, put all together, might be surpassed. Such was Francesco Cenci; and if I have calumniated his memory, may his soul at this moment appear upon the threshold of this tribunal and cry out to me 'Thou liest!' O wretched soul! wherever thou art, listen to me. Leaving to others the care of reproaching you in the presence of God, I here, in the presence of His most Holy Vicar, proclaim thee the most perfidious and the most infamous man that ever lived in the world!"

Farinaccio continued:

"Here we see a corpse, his throat cut with a deep wound. Who is he? A father! Who has killed him? His daughter! She declares it without growing pale; confesses it without remorse. And who is this woman with such dreadful thoughts, and still more dreadful actions? Behold her! A girl whose face seems made by the hands of angels, in order that here below may be kept the type of celestial purity. Mildness beams upon her face, and in her smile. There is no one who does not praise her and laud her to the skies; she has relieved the grief of many, wept for the sorrows of all. What could have instigated this noble maiden to so execrable a deed? Ask the attorney, and he will tell you it was the devil. But let us leave the devil alone, and reason upon more likely causes. Was it the desire of money? At sixteen years of age a gentle maid thinks as much of money as a nightingale that fills the valleys with his melodies on a beautiful summer night; or as much as the butterfly which sports its wings in the rays of a May sun. At sixteen years of age a girl is all love for the heavens and the earth; these two loves are confused within her, so that her first love for a terrestrial object has in itself something divine. But let us grant that she had a desire for money; how could this have led her to commit the abominable crime? The rich patrimony that she inherited from her mother, her father could not have diminished nor taken away; it would have been a foolish idea for her to trust in obtaining either all or a portion of her father's inheritance free of the entail, since Count Cenci, who had planned no other end than that of depriving his children of their property, their fame—and, if he could, of their lives—would not have probably shown himself generous only toward her; and it would have been more than folly in Lady Beatrice to hope for the entail of the family" (and here he raised his voice more loudly than before) "since entailed property, by the universal consent of all legal authorities, cannot by any cause or pretext, nor even by felony, high treason, or parricide of some of the heirs, be alienated from its legitimate succession from male to male.

"I shudder to narrate the atrocities committed by Count Cenci against his daughter Beatrice. Why did nature refuse me a heart and mind like those she granted to the attorney, so that I might delight in exposing the shameful words with which the old man contaminated the chaste ears of Beatrice, and the impiety with which he strove to deprave her maiden mind? But his flatteries, his immodesty, his blind passion, his fierce madness, the dark imprisonments, the long fastings, the affrighted sleep, the painful awaking, the blows, the wounds and the blood with which he attempted to subdue her, availed him nothing. We see a corpse with its throat cut; we shudder to look at it—but let us dare to investigate what he was before he became a corpse. Opening stealthily, like a midnight robber, the door of the room where his desolate daughter groaned, he approaches the bed of the sleeping girl; she sleeps and weeps because not even dreams are friendly to this unhappy maid. He, the sacrilegous man, first shrouding the lamp which the maiden kept burning before the image of the Mother of Purity, removes her covering and sees the body of his child, which nature has made sacred to the eyes of parents. Whoever is here that has a father's heart, let him think upon an impious old man, with his satyr's mouth, his burning eyes, before which the smoke of hell has passed, trembling, raving, extending his hands to touch the body of the maid, and Beatrice feels the cold skin of the reptile creep over her—she awakes—what will she do?

"What will she do? I, O fathers, have painted before you this spectacle, and not in vain. Answer me—say at this moment how would you have desired Beatrice to act—should she have been impiously degraded as never a Roman maid was degraded, or be most miserable, as she now is? Beatrice saw appalling villainy face to face; she drew her dagger and delivered her name from infamy! We, deploring this great necessity, must admire the courageous girl to whom in other times Rome would have voted triumphal honors, but which now has crushed her with torments and threatens her with an ignominious death.

"Shall I be obliged to attempt to show you how great a crime is incest against one's own child? Can it be compared with other cases of ingratitude, as for example, should a son not redeem his father from slavery, or, if poor, should not aid him? In proof of the enormity of this crime, let me recall to you what the divine Aristotle narrates of an animal that having unwittingly committed an unnatural crime, overcome by shame, threw itself from a precipice.

"Even from the most remote periods of antiquity, in every era of social life among men, the unfortunate, rather than guilty one, who to avoid incest murdered his own parent, always went unpunished: thus we read of Semiramis, killed by her own son Ninus; of Ciane, who killed her father Cianno; of Medulina, who killed her father without mercy.

"The first law in the final paragraph of the Digest *de sicariis* expressly ordains; 'Whoever kills on account of violence committed against himself or relatives, to be exempt from the rigor of the law.' Hence, Beatrice

Cenci, driven to it by a more extreme necessity, should be deemed excusable. Madness, not to say worse, seems to me the pretension of the attorney, who declares that Beatrice should not have slain but accused her father. I have already said that she, by means of letters, had recommended herself to persons of great credit, in order that they might endeavor to save her from imminent perils. On the day of the banquet of which I spoke, with warm supplications she begged the guests, horror-struck by the ferocity of Cenci, to save her; and finally, she presented an address to the pontifical throne. If the unfortunate girl was not able to raise her voice higher, will you condemn her because thick walls, deep vaults, bolted doors, and a rigid and suspicious watch prevented her? Will you then condemn the supplicating maid because your ears, deafened by the joys of victory, were not able to listen to the groans of misfortune?

"And let us grant even, for hypothesis, that the attorney is right in his suppositions: Lady Beatrice, having killed her father instead of accusing him, would only deserve the penalty of transportation, according to the precepts of the law of the great Adrian, and not that of capital punishment.

"The attorney is in error, also, when he argues that the reasons adduced by me are of avail in case of actual or imminent violence, and not when a certain space of time intervenes between the violence and the murder, and when death has been dealt with one's own hand, and not procured by means of assassins.

"He is in error, I say, since Lady Beatrice confesses it is true she killed her father by her own hand, but in the very act when he was about to consummate the violence; and mark that, aroused by force, between fright and anger, perhaps she did not recognize, as she certainly might not, her father. And let us still grant that she had recognized him. But your Honors know that

I, unaware, have profaned a most holy name; for can this title be given to Count Cenci without a manifest offence to nature, without an injury to those who are deserving of it? When a wretch breaks the boundaries that nature has placed between father and child—when he neither protects nor loves his child, but on the contrary persecutes and hates her, tramples upon her, body and soul—such a man is no longer a father; rather the more is he guilty and deserving of death, as it was his obligation to protect and love her.

"And with her innocence let also her age, hardly three lusters, prevail with you, which does not consent to fierce deeds being conceived, much less committed; let her wonderful beauty, for which she is the admiration of all who behold her, prevail upon you. The orator Hyperides, revealing to the judges the graces of the accused girl defended by him, did so move their hearts that they dared not condemn her. Were Lady Beatrice here, I would show you a head made by the hand of God, all candor, all gentleness, placed in this world to be a witness of what must be the face of innocence in heaven, and then I would say to you: Now, brand upon it, if you dare, a mark of infamy! When we shall all be no more, and of our bones not even the ashes shall be found—when our times and our affairs shall be forgotten, the name of Beatrice Cenci will stir the hearts of all those who will then be living. Beatrice, surviving us in fame, will recall these inglorious years fallen irrevocably within the abyss of the past. Since from her this age will have a title and a name, it is in your power, O judges! to act so that the recollection of it to posterity may be either acceptable or abominable.

"Let it not be said that here, in Rome, the courtesan had an altar in the Pantheon, while Beatrice, the most courageous of girls, went to the scaffold—that wantonness found divine honors, and chastity, death. Why do we remain any longer to discuss whether she is guilty or innocent? Let us go, honorable judges, defenders and people, to the Vatican, to thank God for having reserved this illustrious girl to our time."

Then he spoke of Bernardino, and said:

"In faith, I was about to forget it; and in fact the accusation against him is not worth the merit of a defence. Blessed God! how is it possible to suppose a child of twelve an accomplice in a murder? Believing either the assertion of the attorney, which is false, or accepting the confession of Lady Beatrice, which is true, we still find the accusation to be absurd. If Lady Beatrice, moved by a sudden emotion of her soul, killed the wicked violator, she could not have had any counselors or accomplices. If, on the contrary, as the attorney imagines, the murder of Count Cenci was perpetrated by assassins, why admit Bernardino to the secret of it? For advice perhaps? Twelve years does not seem a suitable age to furnish advice in a matter of parricide! I should fear to insult you if I should stop longer to speak of the boy—let his accusation be among the monstrous visions which man, drunk by the spectacle of human crime, sometimes dreams in closing his eyes upon the bench of justice."

Here he ceased. Either by the effect of the words of Farinaccio, or by the boldness of his face, his sonorous voice, and the eloquence of his delivery, the bystanders were deeply impressed. A suppressed whispering flew from mouth to mouth; and had it not been for the respect due to the presence of the Pope, and more probably for fear of the halberds of the German soldiers, the hall would have resounded with applause. The judges retired to consider their sentence.

After a long delay it was rumored that the decree would not be issued until late in the night. The bystanders retired, some hoping, some fearing, according to the variety of minds and feelings; all, however, beseeching the Madonna of Good Counsels to inspire the minds of the judges.

Farinaccio, intoxicated by his own eloquence, no less than by the praises which from every side rained upon him, and trusting reason would prevail in the issue of the case, gave himself up as usual, even until a late hour in the night, to his accustomed companions, who never were weary of praising the chastity, the courage and beauty of the Latin girl. When Farinaccio returned home, very late, a servant handed him a despatch with the papal seal, which he said had been brought by a valet of the palace at midnight exactly. At that hour the destiny of the Cenci had been decided: he opened it tremblingly, in the hope of finding the acquittal of the prisoners; but he was deceived. It was a brief from the Pope, creating him a Counselor of the Holy Roman Rota, with the prerogatives, honors, and emoluments annexed to that office. The brief, dictated with the grandiloquence and fine words of the court, praised the learning and even the virtues of the new Counselor.

"Very good!" exclaimed Farinaccio; "it is not what I had hoped, but it seems to promise well. If I had displeased him, His Holiness would not have hastened to give me this splendid token of his approval."

In such trust he slept with golden dreams upon the welcome bed.

At about eleven o'clock at night the judges had met in the same hall where the advocates had pleaded. One chandelier alone, veiled in a circle of dark silk, shone in the middle of the table; all were seated, and they whispered to one another. The veiled light illumined, and at the same time darkened, sensations which they feared, and which, timidly wavering in their minds, threatened to let their thoughts appear on their faces; yet the hour, the place, still seeming to resound with the words of

Farinaccio, and their own consciences, all disposed them to pity.

Suddenly the Chief Justice glanced at a paper not before noticed by him, and supposing it to be some part of the process, he opened and read it. His face from pale turned to a livid hue: he took it with a trembling hand and passed it to the colleague who sat next to him, and this one to another, and so on until, having made the tour of the bench, it returned to the Chief Justice. His shuddering and paleness were diffused like an electric spark upon the faces of his colleagues. All, with heads bent and eyes fixed upon the red carpet were absorbed in the same thoughts: it seemed as if an iron yoke weighed upon their necks. The paper seemed to possess the power ascribed to the head of Medusa: it had petrified them. Indeed it was such as to change into stone every heart of flesh; for it contained the sentence that condemned the entire family of the Cenci to death:

Lucrezia, Beatrice, and Bernardino to be beheaded; Giacomo to be killed by the club; then all torn with hot pincers and afterward quartered; their property also to be confiscated in favor of the Apostolic Chamber.

Long, deep, and terrible was the silence. One could distinctly hear the crackling of the candles; the sand of the hour-glass was heard, grain falling upon grain; the noise of the moths on the beams of the hall struck upon the ear.

The Chief Justice seized the pen desperately; shuddering he dipped it into the ink, which seemed to him like blood; shuddering he signed—and then, without turning his face, with his hand he pushed the paper to his colleague, and this one also signed it and passed it to the others. If the angels saw this infamy, they must have covered their eyes with their wings and wept. But the judges signed, and then went out.

Without, the judges separated silently, each one detesting himself and the others. In the darkness of the night, some here, some there, stole away with wary steps, like thieves afraid of being met by the watch. All received the price of blood: promoted to more eminent offices, they received greater salaries. Not one showed his remorse by hanging himself upon the first tree that came in his way; but they lived and died despised and hated.

CHAPTER XXVI

THE CONFESSION

THE Pope had placed the sentence in his bosom and watched the time and place to use it. The complaints of the people reached even to the Vatican, like the roaring of the sea in a tempest, and he was waiting until the swelling of the popular storm should somewhat abate, in order to accomplish his fixed purpose.

While speculating thus he was waiting the occasion; fortune put it into his hands, nor could either a more ready or a better one have been devised. Count Cenci, as he himself had often wished, was fatal to his family; not only in life, but even after death he seemed to stretch his hand out of the tomb to grasp his relatives, and drag them into it with himself. Paolo Santa Croce, relative of the Cenci family, of whom we spoke in the beginning of this sad history, decided in his intention of killing his mother, Lady Costanza, had not been able until now to do it without open danger. It happened that this unfortunate lady retired into Subiaco, to recruit with the pure air of the country her failing health. Don Paolo, aware of this, went there secretly and killed her without mercy with a dagger: then taking what money he could find in the palace, fled the justice of the world, but not that of God; since we read in the history of Novaes that a short time after he died by a violent death. On this account a terror spread throughout Rome; and the Pope, to take advantage of it in his own favor, was disposed to use great rigor.

The Orsini family, very powerful in adherents and credit, upon whom, by the natural and civil death of the Santa Croces the estates of Oriuolo would devolve, spoke in high terms of praise of the Pope's salutary rigor, and drew with them a great part of the nobility. These eulogiums increased greatly afterwards, when the Apostolic Chamber, without any opposition, consented that the above mentioned estate should pass to the Orsini family; and this was done with the cunning intention of escaping the charge of avarice, and smoothing the way to grasp the property of the Cenci family, at which the Aldobrandini aimed: the Cardinal of St. George also purposely added fuel to the flame, by artfully spreading round reports to terrify the already frightened citizens. "No fathers, no mothers," cried the infuriated people, "are now safe within the domestic home; every tie of nature is broken; it is dangerous to beget children, dangerous to nurse them, imminently more dangerous to keep them in the house when adults. Yes, nowadays poor fathers run the risk of going to sleep alive, and waking up murdered."

Popular sympathy had accompanied Beatrice even to the threshold of her prison: there, the doors having been shut in its face, it remained like a sentinel, and watched all that day and even a great part of the night: finally it felt tired and hungry; sleep weighed down its eyes, hunger took possession of its vitals: add that the night was dark also, and no one could see it. Going home, it ate, drank, and went to bed: next morning after arising, it had almost forgotten Beatrice, and in the streets it met with a new excitement that made it weep, and the more recent one had the power of making it forget the one it had committed to memory.

When the Pope thought the proper time had come to move the ship and unfurl the sail, he summoned Monsignore Ferdinando Taverna, who was in agony for the Cardinal's hat (conferred on him soon after under the title of St. Eusebius), and gave the order, saying:

"I put in your care the case of the Cenci, and as soon as convenient you will execute due justice."

Monsignore Taverna, a very docile instrument to the papal will, went hastily to the palace, and, assembling without delay the congregation of criminal judges, they planned together the manner of giving execution the next morning to the sentence.

In the old extract of the *Journal of the Brotherhood of St. John, beheaded in Rome*, book xvi., page 66, is recorded: "On Friday the 10th of September, 1599, at two hours after midnight notice was given us that the following morning several prisoners in Torre di Nona and the Savella prison were to be executed; thereafter at five hours after midnight I assembled the brotherhood, chaplain, sexton, and assistant, and having gone to the prisons of Torre di Nona, and performed the usual prayers, there were consigned to us condemned to death the undernamed:—Don Iacomo Cenci and Don Bernardino Cenci, sons of the deceased Count Don Francesco Cenci. In the Savella prison at the same hour one portion of our brotherhood went, and having entered into the chapel, and performed the usual prayers, there were consigned to them the undermentioned Roman ladies condemned to death: namely, Lady Beatrice Cenci, and Lady Lucrezia Petroni, wife of the deceased Count Don Francesco Cenci."

And because it seems a duty, after the lapse of centuries, to give to the present generation the names of those who assisted at the horrible tragedy, we transcribe them here as registered in the same extract.

"In the above-mentioned prison of Torre di Nona were present Sir Giovanni Aldobrandini, Sir Aurelio del Migliore, Sir Camillo Moretti, Sir Francesco Vai, and Sir Migliore Guidotti; and in addition Domenico Sogliani, secretary, and the Lord Chaplain. To those of Corte Savella went Sir Anton Maria Corazza, Sir Horazio Ansaldi, Sir Anton Coppoli, Sir Ruggiero Ruggieri, comforter, Giovanbattista Nannoni, sexton, Pierino, assistant, our chaplain, and myself, Santi Vannini, who wrote this."

While this company of pious Tuscans are preparing to render her death less sad, what is Beatrice doing?

She is sleeping as on the night in which she was awakened by the groans of her father, murdered at the foot of her bed. Let us not awake her; only approach quietly to look once more upon her divine beauty. Does she not seem a celestial creature? Look at those smooth cheeks, which have not yet lost all the hue of her pure soul; a tranquil sleep colors them with a more rosy tint, and gilds them with the reflection of the white wings that it extends over her person. Look at her lips; they have drunk many of her tears, and yet they smile a sad but sweet smile. Listen! she speaks.

"Why, O God, art thou so unfriendly to me? what have I done?"

Raising her hand suddenly, the chains with which they had bound her for several days sent forth a sound which, striking sharply and slowly, dispersed itself through the darkness of the prison: yet it was not able to awaken her; she groans and sleeps. Then stood before her a phantom, which seemed like her brother Don Giacomo; and approaching softly her bed, it said: "Come, arise, it is the hour." To which she replied by asking: "Where are we to go?" The phantom leaned over her as if it wished to whisper it in her ears, but the head, with a profusion of blood, fell from its shoulders, rolling over the bed. Then Beatrice uttered a desperate cry, and awoke.

Rising resolutely she looked around her. Nothing appeared changed: the lamp was still burning before the image of the Virgin at the head of the bed; beyond her bed she could discern but little; a profound silence pervaded the prison, yet in one corner, though she had not seen them, two persons kneeling prayed to the Lord for her soul.

She heard a step, then another; then from the black figures a form appeared, approached very slowly within the rays from the lamp, and revealed the venerable aspect of a Capuchin friar, emaciated by fasting and years. Beatrice looked upon that pale face, and spoke not a word. The old man raised his hands as if blessing her, and recited the prayers that have the power of expelling, in the name of the Father, the Son, and the Holy Ghost, the evil spirit from the body of the possessed. She allowed him to finish his exorcism, then in a sweet voice said:

"Father! the devil never has dwelt within me."

"Amen, my daughter! but he is always going about like a roaring lion, hence it is better always to be prepared to meet his assaults. My daughter, do you wish to approach the tribunal of penitence? I am here ready to listen."

"To-morrow."

"To-morrow! And why should we postpone to the morrow what we can do now? Is man master of the morrow?"

"So unprepared—thus taken by surprise—suddenly awaking from a terrible dream!"

"Does death assign us the hour in order not to surprise us? Does it not come unexpectedly, like a thief in the night? Christ has said so."

At this moment the door opened, and by the light of the torch were seen entering the substitute of the attorney, accompanied by several sheriffs, who, with cruel faces, without roughness, as without kindness, approached the bed of Beatrice. Sir Ventura, for such was the name of the substitute, began:

"If by deferring the notice I could, noble lady, change your destiny, I would willingly do so. My painful office obliges me to read your sentence to you."

"Of death?" exclaimed Beatrice.

The Capuchin friar covered his face with both his hands; the others bowed theirs. Beatrice convulsively grasped the tunic of the friar, and groaned from the depth of her soul:

"Oh, God!—God! how is it possible that I should die so young? I am hardly born—why do they wish in such a horrible manner to take me away from life? Lord! what crime have I committed? Life! But do you know what life is at sixteen years?"

"Life," replied the Capuchin to her, "is a weight which grows with our years. Happy those who are not born to carry it! After them, happy are those to whom God grants they may lay it aside soon! What do you find, my daughter, in your past years that would induce you to prolong the sum of it?"

"Nothing," replied Beatrice hastily; then she stopped as if memory seemed to present her a glimpse more bright; but hardly remembered, it vanished; she then, with a low voice more humbled, added:

"Nothing—nothing!"

"Ah! well, then, courage! let us soon rise from this table where the viands are ashes, the drink tears."

"But the manner, oh, father! the manner—oh!"

"Providence has furnished a thousand ways to leave life—only one to enter it. The speediest way to leave it is best; but all are blessed, if they lead to Heaven."

"But the infamy, father—the shame thrown upon my memory?"

"Those are thoughts of the dust. Before the judgment of God, what does the judgment of men matter? What are ages before the breath of the Lord? Fame passes, and time carries it with itself. Upon the threshold of the Infinite, years are not even distinguished as dust. Turn, my daughter, to Heaven, and forget worldly things."

"Alas! death!" murmured Beatrice, and the fatal word passing through her red lips froze and whitened them; a cold perspiration covered her forehead, her limbs shuddered, and her eyelids drooping heavily shadowed her wandering eyes.

"Help! help!" cried Virginia; and was on the point of going for spirits and salts to revive her, when Beatrice, recovering, said:

"It is passed;" and with her own hands she threw back her hair from her forehead bathed with perspiration. Then, turning to the bystanders, she continued: "Pardon me, gentlemen, it was a moment of weakness. Our Saviour had it—excuse it, then, in me, who am a sinner. Now, sir, you may fulfil your office; I am listening."

Sir Ventura then read the sentence, not omitting a hyphen, with slow, monotonous, mournful voice, like the tolling of the bell that knells for the dying. When he had finished, he went out with his sheriffs to repeat this office with the other condemned.

"Virginia," said Beatrice, taking the girl by the hand, "please to go out a moment. Time, as you see, is short—and before dying I must confess and prepare my soul. Go. I will call for you."

Virginia felt her beart breaking; she left the room without saying a word, and even if she had wished to speak she could not. Beatrice, her eyes accustomed to the darkness, saw in the corner of her prison a kneeling man who kept his face hidden in his hands; he was covered with his hood also, so that not a part of his face could be seen; he remained so motionless that he resembled an inanimate being.

Why does this man stay? And who is he, that would presume to have the secrets of heaven revealed to him? Confession can be heard but by one man only: thus it is a sacrament—otherwise sacrilege.

She kept silent; the Capuchin also dared not open his lips. Beatrice looked at one, then at the other; not being able to penetrate the mystery, she remained silent.

That kneeling man was Guido Guerra, the desperate lover of Beatrice. And why has he come in this solemn hour? Why does he wish to sadden her last moments? Has she not suffered enough? To no being was the hatred of others so fatal as his love to Beatrice. It was he who kindled in that maiden's heart an affection, which he afterwards drowned in blood. It was he who, with the intention of saving her, but incautiously, took away not only life, but her fame, the last relic of those unhappily betrayed. Let him leave her to die in peace; for, even living, they would be divided (and she has told him so) by a river of blood, and they would wander perpetually along its banks without ever being able or willing to ford it?

But Guido had come into the prison of Beatrice. Whether a god or a devil urged him, he minded not, he knew not. He wished to see Beatrice, and he does see her: he is regardless of everything else; and now he feels that he would willingly press the hand of the maiden, if it were extended to him, although at the very moment the falling ax might sever them both thus grasped.

Guido rose to his feet; he moved a few steps forward, staggering; then he stopped, and wept. The girl felt those tears descend into her soul as sweet as the tears of a mother.

"Who is weeping?" she said; "I would not have believed that in this place there could be a soul more desolate than mine."

And looking to heaven, she sighed sadly.

These words from the affectionate lips of Beatrice sounded in the ears of Guido like harmony of Paradise. What his passion had dared not, her voice had overcome: throwing aside every fear, he hastily drew back the hood, and showed his face, speaking and beautiful as a head of Correggio's. Silently and tremblingly he approached Beatrice: she recognized him, and started affrighted; then Guido also started back a step. Neither the unhappy lover nor the maiden dared to utter a word, nor breathe; the rattling of chains, shaken by the convulsive heavings of Beatrice, alone disturbed that silence.

Like young birds, fluttering their wings, then drooping them fatigued, these unfortunate lovers raised their eyes only to lower them immediately upon the ground. Their souls were in their glance; from their lips not even a sigh escaped. The lips of Beatrice will not speak; her eyes have spoken enough; the spirit of love passing before her like that of god, said: "You accused your father to him; you poured in his breast an implacable fury; had he loved you less, he would not have become a murderer: he showed his great love when he severed at the same time another's life and his own hope; Guido preferred your purity to his own happiness." And the spirit of love sparkled in her eyes with tenderness and pardon.

Beatrice, yielding to the instinct that urged her, moved to embrace him; then she stopped, blushing, and wept, and at her tears the others wept. Her lips opened to speak; but the monk, who standing near watched their emotions, placed his head between theirs, and with a low voice said:

"Silence! A word escaping from your lips would be death to him and shame to me. You are joined in matrimony. That which God binds in heaven, man may separate, but not put asunder. Now, my children, it is enough."

And with a strong arm he separated them. The mild Beatrice easily consented to the prayer; but Guido passionately repulsed the brother, who with a gentle reproof said:

"Then you wish to pour shame upon my white hairs because I was merciful to you!"

Guido bent down and kissed the iron handcuff which bound the right wrist of Beatrice; he saw the gold ring which he had sent her by means of Farinaccio, and he sighed forth a word, which Beatrice either did not hear, or did not wish to notice. The friar meanwhile arranged the hood upon Guido's head, and passing his arm around his waist dragged him toward the door.

The friar said to the suspicious keepers that his companion, weakened by watching, had not been able to bear the sad spectacle, and consigned him to the care of the Brothers of Mercy, who, receiving him with kindness, led him out of the prison. He descended those winding stairs bathing every step with tears.

Beatrice, like one petrified, stood looking at the door whence Guido had disappeared; she thought herself dreaming; except that the chain, shaking from time to time, gave her assurance she was indeed awake. Involuntarily she looked at the handcuff kissed by Guido, and saw his tears upon it glistening like iris by the light of the lamp; they looked like gems, and so they seemed to appear to her, for, sighing, she exclaimed:

"Behold the wedding jewels that my bridegroom has given me."

When Father Angelico returned, she asked kindly:

"And now where has he gone?"

"To the convent!"

"Ah, how miserable he is!"

"Very miserable! He does not always stay in the convent; often, in the middle of the night, a light knock is heard at the doors, and Guido presents himself. The friars receive him, and hide him through charity and gratitude, on account of the many alms with which he and his ancestors were generous to the convent. He asks for neither food nor rest: he goes into the church, kneels before the great altar, and passes hour after hour upon the cold steps as if in a trance; and were it not for his tears, he would not seem to be alive. Great is the misery of the man whose only manifestation of life is his tears. I think were his worst enemy to see him so reduced, he would feel pity for him."

Thus spoke the monk, and his words canceled from the mind of Beatrice the last traces of that fatal night, when she saw at the foot of her bed her father murdered by the hand of her lover.

"But in the daytime where does he hide? Father, when you see him, I implore you to tell him to go far from Rome; this air is fatal to him; here, I know, cruel men live. Do you know who alone feels pity in priestly Rome? The executioner!"

"I will tell him."

"And if he hesitate, add that I beg him to do so."

"Very well. Now, my daughter, is the time to turn your thoughts to Heaven: prostrate yourself, for so much as you humble yourself, so much you will be exalted. Contrition is born of mercy; and when they present themselves together at the throne of God, it rarely happens that justice does not lay aside her sword."

Beatrice kneeling, opened to the confessor the secrets of her soul. Light faults, little errors, which she considered very heavy, showed how spotless was the innocence of that courageous but gentle spirit. The friar, in listening, bewailed the hard necessity that had forced her to stain her hands with her father's blood. Beatrice was silent, and had not yet confessed the parricide. The friar, skilled in human passions, attributed her silence to shame, and for this, instead of being offended, thought better of her; hence he discreetly entreated her to reveal all her sins, encouraging her to throw off all her shame; but she sincerely replied:

"My sins, as many as I have been able to recollect, I have confessed; for those which I involuntarily omitted, may the Divine Goodness pardon me."

"Still, search."

"I will search again;" and remaining in a thoughtful attitude, she prolonged her silence beyond the expectation of the friar; who, imagining that now to be dissimulation which he first thought bashfulness, not without a little harshness, asked her:

"And tell me, by whose hands was Count Cenci murdered?"

"I must not confess the sins of others." And she said these words with so much candor that the Capuchin looked astonished.

"And you did not kill him, then?"

"I?—I killed him not."

"And why did you, then, accuse yourself of it?"

"I, father, have suffered such painful torments that to think them over I shudder, and can hardly believe that my body was able to bear them without expiring; and yet I was fully resolved to die in the torture in testimony of the truth; but with infinite prayers my relatives, my friends, and the advocates begged me, and with abundant reasons urged me, to assume upon myself the crime; for in this manner, they hoped, I would be able to save my mother and brothers. As to myself, they said it would then have been easy to declare me excusable on account of the persecutions and attempts of Count Cenci. The reasons certainly did not persuade me much, nor would even the prayers have conquered me; but, fearing to show too much harshness against my relatives, I bowed my head, and offered the sacrifice of my life and fame in order to attempt to save that of Lady Lucrezia and my brothers. I had a presentiment that I should lose myself, and not save them, and I said so: the fact has proved that I imagined right. Patience! So it pleased God, and so be it—it was not my fault that those dear ones were not saved."

"But did you not affirm your crime upon oath?"

"The advocate persuaded me that before human and divine laws it was not a sin to defend one's own life by means of the death of others, much less could one offend God by defending it with a false oath; and I swore."

"O sophists! When is anything lost by speaking the truth?"

"It seemed so to me; but he recommended me to place entire confidence in him; and so great is the reputation of learning that he enjoys, I feared to appear too presumptuous in preferring my opinion to his."

"And who was he that recommended it to you?"

"He—Guido, who sent me this ring—the ring which was to be blessed at our marriage." And while she thus spoke, her face through modesty had become crimson. The brother continued:

"Expose fully, my daughter, the entire truth; perchance you may have sinned, more than you think, against yourself."

"But the secrets of God?"

"The secrets of God," replied the Capuchin severely, "are buried in the heart of man; and from man, you know, one can tear out the heart, but not the secret."

Then Beatrice told all the truth, without omitting the slightest particular. The monk, who had begun to listen incredulously, by degrees was forced to believe in the sincerity of the magnanimous girl; and while she still spoke, the monk struck his forehead, exclaiming:

"O God! was there ever seen in the world a more blessed soul than this?"

When Beatrice had finished her confession, the astonished friar said:

"Holy soul, I absolve you, since this is the duty of my ministry; but I protest that I ought to kneel before you and beg you to recommend me to God. From whose lips can prayers be more acceptable to Him than from these most pure and innocent ones of yours? Pray to God by yourself; I will join my prayers to yours, which must certainly reach heaven; nor will I indeed pray for you, for you have no need of it; but rather for this unhappy city, and for the safety of those who have condemned you."

The girl knelt before the sacred images which hung from the wall; and turning, as women are more accustomed to do, toward the Blessed Virgin, gave thanks for calling her so soon from this life, and above all for having granted to her the favor of seeing her dear Guido once more, who, not being able to be her companion on earth, she hoped might be united with her eternally in heaven.

But here she stopped, as if she had trodden upon a viper, and frightened, she asked:

"Father, tell me, for pity's sake, will Guido be pardoned? Will he be made worthy of eternal salvation? Shall I not tremble at his aspect? Will it be granted me to grasp that hand which has murdered my father?"

"Do you suppose, my daughter, that we should be able to enjoy paradise if we did not forget earthly sorrows? To an immortal soul, the memory of having once been a prisoner within a cell of clay would not only be a wearisome thought, but one of shame."

"Ah!" replied Beatrice sighing, "yet I would not have wished to forget my love, although full of sorrows."

Then she began again to pray fervently to God; and

the monk by her side begged Him, silently, never to let the courage of the innocent girl fail.

A Brother of Mercy appeared at that moment upon the threshold of the prison; he beckoned the monk and whispered a word to him; the latter returning to Beatrice, said to her:

"My daughter, if you desire to be in company with her ladyship, your mother, it will be allowed you."

"Let her come—oh! let her come, poor mother—we will console each other."

CHAPTER XXVII

THE GARMENTS

BEATRICE and Lady Lucrezia threw their arms eagerly about each other's neck. Alas! the chains prevented them from embracing freely. I leave untold the convulsive sobs, the desolate words, the long and painful sighs;—so much yet remains to be told of such miseries, that even to think of them the wearied soul trembles.

But everything has an end here below; even tears, although the most abundant inheritance left by Adam to his children: at last both were silent.

Beatrice, observing Lady Lucrezia in a showy robe of satin trimmed with lace, happened to look at her own; and with great wonder saw that, inadvertently, she was dressed in a green gown embroidered with gold, which she was accustomed to wear, in her more peaceful days, in preference to any other.

Memory, often a very importunate friend, recalled to her mind that she wore this very gown when she first saw Guido, and was seen by him; and it reminded her also that he (with his young mind full of the songs of Petrarch) had often said to her that at her first appearance to him she looked like Laura. But this was no time to cherish such happy recollections: expelling them from her mind, she began to consider how unbecoming it would have been to go to death in such gay garments. And thinking, as indeed it was true, that Lady Lucrezia, immersed in grief, had not even noticed it, she said:

"Mother, when we women undertake the voyage of life, our censors say that we take vanity for our provision; and if any danger threatens us, we would rather let the ship sink than throw away the cargo. And they are not wholly wrong. Women, when willing, can reform themselves of every other vice except vanity; because the former are known, but vanity very seldom, or never is; and it cannot even be fought against, because it does not sustain any assault; it yields and flies away, or flying, hides itself under our persons like our shadows at noon."

"Beatrice, I do not understand you; for me these are too abstruse matters."

"A glance, which you may cast upon yourself, will render it plain; look how, without paying attention, you have dressed yourself."

"O, Mother of mercy!" exclaimed Lady Lucrezia, astonished, seeing herself in such apparel—"it may indeed be said that I have lost my senses!"

Beatrice remarked the simple words, and almost smiled; but soon after she added in a dignified manner:

"To show ourselves thus would seem like vain-glory on our part to challenge death, which is far from our hearts. We bear it with resignation, because God sends it to us; is it not true, mother?"

"You speak like the wise and good girl I have always known you to be."

"Now, Virginia," continued Beatrice, "you must try

to provide us with any kind of cloth, enough to make two loose garments; one for myself, the other for my mother, two cords, and two veils—Virginia, my dear girl, why do you not answer?"

Virginia felt a weight on her heart, which prevented her from uttering a word; but after sobbing a long time, she answered:

"I have a piece of bombazine of dark color, and another of violet taffeta, which my father bought in Viterbo at the fair;—but I never made a dress of them—because it is best for me not to be observed—nor known—if you wish them."

"Certainly; and I will give you money enough to buy some less mournful ones; for a girl of your age ought not to wear either dark or black clothes;—you see that when I lived I wore green. And what shall we do for the cords?"

"My father has some."

"And the veils?"

"They are furnished by the Brothers of Mercy," and here Virginia burst into tears again.

Beatrice pressed her hands upon her bosom as if to repress the outburst of passion ready to break forth, and said:

"We shall then have to think of fewer things than I supposed. Haste now, Virginia, for our hours are numbered."

Virginia returned with the cloth, and Beatrice, without losing any time, began to cut it. She held one edge, Virginia the other, and the scissors flew with wonderful celerity, cutting the threads.

The tears of Lucrezia rained down more plenteously than before. This new outburst of sorrow came so unexpectedly that Beatrice felt discouraged. Her courage, which she had drawn from the examples and teachings of philosophers, already began to fail; she rested her head upon her hand, and the rays of the lamp burning before the image of the Madonna fell upon her. Then she exclaimed:

"Ah! it is true, and I had forgotten it; when every other comfort fails, Thou art the star of all storms. Faith is the reason of spiritual beings, and we are already touching the gate of eternity."

All three women suddenly arose, as if urged by the same feeling, and had recourse to the celestial image as the swans fly under the maternal wings, when the roaring of the thunder frightens them: and, having drawn from that inexhaustible source waters of consolation, they returned again to prepare the funeral garments.

An assistant of Master Alessandro now presented himself, holding in his hands a large pair of scissors. He looked long at Beatrice, and seemed dazzled by so much beauty; she looked at him, and shuddered; reassuring herself she thought: "A voice of mercy may perchance have touched the heart of the Pope? Is the spectacle of blood to be taken away from the crowds, which causes them to become more ferocious?" Then turning to the assistant, she said: "Speak!—why do you remain there as in a trance? Speak, we are prepared for anything."

He hesitatingly answered:

"Your ladyship—you know—it is a custom—the hair."

"The hair!" She exclaimed, and immediately raising her hand, she pulled out her comb, and her magnificent golden hair fell down like a wave all over her body. "Look! this is my hair; what do you wish to do with it?"

But the assistant, more embarrassed than before, was silent. She continued:

"Every might has its right;—the right of the ax is in not being impeded in its blow:—I understand—cut it off, and do it quickly."

And the hair fell to the ground.

Beatrice gathered up the glorious mass, and one hand alone was not enough to hold it. She looked at it a long time, and then, as if it were a person, addressed it thus:

"Faithful companion in all my misfortune! I could have wished that you might descend with me into the tomb. But since God has not granted this, you shall not survive me in the world, perhaps to hide the baldness of mature age, or to increase the deceit of vanity—born and grown upon a maiden's head, you shall not become an instrument of falsehood—and besides, all within you is pregnant with misfortune, and you would carry it to whomsoever it might be who should use you. It is better, then, that you should be destroyed, like me, in the elements that compose you; let our fatal particles be dispersed in the immense fatality of the world—united we have done harm, and perhaps might do still more. I will except only this lock—let the rest be consumed."

And she threw it in the fire that burned in the grate. In a short time, of her magnificent hair only a small handful of white dust remained.

"Virginia," continued Beatrice, "I divide this lock of my hair in two parts, and consign it to you. If some day you should ever meet a tall and handsome man, with blond hair, and the mark of fatality on his face—you will recognize him, since all the unfortunate present in their faces a certain family resemblance; and I, you remember, when first I met you, recognized you for my sister in sorrow; listen" (and she whispered a word in her ear)—"you will give him this lock: the other you will keep for yourself. I can leave money, dresses, jewels, and I will leave them to you; but these are not part of myself; by carrying about you my hair, you will always have a fragment of my being—as long as it lasts, at least—since even the dead are destroyed, and their relics are found no more. They cannot bring you misfortune certainly, because you, poor girl! are already unfortunate enough. If I could change your state, God knows I would do it. I wish you all happiness; but if you also are to pass days full of bitterness, let death be as sweet to you as this last kiss which I impress upon your lips."

CHAPTER XXVIII

THE PARDON

BEATRICE, approaching Father Angelico, who was kneeling with his face concealed by his hands, praying and weeping before the image of the Madonna, touched him lightly on the shoulder, and said:

"Father, would you please to call the Brothers of Mercy, since to them and to yourself I wish to intrust new requests?"

"Willingly, my daughter." The friar went out, and returned soon in company with the Brothers. They held their cowls drawn over their faces, so that nothing could be seen of them but their eyes, sufficient to reveal the passions of their souls. It would have been in vain to recognize from these small openings Brother Aldobrandino, who had come there less to comfort than to spy—his dry, curious, glittering, yet anxious glances wandered around.

When they were ranged about her, Beatrice said:

"Brothers in Christ! For the charitable office you render me, I give you with all my heart those thanks which my lips cannot pronounce, and I pray God that He will recompense you according to your merits. So much the more I feel touched with veneration for you, since, by remaining hooded, you are unknown to me, thus signifying that you do not aid the individual, but the suffering creature. Yet I need greater help than you are accustomed to give; and I dare to ask it both from you and from this most pious spiritual father. Let my new request, I pray you, be an argument, not of indiscretion on my part, but of necessity. With the aid of the notary of the Brotherhood of the Sacred Wounds, I have made my will. Now, fearing lest the tribunals might put some obstacle in the way of its execution, I beg that you will intercede with all your might with Pope Clement, and induce him to allow my dower to be disposed of as I have written there. You will also cause two hundred masses to be celebrated for the repose of my soul, a hundred of them before my burial, and a hundred afterward; for such purpose may it please you to receive these forty-five ducats, which I have with me now, and for the remainder, which you may need, please to have recourse to Sir Francesco Scartesio, my attorney, who will give it to you. To Virginia, who has served me with sisterly affection, and has comforted me in my saddest days of trial, besides all that which I leave her in my will, let her have all my linens, woolen, and silk clothes, and my gold ornaments, which will be found in this prison. But where is Virginia? What is she doing, that I see her not?" And she cast her eyes around, but not seeing her she continued:

"Unhappy girl! She had not the courage to contemplate what I am destined to suffer. Poor girl! indeed worthy that heaven should give her either another soul or another station! I know not whether I should desire to see her again; but in case I should not, salute her tenderly for me, and tell her that I hope to meet her in heaven, where all angels are equal, and draw one origin, holy and immediate, from the Most High God. When," and she placed her hand upon her breast, "when this heart shall have ceased to beat, you will bury me in the Church of Santo Pietro in Montorio; there the sun, rising from the summit of Montecavi, sheds its first beams; and although the dead do not feel its warmth or see its light, yet it is consoling in the hour of death to know that your tomb will be visited by the light of heaven. Upon the same hill, farther toward the sea, four years ago they buried Torquato Tasso. In Santo Pietro in Montorio is the Transfiguration, the last picture of Raphael, which death prevented him from finishing. And now, while I go to commune with God, grant, dearest brothers in Christ, that I may confide in the assistance of your prayers."

Lady Lucrezia, imitating the example of her step-daughter, disposed also of several things in masses for her soul, no less than for her relatives.

Prospero Farinaccio was sleeping most profoundly, pleased by gay images of triumphs, honors, and riches; and all this pyramid of rose-colored visions appeared to him crowned by a magnificent cardinal's hat, which he playfully placed upon the light tresses of a woman, whose countenance resembled that of Beatrice. Suddenly he was awakened by the noise of a glass broken by the throwing of a stone against the window of his chamber. At the same time a mournful voice cried from the street below:

"Why do you delay? why do you delay? While you sleep, all the Cenci are led to death!"

He sprang from the bed and threw open the window. Dawn had hardly broken; he strained his eyes, but could not perceive anyone. The voice kept repeating the sad exclamation:

"All the Cenci are dragged to the scaffold—and you sleep!"

He dressed himself hurriedly, got into a carriage, and

hastening to the prison of Corte Savella, heard the news confirmed. He reentered the carriage and hurried to the Quirinal palace. Breathless, he ascended the stairs two or three at a time, and reached the ante-chamber of the Pope. Having arrived there, he asked the chamberlains to procure him access to the High Pontiff on most urgent business: it was a matter of life and death, and for the love of God to do it quickly.

A chamberlain very leisurely taking him by the arm, and holding him firmly before him with a jesting tone, but with perfect politeness, said to him:

"Dear Sir Advocate, you must know that His Holiness still sleeps."

"But I know that the Holy Father rises very early."

At this another chamberlain, seizing Farinaccio by the other arm, caused him to turn toward the left, saying:

"But be assured, my dear sir, that the Pope sleeps yet."

A third chamberlain, in his turn turned him again to the right, saying:

"You must understand, most worthy Sir Advocate, that His Holiness wishes to sleep—for he has not closed his eyes all night."

In this manner was Farinaccio turned now by this one, and now by that, until he found that he had described a perfect circle round the room, and had not obtained what he wanted. Fortune, as if wishing to give the lie to these new Pharisees, caused the cup-bearer of the Pope to appear in the ante-chamber at this moment with a cup of smoking chocolate for his master, and he passed directly across the room to go and give it to him.

The chamberlains, in order not to have their assertions denied, signed him to stop; but he said artlessly:

"I do not understand you; you called me as if the end of the world had come, to order me to carry the chocolate to His Holiness, who has been up some time, and now you wish me to stop."

"You are crazy; we have not heard his bell ring. His Holiness certainly sleeps."

"If you, who are so near, have not heard it, how comes it that I heard it from a distance?"

At this moment, they heard the bell, as if it were rung by a person out of patience with waiting.

"I told you so!—Room, I say," continued the cup-bearer, "for His Holiness gets into a passion easily, and I shall have to take it first."

And he pushed aside the chamberlain in order to pass. Farinaccio, readily imitating his example, in spite of opposition, took the tray from his hands, opened the door, and walked boldly into the chamber of the Pontiff. The cup-bearer was about to cry "Stop thief!" But thinking a robber would not have sufficient boldness to enter there, much less to take refuge in the very room of the Pontiff, astonished, he kept still; and the Pope himself made a motion with his hand that he should leave.

Farinaccio, placing the tray upon the table, knelt at the feet of Pope Clement, saying:

"Let it not be ascribed to me as a fault, most blessed Father, I beg you on my knees, that I have assumed the part, most honorable for me, of the humblest of your servants."

"Rise!"

"Ah, no! Your Holiness, leave me thus with my head in the dust, for such ought to be the attitude of a disconsolate man who supplicates; great sorrow now oppresses me."

He expected the Pope would interrogate him concerning the cause of his coming, intending to discover from the tone of his voice what might be hoped or feared from him; but he stood as silent and impenetrable as a sphinx; so that Farinaccio had to continue in the most piteous voice, still kneeling, with bent head, and hands clasped in supplication.

"A cry, I swear it on the faith of a Christian, a mournful cry awoke me, calling loudly: 'Miserable man! do you sleep, while all the Cenci family are being dragged to the scaffold?' I could not say, most Holy Father, whether this voice came from heaven or from a spirit of darkness."

"Why do you fear that it came from the Evil One! Truth does not dwell in the mouth of the devil."

"Ah! then the voice was really true? Ah! pardon, pardon, Your Holiness, for so much innocent blood, which is about to be shed. Rome never has seen, since its foundation, such a frightful tragedy."

"How innocent? Have they not all confessed the committed crime?"

"*Mea culpa*" pursued Farinaccio, striking his breast with his closed fist; "*mea culpa, mea maxima culpa.* God has wished to humble me. God has wished to give me cause to weep, until, like Saint Peter, tears have made furrows down my cheeks. The wisdom of a man, presumptuous in his science compared to the intellect of love in a maiden, has proved to be a folly, and a snare of death. It was I, Your Holiness, who persuaded the gentle girl, Beatrice Cenci, to confess herself, although innocent, guilty of the parricide: she was ready and disposed to die amidst tortures in witness of the truth; it was I who drew her from her purpose; I who promised that, by inculpating herself and excusing the others, she would easily procure safety for herself and them: for them as being innocent of parricide; for herself, as being forced by extreme necessity to defend herself from violence. She refused; she maintained that the best defence for innocence consisted in telling the truth, and nothing but the truth. Oh, holiest words inspired by God! But I conjured her, I forced her with tears in my eyes; I endeavored to move her by domestic affections, by the generosity of the sacrifice, by the virtue of charity; and I, and her relatives, kneeling around the bed where she lay with her bones broken and her flesh torn by the cruelty of the tortures which she had suffered, extended our hands in supplication until, conquered in spite of herself, and notwithstanding her presentiments, she promised to confess herself guilty in the way she has done, and in the manner which I dictated to the betrayed girl. Pardon, then, Holy Father, pity! Oh, if she were to die thus for my fault, my desolate soul would despair of its eternal safety."

"Do not be disheartened about that; we will easily find a way to send you to heaven."

"And who will save me from my conscience?"

"Your own conscience!"

These words, uttered in a tone of unspeakable scorn, fell upon the head of Farinaccio like a flame: he raised his eyes to fix them on the countenance of the Pope, but that face appeared like stone.

"My conscience," replied Farinaccio dejected, "tells me that I shall have no more peace."

"You shall have it, believe me; I understand these things, you shall have it. Most worthy Sir Counselor, I know you for a man of much perspicacity, and noted in your profession. You—and in this I only give you the deserved praise—fulfilled your noble office with zeal and perseverance, which could hardly be equaled, never surpassed. Now, since you know so well how to perform your own duty, suffer in peace others to do theirs."

"And for this very reason, Holy Father, because not only the sentiment of your duty, but affection and the necessity of your elevated nature urge you to justice, I have made bold enough to explain to you all this, and warn you to be careful lest you commit an error that may cause an eternal stain upon your name."

"We have respected in you" (and here the voice of the Pope sounded somewhat threatening) "the office of advocate; now respect in us that of judge."

Farinaccio, still at the feet of the Pontiff, looked like one of those Israelites who, at the foot of Mount Sinai, waited in expectation for the word of God, and, like them, he heard the words pronounced over his head, amid thunder and lightning. But he did not yet give himself up for lost, and making a desperate effort he said:

"Where justice does not reach, let mercy!"

"They *must* die!" concluded the Pontiff.

"*Must!*" exclaimed Farinaccio, springing to his feet. "Ah! if they *must*, then the affair wears a different aspect. Pardon me, most Holy Father, if I was ignorant of such a necessity, and grant me to go away with death in my heart."

The Pope perceived that he had said too much, and saw that it was necessary to amend, as well as he could, his incautious words.

"Yes;—certainly, in spite of myself—they *must*. The spirit of the people, the fame of Rome, the security of the citizens, the religion of the Papal Mantle command me to shut my ears to mercy."

"Do they command that all should die on a wheel, and be quartered?"

"You, as a man of much learning, know, Sir Counselor, that the Egyptians condemned the parricidal son to be pierced by a number of sharp sticks, and then burned upon a pile of thorns; the father who killed the son, to look for three successive days at the corpse of the slain. Here in Rome, in the early times of paganism, no laws against parricides were known: the malice of men, however, increased afterward to such a degree as to commit such excesses that the horrible punishment of the Pompeian law appeared too mild. In our times, be pleased to turn your eyes toward the kingdoms of Spain,

France and England, and you will not find any milder punishments. If we cut off the head of the man who commits homicide, reason dictates that there should be a difference of punishment between him and the parricide. Nevertheless, to favor you, we will absolve the women from the tortures and quarterings; but the decapitation must be executed."

"Even the child must be beheaded?"

"What child?"

"Bernardino Cenci, Holy Father; you know he has barely reached his twelfth year, should he also undergo the punishment of a parricide? I hardly defended him, thinking that the best advocate for him would be the date of his birth; but I have been deceived."

"But did he not also confess that he participated in the crime?"

"He confessed, certainly, he did confess; but at his age can he know what parricide is, and what matters confession? Did he not confess in order that the tortures might cease, and by the promise that he should be saved? Holy Father! for once listen to the voice of your heart, which persuades you to mercy; give ear to it, for one day we all shall have need of mercy."

"You make me have a scruple about Bernardino Cenci."

And the Pope bent his head, meditating. After he had remained some time in this posture, he continued:

"Generally, wickedness does not outgrow age; sometimes it does, and we read examples of this; nor does age save one from the most atrocious crimes—on this question, however, I have some scruples, and I would wish to be able to satisfy you, most worthy Sir Farinaccio; in order that you may not go away discouraged, but rather that you may be convinced of the great esteem we have of you, we will grant the life of Bernardino Cenci. Now go in peace, and leave us to finish and send the *placet* speedily, in order that it may not arrive too late. You see, Sir Farinaccio, that it is not our fault if you do not call yourself contented. Go in peace!"

Farinaccio thought his case much like that of the patriarch Jacob, when his treacherous sons placed in his hands the bloody garment of Joseph, and he was obliged to say to them—thanks! He departed with a broken heart. With head bent and hoarse voice, he returned thanks to the Pontiff for his complaisance, while the latter said:

"We will send the *placet* immediately, and we authorize you to announce it openly that we have granted it for the merits of your lordship."

"*Ex ore leonis*," murmured Farinaccio, descending from the Quirinal palace; "our ancestors used to consecrate to the gods the remains of the lamb snatched from the wolf's mouth."

So he thought then; but more so afterward, when he understood what kind of pardon had been granted to the little Bernardino. Yet, with the flight of time, with hearing it repeated to him everywhere, and by receiving most sincere thanks, not only from others, but from Bernardino himself, and finding it for his own interest to believe thus, he ended by believing truly that he had snatched this child from death. His light loves, the alternate changes of luck in gambling, and low pleasures first softened, then rendered wholly blunt, the sense or sorrow. The wealth he received from the office of Counselor, the great credit that he enjoyed in the court, persuaded him afterward to abstain from the defence of the Cenci for the reacquirement of the entails confiscated in benefit of the Apostolic Chamber. He excused himself by saying that he had done enough—now others should try.

This and other things he said with the semblance of truth, but they were false. The only truth was the presage of the sceptered priest, who, when Prospero Farinaccio asked him who would save him from his conscience, had replied: "*Your own conscience!*"

CHAPTER XXIX

THE WIFE

BUT love did not sleep. Guido had had means of knowing the fatal sentence as soon as it was signed. Not expecting it so soon, he was surprised; but his soul did not despair, and, having recourse to his new friends the banditti, he urgently prayed them, even ordered them (for his authority over them increased daily) to disguise themselves in various ways and assemble without delay in the Flavian amphitheater.

Two hours before dawn the bandits began to collect in groups, some dressed as abbots, others as friars, some in country clothes, and others as gentlemen; showing the falsity of the proverb, "The tunic does not make the monk," for no one could have distinguished them from true gentlemen cleanly washed and shaved. But, on counting them, they were found to amount to only forty, too small a number for so hazardous an undertaking. But Guido and the rest were not easily discouraged from so great a risk—Guido himself would have rushed into this danger alone. All opinions having been heard, Guido commanded that all should put sprigs of grape-leaves in their hats or hoods as a sign, and, provided with arms, should attack the procession as it approached the scaffold. Having there got free of the Brotherhood of Mercy, the constables and the soldiers, they should seize upon Beatrice and transport her to a place where he would be, mounted upon a swift horse which would carry her behind him beyond the walls of the city; they, profiting by the tumult, should disband, and endeavor to reach Tivoli, where he would await them. The bandits agreed to this arrangement with their whole hearts, for not only by nature were they willing to undertake such bold deeds, but, knowing the compassion all Rome felt for Beatrice, they trusted to gain great renown, of which they were desirous; finally, the promised reward, should they succeed in saving the girl, was Cæsar-like, as they had occasion to say many times afterward.

A wonderful thing—yet mentioned in the records of that time— a little while after, in Rome itself, others meditated the same design! It was believed that these were secretly urged by Cardinal Maffeo Barberini and some of his friends—perhaps it was not true, but he manifested great solicitude in the affair. Beatrice's fate and her great beauty had moved him deeply. The care he took to procure her portrait, and the permission he obtained to render due honors to the corpse of the noble girl, showed it plainly.

Could Guido have had his forces united with those of Cardinal Maffeo, the plan might have succeeded; but thinking he had already trespassed too much on his friend, he did not wish, with unreasonable imprudence, to involve him in an undertaking so difficult and fraught with danger.

This other conspiracy to save Beatrice was composed of artists, who, although accustomed to delineate physical beauty alone, by that secret bond of relationship which unites all good and beautiful things, were easily enamored of moral beauty. As leaders of this company were many intimate friends of the most noble families in Rome, secretly sent by their patrons, who felt as if receiving a great wrong themselves in this Cencian slaughter. Among many others, the history of the times relates how Ubaldino Ubaldini, a young Florentine artist of great expectations, who would have attained great fame had not death unfortunately closed his career, was roused almost to madness: he was the painter who sketched the head of Beatrice, as hopeless love had pictured her face upon his heart, at the very moment she was led to the scaffold. Guido Reni had not yet moved from Bologna, his native place, to Rome: he went there toward the end of the year 1599, or the beginning of the year 1600, as is proved in his life published in the *Felsina pittrice*. Tradition says that Guido painted the portrait of Beatrice on the eve of her death; but as this is erroneous, it should be corrected; for if true, it would stain the reputation of the girl as well as the painter. Upon Beatrice it would lay the blame of vanity, since her soul in those last solemn moments should have been, as it truly was, absorbed in thoughts of God and the purest affections. It would have shown that Guido possessed an unfeeling or a hard heart to have been able, without trembling, to paint this unfortunate, lovely girl, ready to be dragged to an unmerited death. This picture, painted by Guido, is now preserved in the palace of the Princes Barberini at Rome, and was finely engraved by Volpatio, and better still by Morghen.

The design of these consiprators also was to rush upon the procession, seize Beatrice, and the other condemned, put them in a carriage drawn by powerful horses, and transport them to the sea. These exceeded the companions of Guido in number, but were surpassed by them in valor, for the latter were accustomed to mix in the bloodiest frays. A white tassel upon the head was their badge. Ubaldini was to hold the door of the carriage ready, the reins being held by a certain French artist, who had boasted he could drive the sun's chariot without danger of plunging into the Po.

CONTEMPORARY PORTRAIT OF BEATRICE CENCI

From a Painting by Guido Reni

"*Per Dio!*" cried Ubaldini, striking the table heavily with his fist, "she must not die!—she must not die!—it would be better"——

As he hesitated, a companion said:

"What would be better?"

"To break the Apollo Belvedere or the Laocoön."

"And the cupola of the Vatican, too," added a third.

"Much better. for we can rebuild these things," observed the Frenchman who had offered to enact the part of Automedon; but Ubaldini, looking askance at him, said between anger and laughter:

"No, Frenchman, true son of France! these things *cannot* be rebuilt, but better they should perish than an innocent creature."

The sun's first rays peeping over the hills of Rome fell in the prison of Torre di Nona upon a sorrowful sight. Giacomo and Bernardino having met, ran to embrace each other: in order to mingle their tears and kisses, they had come within each other's chains.

"Come, dear one, embrace me, I feel as if embracing my own children. You are happy, Bernardino, in not having children! You do not feel more than half the anguish of death."

"But have I not nephews?"

"Alas! my children—orphans—children of a parricide, pursued by a cruel man who can do all he wishes, and who wants their patrimony! Everyone, to please the powerful, conceals his own baseness under the semblance of holy abomination, and hunts down the unfortunate. Where are their friends? They have become enemies, and will make the children bear the shame of their acquaintance with the father. They will take the bread from their famishing mouths. Who will defend them? They will beat them, and they will cry, and to make them quiet they will beat them again. Their mother, ill-used like them, will be ashamed that her bosom has become a nest for vipers. Ah, no, no! Luisa, my Luisa never will abandon my children, and when milk fails her, she will nourish them with her blood."

"Poor little children! And will they deprive them of all their own property? And take away my estates also? But I know nothing about these wicked affairs, and so I told the father confessor a short time ago, but he would not believe it. He obstinately insisted: but 'No,' I firmly called out—until they came and took me away."

"Who knows better than I, my brother, that you are wholly innocent? You at least have one consolation, that you will pass from this life to heavenly joys. As for me, I doubt whether that wil be granted to me; for although I had no part in the death of Count Cenci still I must acknowledge the crime of having at another time conspired against his life, and consented to his death."

"And yet we confessed we stabbed him ourselves! I murder the man only the sight of whom made me tremble? But, although I am a boy, I saw well enough that if we denied it, they would kill us with a thousand tortures; so, by confessing, we should gain something—death at one blow. Tell me, brother, you who have lived longer in the world, is justice always thus?"

Giacomo replied only with sighs; the boy listening, said:

"Hear, Giacomo, hear! what bell is that which sounds over our heads?"

Giacomo, pressing Bernardino more closely to his bosom, asked sadly:

"How do you feel, Bernardino?"

"I? Very well."

"And are you not sorry to die?"

"Yes, because I love the birds, the butterflies, and the flowers among which they fly, and I love to see the Tiber flow when it is swollen—I love everything. Here I can welcome the sun, which is bright and warm; and there beyond it, I feel that all is dark and cold. Here, I know where I am; but there, where I am going, although they tell me about it, and it may be so, still I am not sure."

"Now listen; that bell knells the last hour for us, who are full of life. That bell proclaims that we must depart, we who wish to stay."

As if in confirmation of his sad words, the confessors and the Brothers of Mercy appeared at the door.

"Come, courage, brothers! the hour draws nigh;" said a mournful voice.

"God's will be done!" replied Giacomo; but Bernardino said:

"And is this God's will, Giacomo?"

"Yes, certainly; for nothing happens without God's consent; and you sin grievously by doubting it," replied a confessor, instead of Giacomo.

"If it be so, father, I repent; and also to gain favor in Heaven, I will believe that I, although most innocent, am sent to my death by the will of God."

"Who of us are sinless? we are all guilty in the eyes of God."

"But not all are dragged to death at the age of twelve."

"God chasteneth whom he loveth; and you, my son, should thank Him with your whole heart for having chosen you from among a thousand to profit by His infinite goodness."

"Father," replied the boy, with simplicity, "if you would like to take my place"——

And the friar, as if remorsefully, raised his hands and eyes to heaven, saying:

"With all my heart, my son, if it could be done; but it cannot."

Master Alessandro, with his iron visage, cut short the delay. It seemed impossible, yet he showed in his face great sorrow—savage—threatening to those whom fortune had thrown into his hands; but yet sorrowful. He wrapped the condemned in two black cloaks furnished by the Brotherhood of Mercy; the very one on the back of Giacomo had formerly belonged to Count Cenci, who had once been enrolled in that holy institution.

All with slow steps passed out of the prison. Giacomo stopped upon the threshold of the room he was leaving, witness of inexpressible agonies, and uttered these words:

"Seventy and seven times accursed be the man, who condemned another man to despair within this living tomb; let him who with only one blow hurries him to his grave be only seven times accursed."

The bells continued to peal a dirge for the dying. The drum sounded discordantly; it seemed as if heaven and earth exchanged in these sounds the news of the slaughter about to be fulfilled, and were stupefied by it. In the courtyard below, several troops of cavalry stood ready, a crowd of constables on foot, the Brothers of Mercy, the executioner and his assistants—in short, all the miserable preparations of power with which Justice must surround herself when she is not justice.

Bernardino looked at all these preparations in a bewildered manner, but more particularly did he notice two carts, within which were furnaces of burning coal with iron pincers heating; and with boyish curiosity he asked:

"Giacomo, what are those pincers for?"

Giacomo did not reply, and many of the friars wept beneath their cowls; but the boy again inquired:

"I wish to know; come, tell me, Giacomo; you will not frighten me in the least, since I know I must die."

"They are for us;" replied Giacomo, and he could say no more.

"Oh! I did not think so many implements were necessary for me; it will be short work with me, you see, I have a neck as slender as a reed, I do not think the executioner will labor very hard."

He then saw a nail, a hammer, and a *red mantle embroidered with gold*, all which objects, as being instruments of the crime, were borne upon one of the carts to be exposed to the public.

"Giacomo, is not that red mantle the one our father used to wear? This red mantle seems to haunt us."

The comforters, in order to prevent the mind of the boy from wandering from religious thoughts, put upon him, as also on his brother, what was called the *tavolette*, a kind of wooden box in which the heads of the prisoners were enclosed, obliging their eyes to rest upon the image of the crucifix, and certain holy prayers made for these occasions by a learned and pious Capuchin, and pasted upon the sides. The boy shrieked, and cried out for them to remove this encumbrance and not take from him what God alone could give—the sight of heaven.

Just then there was a movement among the people at the door of the courtyard, a stir among the soldiery, and a carriage was seen slowly moving in the midst. The voice of the crowd resounded noisily against the prison walls, like the waves of the sea in a tempest.

"Pardon! pardon!"

A thrill of life shone from the eyes of Giacomo, and his head rose. The noble Sir Ventura descended from the carriage, and standing opposite the prisoners, drew a paper from his bosom and read:

"Don Bernardino Cenci, our lord grants you your life. *Be pleased, however, to accompany your relatives, and pray to God for their souls*"*

The comforters then took off the *tavolette* from Bernardino's head; and the executioner, having read the *placet* of the Pope, freed him from his handcuffs, and not

* These were the precise words, as preserved in the chronicle of the times.

knowing what to cover him with to remove from him the appearance of being condemned, he took the red mantle of Count Cenci, and wrapped him in it. Thus fate ordained that the last sons of this wicked man should approach the scaffold, one in the black hooded robe with which he betrayed his God, and the other in the red mantle with which he had tried to betray Marzio. Even his clothes were fatal to his family: like Nessus, he left his garments impregnated with hate.

Bernardino, seeing the bright sun and feeling safe, clapped his hands, and leaped and shouted for joy, the instincts of life prevailing at this moment more powerfully than any other passion; but he soon remembered how many causes for tears were left to him, and how base it was to exult; he crouched low at the feet of Giacomo, and humbly begged his pardon.

In Giacomo the pallor of death had succeeded to the ray of life; his eyes were already glassy and wild; yet from his parched throat came these words:

"Rejoice, my brother; if you could see my heart, you would know it exults more than you can. The Lord begins to be merciful unto me, since he sends another father to my children. Take them to your care, for you alone can receive them. I entrust my blood to you with the same affection that I entrust my soul to my Creator."

"Giacomo," replied Bernardino, embracing his brother's knees, "I swear to make a vow of celibacy, that other loves may not prevent me from having a father's feelings toward the children you leave me."

"And now, blessed be God, gentlemen, let us go."

The procession, having left the courtyard, proceeded toward Santa Maria in Posterula. In the middle of the street of Orco the executioner unloosed the robe of Giacomo, exposing him naked even to the waist, then, having taken hold of the red-hot pincers, he tore his flesh with them.

The flesh shriveled beneath the heat of the iron; the iron smoked, a fearfully painful wound was made, which sent forth an insupportable odor. Heart, sight, hearing, smell, were alike wounded.

Bernardino sprang furiously to his feet, and tried with his hands to seize the pincers; but the executioner drew them back: then, seeing the uselessness of the attempt, he threw himself on his knees, and joining his hands together, prayed:

"Oh! for pity's sake, do not touch him; it is enough, too much for him—for Christ's sake, do it also to me!"

And as Master Alessandro, not heeding, turned to renew the torture, Bernardino cried:

"For pity's sake, Brothers of Mercy, give me back the *tavolette*—that I may not see—I may not hear—it pierces my heart."

And the boy fell in a swoon.

Cruelly lacerated in this manner, the miserable man proceeded through the squares of Nicosia and Palomba, even to the Church of Santo Apollinaire; whence they bent their course to Piazza Navona, anciently called Circolo Agonale, and hence through San Pantaleo, Pollacchi, and the square of Pallottole, even to Campo di Fiore, the broker's exchange, where, by a privilege, those condemned by the tribunal of the Holy Office were executed.

The procession now reached a burning soil; it was the Cenci square. Giacomo, stupefied with pain, neither noticed nor knew where he was dragged. Having arrived at the foot of the archway where the steps begin which lead to the church of San Tommaso dei Cenci, such piercing cries struck upon his ears that they had the power of overcoming the acute pain with which even his brain was seared. He raised his eyes, and as through a veil he saw upon the terrace, which overlooked the arch, the outstretched arms of his wife and children. The shame of appearing in such a state of dejection and misery before his family roused all the blood in his veins, which rushing back impetuously to his heart made him reel. But love conquered shame, and he exclaimed with an affectionate voice:

"My children! Oh, my children! Give me my children!"

The official charged with the execution of justice intended to go on; but the people, touched by pity, shouted unanimously:

"Give him his children!"

And as the officials hesitated to obey, a rush of people barred the procession and approached the cart shouting; on this account the officials, finding the desire of the people just, proclaimed with loud voice that the universal wish should be granted. They let Giacomo descend from the cart, and throwing a cloak over his shoulders to conceal his wounds, led him up the steps into the courtyard of the palace. He suppressed his groans in pity for his family.

Luisa, with her hair unbound, was seen hurrying down the broad staircase holding one little child in her arms, another by her hand. Angiolina followed leading the other children; and when they met Giacomo in the little square, Luisa placed upon his neck the little child, who clung to him desperately, then she tried to kneel and embrace his knees; but at the first sound that came from Giacomo's lips her limbs failed, and, overcome with grief, she fell prostrate at his feet. Giacomo did not see her, for the child hanging about his neck prevented him: and with a voice sufficiently firm he said:

"My children, in a short time one blow will deprive you of a father, and your mother of a husband. I leave you a sad inheritance. This thought torments me, alas! more than my punishment. When they shall have buried me within this Church of San Tommaso, you will remember, although they may hunt you from your home, that no one can shut the door of the church, built by your ancestors, upon you. Come at night, let no one see you, and pray for the soul of your poor father. Luisa, I do not commend to you your children, and mine; I know that before reaching them it will be necessary to pass over your body. My dear Luisa, where are you?"

Hearing no reply, he bent and placed his child upon the ground, for he could not use his arms. Then he saw her lying senseless at his feet, and raising his eyes to heaven, he said:

"Lord, I thank Thee, that in having given me the satisfaction of seeing her again before I die, Thou hast taken from her the grief of this last separation." Then, kneeling on the ground, he kissed her face, bathing it with tears and blood. He then kissed his children one by one, who pressed around him trying to retain him with their childish hands, and uttering such piteous cries that they pierced his heart.

"Farewell—my children!" said the miserable man between his sobs; "farewell, we shall meet again in heaven. Bernardino, remember they are your children now."

Bernardino, bewildered, kissed and embraced the little creatures, and to quiet them, promised he would soon return home.

The mournful procession resumed its course.

Angiolina, left alone with the desolate Luisa, was too much overcome to be able to carry her to her chamber. Not one of the many servants, partisans, or friends of the Cenci family was there to aid her in her pious duty. Men and beasts fled from a house that tottered to its fall. She went into the street, waiting there for some to pass. At last she saw the old Hebrew, Jacob, who kept a broker's shop within a short distance of the palace (for I believe I mentioned before that this palace was near the Ghetto). At first Angiolina felt a repugnance to ask help of a man who was esteemed in those times somewhat less than a dog; but overcome by necessity, she asked him somewhat roughly to help her to carry the poor lady into the house. Jacob, by whom the haughty words and rude tone had not passed unnoticed, replied:

"Willingly, my lady. The Lord in His own way has visited this house, and all miserable people are brothers."

Jacob, walking within the group of children, who were kneeling around their mother and weeping, thinking she was dead, took Luisa in his arms, consoling and assuring the children she was alive. He placed her upon the bed, put a pillow under her head, and, standing near obsequiously, said to Angiolina:

"Born to suffer and to die, we, whom you curse, have also hearts within us. If you wish anything more of me, ask it, I pray you, that the creatures of God, divided by injustice, may at least be united in sorrow."

Angiolina dismissed him, pressing his hand in thanks. Luisa, after a long time, came to herself; looking around her bed, she saw her children, as once Niobe gazed on hers, pierced with the arrows of misfortune. Leaning upon her arm, slightly rising from the bed, she said:

"We never shall see him more! Indeed, my children, we shall no longer have a roof to cover us:—we have lost everything in one moment; father, relatives, friends, fame, and property. Do not curse your father, for he was unfortunate, not guilty; and even were he guilty, it is not for children to judge their own parents. But I affirm that he was unhappy and innocent; therefore, pray God that as he can no more come to us, we may all go to him. We are alone; let us redouble the ties of love within us, and then we shall not see our solitude."

Hardly had she pronounced these sad words when she heard sobs behind her. Luisa, turning round, saw Angiolina, who, kneeling at a respectful distance, had joined together the little hands of the infant, and raised them with her own toward heaven, praying and weeping. Thus the kind woman wished to intimate to Luisa that not every heart had deserted her, and that one remained who would always participate in and weep for the misfortune of her family.

CHAPTER XXX

THE LAST HOUR

THE procession that led the Cenci to the scaffold, after passing through several streets, arrived at the end of the Strada Giulia, where it stopped before the prison of Corte Savella.

Beatrice and Lucrezia were meditating in silence. Father Angelico prayed; listening attentively he heard a noise, which drew nearer and nearer. He looked up, and saw a figure at the door that made him a sign with his hand, and he well understood that sign. Although he had long since worn out his life in the bitter work of giving comfort to the unfortunate reduced to such a sad fate, still he had not courage enough to inform Beatrice that it was time to go. While he felt perplexed what to do, the maiden offered him means by the prayer which she was then addressing to God.

"And if," said she, "this immense desire which urges me out of life into Thy arms, O Lord! is a sin, forgive me. How weary I am of waiting! I am like an exile, who upon the sandy shore would hasten with his wishes the ship that is to reconduct him home. O heaven! a truly happy home of all those who suffer!"

"Daughter, if you feel so strong, the Lord is coming—He has come to take you. Let us go."

And rising to his feet he offered his bony hand to the soft one of Beatrice, who, also rising, exclaimed:

"Here below to suffer is martyrdom; in heaven it is glory—let us go!"

In this place, through either curiosity or pity, the people were collected in greater numbers, and hardly gave room for the ill-omened procession to move.

First appeared Lady Lucrezia, with her black veil wrapped round her head and falling to her waist, and her black robe of cotton cloth with large open sleeves, the under sleeves of very fine linen folded in the most minute plaits and fastening at the wrist, as was then the fashion. She did not wear around her waist the white badge, which in those times Roman widows were accustomed to wear, but a cord, within which her arms were bound, not so tight, however, as to prevent her from raising to her eyes a crucifix. She wore slippers of black velvet, with large bows of black silk.

Long suffering had not been able to wither the divine beauty of Beatrice. Like a light nearly extinguished, she seemed to have gathered all her splendor to sparkle more brilliantly. She was still upon the earth, but appeared like an angel spreading her wings to take flight to the throne of God. She was dressed somewhat differently from her step-mother: her veil was white; over her shoulders she had a silver tissue robe; her dress was of taffeta of a violet color; and her high-heeled shoes were of white velvet with large tassels, the laces and heels of crimson.

"Here she is! here she is!" Like lightning this word ran from mouth to mouth; and, as if they had neither heart nor eyes except for her, all looked at Beatrice.

As soon as she put her foot out of the door, the crucifix of the Brothers of Mercy, wrapped half-way down in a long black veil, was blown by the wind, and seemed like a sail puffed by a propitious breeze for the departure.

The crucifix bowed before her as if to salute her, and both ladies knelt. Beatrice, praying with a loud voice, said:

"Since Thou comest toward me with open arms, be pleased, O Christ my Redeemer! to receive me with the same desire with which I come toward Thee."

Giacomo and Bernardino, having seen from the top of their carts the beautiful, innocent girl, with remorse in their consciences for having induced her to confess herself guilty for the sake of saving them from death, seemed to themselves the cause of her execution, and urged by the same desire, they rushed down from the cart before any were able to prevent them, and throwing themselves at her feet, exclaimed:

"Pardon! pardon, sister; you go to death innocently on our account!"

Beatrice, seeing the shocking laceration of her brother's flesh, shuddered, and supported herself upon the arm of the Capuchin; but soon regaining her courage, with serene aspect she replied:

"What have I to forgive you, my brothers? Neither my confession nor yours sends us to death, but *our property;* and you should have known this before. For what should I forgive you? Because you have caused me to abandon this forest full of wild beasts with human faces? But I am impatient to leave it. For I go where there are neither oppressors nor oppressed? Come then, courage, Giacomo! They may torture you much, but only for a short time. Why do we delay here? Let us hasten to gain the bosom of the Consoler, who awaits us —in eternal peace—in peace!"

Encouraged by this new comfort, which the wonderful courage of the maiden infused into their souls, they reascended the cart.

Beatrice walked light and fast, as a person desirous of reaching in time the place of appointment; and passing before the churches which were in great numbers all along the road, she knelt and prayed with such fervid prayers that those who heard her said that never had they felt such a painful compassion in their hearts, and desired that God would grant them on their deathbeds to go from this life with so much faith and joy.

From the street St. Paolino the procession came out at last upon the square of the Castle St. Angelo, otherwise called the tomb of Adrian.

In the midst of the square arose the scaffold, and here upon a board was a block; upon the block an ax. The rays of the declining sun shone upon the polished iron, which gleamed like fire; the eyes of those who looked were dazzled. The dense crowd waved like a field of ripe wheat blown by the winds; by this motion might be understood that the storm was there, but at that moment it was silent.

A band of men, distinguished by vine-leaves in their hats, advanced close together and silently, thrusting their poniards right and left. It would be impossible to describe with words the great fear which spread around, the confusion, the loud and desperate noise. The esquires tried to rush upon them with their horses, but they, being frightened, shied; the officers, knowing very well what a load of hatred weighed upon their heads, thought only of saving themselves. The Brothers of Mercy, priests, torches, crucifix, flags—all were in confusion.

Master Alessandro, standing upon the cart, kept under his hands Giacomo and Bernardino Cenci, like a falcon that grasps two birds in his claws. Wonderful were the attitudes and expressions of passion, of both men and women, upon the roofs, the balconies and platforms; pitiful cries resounded from the people pushed hither and thither in the square. To add to the confusion, several platforms, having been raised in haste and overcrowded with people, broke down amid the terrible tumult; and of those beneath one had his head broken, another his leg, another his arm, and not one remained without some bruise.

Guido, upon his fiery horse, saw these things and felt impatient for the consummation. Behold, his companions, moving, approach Beatrice; behold, the last obstacle is removed; now they take her—they have taken her, they lift her up, and carry her away. She is safe! The people burst forth into a great cry of joy: they crowd over behind the assailants, and had they not entangled themselves in their own movements they might have helped them better.

Guido, not being able to restrain himself, extended his arms, as if he wished to shorten the space which separated him from his Beatrice. As chance willed, in his hasty movement he pressed the spurs into his young horse, which, already frightened by so much confusion, shied; and, as if this had not been enough to excite him, a platform that stood before him suddenly broke down with a tremendous noise, where the same unfortunate accidents as before were renewed. The horse then, with ungovernable fury, threw off his reins and leaped like a thunderbolt; and, breaking through the crowd, biting and trampling, transported the unfortunate lover with him at his mercy.

In spite of this accident, the companions of Guido would have saved Beatrice, as they were not people to lose courage soon, and taking possession of the first carriage they happened to meet, they would have striven to carry her away in it; but the obstruction came from another side; it was the unhappy fate of Beatrice that the affection of men should be more injurious to her than their hatred.

The people turned back impetuously, pushed by a band of armed men distinguished by a white tassel in the hat; these also were in earnest, for they managed their swords so well as to drive from side to side whomsoever stood in their way.

Beatrice, in the midst of this struggle, seemed like a little boat in the middle of the sea in a tempest. Now she would appear over the wave of the heads of the people, now disappear, now advance, now draw back;—one step toward flight, one step toward the scaffold.

The young Ubaldini, from the door of the carriage prepared to receive Beatrice, saw all, and observed that others were striving to save her, and, through want of concord, instead of aiding were impeding each other, to the manifest ruin of the enterprise. Afraid of the imminent danger, he rushed down to warn his companions to stop from advancing any farther; rather to turn back, if they did not wish to lose Beatrice. But the good young man, between the confusion and cries, was not able to make himself understood by any, and the few that heard him, not knowing what he desired and seeing him deserting his place, thought the undertaking desperate and were disheartened.

Meanwhile the scattered horsemen, availing themselves of the clear ground, came together, with the officers behind them. The squadron having formed again, the captain ordered them to charge; which succeeded very easily, as they were assaulting a disordered crowd. Young Ubaldini, as love counseled him, struggled all alone to oppose the charging horses, and thrust his sword even to the hilt in the first that came before him; but the others gave him two blows, one of which cut his head, another the shoulder, so that he fell upon the ground. The foot-soldiers, having formed themselves into a square, presented a mass impossible to be broken. In this manner, threatened from behind and assailed in front, no alternative remained for the companions of Guido except to save themselves at the sides, which they did with incredible swiftness when they knew the undertaking to be ruined. Beatrice, by the diverse and contrary movements of her own defenders, was dragged to the very foot of the scaffold.

What was in her heart in the midst of these vicissitudes? Did Beatrice reopen her bosom to hope? Did she nurse the fond idea of life? Did love smile upon her? Love did smile; but still she no more desired life. Too far had she gone on the road to the grave to wish to return; for all that she had said about dying had really come from her heart. She now was overwhelmed, I will not say by a craving, but by a sincere desire to rest her head in the bosom of God. Notwithstanding this, love smiled upon her, and even upon the edge of the tomb, human creatures, especially women, are pleased to know themselves loved. They err when they sculpture Love as tearful over the tomb of a loved maiden. Love descends into it together with her, and dwells in it. Beatrice saw Guido, and sent to him, though far away, her last farewell. Guido saw her, and in spite of the space which divided them, they embraced each other with their looks.

Thus were the condemned brought within the chapel. The time granted for the adoration of the Host, in order that they should experience all the indulgences liberally awarded by the Pontiff, having expired, the Brothers of Mercy with the crucifix dressed in mourning came for Bernardino. The poor boy went, more dead than alive; when he arrived at the foot of the steps of the scaffold, they ordered him to ascend.

"O God!" he exclaimed in anguish; "how many deaths must I die? Twice you have promised me life, and twice have you betrayed me. Alas! what new torture is this?"

Nor were words able to persuade him to the contrary, for he thought himself lost; and as soon as he was upon the scaffold, at the sight of the ax placed upon the block his hair stood on end, and he fainted for the second time.

The Brothers of Mercy assisted him with spirits to revive, and when he came to himself, they placed him by the side of the block, assuring him that he was not to die; only to remain there to look upon the execution of his relatives!

With the usual ceremonies they went for Lady Lucrezia Petroni. The pious lady, observing Beatrice absorbed in deep meditation, rose softly, and had almost reached the door before her daughter had noticed her departure. Then Beatrice, raising her eyes and seeing her no more, exclaimed:

"Ah, mother! why have you abandoned me?"

Lady Lucrezia, surrounded by the Brothers of Mercy, who concealed the sight of the maiden from her in crossing the threshold of the chapel, answered to the pious question:

"No, I do not abandon you. I only precede you to show you the way."

Lady Lucrezia could ill succeed in ascending the steps, but she mounted as best she could, and finally reached the platform of the scaffold. The executioner removed the veil from her head, and the cloth from her shoulders. The lady, upon seeing her shoulders bare in the presence of so many people, blushed even to the roots of her hair. She stared at the ax, shuddered, and with many tears said:

"Lord, have mercy upon my soul, for now Thy judgment comes," and turning to the people, she continued:—"And you, brothers, pray to God for me."

She then asked the executioner what she had to do, and he answered: "Stride over the plank of the block, and lie down upon it." Lucrezia hesitated to cross her leg over the plank, but at last she fixed herself upon it.

A painful impediment she met in stretching herself, since the plank was small and sharp, and she exclaimed:

"Oh! how hard it is to stretch oneself upon this!"

And these were her last words. Bernardino covered his face with the red mantle. A quick blow made the scaffold resound, and the boy stagger. The head of Lady Lucrezia was severed from her body. The executioner with one hand seized it by the hair, and with the other placed under the severed neck a sponge; and, showing it to the people, cried:

"This is the head of Lady Lucrezia Petroni Cenci."

Master Alessandro, wrapping the head within a black veil, lowered by means of a rope the head and body to the foot of the scaffold. The Brothers of Mercy arranged the limbs in a coffin, and carried it to St. Celso until justice should be fulfilled.

The Brothers returned for Beatrice: as soon as she saw them she asked:

"Did my mother die well?"

"She made a good death," they replied to her. "and now she awaits you in heaven."

"Be it so!"

When she saw again the crucifix of the brotherhood she sweetly uttered these words, noted down and religiously transmitted to us by a listener:

"O Jesus! if Thou didst shed Thy most precious blood for the redemption of human kind, I trust that one drop may have been also for me. If Thou, most innocent, wert vituperated with so many outrages and killed with so many torments, why should I grieve to die, I who have so long offended Thee? Open, through Thy infinite mercy, the gates of heaven, or at least send me to a place of salvation."

An assistant of the executioner approached the noble maiden to bind her hands behind her back: but she, starting back a step, said to him:

"There is no need of it."

Admonished by the monk to suffer yet that last humiliation, with a smiling face she replied:

"Come then, bind this body to corruption; but hasten to loosen my soul to immortality."

Going out into the open air, she found upon the threshold seven maidens dressed in white, who waited to accompany her. These no one sent. Having heard that Beatrice had left in her will all her dowry in favor of the daughters of the Roman poor, they had spontaneously moved to give her this last proof of gratitude. The officers wished to dismiss them, but they were obstinate and would follow her. Then a crier drew a paper from his pocket, and read with a loud voice:

"By order of the most illustrious Monsignore Ferdinando Taverna, Governor of Rome:—Be it known to all present, that whosoever shall, either by words or deeds, attempt to place any obstacle to the great justice which is to be executed against the most wicked Cenci family shall be punished with three rounds of the lash, or a heavier punishment, at the will of his worship the Governor."

The girls, having heard the decree, stood more firmly than before, observing:

"We do not come to prevent, but to console; if we commit a crime they may punish us."

"Be kind! do not take away from me nor from them this sorrowful consolation," said Beatrice; and the Brothers of Mercy took upon themselves the responsibility of granting it.

They all marched on together. Beatrice began to chant with a sonorous voice the litany of the Blessed Virgin; and the girls answered very devoutly: *Ora pro nobis.*

Behold her at the foot of the scaffold! Without cowardice as without boldness she turned to the girls, kissed them, and spake:

"Sisters, may God reward you for this charity shown to me, for I cannot. I left you my dowry, but it is not worth your thanks, because, you see, at the bridal to which I am going, the Bridegroom is contented with only a contrite and humble heart. I would wish to leave you the years which I should have lived, to add them to yours; and more, the happiness which I should have enjoyed. May love be to you a source of love, as it was for me one of bitter affliction. You will become mothers: love your children, and let them be the crown of your life. I recommend to you my memory: hold it dear; and when any one shall question you of me, tell them with honest face: *Beatrice Cenci died innocent!*—innocent, by that omnipotent God in whose presence I am about to appear; certainly not spotless of sin, for who is without sin before the Lord? but most innocent of the crime for which I am condemned to death. Judges have condemned me, historians will write of the crime of which I am accused, as of a doubtful thing: but through your mercy the recollection of my innocence will remain unblotted from the mind of the people. When injustice shall have finished her reign, which is short, eternal pity will erase the mark of infamy stamped upon my name, and at my fate shall sigh many maidens who shall live on this earth beautiful and unhappy. Farewell!"

Jacob's dream is now being acted before the eyes of the Roman people. An angel ascends upon a ladder to heaven. To those distant, at first appeared her veiled head, then her shoulders, then her body; now she has gained the scaffold.

"You have promised to touch me only with the iron," she said to the executioner: "you at least should keep your promise, and teach me what I ought to do."

And he told her.

Bernardino still kept his face covered with the red mantle: she approached him cautiously and quietly, and impressed a soft kiss upon his hair. A shudder ran through the little boy, who, having removed his cloak, looked, and saw the most beautiful face of the dear innocent girl.

And he fainted for the third time.

Beatrice swiftly crossed the board, and stretched herself upon the block. The softness of this act, which Love embellished with his modest graces, touched even the heart of the executioner, who, thinking of his own daughter, hesitated to destroy that lovelv form; she, perceiving some delay, ordered:

"Strike!"

The arm fell. All shut their eyes; and the air around resounded with only one long, heartrending cry.

The severed head did not stir a fibre: there remained fixed upon the face the smile with which she died, flattered by the visions of a better life; the body contracted and struggled convulsively: finally it was still.

The executioner stretched his trembling hand to take the head, to show it to the people; but Father Angelico and the comforters prevented him: one of them placed over it a crown of roses, and, after wrapping it in a white veil, cried to the people:

"This is the head of Beatrice Cenci, a Roman maiden!"

Guido, after using every means to stop the frightened horse, had recourse to the last expedient. He let loose the reins, and, stretching himself along the neck, with both his hands stopped his smoking nostrils. The colt, thus deprived of respiration, stopped; Guido humored him awhile, then, suddenly pulling his bit to the left and spurring him to the right, turned him back in the road, and galloping furiously returned to the square of the castle.

He reached it at the moment in which the comforter, lifting the head of Beatrice, was crying: "This is the head of Beatrice Cenci, a Roman maiden!"

The Brothers of Mercy, after arranging this body also within the bier, carried it to St. Celso. Here, taking the crown from her head, they girded it around her neck. The wound that separated the head from the neck was thus hidden by that fresh and fragrant crown of roses gathered in the morning; one appeared more red than roses usually are—it was tinged with blood.

The Brothers, worn out by fatigue and pity, took a little rest. The scaffold was cleansed; the instruments were again prepared. The execution awaits its third victim.

Ought my history to sadden its last pages by narrating a slaughter which surpasses in horror the most savage imagination? I will narrate it; because such cruelties still exist in several parts of Europe, which boasts of civilization: and it is not many years since we heard of their being practised.

The Brothers of Mercy, after taking some rest, went for Don Giacomo. He came with hasty steps, covered by the tunic and hat of the Brotherhood of Mercy; he ascended quickly the fatal steps; they removed his tunic and hat, and his shoulders were bare as far as the waist, displaying his shocking wounds. It seemed unnatural to those who saw him that he should preserve in that state, not only life, but his senses and speech. He approached Bernardino, who had revived again, his teeth chattering convulsively and staring vacantly with his eyes, unmindful of what they saw. The boy would indeed have given great cause for tears, but tears were exhausted in Giacomo, he had already shed them all; now there remained nothing for him to shed but his blood, and only a little of this. He placed his hand upon the head of his brother, and, turning it toward Banchi, with loud voice exclaimed:

"I protest for the last time, that my brother, Don Bernardino, is entirely innocent of crime; and if he did confess otherwise, he did it by force of tortures. Pray for me!"

The executioner fastened his legs to a ring fixed in the platform; bandaged his eyes, and taking a leaden hammer struck with all his might against his left temple. He dropped at once like an ox felled by the butcher. The executioner then bent down and cut open his body; thrusting in his arm, he drew it back drenched with blood, with the heart of the executed man in his hand, which he showed to the people, crying:

"This is the heart of Giacomo Cenci!"

And then he threw it aside; then with an ax he quartered him. A sprinkle of that sea of blood fell upon the face of Bernardino, and that warm drop gave him sense enough to comprehend the savage slaughter of his brother.

And he fainted for the fourth time.

The people began to believe him also dead. Having re-conducted him to prison, with great exertions they were at last able to make him revive; but raving continually, and suffering from a delirious fever. For many days he lay at the point of death, until by the assistance of the most celebrated physicians of Rome, after many months of dangerous illness he finally recovered.

The people were in doubt then—at the present day they are sure—whether the Pope had condemned to the greater punishment Bernardino or his relatives.

The *placet* of Clement declared: Don Bernardino Cenci shall be pardoned of his life, by commuting the penalty of death into imprisonment for life, and with the condition that he should be present at the execution of his relatives!

At four o'clock the slaughter was ended.

Master Alessandro, surrounded by the horsemen and police, to save himself from the fury of the people, who, according to the old custom of revenging themselves against the stone, and not against the hand that threw it, would have torn him to pieces, went back to the Corte Savella.

The young Ubaldino Ubaldini was transported with much care to the house of his sister, the beautiful Renza, who was wife of Signor Renzi; and here, with as much secrecy as was possible, they strove to cure him; but the affection of his father, and the zeal of the physicians were in vain against the furious fever accompanied by the delirium that assailed him. The physicians, taking aside Lady Renza, with tears in their eyes gave the poor young man up for lost; notifying her that if he should live through the night, he would certainly not reach the noon of the next day. In truth, at dawn the next day the sick man grew worse, and, still delirious as he was, he asked for paper and pencil. They gave it to him in order to quiet him, and with the bandage on his eyes, and raving, he sketched the portrait of Beatrice, wonderful for the purity of its outline and resemblance; and this was the drawing which, coming to the hands of Cardinal Maffeo Barberini, served as a model to Guido Reni, to take from it the famous portrait of which we have already spoken.

Monsignore Taverna, having discovered the asylum where Ubaldino had retired, sent some officers to arrest him. In vain they warned them that the poor young man was at the point of death; the officers insisted upon entering his room. Ubaldino heard them come and recognized them, thanks to the lucid interval which usually precedes the extinction of life. And turning towards them, with feeble voice he said:

"Tell Governor Taverna that you have found a dead man, who would not change his fate with him."

And falling upon his pillow, he gave his soul to God.

It was the custom then in Rome that the removal of bodies to the church should be made at three different times, according to the rank and condition of the person. Citizens were removed at sunset; nobles, priests, and the professional class one hour after dark; cardinals, princes and barons at two hours and a half after dark.

The bodies of Beatrice and Lucrezia, and the miserable remains of Don Giacomo remained exposed until five o'clock at the foot of the colossal statue of St. Paul, raised at the head of the bridge of St. Angelo: thence they were removed first to the Consulate of the Florentines, then to the Church of the Brotherhood of Mercy. At nine o'clock the body of Lady Lucrezia was consigned to Don Lelio, her brother, who, according to the desire of the deceased, buried it in the Church of St. Gregory.

The friends of the Cenci procured permission to have the limbs of Giacomo entombed in one of the sepulchers which the cruelty of Count Cenci had prepared for his children.

The seven maidens did not leave Beatrice after she was dead, but, conquering natural repugnance, they rendered to her the last offices by washing her carefully, dressing her in fine clothes, sprinkling her with perfumes, and spreading fresh flowers over her. They replaced on her head the garland of roses, and girded her neck with another of white, which likewise became tinged with the blood of the gentle girl.

From all sides were seen collecting new crowds of girls, dressed in white, to render homage to the unfortunate maid, together with the orphans, and all the orders of the Franciscan friars. Fifty torches surrounded the bier, and so many were the lights set at the windows of the streets through which the funeral procession passed, so numerous the clouds of flowers scattered upon the bier, that the common people, in comparing it to that of the *Corpus Domini* procession, said that this surpassed that in having nearly twice as many.

With sad psalmodies the procession reached Mount Gianicolo at the Church of St. Pietro Montorio, where a tomb was prepared, and there they deposited her. Then they resumed their chants more sorrowfully, sprinkled with holy water the unhappy body, and with many lamentations gave it the last adieu. But the crowd did not soon leave the church empty; for when some went out others would succeed; and thus they kept on till midnight.

At this hour the steps that sounded on the pavement of the church became less frequent. The sexton announced that the church was about to be closed, and after a short time believing that all had left, he turned the heavy door upon its hinges, and with a strong push he shut it.

Only one torch remained lighted a few steps from the bier. The lamps, which burned dimly at long intervals before the altars of the saints, rendered more solemn and fearful the obscurity of the place.

CHAPTER XXXI

THE SEPULCHER

A FOOTSTEP is heard; it is repeated. It is the step of a living being, who moves toward the bier. By the light of the torch the aspect of Father Angelico is revealed, as pale as the wax of the torch which burns. He seats himself upon the step of the bier near the chandeliers, embraces his knees, leans his forehead upon them, and thus he remains motionless to weep and pray.

From the remotest corner of the church behold another figure comes forth. His steps are not heard, so softly they pass over the marble of the pavement; but they are slow and staggering. The lamps reflect long shadows upon the walls and floor; so that it seemed as if a crowd of people had assembled there, perhaps to accomplish some dark design. But this is a mere appearance; the shadows belong to that person alone—alone, if we except the desperation that accompanies him. He is barefooted; his eyes are staring, and they gleam like fire.

This is Guido Guerra. What thought urges him to that place is manifest by the poniard he grasps in his hand—the same poniard with which he pierced the throat of the father of Beatrice, executed for parricide—that poniard which, before the ax of the executioner, had cut the thread of her youthful days.

He already touches the hem of the cloth, and is about to lift it. "I expected you!" said Father Angelico, starting suddenly to his feet and placing his hands upon his shoulders.

A long time they stood motionless and silent beside the bier of the beheaded girl. Father Angelico broke this silence by saying:

"Beatrice commands you to live.—Her last thought, ah! her last thought was not of God—it was of you. She died happy in the hope of seeing you again in heaven; this she imposed upon me to say to you—and more, she commanded me to remind you that you have committed heavy sins, which Divine Justice cannot forgive without your long repentance. Do you wish to betray the hope of the loving maiden? Do you wish, unfortunate man! to shut to yourself the way of rejoining her in the bosom of God? Give me that weapon, that I may deposit it within her tomb, and live. Take this instead—it is her hair, which the unhappy one sends to you that you may wear it over your heart—and this image of the Madonna before which she prayed her last prayers, in order that you also might pray before her, and through her mercy obtain that pardon which your bride Beatrice is now begging before the throne of God. Now go, my son, go:—do not disturb the peace of the dead—Beatrice is not here. Raise your eyes to heaven, and there you will see her again."

The hand of Guido opened, and let the poniard fall. He took the hair and placed it in his bosom; he took the image also, and bowing his head wept bitterly.

The friar, gradually forcing the desolate lover, took him away forever from that bier.

Guido moved slowly, and unconsciously approached the door of the church. The friar opened it and, going out into the open air with Guido, began to quiet him with consoling words; but he, maddened, suddenly rushed away, and silently wandered through the country, where the oblique rays of the setting moon rendered the shadows more frightful.

Tradition narrates that with the rising of the sun his madness greatly increased, and he cursed the hour in which he was prevented from accomplishing his design; but, since he had been forbidden to pour out his blood upon the tomb of the beloved girl, he swore to propitiate her shadow with the blood of others—miserable vow, which he kept too well! Making himself the head of a band of outlaws, he became terrible, not only in the Roman Campagna, but with subtle skill he plotted against and took several lives in Rome itself, in the very midst of guards, and even within the security of domestic walls.

One day Guido, looking at the hair of Beatrice, felt ashamed of the degraded life he was leading; and, aspiring to a nobler revenge, went from Rome to Flanders, where war was still raging, which its people maintained for independence and liberty. But he arrived too late, for the war was drawing to a close, and after his arrival nothing of consequence occurred, so that in a short time he found, with inexpressible grief, that he had come only to be present at the peace. Then he considered his past life, and he saw that all his steps had ever dragged him away from that path which the maiden of his heart had recommended to him before dying. Listening to the voice of conscience, he thought it not well to loiter in a cloister drowning his thoughts in corpulence and idleness; but still hoping to appease Divine mercy, he retired to the Alp of St. Bernard, where, for the indefatigable care and wonderful courage shown in placing himself in the fiercest dangers for the safety of the unhappy ones buried by the avalanches, he came into high repute for his piety, as well as his courage; and we may hope that appeased justice may have granted him to see again, in the dwellings of the just, the maiden he loved so well.

Where does the body of Beatrice now rest? From the Church of St. Pietro in Montorio the Transfiguration of Raphael has disappeared, and with it the tombstone of the betrayed girl. But the picture of the Transfiguration, placed in a worthier situation, still receives the homage of posterity; while the devout pilgrim searches in vain for the sepulcher of Beatrice. The monks, like the good son of Noah, ready to cover the shame of the Court of the Popes, have turned the stone upside down, and the inscription has disappeared! A far thicker mantle is required to hide the wicked and detestable sins of avaricious Babylon; nor can records be canceled, as can lives and marbles. Let the pilgrim whom love may urge go to St. Pietro in Montorio; stop before the greater altar behind the balustrade. There, on the right, at the foot of the steps of the altar, let him look upon the flat, broad stone of Pentelic marble that makes an angle with the lateral stones; beneath this lie in peace the bones of Beatrice Cenci, a maiden of sixteen, condemned by Clement VIII, Vicar of Christ, to an ignominious death, for parricide not committed!

This should be enough to enable the devout pilgrim to recognize the place where the maiden lies; but if not sufficient, let him look closer, and he will read upon the stone the following epitaph, which, substituted by the hand of God for that which men had carved on it, never will be erased even in the consummation of ages:

Avaricious cruelty drank the blood and devoured the property of the betrayed one who lies below.

On Tuesday, September 14, 1599, the Brotherhood of St. Marcello, enjoying the privilege of freeing one prisoner on the festivity of Santa Croce, obtained permission that Don Bernardino Cenci should be restored to liberty, on condition that within one year he should pay twenty-five thousand ducats to the Brotherhood of the Most Holy Trinity of Ponte Sisto. How Bernardino, despoiled of all his property, would be able to pay this sum, could not be clearly understood; but the still greedy Court spread a net to obtain the money from the noble and powerful relatives of the Cenci in Rome and elsewhere. The fact is, this money never was paid. The indignation in the public mind increased at seeing the greater part of the Cenci property grasped by the Aldobrandini family; the Pope, by an act of the 9th of July, 1600, was forced to restore to the children of Don Giacomo the property of several confiscated possessions, as they were under the bond of entail, but not without the compensation of a goodly amount of money, as is proved in the order sent to Monsignor Taverna to transact this business, in which occur the following words: "*Pro aliqua condecentiori Cameræ pecuniaria summa per eosden Jacobi filios persolvenda transigas.*" In July, 1601, the same suit being pursued still further, it was necessary to restore all the other plunder, except the vast estate of Casale di Torre Nova, which the Pope had bestowed on Giovanfrancesco Aldobrandini, for a payment of ninety-one thousand ducats. After the death of Clement VIII and Paul V, Luisa Vellia, the courageous widow of Don Giacomo, intent on recovering the stolen property of her children, brought a suit to show the iniquity of this sale; complaining of it as of a notorious injustice, she asked either its restitution, or liberty to show the most enormous fraud and perjury of that instrument against Pupissa Aldobrandini, Paolo Borghese, and others mentioned in the address to Gregory XV. The lawsuits between the heirs Cenci, Aldobrandini, and Borghese lasted for centuries; and so recently as the early part of the nineteenth century the Roman tribunals heard again renewed the ancient quarrel between Prince Borghese and Count Bolognetti Cenci.

If it seems that the writer has acted unadvisedly in making these charges, I request the reader to consider two things: first, that such infamies in those days were neither new nor rare; secondly, that when the gold of the condemned is poured into the coffers of the judge, the latter ought with the clearest proofs to satisfy the people that he did not make common cause with the executioner.

Printed in Great Britain
by Amazon

18469896R00249